P9-CDV-671

*T*ess gazed mutely up at Rotham, searching his face. He had intense eyes. Vivid, dare-the-world eyes. Just now she felt as if she could drown in those vibrant gray depths.

He was far too masculine and desirable, devil take him. She knew she should turn and run, yet she couldn't move.

And then he took the decision from her. Raising his hands, he slowly slid his fingers along either side of her jaw. When his mouth covered hers, Tess completely forgot to breathe. She could only remain rooted there, absorbing the jolting delight of Rotham's probing kiss.

His lips had the texture of heated silk, his exploring tongue a scalding wildness. *What a wicked, marvelous sensation.* Her head swam with drugged pleasure, her body trembled.

He kissed like a possessive lover—or what she imagined a possessive lover to be. A whisper of a sigh escaped Tess. She had suspected that kissing Rotham would be remarkable, but she'd vastly underestimated how wonderful, how intensely glorious, it would be. The impact left her too flustered to think, too dazed to stand on her own. Reaching up, Tess weakly clutched at his shoulders. . . .

Books published by The Random House Publishing Group are available at quantity discounts on bulk purchases for premium, educational, fund-raising, and special sales use. For details, please call 1-800-733-3000.

To Desire a Wicked Duke

A Novel

Nicole Jordan

Wood County Public Library
Bowling Green, Ohio 43402

BALLANTINE BOOKS • NEW YORK

Sale of this book without a front cover may be unauthorized. If this book is coverless, it may have been reported to the publisher as "unsold or destroyed" and neither the author nor the publisher may have received payment for it.

To Desire a Wicked Duke is a work of fiction. Names, characters, places, and incidents are the products of the author's imagination or are used fictitiously. Any resemblance to actual events, locales, or persons, living or dead, is entirely coincidental.

A Ballantine Books Mass Market Original

Copyright © 2011 by Anne Bushyhead

All rights reserved.

Published in the United States by Ballantine Books, an imprint of The Random House Publishing Group, a division of Random House, Inc., New York.

BALLANTINE and colophon are registered trademarks of Random House, Inc.

This book contains an excerpt from book one of the forthcoming Legendary Lovers series by Nicole Jordan. This excerpt has been set for this edition only and may not reflect the final content of the forthcoming edition.

ISBN 978-0-345-51009-9

Cover illustration: Alan Ayers

Printed in the United States of America

www.ballantinebooks.com

9 8 7 6 5 4 3 2 1

For Sandra Chastain and Ann Howard White
Dear friends and sisters at heart
Love you bunches

To Desire a
Wicked Duke

Chapter One

❖

*Although I have been off the Marriage Mart a good
while now, I am quickly relearning an indisputable
rule of engagement with the opposite sex: When you
play with fire, you are likely to be burned . . . and
Rotham is the hottest sort of fire.*
                    —Diary Entry of Miss Tess Blanchard

Richmond, England: October 1817

The kiss was amazingly insipid.

Disappointment surged through Tess Blanchard as
Mr. Hennessy drew her more fully into his embrace.
She had expected so much more when she acquiesced
to his impulsive gesture.

More excitement, more pleasure, more *feeling*. In
short, she had secretly longed to be swept away by romantic passion.

Instead she found herself logically analyzing the
construction of his lovemaking. The precise pressure
of his lips. The exact angle of his head. The unarous-
ing feel of his arms around her.

There was no spark, no *fire* between them at all,
Tess realized sorrowfully. The entire business left her
remarkably cold.

Oh, Patrick Hennessy certainly *seemed* skilled in
the art of kissing, she mused as his mouth plied hers
with increased ardor. But surely a man who counted

himself such an expert lover should have elicited a stronger response from her?

Not that she had much basis for comparison. This was only the second man she had ever romantically embraced in her three-and-twenty years.

It had happened purely on a whim. One moment they were laughing together over a line in the comic play Hennessy had written. The next, an arrested expression claimed his features as he gazed down at her. When he stepped closer and bent his head to capture her lips, Tess had no thought of stopping him. For too long she had let herself languish on the shelf in the game of love, refusing to open herself up to renewed heartbreak. But it was past time to reenter the lists.

Admittedly, in Mr. Hennessy she was drawn by both curiosity and the lure of the forbidden. She knew better, of course. A proper lady did not indulge in scandalous experiments with libertine actors behind the stage curtains. Hennessy was known as something of a Lothario among the London theater crowd, although in addition to being a brilliant performer, he was also a successful manager of his own troupe, a budding playwright, and the talented director of Tess's two recent benefit concerts, which had raised vast sums for her charities.

Then again, perhaps she was not giving him a fair chance.

Closing her eyes more tightly, Tess made a stronger effort to enter into the spirit of the kiss. In response, Hennessy's hand stole lower down her back, over her derrière, to pull her closer. Despite her own lack of enthusiasm, she had evidently affected *him,* judging by the swelling hardness she felt pressing against her lower abdomen—

"Well, well, are you practicing to play the part of lovers in your production, Miss Blanchard?"

At the sharp-edged drawl, a startled Tess tore her mouth away from Hennessy's—and froze in mortification upon recognizing that sardonic male voice. Obviously she had failed to hear anyone enter the ballroom where their makeshift stage was erected.

Good Lord, what utterly dreadful timing, to have her transgression discovered by the arrogant, infuriating Duke of Rotham, elder cousin of her late betrothed. Rotham had stepped behind the stage curtains to find her locked in a clandestine embrace with the man she had hired to produce her amateur theatrical.

Scalding heat flooded Tess's cheeks as she pulled away from her partner in crime. Hennessy had also reacted to the duke's unexpected appearance by releasing her instantly. Yet the actor looked not only guilty but somewhat alarmed, as if he'd been caught in a hanging offense.

Squaring her shoulders, Tess turned to face Ian Sutherland, the tall, lithe Duke of Rotham. His handsome face was an enigmatic mask in the muted daylight seeping over the stage curtains from the ballroom windows, but his mouth held a tightness that signified displeasure, perhaps even anger.

He had no right to judge her, she told herself defiantly.

"You are mistaken, your grace," Tess said, striving

to keep her voice calm as she responded to his mocking tone. "There are no lovers in Mr. Hennessy's play. It is merely a comedy of manners about a mischievous ghost."

"You were testing out a new role, then?"

"What may I do for you, Rotham?" Tess asked, ignoring his jibe. "We have only just concluded the dress rehearsal and still have a great deal to accomplish before this evening's performance."

They had constructed a stage at one end of the ballroom of her godmother's country mansion for the theatrical—the crowning entertainment of the charitable benefit Tess had organized. Tess had engaged Hennessy and his troupe to put on the one-act play and direct the houseguests in their respective acting roles.

"I doubt your preparations entail kissing the hired help," Rotham drawled in that annoyingly cynical tone of his.

Tess stiffened. "It is hardly any of your business whom I kiss, your grace."

"I beg to differ."

Renewed ire rose in Tess. She would not allow him to dictate to her, as he was regularly fond of doing. Indeed, they had had similar arguments before. The Duke of Rotham was head of the family she would have married into had her betrothed not tragically perished two years ago at the Battle of Waterloo. But they had no real blood ties, and Rotham was mistaken in thinking that he had any say over her affairs. Particularly her amorous affairs.

Shifting his attention, Rotham turned his piercing gray gaze on Mr. Hennessy, who still seemed wary and on edge. "I expected better of you, Hennessy. You were supposed to be protecting her, not assaulting her. Is this how you fulfill your duties?"

The actor shot the duke a chagrined look of apology. "I beg your forgiveness, your grace. I fell down in my duties disgracefully." Rather sheepishly, he turned to Tess. "A thousand pardons, Miss Blanchard. I was vastly out of line."

Tess started to respond, but Rotham interrupted her. "I'll thank you to leave us, Hennessy. I shall deal with you later."

Her jaw dropped at Rotham's arrogant dismissal, but before she could voice her objection aloud, Hennessy gave her a brief bow, then pivoted with alacrity and disappeared through a part in the curtains.

She remained speechless as she listened to him bound down the stage steps and hurry away across the ballroom. It was hardly chivalrous of him to abandon her to the mercies of the duke, Tess thought resentfully. No doubt he preferred not to challenge a nobleman of Rotham's station and far-reaching influence.

However, when she at last gathered her wits enough to protest, Rotham held up an imperious hand, forestalling her. "You should know better than to indulge in trysts with libertines such as Hennessy."

Prickling with indignation, Tess returned a mutinous look. The nerve of him, scolding her for a sin she had not even committed. "I was not indulging in any *tryst,* your grace. It was just a simple kiss."

The corner of Rotham's mouth curled. "It did not look at all *simple* to me. You were participating fully."

He sounded almost angry, although why he would be angry with her for returning the actor's kiss, she couldn't fathom.

"What if I *was* participating? It is no crime—"

Realizing how high-pitched and flustered her own voice sounded, Tess took a calming breath and forced a cool smile. "I truly cannot believe your gall, Rotham. How someone of your wicked character can deride another man for rakish behavior—or criticize me for something so innocent as a mere kiss—is the *height* of irony. Do you even recognize your hypocrisy?"

A hint of satirical amusement tugged at his lips. "I acknowledge your point, Miss Blanchard. But I am not the only one concerned about your relationship with Hennessy. Lady Wingate is worried that you have become overly attached to him. In fact, she sent me to find you."

That gave Tess pause, as doubtless Rotham knew it would. Baroness Wingate was not just Tess's godmother but chief patron for her various charities. She could not afford to offend the noblewoman whose generosity impacted so many lives for the better.

"I have not become attached to Hennessy in the least," Tess finally replied. "He is a valued employee, nothing more."

"Do you make a habit of kissing all your employees?" Rotham taunted. Before she could reply, he shook his head in reproach. "Lady Wingate will be severely disappointed in you. She arranged a lavish house party solely for your sake, so you could dun her guests for your assorted charities. And *this* is how you repay her?"

Unable to refute the charge, Tess regarded Rotham in frustration. Her godmother had long disapproved of her endeavors to promote her charitable organizations and had only recently relented and invited some four dozen wealthy guests to a weeklong house party, thereby providing Tess with a captive audience. She'd spent the past week attempting to persuade each one of them to contribute to her causes.

"Do you mean to tattle to her?" she asked Rotham.

His answer, rife with mocking humor, disturbed her. "That depends."

"On what?"

"On whether or not you intend to continue your liaison with Hennessy."

"I tell you, I am *not* having a liaison with him! You have completely misconstrued the matter."

"Who initiated the kiss?"

"What does that matter?"

"If Hennessy took advantage of you, I will have to call him out."

"You cannot be serious!" Tess stared at him, appalled to think he might not be jesting. The last Duke of Rotham, Laurence Sutherland, had ended his licentious career when he was killed in a duel over a married woman by her jealous husband. His son Ian had followed a similar reckless path all through his youth, generating wild tales of gambling and womanizing. Ian Sutherland's scandalous endeavors had earned him the nickname "the Devil Duke" when he came into the title eight years ago. But surely he would not actually *shoot* Hennessy for the mere act of kissing her.

"You know very well that dueling is illegal," Tess

objected, "in addition to being dangerous and possibly even lethal."

Rotham's mouth tightened again, as if he too had recalled his sire's ignominious end. "Indeed."

When he said nothing further, Tess suddenly recalled the confusing remark he'd made before ordering the actor from the ballroom. "What did you mean when you said Mr. Hennessy should have been 'protecting' me?"

Rotham waved a careless hand in dismissal. "It is of no import."

"I should like to know." Tess fixed him with a stubborn gaze, determined not to back down.

He must have sensed her resolve, for he gave a shrug of his broad shoulders. "When you began spending so much time at the Theatre Royal in Covent Garden in preparation for your last charity event, I charged Hennessy with keeping an eye on you. The theater district is a dangerous area, especially for an unescorted young lady."

Her eyebrows lifted in puzzlement. "So you asked him to look after me?"

"Yes. I paid him a significant sum, in fact."

So *that* explained why Hennessy always insisted on escorting her to and from her carriage, Tess realized, and why he had hovered around her whenever she attended rehearsals. She had thought it was because the actor was growing enamored of her company. Irrationally, she couldn't help feeling a prick to her self-esteem.

"My companion usually accompanies me to the theater," she pointed out to Rotham.

"Your companion is an aging spinster with all the substance of a butterfly. She would be no help whatsoever if you were confronted by trouble."

That much was true, Tess conceded. Mrs. Dorothy Croft was tiny and gentle and soft-spoken, in addition to being a bit scatterbrained. The impoverished friend of Tess's late mother, Dorothy had needed somewhere to live after being widowed, so Tess had opened her home in Chiswick to her. The relationship had also benefited Tess. With a genteel, elderly lady to lend her single state respectability, she had much more freedom to conduct her charitable endeavors.

"I have a sturdy coachman and footmen to provide me protection should I require it," Tess argued.

Rotham's vivid gray gaze never faltered. "Even so, I thought it wise to ensure your safety. And you would not readily have accepted any edicts from me."

That was also certainly true. They had long been at odds—which is what made Rotham's current interest in her safety so startling. That he might be seriously concerned for her welfare had never crossed her mind.

"Well, you needn't worry about me, your grace. I am capable of providing for my own protection."

"Then you should refrain from kissing the likes of Hennessy. And he had best keep away from you. If he dares to touch you again, he will answer to me."

At the edge of possessiveness in the duke's tone, Tess's eyebrows narrowed in disbelief. He could not possibly be jealous. No doubt he was merely angry at

Hennessy for disobeying a direct order, and at her for daring to contradict him.

"Your transgressions are a thousand times worse, Rotham."

"But I am not an unmarried young lady, as you are."

"I am not so young any more," Tess rejoined.

Instead of replying, Rotham hesitated, as if suddenly aware how sharp his tone had become. Shaking his head, he seemed visibly to repress his emotions, as if distancing himself from their argument.

His succeeding laugh was soft and laced with real amusement. "You are hardly ancient, Miss Blanchard. You only just turned twenty-three today."

Tess eyed him with suspicion. "How did you know it was my birthday?"

"As head of the family, it is my business to know."

"You are not head of *my* family."

"For all practical purposes, I am."

There it was again, that ironic drawl that convinced her he was deliberately attempting to provoke her.

It was infuriating, how Rotham always seemed to get under her skin, Tess reflected. Particularly when she was normally serene and even-tempered.

She had always thought him vexing—and deplorably fascinating. Rotham not only had a wicked reputation, he even *looked* wicked. He had striking gray eyes fringed by dark lashes, with lean, aristocratic features that were handsome as sin. His hair was a rich brown shot with gold threads, several shades lighter than her own sable hue, and held a slight curl. He possessed the muscular build of a sportsman, but with a lethal elegance that proclaimed his nobility.

Yet it was Rotham's powerful personality that made him utterly unforgettable.

At the moment his features were mainly in shadow, since it was barely noon on a dreary, rainy autumn day and they were shrouded by stage curtains. Yet he still had the strange ability to affect her, Tess acknowledged.

She'd felt that same magnetic allure the first moment of meeting Rotham during her comeout four Seasons ago, when he'd deigned to dance with her. But shortly afterward, she'd fallen in love with his younger cousin Richard.

Ever since, she had felt guilty for her forbidden attraction to the Duke of Rotham. He was every inch the fallen angel. And lamentably even now, she felt his hypnotic pull as his gray gaze bored into her. . . .

In an effort to break the spell, Tess abruptly changed the subject. "What are you even doing at this house party, Rotham? You never attend my functions, even when you are invited."

"Lady Wingate requested my presence for your birthday celebration this evening."

"So *that* is how you knew my age. She told you."

"No. I've known for some time. Richard was third in line to become my heir after two of our uncles. When you became betrothed to him, I made it a point to learn a great deal about you."

It made Tess profoundly uncomfortable to think that Rotham had such detailed personal knowledge of her, or that he was privy to any of her secrets. But his next statement disturbed her even more.

"Given your history with my cousin, Miss Blanchard, it is only reasonable that I feel a certain responsibility toward you."

Her tone was sweetly spirited when she replied. "I told you, you needn't concern yourself with me."

"But Lady Wingate has every right. She fears you have been spending more time with Hennessy than is wise. It appears she has ample justification. What the devil were you thinking, kissing him?"

Tess's vexation returned full force. "I was experimenting, if you must know," she retorted defensively. "I have grown another year older without any prospects of romance or passion, and I wanted to see if I could change my fate. The sad truth is, I had forgotten entirely what it feels like to be kissed, and I thought Hennessy could remind me. Is that so wrong, your grace?"

A strange look settled over Rotham's face. She was surprised that he didn't return a mocking rejoinder. In addition to being impossibly arrogant, he possessed a cutting wit that could slice an opponent to ribbons. She'd seen victims of his acerbic tongue quail from him in tears. And more than once she herself had been on the losing end of their verbal battles. Normally it was all she could do to hold her own with him.

"I lead a very tame existence," Tess added grudgingly. "All very proper. My charities are extremely rewarding, but on the whole, my life is not particularly fulfilling."

When still he made no reply, Tess bit her lower lip. How could she explain to a man like Rotham the restless yearning inside her? *He* had never been hemmed in by stifling rules of conduct, forced to subjugate his very nature to propriety. Even her charitable endeavors were subject to censure. Because she was a woman—and a lady, at that—even her dear godmother objected to her efforts. All she wanted was to make a difference in people's lives, but she had to fight for every single success.

Yet the chief source of her dissatisfaction went far deeper. For the past two years, her life had been barren of passion and joy. It was primarily her own fault, of course. She not only had gone into mourning for Richard, she'd practically buried herself with her late betrothed. But now she was determined to return to the world of the living.

The fact that this particular day was her birthday only made her more defiant than usual.

"In all honesty," Tess resumed her confession more quietly, "I suppose I was indulging in a touch of melancholy. I am practically a spinster, languishing on the shelf while life passes me by—a rather lonely way to live."

For a moment, Rotham's sensual features seemed to soften further . . . but only for a moment. "So you were feeling sorry for yourself?"

Tess gritted her teeth. "Yes, I was," she snapped.

Rotham looked strangely gratified by her acrimony, as if he preferred sparring with her to hearing her admit feeling any weak emotions such as sadness or loneliness.

"And what was your verdict?" he asked unexpectedly after a brief silence.

"Verdict? About what?"

"Did you enjoy kissing Hennessy?"

Color rose to bloom in Tess's cheeks. "Not particularly—not that it is any concern of yours."

She'd been extremely disenchanted with the actor's efforts. As kisses went, his were exceedingly dull. Although sadly, Richard's kisses had not been particularly thrilling either—

Tess winced inwardly. It was a betrayal to Richard's memory to voice such disloyal thoughts. Her self-reproach was distracting enough that she almost missed Rotham's casual statement: "You should have come to me."

"I beg your pardon?"

"If you wanted to know about passion, you should have applied to me. I can show you all you need to know about kissing."

She stared at Rotham, her jaw slack. Once again he had startled her into speechlessness. But perhaps he was simply mocking her.

"You think you could do better than Hennessy?" Tess asked archly.

A gleam of humor entered his eyes at her challenging tone. "Certainly I can."

She shook her head in bemusement. "If I were to kiss you, my reputation would end up in shreds," she remarked absently.

A wry half smile curved Rotham's mouth. "I am not quite that sullied."

"Yes, you are."

When he merely continued to smile that infuriatingly knowing smile, Tess finally grasped that he was serious.

Rotham is actually offering to kiss you, to show you passion himself.

Nervousness suddenly swamped Tess. She ought to tell him to go to the devil, so why was she even hesitating? And why was a rush of excitement sweeping her senses at the possibility of kissing him?

She knew better than to accept his offer. Rotham was infinitely dangerous. More hazardous than any man she had ever encountered in her life. And her long-standing sexual attraction to him was shameful. She'd spent the past four years trying to deny her fascination with him.

Even worse, he was fully aware of his spellbinding effect on women—including herself.

On the other hand . . . the thought of kissing him was sinfully intriguing. This was her chance to learn from an acknowledged expert, urged a scandalous voice inside Tess. He could indeed show her everything she longed to know about passion—and probably much more.

Swallowing past the dryness of her throat, Tess glanced around her. The stage was set to resemble a Green Room at Drury Lane Theatre, since Hennessy's play centered on the legendary spirits who haunted that renowned theater, benevolent ghosts who appeared before performances to bless and encourage the actors. Behind her was a dressing table laden with cosmetics for applying stage makeup. Next to that stood a floor-length looking glass. And on the far end of the stage sat a chaise longue and several chairs for entertaining patrons and admirers.

Still debating, she turned back to face Rotham. When he took a step closer, decreasing the distance between them, fresh awareness assaulted Tess at the realization that they were wholly alone together.

She gazed mutely up at Rotham, searching his face. He had intense eyes. Vivid, dare-the-world eyes. Just now she felt as if she could drown in those vibrant gray depths. His high cheekbones and chiseled jaw-line, too, held a stark beauty that entranced her.

He was far too masculine and desirable, devil take him. She knew she should turn and run, yet she couldn't move.

And then he took the decision from her. Raising his hands, he slowly slid his fingers along either side of her jaw. As he lowered his head, her heart pounded so hard, her chest hurt.

When his mouth covered hers, a shock of surprise speared through Tess. She completely forgot to breathe. She could only remain rooted there, perfectly motionless, absorbing the jolting delight of Rotham's probing kiss against her lips.

Then he made her open for him. The scent of him filled her senses, the taste of him stole her reason. His mouth had the texture of heated silk, his exploring tongue a scalding wildness.

What a wicked, marvelous sensation. Emotions whirled and clashed within Tess, leaving her giddy. Her head swam with drugged pleasure, her body trembled. At her unconscious reaction, he thrust his tongue even deeper, inciting that delicious, melting weakness throughout her entire body.

He kissed like a possessive lover—or what she imagined a possessive lover to be. A whisper of a sigh escaped Tess. She had suspected that kissing Rotham would be remarkable, but she'd vastly underestimated how wonderful, how intensely glorious, it would be. The impact left her too flustered to think, too dazed to stand on her own. Reaching up, Tess weakly clutched at his shoulders.

Rotham only drew her closer.

The sinful thrill of being captured against that hard male body sent another hot ripple of weakness surging through her. The beguiling friction of his chest against her breasts only made her want more.

How was it possible to be so desperately attracted to a man she disdained? Tess wondered. No, her feelings went far, far beyond attraction. This was sheer yearning.

She felt stunned by the sparks of fire between them. She had never before been struck by such lightning bolts of need. Richard had never once kissed her like this. His kisses had been tender and gentle. Not this magical, overwhelming, enchanting fervor. . . .

Rotham must have felt her shiver of helpless excitement for he suddenly broke off and raised his head.

Tess felt slightly stunned by what she glimpsed in his hooded eyes. Desire shimmered there, she was certain of it. *Unwilling* desire.

Rotham stared down at her, as if trying to come to terms with the passion that had exploded between them. His gray eyes had darkened to smoke, and she could see the struggle on his face. His fierce resistance matched her own, she knew.

Yet he must have been affected by the same weakness, for he abruptly gave in with a curse.

His wonderful mouth possessed hers again. To her delight, his kiss turned even more fiery, seizing, claiming, demanding, making her very blood sizzle.

Tess whimpered when she felt him start to pull away again, but thankfully his lips never left hers as he swept her up in his arms and carried her across the stage to the chaise longue.

Still holding her, he turned and sank down so that she was cradled in his lap, one strong arm supporting her back, the other hand keeping her face immobile for the attentions of his marvelous mouth. Her mind reeling, Tess was utterly powerless to protest, nor did she even wish to. Instead, she wrapped both her arms around his neck and returned his kiss measure for measure.

Her nerves drank in sensations while exhilaration sang in her blood. She was pressed against a body that was rock hard and lean as he ruthlessly explored her mouth. His tongue teased her relentlessly . . . thrusting, retreating, returning. At the same time, his hand began to roam the bodice of her blue merino gown.

When he cupped her breast, Tess drew in a shuddering gasp. She ought to stop him, she knew, but heat scorched her, incinerating any remaining fragments of common sense she possessed. Thus, rather than push him away, she curled her fingers in Rotham's thick dark hair, clinging with her remaining strength.

At her obvious eagerness, he shifted his wicked mouth from her lips to graze over her cheekbone, then lower, beneath her jaw and along her bare throat, leaving a trail of fever on her skin. Enraptured by his caresses, Tess bent her head backward to give him better access.

"I can't catch my breath . . ." she fretted in a rasping voice.

"You don't need to breathe, angel. Just feel."

His husky half-whisper was as seductive as it was dangerous, but she obeyed his beguiling command, straining against his arousing palm as he caressed the swelling mounds of her breasts beneath the fine wool fabric. Within the constricting confines of her corset, she could feel her nipples peak to a tingling ache—a result he seemed determined to encourage.

When his hand continued molding the contours of her breasts, Tess moaned out loud. Sweet shocks of reaction compressed her chest, while her bones melted beneath the sensual onslaught.

"So beautiful," he murmured as he drew back.

Lifting her heavy eyelids a fraction, she glimpsed his face above her and saw that he was watching her every response. Her dazed gaze locked with his hypnotic one.

"Bloody hell, how I want you. . . ." His gruff declaration somehow aroused her even more.

She wanted him, too. She felt as if she'd never lived until he touched her. The surge of want, of need inside her, overwhelmed Tess. She shuddered with the excitement of yearning as Rotham's hand abandoned her breasts and reached down to raise her skirts, baring her legs to mid-thigh. Then his dexterous fingers began to glide upward along her skin—

"*Good God,* what is the meaning of this?"

Even through her stupor, Tess recognized her god-mother's outraged voice.

When she jerked her head up, she saw that the stage curtains had parted and the baroness stood there, the picture of wrath.

On the stage steps behind Lady Wingate stood several of her patrician houseguests, gaping at the sight of Tess sprawled on the Duke of Rotham's lap, her skirts in total disarray, his palm fondling her bare inner thigh. Their scandalized expressions presented a fitting complement to the baroness's furious one.

Aghast, Tess scrambled to right herself, awkwardly trying to push off Rotham's lap and struggle to her feet. She felt his strong hands on her hips, helping her to stand, then steady her when she swayed from dizziness.

He rose more slowly to face their horrified audience.

Lady Wingate was practically quivering with rage, her eyes shooting virtual daggers at them both. In a similar vein, Sir Alfred Perry and his high stickler wife, Lady Perry—who were among Tess's largest contributors—eyed them with supercilious scorn.

Tess felt her cheeks flush scarlet. When she glanced guiltily up at Rotham, she saw that an enigmatic look had settled over his features, yet his sensual mouth held a grimness that acknowledged the gravity of their social infraction.

In disbelief, Tess raised a hand weakly to her temple. How could she possibly have failed to hear their approach? No doubt her moans of pleasure had drowned out the sound of their footsteps.

Renewed shame flooded Tess. For the second time in half an hour, she had been discovered locked in a passionate embrace with a wicked gentleman.

Yet this time she had the sickening feeling that she'd sunk herself utterly beyond repair—and worse, that there would be no escaping the consequences.

Chapter Two

*How is it possible that Rotham makes my blood boil
and race at the same time?*
— Diary Entry of Miss Tess Blanchard

"Tess Blanchard, how *could* you?" Lady Wingate admonished in continued fury, pinning her appalled gaze on her goddaughter.

Swearing under his breath, Ian glanced down at Tess. Her cheeks were hotly flushed as she stood frozen in consternation. Despite the difficulty of covering his own aroused state, he stepped protectively in front of her to draw the baroness's fire.

Consequently, Lady Wingate shifted her fierce gaze to him. "And *you,* Rotham . . . I trusted you with her, yet you betray me in this scurrilous fashion."

At the charge of betrayal, Ian's jaw muscles tightened. Yet he couldn't honestly argue against the allegation. Not in front of an audience, at any rate. Particularly such notorious gossips as the Perrys.

Noting the avid interest of the spectators, he spoke evenly. "This matter is best resolved in private, Lady Wingate, wouldn't you agree?"

As if recalling her surroundings, the noblewoman gave a start. "Yes, of course." Compressing her lips in a tight line, she turned to her houseguests. "If you please, I should like to speak to the duke and my god-daughter alone."

"Certainly, Judith," Lady Perry said curtly, taking her husband's arm. "Come, dear, we are obviously *de trop*."

Sir Alfred seemed reluctant to leave—or at least the disdain on his florid face had lessened to something resembling intrigue. "Must we go? I fancy this will provide better entertainment than the play we are to perform tonight. A theater haunted by spirits cannot hold a candle to a real-life scandal."

Lady Perry shot her spouse a sharp glance of disapproval and tugged on his arm, compelling his obedience. When she led the way back across the ballroom, the other guests trailed after them.

The moment they were gone, Lady Wingate resumed her chiding. "I expected so much better of you, Tess. How is it that I find you behaving like a trollop in that indecent manner—and with Rotham of all people?"

"I am wholly to blame, Lady Wingate," Ian interrupted, wanting to shield Tess from her wrath.

"Oh, I have no doubt *you* were the instigator, your grace," her ladyship snapped, her tone caustic. "I was willing to forgive you for being a rakehell, but I can never forgive you for *this*."

He couldn't forgive himself either. In a moment of blind temptation, he'd let his damnable desire for Tess Blanchard flare out of control, and then he was caught seducing her.

Ian voiced another low oath, although this time his curse was directed at himself rather than the intruders. He should have exercised more restraint, but he'd been unprepared for his body's reaction to the tantalizing taste of Tess, to the yielding softness of her mouth and form. The jolt had been electric. She'd felt it too, judging from her shiver of startled awareness the moment their lips touched. Against the shouted warnings of his conscience, he'd given in to the fierce rush of primal lust she aroused in him, unable to stop himself.

The baroness regarded him with scorn. "Of course, you *will* do the honorable thing, Rotham."

Ian narrowed his eyes momentarily. He knew what she meant by "honorable." His gut tightened, yet he nodded solemnly. "Naturally I will. You needn't worry."

"There is no hope for it," Lady Wingate added, so there would no misunderstanding. "You must wed her at once."

"I agree."

Behind him, Tess gasped. Stepping out from his protective shield, she stared up at him in stunned dismay. Ian suspected her distress now was not merely because she had disappointed her godmother and patron.

Her mouth opened and closed as she struggled to find her voice. Ian might have felt a measure of amusement at her response had the circumstances been less serious; it was rare that he rendered Tess speechless. Clearly he had shocked her by agreeing to wed her without a word of protest or debate.

Yet there was no need for either, Ian knew. He had exposed her to scandal and ruin, so he was obliged to make amends—and quickly, before she became mired so deeply in shame that she could never recover. Whatever his feelings about wedding Tess, he intended to protect her from hurt. She had been hurt too much already.

Tess apparently was not of the same mind. Her voice was hoarse, but held unmistakable adamancy when she spoke. "There is certainly no need for such drastic measures, your grace."

Ian left it to the baroness to reply, which she did with alacrity.

"There absolutely *is* a need," her ladyship insisted. "Marriage is the only way to save you from ruin. You will indeed wed Rotham." Before Tess could reply, Lady Wingate held up an imperious hand. "You, miss, are nearly a spinster. More than two years have passed since Richard's death, and it is time that you secure a husband."

"My lady," Tess said with heightened distress, "You cannot truly expect me to marry Rotham—"

"You will, or I will withdraw my support for all of your charities and leave you to face the scandal alone. Just see how quickly your organizations shrivel without my patronage."

At the harsh ultimatum, Tess flinched as if struck by a blow. She gazed back at Lady Wingate in stunned disbelief, but the baroness returned her regard without mercy.

The silver-haired noblewoman was every inch an aristocrat—tall, regal, commandingly haughty, and accustomed to getting her own way, but Ian knew she was deeply concerned for Tess's welfare. What was more, the baroness understood how vicious society would be in rendering judgment on an unmarried young lady who had sinned in a public display of wantonness.

When Tess remained mute, Ian stepped into the breach once more. "Lady Wingate, if you will allow us a moment alone, perhaps we can come to a resolution on our own."

"Very well, your grace. I trust you will talk some sense into her. I should like to announce your betrothal this evening, before the performance. Meanwhile, we will have to devise a story to explain your transgression in hopes of minimizing the damage. . . ."

Her voice trailing off, she frowned, deep in thought. "I have it. Rotham, you can say that you have been enamored of Tess for some time now, but that you properly waited until she was out of mourning for Richard before asking for her hand. When my friends and I interrupted your lovers' tryst, you had just proposed and Tess had accepted. In your delight, you were both carried away by passion. The fact that you were overly eager to celebrate your nuptials will perhaps be more forgivable if you adopt the pretense of being in love with each other."

When Tess made a faint sound of protest, Lady Wingate shot one last glance at her. "I know you will not fail me, my dear, after all I have done for you."

With that she turned away and disappeared beyond the stage curtains. Eventually Ian heard the faint echo of the ballroom door shutting. Otherwise, the resulting silence was deafening.

Tess still stood frozen, looking as if the sky had come crashing down upon her unwitting head.

To fill the uncomfortable void, Ian strode across the stage and flung the curtains open wide.

"What are you doing?" she demanded in low voice, her tone suspicious.

"Making it harder for anyone to eavesdrop again. I should think you've had enough of bystanders sneaking up on you for one afternoon."

She had no retort for that, yet Tess's defenses rarely were lowered for long. Deciding it was best to take advantage of the moment, Ian came straight to the point. "You heard Lady Wingate. Are you prepared to be sensible, Miss Blanchard?"

"I am always sensible," she retorted with a hint of her usual spirit. "But you are quite mad if you think I will wed you."

"Perhaps I am mad." Ian shook his head, a short mirthless chuckle escaping him.

"Surely you do not find this abominable situation amusing!"

In truth, he found a measure of cynical humor at their predicament. He most definitely had not expected to be making a proposal of marriage when he set out this morning to drive the five miles between Wingate Manor and Bellacourt, his family seat. It was even more ironic that after all his amorous liaisons in the past, coupled with all the years of eluding grasping matchmaking mamas, a simple bout of kissing should prove his downfall. Although there had been nothing simple about kissing Tess . . .

"Amusing?" Ian murmured. "Somewhat. Frankly, I find it unbelievable that I was so inept as to be caught kissing you. I must be losing my touch."

Her sniff was eloquent. "Well, *I* find it unbelievable that you would allow yourself to be coerced into matrimony," Tess rejoined.

"There is no coercion involved."

"Then why would the threat of scandal concern you? You have never cared one whit what polite society thinks of you."

He didn't give much of a damn about respectability for himself, but Tess was another matter entirely. "I care what happens to you. Lady Wingate is right. Your reputation will be in ruins if you don't marry me. The Perrys will see to it."

Her frustration, her utter dismay, was manifested in Tess's expression. Backing up a step, she sank down on the chaise and covered her face with her hands. "I assure you, *I* am not laughing," she muttered. "I only want to cry."

"Don't let me stop you."

Tess stiffened, as he had meant her to do; her chin snapped up so that she could glare at him. Ian was rather relieved by her feisty reaction. Needling her had always been the surest way to maintain the upper hand with her.

"If you mean to turn into a watering pot," he continued in a pleasant drawl, "I advise you to indulge now so that you can recover your appearance. If your eyes are red and swollen when you become a blushing bride, you will convince no one that we are making a love match."

Tess's glare deepened. "You are without a doubt the most provoking creature alive," she said through gritted teeth.

"I suppose that depends on your perspective."

"Mine is the only perspective that counts with me!"

"You are forgetting arbiters of the ton such as Sir Alfred and Lady Perry."

She hesitated, even though her dark eyes still glittered with helpless anger. "I should think you would want to help me get out of this awful predicament, Rotham."

"I suspect it isn't possible."

His fatalism seemed to disturb her even more. "How can you remain so calm?" she demanded in disbelief.

"I assure you, I am far from calm, but there is no use bemoaning fate if it can't be changed."

"*You* are capable of changing our fate. All you need do is tell Lady Wingate you refuse to wed me."

"I fear I will have to disappoint you, darling. My transgressions are vast, but I draw the line at ruining you. I compromised you, so now I must make amends." *And I feel guilty as hell for it,* Ian added to himself.

Tess's hands clenched in impotent fury. "It isn't right that I should be forced to marry you. I did not ask you to kiss me."

"But neither did you object."

"I intended to, just before we were interrupted."

Ian raised a quizzical eyebrow. Tess's flush indicated she knew very well she had been a willing participant in her seduction.

"Granted, I never should have taken it so far," Ian conceded. "But the damage is done now. You need the protection of my name."

When distress crossed her beautiful face once more, he softened his tone a measure. "Take heart, sweeting. No one who knows you would hold you to blame for our transgression. Everyone believes you to be a saint."

Her mouth twisted. "I am hardly a saint."

"But you are a pattern card of respectability."

"Until now I have been. It is utterly unfair that my one lapse should result in a life sentence."

Ian agreed, it was unfair that she would bear the brunt of society's disapproval. On the scale of social infractions, his were infinitely worse, but would be judged minor compared to this one slip from Tess. He'd been a rebel most of his life, but he had paid little price for his reckless scandals. Certainly his wickedness had not made him an outcast. He was a duke after all. Without an act of Parliament, he could literally get away with murder and scarcely suffer for it.

Ian shook his head sardonically. He disliked society's rules even more than Tess did, and he sympathized with her resentment of the hypocrisy. But the double standards employed for unmarried young ladies and powerful, wealthy noblemen were a fact of life.

He moved back across the stage to stand before her, holding the advantage since from her seated position, she was forced to tilt her head to look up at him. "I won't go down on bended knee, but I should make my offer formal. Miss Blanchard, will you do me the great honor of giving me your hand in marriage?"

"*No.*"

He bit back a smile at her succinct response. "This is no time to be stubborn. When an eligible suitor asks a lady to marry him, she should simper and blush and say, 'Lah, sir, but of course I will.'"

"Lah, sir, I will *not*," Tess insisted.

His amusement disappearing, Ian exhaled an exaggerated sigh. "Let me remind you of the consequences if you don't accept. The gossips will rip you to shreds. Contributions to your precious charities will end, not to mention losing your chief patron. And after this, your chances of marrying will be significantly diminished. They may even be nonexistent."

Of all those threats, he knew the second would be the most crucial to Tess. When Richard first entered the army, she'd become involved aiding families who had sent their men off to war. Then, upon her betrothed's death, she'd buried herself in her work as a way to lessen her own grief, to the point that her charities had become a passion for her.

Looking chagrined, Tess leapt up from the chaise and began to pace the stage. "There must be some alternative. Perhaps if we simply became betrothed and then later called off the engagement . . ."

"That would only postpone the inevitable scandal," Ian replied. "Given my reputation, a betrothal that doesn't lead to marriage would be even worse for you in the end, especially after what Lady Wingate's guests saw today."

Tess clenched her teeth and continued pacing. Watching her, Ian decided he would do better to let her rant for a while, to burn her anger out. In the end, she would see there was only one course open to her.

Turning, he sat down in a chair, then stretched out his long legs and crossed his boots at the ankles. "Pray tell me, what objections do you have to becoming my wife?"

She shot him an incredulous look. "You must be

jesting. There are countless reasons, but the chief one is that you don't love me, and I don't love you."

"You have far too many romantic notions. Members of our class marry for a host of socially accepted reasons, but love is rarely one of them."

"*I* planned to marry for love, and you are not the sort of man I could ever love."

Ian winced inwardly at her stinging avowal, although outwardly he shrugged. "I suppose you are still in love with Richard."

"Of course I still love him."

He had suspected as much. Even if Tess was officially out of mourning for her late betrothed, she was still devoted to his cousin's ghost. "I'm afraid that can't be helped."

When she made no reply, Ian adopted his same provoking drawl. "Your trouble, Miss Blanchard, is that you are overly idealistic."

"And you are an unabashed cynic."

"No doubt I am."

Cynicism was bred into him; he'd learned it by imitating his illustrious father. But love was a concern all on its own.

He was not enamored of Tess. Oh, he desired her . . . intensely. It shocked him how much he wanted her. But desire was not the same thing as love.

His attraction to her had always irritated him, Ian acknowledged. And it would likely be even worse now that he knew what it felt like to have Tess in his arms.

He shifted in his seat, recalling the rioting of his senses when he'd embraced her on the chaise a short while ago. His first taste of her had been beyond all expectations, and so had his reaction to her. Even though she kissed like an innocent, he'd never felt such hunger, such fierce impatience with a woman before. Admittedly, he'd lusted after Tess for years. He'd fantasized about claiming her, about losing himself in her—

Sharply, Ian disciplined his thoughts. "Love is vastly overrated," he told her.

"Even if it is, you know very well we would never suit," Tess retorted. "We would make each other extremely unhappy."

That was indeed a possibility, Ian thought, although he made no comment.

"Besides, you obviously dislike me."

That wasn't the case at all. "I don't dislike you."

"You always act as if you do."

Only because he was determined to hide his desire for her.

Aloud he said, "Your fierce aversion to me is hardly flattering."

"I have no wish to contribute to your self-conceit."

"Don't turn waspish, darling," he remarked in a light tone.

She blushed, even as her defensive gaze met his. "I am merely stating a fact. No doubt there are legions of females who would be enthralled by your proposal, but I am not one of them."

Ian wondered how many women would leap at the chance to wed him, not to mention bed him. But not Tess. She was unique in that respect, along with many others.

"You have made your point," he said evenly. "You

don't wish to wed me. But you are forgetting the advantages."

"What advantages?"

"You will find there are significant benefits to becoming my wife. A duchess can get away with a great deal more than a mere young miss."

"I know that," she answered, an edge of bitterness in her tone. "But I will gladly forgo such pleasures."

"Can you afford to turn down my fortune when your chief patron has given you an ultimatum and vowed to abandon you? I am quite wealthy, Tess. I will promise to contribute generously to your causes, and I am prepared to make you a substantial marriage settlement, every farthing of which you may spend on your charities if you wish. Just think of all the good you could do. It should be some consolation that you can continue tilting at windmills to your heart's content."

His argument didn't seem persuasive, judging by her grim silence as she continued stalking back and forth across the stage.

"Sit down, sweeting," Ian said dryly. "You will wear out your slippers."

To his surprise, Tess obeyed and returned to sit on the chaise, although she perched on the edge, straight-backed and rigid with frustration.

"If you reflect on it unemotionally," Ian suggested, "you'll see the wisdom of our immediate nuptials."

"I don't *wish* to be unemotional. We are talking about *marriage* . . . a lifelong, irreversible union. This will change every aspect of our lives irrevocably."

"Would it comfort you any if I said we could treat

our marriage strictly as a business contract? After a suitable interval, we can live separate lives if you wish."

Her look turned guarded. "Do you mean that we would be husband and wife in name only?"

That was not quite his meaning. "The marriage must be consummated for it to be legal, but afterward, we needn't share a bed or even a home."

Ian didn't expound further. He would eventually be expected to sire an heir to carry on the title, but he thought it unwise to mention that obligation to Tess just now.

As for his choice of brides, he had planned to make a marriage of convenience someday, to a gentlewoman with a dispassionate nature and similar background to his.

Not a woman like Tess, who was warm and spirited and filled with passion for her causes. She was no meek, simpering young miss, even if at the moment she was at a severe disadvantage, trying to come to terms with her unwanted fate. Otherwise, she fit his requisites for his duchess quite well. And he suspected that the physical aspects of their marriage could be more than satisfactory.

An image entered Ian's head of them together in the bridal bed. He could picture Tess's long, glossy-dark hair flowing around her lovely bare body, her legs wrapped tightly around his hips as he took her—

Cutting off the unwanted vision, Ian said more curtly than he intended, "We will both have to make the best of a difficult situation."

After a long silence, Tess spoke in a weak voice. "I fear you may be right."

"We should be married on the morrow, before the gossips can savage your reputation."

Renewed dismay claimed her features, but at least she didn't argue. Ian pulled out his pocket watch, noting that it was nearly one o'clock. "I had best leave now if I hope to reach Doctor's Commons in time."

"In time for what?"

"I need to procure a special license to wed. I will likely remain in town overnight to visit my solicitor and make the financial arrangements we discussed. But I should return by late tomorrow morning."

Tess bit her lower lip hard. "You are just going to leave me here to face Lady Wingate and her house-guests alone?"

"You needn't face them unless you wish to." He cocked his head. "In fact, you are welcome to accompany me to London if you like, but I should think you would rather remain here and prepare for our wedding."

She flinched at that. "I expect I should attend the play's performance this evening if I hope to maintain my contributors' goodwill, although it will be difficult to carry on as if nothing has happened. And it will be utterly impossible to pretend we are making a love match as Lady Wingate suggested."

Ian didn't reply directly, not wanting to delay his departure with a futile discussion about love and love matches. "Where would you like the ceremony to be held?"

Looking stunned again, Tess gazed mutely back at him, as if finally accepting that this was really happening to her.

Rising, Ian said in a bracing tone, "You may decide

where the blessed event is to take place. Any of my homes might do . . . my house in London, the chapel at Bellacourt, here at Wingate Manor, your own house in Chiswick. Or you may prefer a church wedding. I doubt if St. George's in Hanover Square is available at this late date, but you may have other ideas. If I recall, you planned to wed Richard in the village church in Chiswick."

"No, not there," Tess said. "It would be a mockery to wed in a holy church for an unholy union."

She shuddered slightly, evidently an involuntary response. Even so, Ian couldn't help wincing again, in addition to feeling another wave of guilt along with a fresh desire to comfort her. It would take a harder heart than his to be impervious to this beauty with the passion-bruised mouth and vulnerable eyes.

Stepping closer, he reached down to touch the backs of his fingers to her cheek. His voice lowered as he gazed down at her. "I truly regret that it has come to this pass, Tess."

"So do I," she whispered, drawing back and looking away.

Remorse was Ian's chief sentiment as he waited in the entrance hall of Wingate Manor for his carriage to be brought around. He deeply regretted forcing Tess to the altar. In fact, he regretted the entire damned morning.

His first mistake was overreacting when he parted the stage curtains to find her kissing Hennessy. He'd felt an instinctive rage, a deep-seated, primal male possessiveness that he'd never felt with any other woman.

Then he'd compounded his error by taking Tess to task for her wanton conduct and revealing the extent of his jealousy.

It wasn't that he harbored any deep feelings for her, Ian reasoned. He simply wanted to save her from a Lothario. Yet he couldn't deny that he savagely disliked the idea of Tess giving herself to another man, particularly one of Hennessy's hedonistic tendencies.

He hadn't liked the idea of his cousin Richard having her either, Ian remembered. He could still recall his first sight of Tess at her comeout ball. She was laughing with Richard with the intimacy of old friends, the expression on her face one of fond delight.

Her delight had suddenly arrested, however, when Ian stepped forward, as if she'd become sharply conscious of the sexual awareness pulsing between them. When Lady Wingate made the introductions, Tess stared up at him warily through a fan of dark lashes. She wasn't intimidated by him, Ian thought, merely cautious. And given his wicked reputation, he couldn't blame her.

He'd wanted her from that first moment, though. When he danced with Tess at Lady Wingate's urging, the heady sensation of being so near to her had gone straight to his head—and to his loins as well. He'd been immediately, shockingly aroused.

His wild physical response to Tess had no justifiable rationalization. The sensual hunger she stirred in him was far out of proportion to their respective ages and experience.

He'd been twenty-six at the time, well on his way to becoming a rake like his late father. As a genteel young lady making her bow to society, Tess was much too innocent and proper for his tastes.

Oh, she was an acknowledged beauty, no doubt about it. Her thick, glossy hair was mahogany dark and rich; her face fine-boned and captivating, her complexion pale and perfect. Her figure was slender but enticingly ripe in all the right places.

She had a serene loveliness about her, an unmistakable feminine allure that drew Ian against his will. She'd left a deep mark on his memory that night, a mark that had only increased over the years since. But even though Tess's magnetic beauty bowled him over at a physical level, it was her passionate warmth and spirit that touched him on a much deeper plane—as did, ironically, her genuine goodness.

Perhaps because it was such a contrast to his own misspent youth, Ian suspected, when he was a wild, moody lad with a tree-sized chip on his shoulder.

He had wasted his younger years living on the edge of compulsive excess, defying society's dictates and living down to his licentious father's expectations. After inheriting the title at twenty-two when his ducal father was shot in a duel by a jealous husband, Ian had further tarnished his reputation by spending all his time in gaming hells winning enormous fortunes, and in various bedrooms indulging in amorous affairs with women who pursued him primarily for his title and wealth.

Compared to him, Tess Blanchard was a saint. Even without the comparison, she was laudable. She had a giving heart that was unfeigned, and an indomitable spirit that had earned his admiration. Even though she had suffered bitter disappointments in recent years—having lost both her parents and then her beloved betrothed—she'd risen above her own misfortunes to lessen the misfortunes of others. Ian couldn't help but be impressed by her strength and resilience, by her tenacity and courage.

Tess was a fighter as well as being a pioneer of sorts. Like other young ladies of her genteel station, she made up baskets of food for the poor, stitched shirts and knitted stockings, and collected donations from the neighboring gentry. But her efforts went much farther and had a far greater impact.

One of her chief causes was the Families of Fallen Soldiers, relatives and loved ones of those who had died fighting in the decades-long war against French tyranny. She also visited soldiers' hospitals in London to comfort sick and wounded veterans. And over the past summer, she had expanded her solicitations to the entire Beau Monde and organized several charitable benefits that drew the cream of the ton, including the Prince Regent.

It amused Ian to watch Tess at work, soliciting funds from the wealthy denizens of the ton. She was sweetly ruthless, persuading with charm and common sense, and if that failed, shaming them into opening their purses. She frequently managed to get her way, despite the obstacles in her path.

But admiration or not, Ian had done his utmost to quell his attraction for Tess because Richard had laid claim to her the night of her comeout ball. He might covet what his cousin had, he might still feel the pull of desire every time he looked at her, but he possessed enough honor to consider her strictly off-limits. He'd even helped Richard salvage his courtship of Tess four years ago, Ian recollected.

And while Richard was abroad fighting a war, he'd kept away from her as much as possible. If he was forced by family duty or social convention to interact with her, he made certain he always riled her—picking fights, dictating to her, generally throwing around his weight as head of Richard's family—in part to conceal his craving for her, but also because his state of arousal around Tess frequently put him in a foul mood.

Even after his cousin's death, Ian kept up the pretense of being at odds with Tess and only backed off a little out of consideration for her grief.

He hated to see her grieving, though. He'd been the one to break the news to her of his cousin's death two years ago, conveying the letter from the War Ministry commending Richard's valor on the battlefield at Waterloo.

It was the second hardest thing Ian had ever done. The hardest was seeing the resulting devastation in Tess's eyes. Her sorrow had ripped through his chest. Even though he'd brought Lady Wingate with him to try and console Tess, she had proved inconsolable, then or in the months that followed. Her betrothed's untimely death had changed her, had stolen the laughter from her eyes.

A fierce protectiveness had welled up inside Ian that day. And he still felt protective of her, whether he wished to or not. As a consequence, he'd made certain that Tess was well guarded by her servants whenever she went to London to visit hospitals or asylums to care for wounded war veterans. And more recently, he'd commissioned actor Patrick Hennessy to look after her when she visited the theater district to foster clever new projects that generated income for her charities.

He hadn't wanted Tess to know he was so concerned for her welfare. There was no point in advertising his involvement with her charities either. As soon as he returned from London, he would remind the actor of his promise to keep quiet, Ian noted.

His outsized protectiveness was largely the reason he hadn't fought having to wed her. He felt obliged to save Tess from a scandal he had caused.

By marrying her, he would also be making reparations of another sort. Although for good reason, he'd been the one to send Richard off to war in the first place, thus changing Tess's fate irrevocably.

At least Lady Wingate should be pleased by the marriage, Ian surmised. The baroness's violent reaction to their wanton conduct had seemed a bit overplayed, now that he had time to consider it. In fact, he suspected her ladyship of trying to throw them together, much as she'd done four years ago at Tess's comeout ball. But if she wished to promote a love match between them, this was hardly the way to go about it, forcing Tess to choose between her beloved charities and ruination.

"Your carriage is ready, your grace."

His reflections interrupted by the Wingate butler, Ian donned his greatcoat and beaver hat and stepped out into the rain.

He likely wouldn't sort out his complicated feelings for Tess any time soon. And just now he had to drive to London to procure a special license for a marriage neither of them had anticipated . . . and she, at least, violently opposed.

The impending termination of his bachelorhood didn't exactly fill him with delight either, Ian admitted. Yet he couldn't deny that it had crossed his mind recently to court Tess himself. Indeed, for the past several months—ever since Lady Wingate had insisted her goddaughter was coming out of mourning—he had toyed with the notion of seriously considering matrimony, and of making Tess his first choice.

He'd doubted she would be amenable to his suit, though. He had done too good a job of deliberately antagonizing her.

And now, Ian thought with a sardonic twist of his lips, it probably served him right that he had to deal with the extreme ill will he had purposefully sown.

Shaken and dismayed, Tess was grateful to reach her bedchamber at Wingate Manor without encountering anyone. She couldn't bear to face the baroness or any more gawking houseguests just now. Not when she had to struggle with such a life-altering decision.

As Tess let herself into her room, the weight settling on her chest made it difficult to breathe. She was aghast to think she would have to marry Rotham despite their mutual antagonism—and furious at herself for letting this disaster come to pass.

Yet you will be facing a worse disaster if you don't accept his offer, she reminded herself. Not only would scandal render her an outcast in society, her precious charities would be devastated.

Tess didn't doubt that Lady Wingate would carry out her threat to ally with the entire ton against her. The baroness actually had ties to Rotham's family by marriage; Judith's late sister-in-law had been his maternal aunt. But they might as well have been related by blood, given their forceful natures. Her ladyship had an acerbic wit just like Rotham, and had regularly run roughshod over her weakling husband before Baron Wingate's untimely demise from a lung ailment several years ago.

Rotham was just as strong-willed as Lady Wingate, perhaps more so, Tess acknowledged. He was a nobleman accustomed to getting what he wanted—which was one of the prime sources of friction between them.

How could she wed a man who was so vexing, so overbearing, so dictatorial? His arrogant high-handedness made her blood boil.

"If anyone could induce me to murder, it would be Rotham," Tess muttered to herself. "How can I endure an entire lifetime of being his wife?"

He was right on one score, however, she conceded grudgingly. It was difficult enough for her as a woman—and a single lady at that—to raise funds for even the most worthy causes. It would be impossible if she lived under a cloud of scandal.

And as Rotham had pointed out, as a duchess, she would be in a much better position to aid her charities. As it was now, she had only a fraction of the power and influence Rotham possessed by virtue of his rank and fortune.

Marriage to him, though, would shatter all her plans and hopes for her future, Tess thought despondently. She had earnestly hoped to find true love again. And recently she'd been encouraged by the success of her closest friends—the three beautiful but staunchly independent Loring sisters—and even her cousin, Damon Stafford, Viscount Wrexham. She'd watched this past year as one by one, they found love and happiness in marriage.

Although Tess didn't know if she would ever love again, their felicity—no, their *joy*—had inspired her to play the matrimonial mating game once more. Besides, she wanted a husband and children someday. Thus, she was willing to risk the whims of fate, even though she knew firsthand how incredibly painful it was to lose a loved one.

Crossing to her valise, Tess pulled out the last letter Richard had ever written to her. *My dearest love,* the salutation began.

Her eyes welled with bittersweet pain as she smoothed the well-worn pages with her fingertips.

She had known Richard Sutherland all of her life, having grown up in the same country neighborhood in Chiswick, partway between London and Richmond. Since he was only two years older, they had played together as children. Surprisingly, their friendship blossomed further after he went off to university, chiefly because they kept up a written correspondence.

Tess was glad to have her dear friend Richard's support at her comeout ball, particularly since she was flustered to meet his handsome elder cousin, Ian

Sutherland, the sinful Duke of Rotham. Rotham had a wild reputation, but had attended her ball at the invitation of Lady Wingate, who had sponsored Tess's entire London Season. His wickedness should have made him anathema at a young lady's debut, but in the eyes of the hypocritical ton, the duke's family connections combined with his high rank and enormous fortune made him a supremely eligible match.

Rotham's powerful physical allure had unnerved Tess, though. In comparison, his younger cousin Richard was a much gentler man, sweet and thoughtful, instead of intense and dangerous to her peace of mind.

When that same night Richard had asked to court her, Tess had welcomed his suit and forcibly repressed her forbidden attraction to his wicked cousin.

She'd always wondered, however, if Richard had acted out of jealousy that night. Certainly he resented his cousin's wealth, since Rotham controlled the purse strings and refused to increase his quarterly allowance.

Richard had chafed at his lack of funds, yet it surprised Tess when shortly after her comeout ball, he had entered the army on an officer's commission purchased by the duke. Richard had never before shown interest in a military life, but he was not cut out to be a clergyman, and a gentleman of limited means had few ways to earn a livelihood other than the military or the Church.

He was off fighting the war when Tess lost her mother to a lung fever late that same year. Richard's letters had comforted her greatly, though, and when he came home on leave and proposed to her, they had agreed to a quiet betrothal. They planned to marry after her official year of mourning for her mother ended, but before the wedding could take place, Napoleon escaped imprisonment and Richard was called back to war. Tragically, he was killed in the Battle of Waterloo in the summer of 1815.

To shut out her grief at losing her betrothed, Tess had thrown herself into supporting various charities, including founding the Families of Fallen Soldiers. She also continued teaching classes part-time at her friend Arabella Loring's Academy for Young Ladies. She had a modest fortune, so she wasn't forced to work for her living, but she wanted to give herself a sense of purpose as well as fill the vast hole in her life.

Now, two years later, Tess had overcome her numbness of spirit and was satisfied with her life for the most part. But she still longed for love to replace the emptiness.

If she were ruined by scandal, though, what chance for love and marriage would she ever have? The lonely dreariness of a life lived in chaste spinsterhood held scant appeal.

That was the chief reason she had kissed Hennessy today, Tess remembered. For two years now, she'd led a colorless, passionless existence, one with no spark, no fire, and she'd vowed to change that.

But her resolve to live life more fully had landed her in deep trouble—

A quiet rap on her bedchamber door startled Tess out of her reverie. Quickly she wiped her damp eyes and returned Richard's treasured letter to its velvet pouch and tucked the pouch into her valise.

When she opened the door, she found the youngest and most passionate of the three Loring sisters standing there. Lily had recently married Heath Griffin, the Marquess of Claybourne, after a spirited courtship. With Lord Claybourne's financial support, she had initiated her own charitable endeavor, starting a home for destitute and abused women, and had attended Lady Wingate's house party to help promote Tess's causes.

"Is it true that you accepted Rotham's proposal of marriage?" Lily demanded as she swept into the room.

"It is true that he proposed," Tess said, shutting the door after the dark-haired beauty, "because we were caught in a compromising position. But I haven't yet accepted his offer."

"What in the world happened, Tess? I heard you were discovered together in a passionate embrace, but I thought you and Rotham were mortal enemies."

"I wouldn't call us *mortal* enemies, although we don't get along."

"Then why ever were you kissing him? And why would you allow it to go so far? Lady Perry said you looked as if you were already lovers."

Tess flushed. "We are *not* lovers, Lily. We just . . . became carried away. The deplorable truth is, Rotham kissed me as a sort of experiment, and I lost my senses. I couldn't help myself."

Lily's expression turned more sympathetic. "When Heath kisses me, I lose all ability to reason, so I am not surprised that Rotham affects you that way. He does have a reputation for being a devil with the ladies. That is partly why they call him 'the Devil Duke.' But I hate to think of you wedding him, Tess. It is such a mismatch."

"I know," she agreed feelingly.

"You are a veritable angel compared to his devil," Lily added with a faint scowl. "But Lady Wingate insists that you will marry him. You know we will stand by you if you choose to defy her."

"In good conscience, I don't believe I can defy her," Tess replied quietly.

She couldn't lightly dismiss her obligations to her godmother, not after all the baroness had done for her. As girls, Judith and Tess's mother, Susan, had been bosom friends and attended school together. With no children of her own, Judith considered Tess more a daughter than goddaughter. After Tess's father died from a fall in a hunting accident when she was sixteen, the baroness had borne the expense of a London Season, and utilized her role as a leader of society to gain Tess's entry to the best circles.

When recently Lady Wingate began pushing her to consider matrimony again, Tess had been willing to do so. But Rotham would have been her very last choice for her husband. . . .

Upon seeing the despairing look on her face, Lily wrapped her arms tightly around Tess, hugging her close. "I suppose you will have to marry him," she said, finally drawing back.

"Yes, I suppose I will. The alternative is unthinkable." Tess forced a smile, despite her feeling of helplessness. "If I refuse, I will dwindle into an old maid and play the fond aunt to your children instead of having children of my own. Worse, everything I have worked for these past years will be totally wrecked."

"What does Rotham say?"

"He wants the ceremony to be held tomorrow. In fact, he has gone to London to procure a special license."

"So soon?" Lily's tone held the same dismay that Tess's had.

"In his view, if we must wed, it is best done quickly, before the scandal has time to set in."

Worry darkened Lily's features. "What do you plan to do now, Tess? Is there any way I can help you?"

"I think I want to go home. I don't feel capable of pretending we are making a love match, as Lady Wingate wishes us to do."

"I will accompany you. You shouldn't be alone at a time like this. Heath can remain here and woo Lady Wingate's houseguests for their donations."

Tess shook her head. "I would rather you stay and assume my role. Dorothy will be at home to console me," she said of her companion, Dorothy Croft.

"Are you certain?" Lily asked, sounding unpersuaded.

"Yes. I can manage on my own, dearest. The most pressing decision is where to hold the ceremony. I planned to marry Richard in the village where we grew up, but it doesn't seem right to use the Chiswick church with Rotham."

"Why not Danvers Hall? You know Arabella will support you in any way possible."

The Loring sisters had lived at Danvers Hall in Chiswick for several years, before the estate was inherited by the new Earl of Danvers, Marcus Pierce.

After Arabella, the eldest sister, had wed Marcus, she continued to make her home there, while Roslyn and Lily had moved out to live with their new husbands.

Tess pursed her lips thoughtfully. "Danvers Hall might work."

"Then I will write Arabella at once and let her know." Lily shook her head in disbelief. "Just think, Tess, by this time tomorrow you could be married and preparing for your wedding night."

At the realization, Tess couldn't suppress a shiver. Rotham had promised they could live separate lives after the consummation, but she still had the wedding night to get through.

Heaven help her.

She didn't want to share a marital bed with him, even for one night. She didn't want him arousing her or tempting her or overwhelming her with his devastatingly sensual kisses. Her wild response to him earlier today had frightened her. Never in her life had she ever lost control like that—

Lily evidently comprehended her reservations, for she offered a suggestion. "If you are worried about the physical aspects of marriage, you know you can apply to Fanny for advice. If anyone can help you defend yourself against Rotham's sensual powers, it will be Fanny. No one knows more about men than she does."

Lily made an excellent point. A dear childhood friend of the Loring sisters, Fanny Irwin had craved a more exciting life than rural Hampshire offered, and so had run off to London at the tender age of sixteen to become a renowned Cyprian. But the sisters had loyally refused to repudiate Fanny for her sins, particularly after their own reputations were irretrievably tarnished by their parents' vivid scandals.

In fact, Tess had discreetly aided Fanny in the past—last summer, when Lily had taught several young courtesans at Fanny's London boardinghouse to improve their manners and grace. Fanny would likely be willing to return the favor, Tess presumed, and advise her how to deal with an expert lover like Rotham.

Particularly what to do on your wedding night during the consummation.

Her heart leaping at that alarming thought, Tess nodded. "I shall write Fanny immediately and have a Wingate footman deliver my message. Hopefully she will have time to meet with me before the ceremony takes place."

She desperately needed Fanny's help in defending herself from Rotham, Tess knew. If his mere kisses could steal her senses and incite her to abandon a lifetime of training and all her moral scruples, what would an entire night in his bed do to her?

Turning back to her valise, Tess drew out her small leather-bound diary and tore out a blank sheet in order to pen a note to Fanny.

She firmly refused to acknowledge feeling anything but dismay just now. Her pulse was *not* thrumming with excitement at the prospect of consummating a marital union with Ian Sutherland, the Duke of Rotham.

This marriage would be a total disaster, for they were utterly mismatched. Rotham brought out the very worst in her, Tess declared silently.

Furthermore, she adamantly ignored the sly voice

in her head insisting that he also brought out an admirable quality in her: The way Rotham constantly challenged her and roused her fighting spirit set her blood to racing.

The only thing she was willing to admit, Tess vowed, was that she was in very, *very* big trouble.

Chapter Three

I rashly longed for sparks in my life and now my wish will be granted in spades. My marriage will be vastly different from the sweet, gentle love match I expected to make.

—Diary Entry of Miss Tess Blanchard

In the end, Tess agreed to marry the Duke of Rotham.

When she sought out her godmother to report her decision, Lady Wingate seemed appropriately mollified by her capitulation, and allowed that since the house party at Wingate Manor was scheduled to last three more days, Danvers Hall would serve best for a small, quiet wedding ceremony.

However, the baroness opined, it would be most fitting for the newlyweds to repair directly to Rotham's family seat afterward, so as to remain out of the public eye for a time. Additionally, such a magnificent estate as Bellacourt would remind the Beau Monde just what a grand match Tess was making, even if it *was* a bit tainted by scandal.

Lady Wingate also softened her condemnation of Tess with something of an apology.

"You may think I am being cruel, my dear, by forcing this marriage upon you—and I do regret that you object so violently to taking Rotham as your husband. But I have high hopes that your union will work out when all is said and done."

Tess shared nothing of her godmother's confidence and saw very little prospect for wedded bliss with Rotham. But she dutifully permitted the baroness to announce their betrothal that evening and asked that her absence from the amateur play performance be excused since she needed to prepare for her wedding the next day.

Patrick Hennessy's apology to Tess, on the other hand, was visibly more abject and heartfelt.

Despite the awkwardness of facing the actor so soon after the debacle of their interrupted kiss, she had to consult with him briefly before leaving for Chiswick in order to settle their account and give him a bank draft to pay for his troupe's services over the past week.

"*Please* allow me to beg your forgiveness again for daring to kiss you, Miss Blanchard," Hennessy implored after pocketing the draft. "I have no notion what came over me."

"It was not entirely your fault, Mr. Hennessy," Tess replied, her cheeks warming in embarrassment at her own willing participation.

"'Tis a wonder you didn't box my ears as I deserved. And that his grace refrained from running me through in a fit of jealousy. At least it seems to have brought him up to scratch and inspired him to offer for your hand after all this time."

Tess's flush deepened. Clearly the news of their imaginary love match had spread through Wingate Manor like an outbreak of ague. "His offer had little to do with jealousy of you, I am certain."

When a skeptical look crossed the actor's face, his response reminded Tess of Rotham's earlier unexpected revelation.

"Why did you never tell me he had hired you to keep an eye on me?"

Hennessy regarded her ruefully. "The duke bade me keep quiet on pain of death because he feared you would take offense at his interference. But he thought concern for your safety was warranted—a lady going about town alone, and in Covent Garden no less, where you could be mistaken for a . . . a . . ."

When the actor hesitated, Tess filled in the missing word. "A lightskirt, you mean."

"Well . . . yes," Hennessy admitted sheepishly. "You are nothing of the kind, Miss Blanchard, but your forays into the thespian sphere open you to certain charges, no matter how admirable your motives. Once you become a duchess, though, your ventures are likely to cease."

Tess frowned at him. "I well know how my forays are regarded, Mr. Hennessy, but I intend to continue holding charitable benefits even after my marriage to Rotham."

"I wonder if you will be permitted to do so," the actor said worriedly. "Especially after today. The duke is no doubt eager to cut out my liver, and he will not wish you to employ my troupe again. Indeed, he could ruin me and my company with scant effort."

"I would never allow that to happen," Tess declared loyally. "I assure you, he will have no say in my future endeavors."

She would make certain Rotham stayed out of her

business dealings, Tess vowed to herself, especially when it came to employing Patrick Hennessy and his theatrical company. With his remarkable talent, Hennessy had been invaluable in orchestrating this week's amateur performance by wealthy houseguests who could then become patrons of her charities, and in raising funds for her two London benefits—deciding on the programs, hiring and managing the actors and opera singers, and building the stage sets. The recent musical evening at the Theatre Royal alone had brought in the enormous sum of two thousand pounds. Tess knew she could never have had a fraction of that success on her own. She was not about to give up Hennessy's organizational skills or relinquish the opportunity to raise even more funds using his creative genius.

The actor obviously held doubts about his continued employment, but he shrugged and flashed a placating smile. "I hope you are right, Miss Blanchard. I expect, however, that I have just missed my best chance to advance my investigation of the spirit world. A recent ghost sighting was reportedly made at the duke's castle in Cornwall, but now in all likelihood, I shall never be granted permission to visit there and examine the truth of the rumors for myself."

"Rotham's castle is said to be haunted?" Tess asked with mild interest.

"Yes. I only learned of it while researching the play I wrote for your theatrical tonight. I have been corresponding with a scholar who is a noted authority on Cornish spirits. The ghosts at Drury Lane have not been spied for years, but those at Falwell Castle are of recent origin—last winter, in fact."

Tess pursed her lips in thought. She vaguely recalled that Rotham possessed a castle in Cornwall, but had never heard of it being haunted.

"Still," the actor added hopefully when she was silent, "might you consider putting in a good word for me with the duke once you are his duchess, Miss Blanchard? If I could somehow garner an invitation to Falwell, I could experience a new ghost firsthand. I would be forever in your debt."

The return of Hennessy's good-natured brashness did not surprise Tess, yet almost made her roll her eyes in exasperation. Her life was in chaos, her future with her soon-to-be husband completely uncertain, and all the actor was interested in was researching ghosts? Moreover, he had to know that after the contretemps this afternoon, this would hardly be the ideal time to ask the duke to help him.

Since she owed Hennessy more than she could repay, however, Tess didn't reject his request out of hand.

"Perhaps a visit to the castle can be arranged, Mr. Hennessy. Meanwhile, I would ask that you oversee tonight's performance and treat our amateur actors with special care, since I will not be here to assist you. You know as well as I how to flatter their vanity and keep in their good graces."

"Certainly, Miss Blanchard. And again, I am grievously sorry for taking liberties, particularly if I precipitated complications with the duke in any way."

As am I, Tess thought as she turned away and headed toward the stables. *As am I.*

* * *

Tess was grateful when her dependable coachman and footmen whisked her away from her godmother's country estate in Richmond to her own home some ten miles away.

After her mother's death, Tess had turned down the baroness's invitation to come live at Wingate Manor. Instead, she'd remained in Chiswick, near her dearest friends, in her family home. Not only was the charming house large and comfortable, it was less than an hour's drive to London—a significant advantage since she visited London so frequently on behalf of her charitable causes.

Tess had taken a companion for propriety's sake, however, in a mutually beneficial arrangement. Dorothy Croft's presence allowed her a vital measure of independence that she could never have had otherwise. And she provided the widow with a home and much-needed income, as well as a large, well-lit studio for painting her precious watercolors.

Dorothy was actually fairly skilled as an amateur artist, and she had the dreamy mentality of an artist as well. Tess found her companion in the attic studio, brush in hand as she contemplated a blank canvas. When told about Tess's impending marriage to the Duke of Rotham, the elder lady did not seem at all surprised.

"That is lovely, dear. I am very pleased for you. It is high time you married, you know." Her eyes clearing, Dorothy suddenly regarded Tess in dismay. "Do you mean to tell me I will soon be out of a home? Will his grace wish to reside here? Do you want me to leave?"

"No, dearest," Tess said quickly. "You may live here as long as you please. I expect Rotham to remain at his family seat in Richmond or his house in London, and I shall likely move in with him."

At least for a time, Tess added to herself. Thankfully, he had promised they could live separate lives and even have separate homes once the sensation of their abrupt marriage faded.

Dorothy looked relieved before returning her attention to her canvas. "Thank you, dear Tess. Now if you will excuse me, I must paint this rosebush before I lose my inspiration. I had the most marvelous concept. . . ."

Tess managed a smile and kissed her companion's soft cheek, then made her way downstairs to her bedchamber. She loved Dorothy dearly, but the absentminded lady was not likely to provide much support in helping her deal with her menacing disaster.

With the aid of her maid Alice, Tess began to unpack her luggage from her weeklong stay at Wingate Manor, then tried to decide what gown she should wear for the marriage ceremony and what clothing she would need once she wed Rotham. Her wardrobe was smaller these days, since she'd given away her mourning weeds of black crepe and gray bombazine as part of her resolve to rejoin the living. She had no wedding trousseau, of course—

Suddenly feeling overwhelmed, Tess sank down helplessly in a chair.

"Are you ill, Miss Blanchard?" her maid asked in a worried tone. "Shall I fetch Mrs. Croft's smelling salts?"

"Thank you, Alice, but I will be fine in a moment. I think perhaps I will leave my packing until tomorrow, when Lady Claybourne will be here to help me choose what to take with me."

Lily, bless her, had promised to bring her two sisters over first thing in the morning. Thank heaven, Tess thought morosely, since there was no possibility of her managing the feat just now. Not when her entire future was on the verge of being shattered.

After dismissing Alice, Tess pulled out her diary and opened it to the last entry, when she had been so hopeful about the outcome of the house party. She was at a loss now about what to write, though, given all her chaotic thoughts and feelings.

"Stop wallowing in self-pity," Tess chided herself. "Throughout history, women have been forced to make unwanted marriages, and most of them survived."

And I will too. . . .

I hope.

Since she had failed to bolster her flagging spirits, Tess eagerly welcomed the crunch of carriage wheels in the drive barely an hour later. A glance out her window confirmed her hope that Fanny Irwin had come in response to her panicked note.

Hugely relieved, Tess hurried downstairs herself to admit Fanny.

As expected, the courtesan had traveled here incognito in a plain, closed carriage, and wore a hooded cloak so as to keep her visit unremarked. Although Fanny appeared quite well-bred, dressing demurely in high-necked gowns of dark fabrics and wearing her raven hair pulled back in a severe knot, she couldn't help looking like the exotic beauty she was.

After handing Fanny's wet cloak to the housekeeper and asking for refreshments to be sent up, Tess led the courtesan back upstairs to the sitting room adjacent to her bedchamber.

"I came at once," Fanny said, crossing to the hearth fire to warm her chilled hands. "Of course I will do whatever I can to help you, Tess. You have done so much for me and all of my friends, I can never repay you."

The Cyprian was famous and expensive, Tess knew, but Fanny's sharp wits and highly-tuned feminine instincts, even more than her sultry looks and lush figure, had brought her to the top of her overcrowded profession at the relatively young age of four-and-twenty.

She was trying to leave the demimonde, however. Her first Gothic novel had just been anonymously published, and she'd begun writing a second one, hoping to establish a new career that would allow her to marry for love as her close friends, the Loring sisters, had done.

Tess had actually fostered Fanny's research for her current novel by introducing her to Patrick Hennessy, who had given them an intriguing tour of Drury Lane Theatre and shared delightful legends about the ghosts of long-dead thespians.

Once they were settled with a fresh pot of tea and biscuits to give them sustenance, Fanny got straight to the point. "From what I hear, Rotham will likely be a difficult husband to manage."

"I don't doubt it," Tess murmured. "It is why I called upon you to advise me."

Fanny had aided and abetted the Loring sisters significantly during their recent courtships, Tess knew. Her own cousin Damon's wife, Lady Eleanor, had also benefited from Fanny's expertise. And most recently, Madeline Ellis, the bride of Arabella's close neighbor, the Earl of Haviland, had sought her help.

"Perhaps," Fanny suggested, "we should begin with what we know about the duke. I understand he began sowing his wild oats at an early age."

"Quite early."

Most of Tess's knowledge about her intended husband she had learned from society gossip and of course Richard, who had complained bitterly about his dictatorial elder cousin. But she gave Fanny an abbreviated version of Rotham's past.

After his mother died giving Ian Sutherland birth, he was left to the tender mercies of his father, who was something of a wastrel as well as a libertine. Ian ran wild as a child, and after he was out of shortcoats, persisted in breaking all the rules of gentlemanly behavior. Yet because he was heir to a dukedom, he was exempted from any serious consequences. Tess actually envied his freedom, even if she couldn't always admire his rebel actions.

After inheriting the title, he'd continued regularly shocking the ton, even vying with professional gamesters in the worst hells. He had uncanny successes at the card tables—the luck of the devil, some said—and won huge sums. Then, through clever investments and ruthless business dealings, Rotham had transformed his winnings into an immense fortune.

"I have seen his skill at the gaming tables for myself," Fanny said at the conclusion of Tess's summary. "He is also known for his mastery over the fair sex, but reputed to be cold and distant when it comes to emotions. You will not conquer his heart easily, Tess."

"I have no desire for his heart, believe me," she vowed. "I only want to know how I can defend myself against him."

"What precisely do you mean? You likely needn't worry about your wedding night. I'll wager you will find the pleasures of the marriage bed exceedingly enjoyable."

Tess took a large swallow of tea for courage. "In truth, that is what I fear, Fanny. I don't wish to give Rotham such power over me."

Briefly she related how she'd fallen victim to her senses this afternoon when the duke had merely kissed her. She was still a little shocked by the intense passion he had made her feel. She wasn't eager to surrender her body to Rotham either, even in the sanctity of matrimony, for carnal intimacy would likely make her that much more vulnerable to him.

"Sexual attraction is normal and natural," Fanny assured her. "Especially with a man like Rotham. So perhaps you shouldn't try to fight your responses, merely control them."

"I would be elated to learn how to control them," Tess said fervently.

Fanny smiled at her impassioned tone. "You should

be glad he is a skilled lover, for it will likely make the consummation go more easily for you. But so the physical aspects of his lovemaking will not take you by surprise, I can tell you exactly what to expect from your deflowering and how to lessen the impact of his sensuality. Forewarned is forearmed."

"Thank you, Fanny," Tess replied in gratitude.

The courtesan eyed her thoughtfully. "Are you not the least bit excited about finally knowing the secrets of passion? I would be, were I in your shoes."

She hesitated, looking down at her teacup. She had accepted Richard's proposal of marriage with joy, yet if she were strictly truthful, she had never quite felt the kind of romantic ardor for him that she'd always dreamed of. Which had left her feeling a trifle guilty.

She felt a similar guilt now because she couldn't help a delicious twinge of anticipation at the thought of becoming Rotham's lover.

"I suppose I am, a little. But I dislike the thought of being at Rotham's mercy. We may have to remain at Bellacourt for an indefinite period. Lady Wingate believes we should absent ourselves from town until the scandal fades—in fact, she suggested we consider going away on a wedding journey for a time. But I cannot contemplate being alone with Rotham for that long."

When an idea struck her, Tess glanced back up at her friend. "I wish you could accompany me to Bellacourt after the wedding ceremony, Fanny. I could use your support and protection. I would ask Dorothy, but she is so meek and mild, Rotham would eat her for breakfast."

Fanny shook her head at Tess's impulsive proposal. "I understand your worry, but your patrons would not look kindly on you having so notorious a house-guest. It is one thing for me to quietly visit you here, where you can rely on your servants' discretion. It would be quite another to brazenly batten myself on you so soon after your nuptials. For your sake, Tess, it is best to let the furor over your sudden marriage die down first."

Tess sighed, knowing Fanny was right. Inviting a famous courtesan to stay with her at her new residence during the initial days of her marriage was not the way to avoid scandal, which was the prime reason for wedding Rotham in the first place. Once she was firmly established as his duchess, she should be able to get away with a good deal more.

"I suppose part of the reason for my anxiety," Tess said, "is that I have so little experience. I never did more than kiss Richard."

"I have never really kissed Basil either," Fanny admitted. "Unless you count the time he helped save me from abduction, when he reacted from relief of the moment."

Taken aback, Tess raised her eyebrows. "Is that so? You have never even kissed?"

The courtesan's mouth twisted in dry humor. "I know—it is supremely ironic, considering my profession. And supremely frustrating as well. I had hoped to be betrothed to Basil by now, but he may never offer for my hand. His pride, you know. It is bad enough that I spent all these years sharing my body with other men, but even if Basil is able to overlook my wicked past, I suspect he cannot dismiss that my wealth exceeds his."

The target of Fanny's affection was her former childhood neighbor in Hampshire, Basil Eddowes. Basil had been secretly in love with Fanny since their youth, before she set out for London to make her fortune, much to his bitter disappointment. Tess had met him this past summer at Fanny's London boarding-house, where he lodged. At the time, Fanny and Basil had sparred and squabbled regularly, until her abduction by a ruthless gamester had roused the hot fires of jealousy in him and spurred him to hint at his amorous feelings.

A scholar and law clerk by education and training, Basil was presently a junior secretary to a nobleman, but he didn't earn enough to support Fanny in her accustomed lifestyle, a circumstance that the courtesan feared embarrassed him and made him feel unworthy of marrying her.

"My relationship with Basil is more like yours was with Richard," Fanny said. "It began as a friendship, not a grand passion, and I am not certain it will ever progress any further. Honestly, I am almost afraid to press Basil by displaying a greater physical affection. What if he doesn't enjoy kissing me, or worse, making love to me?"

"I cannot imagine that he wouldn't," Tess replied faithfully.

As she drank another swallow of tea, she found herself frowning thoughtfully. Listening to Fanny lament her own amorous problems had reminded Tess that as a wealthy duchess, she would be in a position to help her friend as well as her charities.

It was then that Tess remembered what she had learned about her future husband's castle. "Mr. Hennessy told me about some interesting rumors today, Fanny. Supposedly there are ghosts inhabiting Rotham's castle in Cornwall."

"Ghosts?" Fanny straightened, her expression brightening with interest.

"So Hennessy says. If so, it might be an ideal place for you to write your new Gothic novel, since your story is set in a haunted mansion. Even if you won't come with me to Bellacourt, I could perhaps arrange for you to visit Falwell Castle. Cornwall is a long distance away, at least two full days' drive, so the ton is unlikely to take offense at your staying there."

Fanny's face fell again. "It sounds intriguing, but I don't want to leave London just now. Basil might forget me entirely in my absence. Even if I remain, I may never be able to persuade him to propose."

The courtesan suddenly waved her hand in dismissal. "Now enough about me and my romantic troubles, Tess. We need to discuss your marriage to Rotham. Tell me *exactly* what happened this afternoon when he kissed you."

Despite the embarrassingly intimate nature of Fanny's advice, Tess was grateful to have a practical knowledge of carnal relations, and more importantly, ways to fortify her defenses against Rotham's sensual powers.

After they finished their discussions, Fanny stayed for supper. By the time the courtesan left to return to London, Dorothy had already retired to bed. Tess eventually followed her companion's lead, but she lay wide awake, feeling a great dread inside.

She didn't want a cold marriage of convenience. She wanted true love. She wanted to *matter* to her husband.

Rotham didn't even believe in love—he'd as much as admitted his cynical sentiments this afternoon. And he certainly cared nothing for her, other than a professed obligation to protect her from the dangers of London.

Then again, Rotham would likely give her the passion she longed for.

She had never known real passion, just a sweet and tender love. Remembering, Tess squeezed her eyes shut.

She secretly regretted never having experienced physical intimacy with Richard. He had wanted to consummate their love before he shipped out that last time, but she was saving herself for marriage and so wouldn't allow it. She'd been so caught up in appearances, so determined to behave with propriety, that she had missed out on one of the momentous events of womanhood—giving herself to the man she loved. Now she was likely never to know that joy.

Tess rolled over and punched her pillow.

Losing Richard had taught her how trivial and petty society's rules were compared to life-and-death issues, so it seemed particularly galling that once again she had to conform to the ton's dictates for the sake of propriety—and even worse, wed a nobleman who was renowned for his very wickedness.

* * *

Tess spent the night tossing fitfully. The next morning, however, she had no time to dwell on her misfortunes since her friends descended upon her to help make her ready for her wedding. In a flurry of missives from Rotham and Lady Wingate, she learned that the ceremony was set for two o'clock at Danvers Hall. So before she knew it, Tess was entering Arabella's drawing room, dressed in a simple but elegant gown of rose-colored silk, about to speak sacred vows to love, honor, and obey.

When she spied Rotham at the far end of the room, she reluctantly acknowledged the violent fluttering of her heart. He cut a commanding figure, his blue tailcoat molding his strong shoulders and deceptively lean frame, which she knew was all hard muscle. With his devilish elegance, the duke would never be mistaken for anything less than an aristocrat, but the intimidating aura of power about him made him unique.

He moved easily, gracefully, as he approached her. Tess, however, couldn't help recalling her last sight of Richard dressed in his scarlet uniform the day he left with his regiment to fight Napoleon's revived army. Nor could she fail to compare this moment with the wedding nuptials she had long expected.

Thus, when Rotham greeted her with a polite "Miss Blanchard," she merely inclined her head and murmured, "Your grace" in return. They might have well been strangers.

The guest list was small, but included Tess's dearest friends: Her godmother, Lady Wingate; the three Loring sisters and their husbands; Tess's cousin Damon and his lively wife, Eleanor; Dorothy Croft; Jane Caruthers, the spinster who oversaw the daily operations of the Freemantle Academy; and the academy's original patron, Winifred, Lady Freemantle.

Tess's women friends flanked her protectively until it was time to begin the ceremony. Rotham evidently noted their concern, for his gray eyes glittered with irony as he led her to stand before the vicar.

Her mind was a riot of scattered thoughts and feelings just then. How many weddings had she attended this past year, watching her friends and neighbors and cousin become bound to their life-mates? The vicar was the same clergyman who had married Arabella and Lily.

He was getting a good deal of practice, Tess thought irreverently as his gentle voice droned on.

The sense of unreality continued to plague her throughout the liturgy. Some while later, though, it was over and Rotham gave her a brief kiss to seal their vows.

His lips were cool, yet they still stirred the same deplorable heat inside her as yesterday, Tess realized to her regret. So did his casual touch at her back when he guided her toward a side table to sign the marriage lines that would make their union official.

She hesitated for a moment before taking a deep breath and putting ink to parchment. Then glancing up, Tess met her new husband's eyes.

For better or worse—likely much worse—she was now wed to the Duke of Rotham.

The duke's own feelings were a perverse mixture of resignation, triumph, and regret.

Resignation because he disliked losing control of his fate.

Triumph because he now had legal claim to the one woman in the world he'd thought he could never possess.

And regret because once again he had driven the laughter from her eyes.

Ian glanced down at the lovely, vibrant woman he had just wed. There was no trace of Tess's enchanting smile. No expression at all except sadness . . . and perhaps trepidation.

The last thing Ian wanted was for Tess to fear him.

"You might attempt to lighten your expression, love," he suggested in a dry tone. "Pretend for a moment that you are not going to your doom."

Tess's back stiffened for an instant before she visibly made an effort to relax. "Everyone here knows our circumstances. They would disdain the hypocrisy if either of us feigned joy."

"Perhaps, but your friends now look ready to draw their swords and skewer me if I dare take a wrong step."

She glanced around at their audience. The wedding guests were eyeing Ian with various degrees of concern, even belligerence on the part of the youngest Loring sister.

Tess smiled at Lady Claybourne before turning back to Ian. "I believe Lily is unarmed at the moment, but she has recently become skilled with a rapier and would no doubt be willing to use it in my defense."

Ian's mouth curved. "Is that a warning?"

"You might say so," Tess rejoined with a hint of her usual archness. A moment later, she sighed. "You are right—we should keep up appearances. If you will contrive to say something in the least witty or amusing, I would find it easier to comply."

He gave a mock wince. "Meaning my usual wit is lacking. You wound me."

She manufactured a mild laugh, which caught the attention of half the room. Still, there was a spark of humor in Tess's dark eyes that relieved Ian.

"Where will we go from here, your grace?" she asked. "Bellacourt?"

"Yes. Surely no one will object to me taking my bride to my family seat for a measure of privacy. You may invite your friends to visit you whenever you wish—the sooner the better, in fact—so they can be reassured that I am not beating you or starving you or chaining you away in my dungeon."

Surprisingly, interest flared in Tess's eyes. "You have a dungeon?"

"Not at Bellacourt. It was merely a figure of speech."

"What about your castle in Cornwall?"

His eyebrow lifted. "Falwell? Actually it has quite a large dungeon. Why do you ask?"

"A dungeon might prove useful for a friend of mine."

"You have a friend who chains up prisoners?"

Tess's soft laugh was more genuine this time. "Only in the fictional sense. She is a writer of Gothic novels and is currently plotting her latest tale. She hopes to include an element of fright—nothing too gruesome, merely suspenseful enough to make readers shiver. And a dungeon could provide ideal fodder for inspiration, especially one that might be haunted by ghosts. I should like to hear more about yours, Rotham."

"I would be happy to oblige sometime, love," Ian replied. "For now, however, we should join the others before they decide you need rescuing. In any event, I believe Lady Wingate wishes to toast our nuptials."

Tess's smile faded at the reminder, but she accepted his arm without protest, then raised her chin as if girding herself for a losing battle.

My bride. My wife. The words sounded strange to Ian. Stranger still was realizing how impatient he was to be alone with Tess.

No doubt his desire to leave Danvers Hall had something to do with his reception by the company. Since the ton was actually rather small, he knew all the noblemen present, some of them fairly well. But he hadn't expected to be approached by each and every one of them during the course of the next hour.

The first to pull Ian aside was Tess's cousin Damon Stafford, Viscount Wrexham, who said quietly, "I want to offer you a word of warning, Rotham. Should you hurt my cousin in any way, you will answer to me."

"I assure you," Ian replied, keeping his tone bland, "I have no intention of hurting her."

"See that you don't."

No sooner had Wrexham walked away than Heath Griffin, Marquess of Claybourne, took his place. "You should be aware that your new wife has a large number of friends, Rotham."

Ian suspected that Lady Claybourne had prompted her husband to make her and her sisters' concerns known. But the next warning came from Marcus Pierce, the Earl of Danvers.

Ian held up a hand, preempting him. "Don't tell me. You have come to threaten me with bodily injury should I harm a hair on my new wife's head."

"Not a threat, a promise," Danvers said easily.

Ian might have been amused had he not known the noblemen were deadly serious. Even so, he could respect their position and was glad that Tess had so many friends who cared about her welfare, even if *he* was the one who would suffer the consequences of failure.

Last was the tall, fair-haired Duke of Arden, Drew Moncrief. Arden's wry smile of understanding mirrored Ian's sardonic one. "I suspect you know what I wish to say, Rotham."

"I believe I do. Your new duchess is worried for *my* new duchess and has charged you with seeing that I don't hurt her."

"I won't need to lift a finger in her defense," Arden added. "My wife and her sisters think of Tess as their own. You don't want to make them your enemies."

"I expect not. I consider myself fairly warned, Arden."

Then Lady Wingate came up to him and proceeded to express her fears for Tess. "I have begun to wonder if I acted too precipitously," the baroness began. "If you are harboring any thoughts of revenge at being compelled to wed her, you should not blame Tess. I am at fault, Rotham. . . ."

With effort, Ian listened patiently and refrained from lifting his eyes to the ceiling when claiming that he had no thoughts of revenge and promising to treat Tess with consideration and respect.

Lady Wingate did not look entirely reassured, but she left him to rejoin Tess, who was surrounded by the Loring sisters.

Ian studied his bride for a moment, then glanced at the mantel clock, wondering how soon he could escape the intense scrutiny of her friends and have her to himself.

Chapter Four

❦

*I admit Rotham sometimes astonishes me and
contradicts my long-held opinions of him.*
        —Diary Entry of Miss Tess Blanchard

By the time the bridal couple departed Danvers
Hall for Richmond, the chill, drizzling rain had
ceased, but dusk had fallen. Within the relative
warmth of his closed carriage, Ian observed his new
wife.

Tess had spoken little once they were alone together and refused to meet his eyes. A melancholy
frown pursed her lips now as she gazed out at the
darkening countryside, her thoughts obviously far
away.

She didn't stir even when they reached Bellacourt.

"Pray forgive me for interrupting your dismal ruminations," Ian drawled, "but we have arrived."

Seeming finally to become aware of her surroundings, Tess gave him her full attention. "I beg your pardon? What dismal ruminations?"

"You are still stewing about our marriage, are you
not?"

"Truthfully, I was thinking of something else entirely."

Visibly shaking off her musings then, she bestirred herself and accepted his hand to descend the carriage.

Yet when she stepped down, Tess hesitated a long moment, looking up at the magnificent residence of mellow golden stone. Displaying grace and grandeur in every line, Bellacourt boasted four vast wings of four stories each, built around a large central courtyard. Tess had visited there twice before with Richard, Ian knew, but she'd seen only a fraction of the many rooms and few of the numerous outlying buildings on the estate.

He meant to try and make her feel welcome, though. He well remembered what it was like growing up at Bellacourt as a child. The cold, lonely formality of his home had been unrelieved by a procession of nannies and governesses and tutors, or by the presence of his only surviving parent, since his dissolute father much preferred the sinful pleasures London offered.

"I have instructed my majordomo to make a place for your servants," Ian said while guiding Tess up the wide front steps. "Your maid and coachman and footmen will have rooms for tonight. Tomorrow we can discuss what further staff you wish to reside here with you."

She glanced up at him with sharp puzzlement.

"You seem surprised," he remarked. "I am not such a complete ogre that I would deny you your own servants."

"I did not think you were a *complete* ogre," was her mild retort.

Ian bit back a smile at that show of her former spirit. "I will introduce you to my housekeeper and majordomo this evening," he continued, "but meeting the remainder of the staff and touring the house can wait until morning if you wish. You must be fatigued after the unsettling events of the past two days."

Her brows drew together as she studied him with something close to suspicion. "Thank you," Tess replied, reverting to her previous emotionless tone. "I would indeed prefer to wait."

As they reached the front door, it was opened by an imperious, silver-haired man dressed in ducal livery, and a much more congenial older woman.

Ian performed the introductions as promised, making her known to Mr. Gaskell and Mrs. Young, then added once they had handed over their outer garments, "Mrs. Young will show you to your apartments so that you may dress for dinner."

"I trust I will have my own rooms?" Tess queried in a low voice.

A dry smile curled his lips. "But of course. Somehow I knew you would insist upon it."

Bending, he kissed her fingers, which clearly startled her. "Smile for our audience, darling," Ian murmured for her ears only. In a louder voice, he said, "Pray join me in the drawing room before dinner, my love. I will be counting the moments."

When Tess was shown to her splendidly appointed rooms, she was comforted to find her maid Alice there before her. Having a familiar face with her as she prepared for dinner bolstered her spirits—although it seemed strange to hear herself addressed as "your grace," especially with such awed reverence as Alice displayed.

She was the Duchess of Rotham now, however, and as such would have to grow accustomed to the fawning deference afforded ladies of her exalted new rank.

Tess doubted her husband would show her similar deference in his manner of address. Not only was theirs an adversarial relationship, but Rotham had all the advantages in their marriage . . . legal, financial, physical.

There was little point in fretting over her position of weakness, she knew, but Fanny had advised her to start off on the right footing, to establish boundaries from the very beginning. Accordingly, Tess braced herself for the evening ahead and prepared to take the offensive.

Upon descending the stairs, she was met by Gaskell, the Bellacourt majordomo, who conducted her through the large east wing to the drawing room.

Once again the rich furnishings and artwork gracing the walls dazzled her. It was hard to fathom that she was now mistress of such a magnificent estate. But when Tess caught sight of the nobleman standing near the mantel, she only had eyes for him.

Rotham wore a different coat now—this one burgundy—and white satin evening breeches. His own gaze briefly surveyed her rose silk gown, the same one she had worn for their wedding, before he offered a pleasant greeting. When she made no reply, he dismissed his majordomo and crossed to a side table, where a decanter of sherry sat.

Tess watched him as he poured two glasses. His hair was too long for fashion, and the tawny brown

locks curled over the edge of his high collar. The careless touch softened the aristocratic arrogance of
Rotham's chiseled features, with their high cheekbones and forehead.

His tone, however, had lost little of its usual mocking edge when he spoke.

"You might attempt to cooperate in our pretense of
a love match in front of the servants," Rotham said,
handing her one of the glasses of wine.

"I fear I am not skilled enough as an actress to
manage that feat," Tess remarked, keeping to her
plan to begin on offense. "And I certainly see no need
to do so in private."

Rather than respond in kind, he changed the subject. "Did you find your rooms satisfactory?"

"As much as possible under the circumstances."
Tess glanced around the large, splendid drawing
room. "I expected to feel sympathy for the poor female who agreed to be your duchess, but I concede
there are many ladies who would be thrilled to be
mistress of such a grand estate as Bellacourt."

"But you are not one of them." He took a swallow
of his sherry. "You are not exactly my ideal bride
either. You are too managing and independent for my
tastes."

Tess felt stung by his honesty. It was vexing also to
admit that her feminine pride might be a little
wounded, knowing that Rotham had no desire to
wed her.

"No doubt you prefer someone more helpless," she
said, parrying his gibe. "I am sorry to disappoint
you."

She expected him to say something cutting in return, but he merely gestured toward the same side table. For the first time Tess noted the silver tray lying there.

"Those are for you."

Curious, she went over to inspect the tray's contents—several official-looking documents and a small, blue velvet box.

"Open the box," Rotham instructed.

When Tess did, inside she found a lovely gold locket on a delicate gold chain. Lifting the bauble from its resting place, she shot him a puzzled glance.

"Your birthday gift," Rotham replied to her unspoken question. "It occurred to me that your birthday was spoiled, so you ought to have your gift now. I brought it with me to Wingate Manor yesterday, but never had the opportunity to give it to you."

"You brought me a birthday gift yesterday?"

Tess stared at Rotham in near shock. She could not have been more surprised if he'd claimed to have plucked the moon out of the heavens for her.

Tearing her gaze from his, she focused on his gift. The locket was simple, but an appropriate birthday remembrance from a family acquaintance to a single young lady—which was what they had been yesterday before Rotham had interrupted her ill-conceived experiment in passion and set them on the path to marriage with his devastating kisses.

"The Rotham jewels also belong to you now," he added, "and are much more valuable . . . although since many of the pieces are entailed, you cannot sell them. They are in a bank vault in London for you to wear any time you wish."

When Tess fell silent, unsure what to say, Rotham

continued. "Those documents are from my solicitors—various legalities to allow you to keep your own fortune and properties, in addition to the details of our marriage settlement. The last is my wedding gift to you—a bank draft for the Families of Fallen Soldiers. As you recently told your major contributors, with winter coming on, the funds are badly needed."

Tess stared at the draft for two thousand pounds, then mutely lifted her astonished gaze to Rotham. She had been prepared to meet him with defiance and belligerence, but his thoughtful gifts had completely taken the wind out of her sails. Were his magnanimous overtures a peace offering of sorts? An attempt to reduce their constant warfare and call a truce in their verbal sparring?

"Th-thank you," Tess stammered. "I never envisioned such generosity from you."

His mouth curved. "I well know your opinion of me, sweeting. Perhaps that alone spurred me to prove you wrong."

If he had schemed to confound her, he had certainly done so, Tess thought, taking a long swallow of wine. She must have drunk too quickly for she suddenly felt light-headed. Swaying, she brought her fingers to her temple.

Rotham immediately reached out to support her elbow. "Sit down, Tess. Did you eat anything today?" he asked as he led her to the nearest chair.

"Not much," she admitted, consciously responding to his continued kindness.

"Drinking wine on an empty stomach is not wise. We will go into dinner shortly."

"I am not particularly hungry."

"Even so, you should eat."

At his forceful tone, Tess stiffened out of habit, then applauded her instinctive response. She didn't want to live in armed warfare with Rotham, but neither did she want to become even more vulnerable to him than she was now. She was making a poor job of keeping her distance thus far.

"Is that a command, your grace?" she asked airily.

That half-smile etched his mouth again. "A suggestion, merely. But I might remind you that not three hours ago, you vowed to love, honor, and obey me."

Glad to be back on familiar ground, Tess arched a taunting eyebrow. "Surely you do not expect *obedience* from me?"

"No, I know you better than that," he returned with amusement. "Obedience is far beyond my expectations. And you declared yesterday that you could never love me. So that leaves honor." His smile faded, while his eyes fixed on her. "I expect you to honor our marriage vows, Tess, even though they were made under duress. I have no desire to be cuckolded."

The suggestion that she would ever commit adultery, regardless of how their marriage had begun, filled her with indignation. "I would never dream of cuckolding you, your grace. Although it is a matter of supreme indifference to me if *you* fail to honor our vows. Indeed, I expect you to seek your pleasures with your numerous mistresses."

At her adamant reply, he studied her for a long moment, as if trying to gauge her sincerity. Then his expression seemed to lose its intensity and his sardonic humor returned. "My numerous mistresses? How many do you think I have?"

"Rumor suggests that you have several."

"Rumor would be wrong."

"You cannot deny that you have kept mistresses in the past."

"Never more than one at a time. And I have none now."

Tess shrugged, although her show of indifference was pure bravado. She sincerely hoped her husband would not choose to flout their vows so savagely and sully their union—or if he did, that he would be discreet about it.

"I only meant," she explained, "that I am not opposed to having a liberal marriage."

"I never realized you were so broadminded."

"I am, rather. It comes from having several married friends. . . ."

She hesitated, debating whether to mention her friendship with Fanny Irwin.

Just then Gaskell appeared to announce that dinner was served. She allowed Rotham to escort her to the smaller of Bellacourt's two dining rooms. The table was still enormous and sparkled with crystal and china.

Instead of sitting at each end, however, parted by the vast length of the table, Tess found herself seated at Rotham's right. When they had begun the soup course—the first of many dishes and removes—and the liveried footmen had left them alone, Tess returned her attention to Fanny, not only to provide a distraction from her own marital difficulties, but because she sincerely wished to help her friend.

"Do you happen to need a secretary, Rotham?" she began. "I know you are not much involved with politics in the House of Lords, but with your vast business enterprises, you must have numerous tasks that require clerical assistance."

"I have two secretaries now. Why do you ask?"

"I know someone who would be ideal for the position. His name is Basil Eddowes. For the past several years, Mr. Eddowes has worked as a law clerk for a London solicitor, but just recently Lord Claybourne secured him a post as a junior secretary for an elderly nobleman. His salary is not sufficient for his needs, however, and I hoped to improve his prospects."

Rotham's expression remained neutral. "Why such a marked interest in this Eddowes fellow? Is he a former beau, perhaps?"

"Not a beau of mine. His affections are set on someone else entirely." Tess paused before launching ahead with the nascent plan that had been forming in her head ever since last night. "Are you by chance acquainted with Fanny Irwin?"

She could tell her question was unexpected. "The Cyprian, Fanny Irwin?"

"Yes. Fanny is a dear childhood friend of the Loring sisters, and has become a close friend of mine these past few years."

Rotham's eyebrow shot up. "I find it surprising that you claim a friendship with a leading citizen of the demimonde."

"It is actually not so unusual. . . ." A blush rising to her cheeks, Tess told him about meeting Fanny four years previously when the Lorings moved from Hampshire to Chiswick to live with their cantankerous uncle . . . how Fanny's craving for excitement had lead her to embark on a career as a lady of the evening, and how the sisters had refused to give up the connection with their bosom friend even after making brilliant society matches this past year, despite the courtesan's notoriety.

Her tale was interrupted when the soup was removed and the fish served, but once the footmen were gone, Tess continued, explaining about Basil Eddowes's odd courtship of Fanny.

"She no longer traffics with the gentlemen of the ton, but you can see why Mr. Eddowes would be hesitant to propose."

"I believe I can," Rotham murmured, his tone dry.

Tess ignored his remark and went on. "His pride is a large impediment, not only because of Fanny's scandalous past but the issue of finances as well. She has abandoned her expensive lifestyle entirely—recently she sold her grand London residence and moved to her much smaller house in St. John's Wood. But Basil wishes to support his wife in at least moderate fashion. If you were to hire him, he and Fanny could afford to marry."

"Go on," Rotham said evenly.

With that small encouragement, Tess warmed to her theme. "You could give him a job cataloging your library, for instance. I know Bellacourt has a well-stocked library. Or perhaps you could utilize him to good purpose in your business dealings. As a clerk, Basil's main duties were writing out fair copies of legal documents, but his talents were utterly wasted. Although he has more responsibility in his current secretarial position, he is capable and clever enough for so much more. He is also accomplished at ciphering and accounting. I believe he could prove a valuable asset to you."

When Rotham did not leap to agree, Tess hastened to add, "If you have no need of his services, I thought I might hire him to help manage the increasing contributions to my various organizations and the growing demands of arranging benefits and other charitable events . . . at a significantly increased salary, of course. But I don't wish to offend his pride. The offer would be better received coming from you. If I were to ask him, Basil would likely consider it charity on my part and refuse. If you would allow it, we could say that with my new obligations as your duchess, I will be too busy to continue overseeing my former responsibilities in the necessary detail."

His gray eyes surveyed her. "You seem to have put some thought into this."

"Well, I only began forming a plan yesterday. You were mistaken earlier in the carriage. I was not stewing about our marriage. I was thinking about how to unite Fanny and Basil."

A devilish light entered Rotham's eyes. "So you are set on playing matchmaker?"

"What if I am?"

"You know you cannot save everyone, sweetheart."

Tess gave him a quelling look. "Your cynicism is showing again, Rotham."

"As is your idealism. You want to be a champion for true love."

"I do indeed. I am determined to help my friends. Simply because *I* have lost any chance for love and happiness in marriage does not mean that Fanny must."

A muscle flexed in Rotham's jaw, but he made no comment.

Tess softened her tone. "Fanny has been extremely good to me. I owe her a debt for supporting me during the darkest period of my life, when I lost Richard so shortly after losing my mother."

She was not playing on Rotham's sympathies unfairly, Tess thought defensively. It was true that Fanny had helped significantly to bring her back to life and diminish her sorrow.

Rotham's expression had turned enigmatic again, though, making Tess doubt that she was persuading him. Taking a breath, she tried a different tack.

"If nothing else, I believe I can help Fanny become more respectable by offering her my patronage. Until now I have been compelled to avoid her in public. I have visited her home in St. John's Wood upon occasion, but I had to do so in secret. Because of my charities, I could not afford to be seen with a former Cyprian. It was immensely frustrating."

"I imagine it was."

She shot him a suspicious look. "No doubt you find my predicament amusing. *You* have never had to curtail your friendships to protect your reputation. You have no reputation to speak of."

"Thankfully I have not."

Tess couldn't tell if he was mocking her again. "I warn you, Rotham, even if you disapprove of my continued association with Fanny, I don't mean to give up my friendship solely because I am now your duchess."

"I have no intention of dictating your choice of friends, sweeting."

She felt a tension inside her ease.

"So you are set on making Fanny and her suitor one of your projects," he prodded.

"Yes. I may as well use my new position to help them." Tess fell silent for a moment, contemplating her unwanted fate. As a duchess, she might also have more freedom to be her own mistress—at least if Rotham's word could be trusted.

Eventually a sigh escaped her. "I am becoming resigned to our union. You were right. There is little use crying over what cannot be changed."

"I suppose that is progress," Rotham murmured in a dry undertone. "So what do you wish of me?"

"I want your permission to invite Fanny to Falwell Castle. I will understand if you balk at inviting her into any of your main homes, which is your right. In fact, I thought of inviting Fanny to Bellacourt to keep me company here, but she advised against it. Yet allowing her to visit your remote castle in Cornwall is not the same thing. And it could be beneficial for Fanny. . . ."

Once the main course of roasted pheasant and fricassee of venison was brought in, Tess told Rotham more about Fanny's new career as a Gothic novelist.

"And writing about the dungeon at Falwell would benefit her?" he asked.

"Yes. Dungeons are excellent settings for Gothics, and haunted dungeons would be doubly exciting for Fanny's readers. Falwell Castle is said to be haunted. Supposedly your servants have sighted the ghost of one of your late ancestors."

"Where did you hear that?"

"Hennessy told me. He is interested in the spirit world and has investigated ghost sightings around England and Scotland. In fact, he based the play he wrote for Lady Wingate's house party on his research. Is there any truth to the rumors about ghosts at Falwell?"

"My steward has reported hearing ghosts there these past few months, but I haven't had time to examine the matter yet."

Tess decided this was not the time to mention Hennessy's desire to explore Falwell's purported ghost, but Fanny's need was another situation altogether. "Well, haunted or not, your castle could offer the perfect atmosphere for Fanny's creative endeavors and perhaps provide material for her plots."

Tess couldn't quite entirely read the gleam in Rotham's eyes, but it seemed part amusement, part exasperation, and part admiration. "Very well, you have my permission to invite her."

"That isn't all. . . . I want to go to Cornwall with her."

When Rotham's eyebrow edged up again, Tess explained. "You know that Lady Wingate suggested we absent ourselves from London for a time in order to let the scandal subside. Well, if I must be exiled from society to dwell in purgatory, I prefer to do so in Cornwall rather than Richmond. Removing there has a prime advantage. I would not have to endure the gossips criticizing my every move, or Lady Wingate lamenting how my scandalous behavior has dismayed and disappointed her."

"There is that," Rotham agreed blandly. "Would you expect me to accompany you?"

"You needn't bother," Tess quickly replied. "You likely have no wish to visit Cornwall, so I will gladly go on my own—and take Fanny and Basil with me. I want them to have the opportunity to be together and fall in love."

"You seem to have it all plotted out."

"Not entirely, but I am working on it."

"If I fail to hire your friend Basil, will you make me into a villain?" Rotham queried, his tone not so much mocking as teasing.

Tess smiled for the first time since beginning her tale. "I need no excuse to make you into a villain, Rotham."

"I suppose not. But you are asking a great deal, you know—demanding that I sink so low as to play Cupid with you."

Her smile widened a little. "I am certain I can manage without you, but I would prefer to have your assistance in hiring Basil. Will you help me?"

He didn't reply, but his gaze dropped to her mouth. At his continued silence, Tess pressed on. "You said that you regretted making me wed you, Rotham. If you want to make it up to me, you will accommodate this one small request. You have the resources to make a major difference in my friends' lives, and I am asking you to intercede on their behalf."

Rotham leaned back in his chair, observing her over the rim of his wineglass. "Hiring your Mr. Eddowes shouldn't be difficult," he said finally, "although hiding the fact that we are in collusion might be trickier. And your traveling alone to Cornwall is another matter altogether. It is a two-day drive at minimum, even in a well-sprung post chaise when the roads are in good repair. I don't know that I want you hazarding the trip."

Tess grimaced. "I have told you before, you needn't concern yourself with my welfare."

"But I intend to. You are my wife now."

She sobered instantly at the reminder, which at last prompted a positive response from Rotham.

"I will consider all your requests," he said, surprising her, "if you will eat your dinner." He looked pointedly at her plate. "You have barely touched your food tonight, and my cook went to a great deal of trouble to please you with your first meal at Bellacourt."

"Very well," Tess said, feeling a trifle more optimistic. "I would not want to disappoint your cook."

Picking up her fork and knife, she applied herself to her pheasant while trying to forget that this was still her wedding night and that the worst still lay ahead.

Chapter Five

Fanny thinks I should be pleased that my husband is so attractive and reported to be highly skilled at lovemaking. Most women cannot say the same about their husbands or even their lovers. But I would be far happier were Rotham not so gallingly irresistible.
— Diary Entry of Miss Tess Blanchard

Ian kept his thoughts to himself during dinner as he watched Tess employ her persuasive tactics on him like a master. Her use of sweetly reasoned arguments to gain her way with him was new in his experience. He was more accustomed to deflecting ripostes from her tart tongue during their verbal jousts.

Yet he couldn't deny her appeal. Nor could he help noticing the way her lovely eyes brightened when she championed her friends. Her animation, her sheer passion for her causes, made Tess nearly irresistible. Even against his will Ian found himself wanting to agree to her proposition.

In truth, he had little enthusiasm for traveling all that distance to Cornwall in the pursuit of a dubious love for individuals he didn't even know. But he wouldn't spoil his first married evening together with Tess by refusing her request out of hand.

And she did have a point. There might be some advantages to removing themselves from London society for a time—most importantly, to a more intimate setting in which to become better acquainted with his bride. Cornwall would have fewer outside influences to interfere if he attempted to establish a new relationship with Tess.

Ian felt the stir of wry amusement as he wondered if their marriage would always be a series of negotiations.

He was not so amused, however, when after the footmen had served a dessert of fruit and cheese and were dismissed for the final time, Tess began eating even more slowly, obviously delaying the end of dinner.

"What are your plans for your next charity benefit?" he asked, on the theory that encouraging her to talk about her philanthropic endeavors might take her mind off their forthcoming wedding night.

Yet she seemed wise to his strategy. "If you mean to distract me, it will not help."

She relaxed a little when he changed the subject to discuss the servant staff at Bellacourt and her expected role as mistress here, but Tess visibly stiffened when he eventually announced that it was time to retire.

"Must we?" she asked, her tension returning.

"We are newlyweds and should act the part. Couples in love would not tarry at the dining table."

When she fidgeted with her wineglass, Ian decided he'd had enough of her trepidation.

"For appearance's sake, Tess, we must share the same bedchamber tonight, but we needn't consummate our union just yet. If it will ease your mind, I won't make any connubial demands until you are ready."

She searched his face, looking cautiously hopeful

for a moment . . . then nodded in relief, as if she believed his offer to postpone carnal relations. "I would much prefer to wait."

Taking a fortifying swallow of wine then, she added more firmly, "It may be a long while until I am ready. And you should know that after the consummation, I don't intend to share a marital bed with you. You said we could live separate lives, and I mean to hold you to your promise."

"If that is what you want."

"I do."

Ian watched Tess over his own wineglass. He could easily take her declaration as a challenge. Her reticence both annoyed him and pricked his vanity, inspiring a fundamental male instinct to prove his worth as a lover.

His rational side, however, debated with his natural impulses. There was no question that he wanted Tess in his bed—tonight and every night—but it would be far easier to keep his distance from her if he treated their marriage strictly as a legal contract, just as she wished to do.

On the other hand, arousing Tess might be the quickest means of overcoming her fear of him. He was confident he could change her mind about sharing a nuptial bed once she understood the kind of pleasure he could give her.

Ian took a swallow of his own wine. It was ironic that he would have to woo his own bride. He'd never had to exert himself to win any lover he wanted. Women never refused him; indeed, they practically threw themselves at him. And to his knowledge, he had never instilled sexual fear in any of them.

Then again, Tess was utterly unique, he reminded himself. And provoking her was still the most effective means of arming himself against her.

"I am prepared to be patient for a time," he deliberately drawled in that lazy tone that never failed to rile her. "But I trust you realize such forbearance reflects estimable gallantry on my part."

Her gaze narrowed on him.

"I should also point out that you will miss out on an exceptional experience if we don't become lovers."

Her chin lifting, she stared at him. "It amazes me," she finally said, "that entire minutes can pass before I am reminded how insufferably arrogant you are."

Ian bit back a smile. "You will turn my head with all your pretty compliments."

"Adding to your conceit was not my intention, believe me."

Instead of retorting, he stood and moved behind Tess to pull out her chair for her, bending to murmur in her ear.

"I've had no complaints about my lovemaking, sweetheart. But since you profess to have little knowledge of passion, I suppose you can be excused for your naïveté."

"I will forgo the pleasure of ending my naïveté, thank you," Tess snapped, rising to her feet.

His taunting had served to distract her, Ian decided as they climbed the sweeping staircase together. Yet he was somewhat distracted himself.

Tess did have a disconcerting way of keeping him off balance. Her earlier discussion of mistresses, for instance. Her implication that he would so easily commit adultery had stung him. He wouldn't deny that he'd had several mistresses in the past—and more liaisons than he ought. But he'd never been intimate with a married woman. He drew the line at cuckolding another unwitting chap as his illustrious father had been so fond of doing.

And he would never be so liberal where his own wife was concerned, even discounting the fierce possessiveness Tess kindled in him. He was not about to let her give her body to any other man, certainly not now that she was his. They were joined in holy matrimony now and he intended for both of them to honor their vows.

It would require a Herculean effort, though, to sleep in the same bedchamber with Tess and restrain his desire for her. But for both their sakes, Ian pledged, he meant to try. For now he would keep his hands off her if it killed him.

When at last he escorted her up to the ducal apartments and closed his bedchamber door behind them, he saw Tess's nerves visibly return. The suite was quite large, but Ian suspected it felt too small to her, having to be alone with him.

He noted how her gaze swept the room. The furnishings were done in burgundy and golds, with a massive four-poster canopied bed dominating one side. The covers were drawn down and someone—presumably her maid—had laid out her nightdress and dressing gown on the bed.

Despite the welcome fire in the hearth that took away any chill, Tess shivered, evidently still unsettled at the necessity of having to sleep with him.

"Do you need my help undressing?" he asked, keeping his tone placid.

"I can manage."

"The dressing room is beyond that door." He gestured toward the far side of the bedchamber.

Tess hesitated. "It occurs to me that we needn't share a bed at all, even to keep up appearances."

"Where do you propose sleeping then?" When she had no answer, he relented. "There is a chaise longue in the sitting room next door, where you may sleep if you wish. I advise you to take some blankets to ward off the cold. Although it seems foolish when there is a comfortable bed right here."

He waited for her reply to no avail. "I could volunteer to be noble, but I have no desire to endure such discomfort myself. My bed is large enough that we can each sleep on our own side."

When Tess still remained silent, Ian let out a breath in exasperation. "Your nerves are understandable, love, but I assure you, I won't ravish you in your sleep. I am that much of a gentleman."

"I believe you are," Tess said grudgingly. "It is just I have never slept with anyone before."

"That can be lonely."

She gave him a quelling look. "I doubt I will sleep a wink tonight," she muttered under her breath.

"I may not either," Ian murmured with complete sincerity.

After a long delay, Tess emerged from the dressing room uncertain how to act. Fanny had advised her to let Rotham take the lead on their wedding night, but what the devil should she do now that he didn't mean to consummate their union? She never would have envisioned such consideration from him, and yet she was grateful that he didn't mean to force her to honor their vows just then.

When Tess caught sight of Rotham, though, she came up short. Only partly dressed, he lounged in a wing chair, drinking from what looked to be a brandy snifter. Although he still wore his satin knee breeches and stockings, he'd shed his coat and cravat and shirt and had removed his shoes.

Her nerves ran riot at the sight of his bare torso. She wished he would don a dressing robe. It would be far easier to pretend indifference to him if he were not half naked—

Abruptly, Tess scolded herself. Much of the female population of England wanted the sinfully handsome Devil Duke. Perversely, she was determined she would not.

Even so, it was easier to mentally voice such a principle than to stand by it. Simply being alone in the same bedchamber with Rotham made her dizzy and incoherent. It didn't help that he was surveying her as if he could see through her concealing dressing gown. In turn, she tried not to look at his bare, smoothly muscular chest and instead forced her gaze back to his face. His features were leaner and harder than Richard's—

Irritated at herself for making such comparisons, Tess shut off her thoughts and strolled across the bedchamber to hold her chilled hands out to the fire. Yet her eyes were drawn irresistibly back to Rotham. She felt a stomach-tightening awareness of him as a man. His broad shoulders, the long, elegant muscles of his body, the lithe strength that seemed to radiate from him almost as an extension of his powerful personality, all captured her attention with bewitching ease.

He was entirely too compelling for her peace of mind, devil take him. And he knew very well he was affecting her. He looked at her in that perceptive way of his, as if realizing her disinterest was sheer bravado.

Heaven help her if he realized how fast her heart was beating, Tess reflected. It was bad enough that he thought her a nervous rabbit.

She winced, remembering how her vow to keep out of his bed had amused him. At least he was right about one thing. Since his bed was massive, it would be easier for them to stay on their respective sides.

His low voice broke her chaotic ruminations. "Come here, Tess."

"Why?" she asked rather suspiciously.

He held up the brandy snifter in his hand, which was three quarters full with amber liquor.

Eyeing the glass, she pasted a half smile on her lips. "First sherry, then wine with dinner, and now brandy. Are you trying to make me foxed?"

"I am trying to settle your nerves."

Agreeing with his goal, Tess moved toward him, her slippers making little sound on the Aubusson carpet.

"Now drink," he ordered.

She took the glass he offered her and dutifully sipped the brandy, welcoming the burn. Perhaps the potent liquor would indeed help to soothe her rattled nerves, or at a minimum, help her to sleep.

"I don't normally retire so early," she admitted,

making the observation to alleviate the awkward silence.

"Oh? What do you do in the evenings?"

"After dinner I usually spend time with Mrs. Croft, assuming I can lure her from her studio. If not, I keep myself occupied writing letters or with needlework. And I frequently read before bedtime."

She also often wrote in her diary, but she was not about to tell Rotham that, especially when he had recently become the prime subject of her private musings. She'd written four pages about him just since yesterday, after her life had suddenly turned upside down.

"Did you bring any reading material with you?" Rotham asked.

"Yes, but it is in my own bedchamber."

"It won't do for you to go traipsing down the corridor to fetch it."

"I suppose not," Tess conceded.

"We can always sit here and converse."

She didn't think that a wise idea, not when she was so conscious of his bare chest. She drank another long swallow of brandy and tried not to wince at the searing sting in her throat.

"Do you mean to leave your hair pinned up like that?" Rotham asked.

"I hadn't thought about it."

"You should take it down."

"Perhaps so," Tess agreed. When he politely retrieved the brandy glass from her and set it down, she reached up and pulled the pins from her coiffure, sending waves of glossy dark hair tumbling over her shoulders.

Rotham's gaze arrested as he studied her. "I have never seen your hair down before," he remarked, sounding as if the sight appealed to him.

He slowly rose to his feet then. Tess froze in place when he reached out to finger a long tress.

His hand shifted to her cheek next and stroked lightly. Tess shivered. It unsettled her intensely to be touched by this man.

It unsettled her more to think Rotham might kiss her, but she suspected that was precisely his design when he gently lured her chin upward with his thumb.

His gray eyes held her spellbound for a long moment. She could hear her own heart hammering as her gaze wandered to his mouth. Before yesterday she'd thought his lips would be hard like the rest of him, but now she knew better.

When he bent his head to let that hot velvet mouth graze hers, Tess sighed and leaned toward him involuntarily . . . yet somehow she found the willpower to turn her head to one side and press her palms against his bare chest.

"You said you would treat our union as a contract," she exclaimed breathlessly. "Kissing is no part of any contract."

"No, but it is the best way to vanquish your fear of me."

"I do not fear you, Rotham."

He emitted a soft sound of amusement.

"I do not," Tess insisted. "I am suffering the normal sensibilities every young lady has on her wedding night."

"I told you, I won't do anything you don't wish me to do."

"You are kissing me now when I don't wish it."

"Are you certain?"

Of course she wasn't certain. She only knew that she didn't want a disastrous repeat of yesterday, when she'd completely lost her senses.

Yet it was happening again now, just being in such close proximity to Rotham. How could she possibly think when his fingertips were drawing tingling patterns on her throat? When the warm swirl of his breath was caressing her lips and stealing *her* breath?

Tess felt a vivid shock of awareness when Rotham covered her mouth with his again, and yet unlike yesterday, his kiss was soft and sensual this time. She hadn't expected such tenderness from him, but that was exactly what he gave her. He rubbed his lips over hers, measuring their softness, inducing a fresh shiver of delight to slide down her spine and gather low in her belly.

Reality seemed to fade. In its place stole an intimate, overwhelming sensation. Tess felt dazed, as if she were slowly falling headlong into a vortex. She shut her eyes and swayed so weakly that Rotham had to steady her with one hand at her waist. Meanwhile, his mouth was tender fire, sending heat washing over her skin and throughout her body.

She was unaware of the passage of time, but when Rotham finally raised his head, she stood there clutching his bare shoulders.

"What more can I do to set your mind at ease?" he asked in that low, husky, tender-rough voice that stroked her senses.

Dragging her eyes open, Tess blinked up at him. His expression was gentle, his eyes as warm as she had ever seen them. She could not have spoken, though, if her life had depended on it.

When she didn't reply, he smiled again. "We should go to bed, love."

His suggestion was like a dousing of cold water and made Tess go rigid. Jerking her clinging hands away from his half-naked form, she took an abrupt step backward.

At her reaction, Rotham cocked his head at her. "I would never have pegged you for the craven sort."

Tess swallowed and tried to regain her composure. She was *not* craven. And she refused to let her nerves get the better of her, especially in front of this man. "You are right, this is absurd."

Turning, she moved around the end posts to the far side of the bed. She kept her back to Rotham as she shrugged out of her robe, giving him only a glimpse of her concealing nightdress. Then she climbed into the high bed and pulled the covers up to her chin.

The silence that followed was broken only by the quiet crackle of the fire and the whisper of clothing as Rotham undressed. Tess kept her gaze averted until she heard him moving around the room.

Wondering what he was up to, she peered over her shoulder and saw that he was putting out the lamps. Her initial glimpse of him, however, startled her. He was not wearing a dressing gown or even a nightshirt.

To her regret, she couldn't look away. Rotham had always been fascinating and forbidden to her, and in the glow of firelight that still illuminated the bed-chamber, he seemed even more so. He was virile and vital enough to make her breath catch, his nude body lean and sleek with muscle.

But of course he would be well-honed. He was a sportsman and a member of the Corinthian set, his muscles hardened by riding and fencing and amateur fisticuffs at Gentleman Jackson's salon.

"Do you mean to sleep in the nude?" she asked in a high voice as he crossed to the bed.

"It is my custom, yes."

His weight settled on the mattress, and the rustle of covers told her that he had claimed his side of the bed.

Several minutes passed, but although Tess shut her eyes and willed slumber to come, her tension only seemed to increase. She was as far away as she could get from her naked husband, but still he was lying not an arm's length from her.

His nonchalance irked her somehow. Tess resented that Rotham just planned to fall asleep. But then he likely hadn't been affected by the sensual kisses he had just given her.

After another ten minutes, her nerves had grown even more taut. Tess rolled onto her other side, trying to find a comfortable position, but comfort eluded her, as did calm.

Finally she opened her eyes. Rotham lay on his side, she saw, his back to her, his breathing even but not heavy.

"Rotham, are you asleep?" she whispered.

"No."

She raised herself on one elbow. "Perhaps you are right—it is best to have done with it."

"Have done with what?"

"The consummation."

There was a long silence.

"Why?" came the brief question.

"Because then I won't be lying here all night anticipating the worst. I wish you would just get it over with."

"I am not going to rush the consummation, sweetheart. Not until you are ready and willing, even eager."

Tess lay back down and stared up at the canopy overhead, vaguely noting the flickering shadows made by the hearth fire's flames. "How can you simply go to sleep?"

"It doesn't seem I will be able to, with you flopping like a landed fish," Rotham said dryly, rolling onto his back.

"I am sorry," she apologized, without really meaning it. "But I cannot believe you are supposed to be a wicked rake and you are acting nothing like one."

He laced his hands behind his head. "I cannot believe I am showing such remarkable restraint, having a beautiful woman in my bed and doing nothing but trying to sleep."

It was some consolation that he thought her beautiful. But Tess doubted the suspense was as much of a hardship for him.

Why was he refusing to claim her virginity? she wondered. She had thought he was delaying out of consideration for her sensibilities. But he might be stalling simply to torment her. Or perhaps he wanted to make her plead with him to take her.

Well, she would not give him the satisfaction. Except that she would obviously suffer more than he would if she held stubbornly to her vow. . . .

Tess was deliberating what to say when Rotham spoke again. "I should think you would be curious to know what you are missing."

"My friend Fanny told me what to expect tonight . . . how carnal relations are conducted."

"Merely hearing a description of lovemaking is not the same as experiencing the real thing. You have to feel passion for yourself. I can give you great pleasure if you will allow me."

"I don't doubt it. Your reputation precedes you."

He turned his head on the pillow to look at her. "Your friend Fanny cannot be your source. I have never been with her."

"You have been with some of her colleagues."

"What did Fanny say about me?"

"Just that you were a highly skilled lover. And that I should leave the seduction to you."

"You should consider following her advice," Rotham suggested. "You said you wanted to know about passion, remember? You may as well make use of this opportunity. As husband and wife, we can legitimately engage in carnal relations without inviting scandal."

"I no longer fear scandal," Tess replied. "That barn door is already wide open."

Rolling onto his side, Rotham turned to face her. She could see his contemplative expression in the dim golden light. "True. So something else must be making you fret. Shall I guess? You worry that if you enjoy my lovemaking too much, it will give me the upper hand."

How had he known her concern? Tess wondered.

Her surprise must have shown on her face, for he smiled. "I promise not to hold your enjoyment against you."

"How gallant of you."

"It would be more gallant if I overlooked my scruples and consummated our marriage whether you were eager or not."

"You have scruples?" she rejoined.

"A few."

"Imagine that."

That glint of humor entered his eyes again. "Did anyone ever tell you that you have an insolent mouth?"

"No, never."

"Well, you do."

"That is because you bring out the worst in me."

"I didn't say your insolence was a bad thing. In fact I rather admire your sharp tongue. But I think you are purposely using it just now to keep me awake."

She couldn't help but smile in return. "Why should I be the only one tossing all night long?"

Rotham's long sigh held amusement and exasperation both. "If I show you there is nothing to fear, perhaps you can sleep."

He reached out to touch the corner of Tess's mouth then. When he shifted his body closer, her lips parted wordlessly.

Heaven help her, but she wanted him to kiss her again.

When she tilted her face up to his, though, he shook his head. "I won't be kissing you, darling."

"Then what do you mean to do?"

"Simply to arouse you. For you to experience passion, your body must be prepared for it."

Propping himself up on his elbow, he drew down the covers to her waist. Then his hand moved upward again, sliding over the rise of her bosom to the high neckline of her nightdress. "Next time you will have to take the initiative, love, but for now you may leave everything to me."

Tess automatically tensed, but Rotham kept his movements slow and unhurried as he worked the small buttons at the front of her gown, his deftness suggesting long practice at relieving women of their clothing. When he had unbuttoned her bodice, he slipped his hand inside. Tess's breath faltered as his warm palm brushed across her nipples, which were suddenly tight and hard.

For a long moment he merely explored the contours of her breasts at his leisure, cupping the ripe swells, grazing the taut peaks with his thumb. Tess felt herself flushing when he parted the fabric to expose her naked breasts to his gaze.

His eyelids lowering, he stared down at her in the firelight, at the full mounds crested with rosy nipples.

"You are one of the loveliest women I have ever known."

She found it hard to speak past the sudden hoarseness of her throat. "And you . . . are a master of flattery. No doubt your compliments are part of your repertoire."

"You vastly underestimate your allure. Now hush,

love, and allow me to continue. Your sole task is to close your eyes and simply feel."

It was difficult for Tess to trust Rotham enough to give herself over to him so completely, but she obeyed and shut her eyes.

Without the use of sight, her other senses came vibrantly alive. The sweep of his fingers was only a whisper across her skin, but the pressure affected her more keenly than before. The quickening thud of her heartbeat seemed louder as well, as did the husky note in his voice when he asked, "How does it feel when I tease your breasts like so . . . ?"

He lightly traced each aureole before attending the peaks. When he plucked her tautly straining nipples, he dredged a soft gasp from Tess. The tips of her breasts were hard and aching under his curving fingers, and she stirred restlessly.

Her response only encouraged Rotham, for he lowered his mouth to one breast. "How does it feel . . . when I taste your nipples?" he queried, flicking his tongue lightly over one crest.

Tess gave another sharp inhalation as pleasure rushed in to flood her. Then Rotham began to stroke her with his tongue, laving gently. Heat flared inside her. She felt dazed by the sensation of his hand molding the soft flesh of her breasts while his mouth worked its magic. She arched her back helplessly, craving more of his touch.

"Just relax, love, and let me pleasure you. . . ."

How could she possibly relax? Tess wondered as he suckled each of her breasts in turn. She tried desperately to remember Fanny's instructions. *Breathe,* was the first rule. *Think of something unpleasant such as*

*a visit to the toothdrawer or an unruly pupil in one of
your classes at the Freemantle Academy. If all else
fails, count to one hundred.*

She began counting but only reached "twelve" before Rotham shifted his attention from her bare
breasts. Reaching beneath the covers, he skimmed his
hand over her nightdress and down her stomach in a
light, tantalizing massage. When he deliberately
cupped her woman's mound, Tess whimpered and
clutched at his arm.

Rotham, however, easily freed his arm from her
grasp and pushed the covers lower to expose the rest
of her body. Surprisingly, she wasn't chilled in the
least. Instead, she was overheating rapidly.

She thought he planned to remove her nightdress,
but he merely raised the hem to her hips. His warm
palm came to rest on her inner thigh, then glided
slowly upward.

Tess tensed beneath his stroking hand, but made no
protest when he tangled his fingers in her dark curls
at the apex. But when they gently spread to probe the
folds of her sex, her eyes flew open.

"You are wet and swollen for me. A good sign."

He held her gaze as he rimmed the sleek cleft of her
femininity with exquisite care, teasing the tiny bud
hidden there. Tess shuddered at the fire rushing across
her skin, pooling between her thighs. It was sweetly
painful and only made her want more. Without voli-
tion, she raised her hips, straining against his touch,
seeking more of the delicious pleasure his bewitching,
brazen caresses were arousing in her.

Her longing grew as his tender ministrations continued. He caressed her with the skill of a man who

knew women, cupping her naked center with his palm, then sliding his middle finger over her cleft and penetrating inside a fraction of an inch. When his thumb rubbed the swollen bud there, the heavy ache at her core became sharp and focused, and Tess moaned.

"That's it," he murmured in approval. "Let me know how you feel."

Rising slightly then, Rotham shifted his position and knelt between her legs. With his hands he spread her thighs farther apart and bared all her feminine secrets. Tess felt wide open and vulnerable as he bent down to her.

Rotham settled his mouth on her thigh and began moving upward, tracing the earlier path of his hand, trailing searing kisses on her skin. Her stomach clenched in a knot of sensation. Still it shocked her when she felt his warm breath against the heart of her.

Tess trembled violently as she realized his intention. At the tender flick of his tongue over her most sensitive flesh, she jerked, lifting her hips halfway off the mattress.

"Easy," he whispered, his hands slipping beneath her bare buttocks to hold her steady.

He dipped his dark head again and pressed a kiss against her sex. Another tremor rocked her, and she slid her fingers into his thick hair.

His tongue continued to stroke her with infinite delicacy until her body surrendered with shameless wantonness. Her breath coming in hoarse pants, Tess shut her eyes, her head shifting desperately back and forth on the pillow. She was unbearably hot, yet longing for some distant fulfillment that seemed to elude her. It was like being on the edge of a precipice, about to fall off. . . .

She held on to him blindly as his hot tongue dragged back and forth over her sweetly aching flesh, plying the bud of her sex in a soft, clever rhythm. With a whimpering cry, Tess arched upward against his mouth, seeking surcease.

However, it wasn't until his lips closed over the taut nub and gently sucked that the first fierce jolt of ecstasy hit her.

Tess sobbed, her lungs laboring wildly. She had no control over her body's responses any longer. Every part of her pulsed with a hot passion she had never before experienced.

One last relentless kiss from Rotham sent her completely over the edge. She cried out as she shattered and burst into flames, the fire burning her from the inside out.

When finally she stilled, the aftermath left her throbbing with hot pulsations. Her limbs felt weak, utterly limp, her body boneless with pleasure.

With one final, tender kiss on her thigh, Rotham stretched out beside her again and gathered her in his arms, her face tucked against his shoulder.

It seemed an eternity before Tess regained her senses enough to become aware of her position. Her hand rested on Rotham's warm, hard chest, while below, the heated maleness of him pressed against her thigh.

When he eased away from her a moment later, Tess opened her eyes to find Rotham had closed his, as if he were in pain.

Her gaze slid downward toward his hips, to his naked loins. He wasn't as indifferent as he pretended, she realized. He was fully, hugely aroused.

Her breath went shallow at the sight of his long shaft so large and swollen. Thick and darkly rigid, it jutted out from a sprinkling of crisp black hair at his groin, with heavy sacs beneath.

"Do you want . . ." Her voice came out as a husky croak so she stopped.

His eyes opened. "Do I want what, love?"

Tess swallowed and tried again. "To seek your release? Fanny said it can be painful for men to remain swollen like that."

"I will survive."

She wasn't certain she could believe him. When she reached out tentatively to touch his male member, though, he caught her hand and held it away, as if he couldn't bear to have any contact with her.

Tess felt her face flush with heat, this time from embarrassment instead of passion. Her shame only increased when Rotham's low drawl broke the silence.

"Your blushes are charming, sweeting, but hardly necessary now that we are wed."

When Tess stared at him mutely, Rotham sat up long enough to draw the covers over them both, then reclined on his back and shut his eyes again.

Tess bit her lower lip hard. How could he just act as if nothing had happened? Passion had been a stunning discovery for her, a raw awakening. Rotham's incredible tenderness had only confirmed her suspicion that lovemaking could be wonderful with a considerate lover.

His consideration had completely disappeared now,

though, while she lay there shaken, trying her best to act as if she had not just felt the most earthmoving sensation of her life.

Worse, the stunning experience only left her yearning for more of his caresses. Far more.

Yet Rotham was completely ignoring her again.

She could play his game if she had to, Tess vowed to herself. Indeed, she would be better off if she could pretend the same disinterest he was showing her.

"Thank you," she said, infusing blandness into her tone. "That was . . . an edifying experience."

There was a long pause. "Merely edifying?"

He sounded almost disgruntled, which made Tess feel better.

"Actually, it was quite nice—but generally what I expected, given what Fanny has told me." She let that sink in, then managed a smile. "You were right, Rotham. It did help to soothe my nerves. I find I am rather fatigued after all the strain of the past two days. Perhaps now I can sleep."

She had the immense satisfaction of seeing a muscle in Rotham's cheek flex as his jaw clamped shut.

Feeling more like herself for the first time since realizing she had to marry him, Tess rolled over onto her other side. She doubted she would sleep much, but at least Rotham's slumber would not be very restful either.

Chapter Six

There is a reason they call him the Devil Duke.
        —Diary Entry of Miss Tess Blanchard

Ian awoke in the gray light of dawn, painfully hard. He lay on his side cradling Tess's back, his arm around her slender waist, his throbbing erection nestled against the softness of her buttocks.

For a moment he savored the sweet ache. *Torment* was the word that came to mind. It had been pure torture to sleep beside Tess for an entire night without giving in to his craving for her. Obviously he hadn't completely succeeded, either. Betrayed by his primal instincts, tempted by the potent sensuality of her body, he'd unconsciously drawn her to him while they slept.

A damn fool thing to do, Ian thought with a silent oath.

Taking care not to wake her, he twisted away from her warmth. Tess shifted in protest and turned toward him, as if seeking his embrace. Ian froze, but she remained slumbering peacefully.

Against his will, he lay there watching her in the faint light of morning. Her hair—a glorious deep sable—tumbled around her face and shoulders in lovely wanton disorder. He'd always wondered about the texture, how it would feel to bury his hands in those rich waves. In truth, he could remember past nights when he'd lain awake wondering what her skin would feel like, how her mouth would taste. He'd also imagined pleasuring her, pictured her beneath him, writhing in the throes of desire he'd awakened in her. . . .

Now he knew. And that stunning knowledge would make it even more difficult to resist her allure. Touching her, tasting her, had left him burning for Tess with the kind of desperate hunger reserved for green youths.

The irony of it didn't escape Ian, either. He'd spent the better part of four years learning to subdue his fantasies about Tess, ruthlessly restraining his impulses. Yet even though he finally had her in his bed, even though he could *legally* assert all the rights of her husband, he couldn't satisfy his fierce urges. Not when he'd vowed to delay the consummation until she was eager for it.

His unrelenting desire for Tess still annoyed the devil out of him, Ian acknowledged. At least his lust was understandable, though. What worried him more was the strange stirrings inside his chest.

He shook his head in bemusement. It shocked him that he could feel such bewildering tenderness for any woman. He was supposed to be a coldhearted bastard like his late father.

He didn't feel at all coldhearted just now, with Tess looking all sleep-tousled and warm.

Ian reached out to touch the vibrant cloud of her hair, feeling the silk of it slide through his fingers. His gaze moved over her face, admiring the elegant sweep of her cheekbones, the heart-shaped fullness of her mouth. *That luscious mouth*. The taste of her would be forever branded on his memory.

He wanted to taste her again. . . .

Berating himself, Ian drew back his hand. Forcing himself to leave their marriage bed would require extreme willpower, yet he'd managed to hide his weakness for her all these years. He could continue to do so for a while longer.

It was some consolation that Tess was not as impervious to his lovemaking as she pretended, Ian thought as he eased from the bed. She had professed not to want him, but her body had told him differently. And he was gratified that her innocence and inexperience was no pretense. He'd been afraid Richard had taken their betrothal beyond genteel bounds.

Silently, Ian carried his dinner clothes into the dressing room and donned breeches and boots and riding coat. When he escaped the bedchamber, he descended the stairs and headed directly for the stables. After ordering his favorite mount saddled, he indulged in a long gallop. It was a chill autumn morning, with rolling blue-gray mists covering the verdant hills and dales, but the brisk exercise helped to ease his frustration and restlessness a small measure.

He returned to Bellacourt in a marginally better mood—until he reached the breakfast room and found Tess there before him. Ian halted on the threshold momentarily. He wasn't accustomed to sharing his breakfast table. In fact, he liked the solitude of his bachelor's existence.

His solitary habits would have to change, of course.

He was a married man now, and he had a wife whose interests he would have to consider in addition to his own.

Tess looked fresh and lovely, a sight to warm any man's loins. Her feminine figure was garbed in a long-sleeved morning gown of jade green muslin, while her skin had an enchanting flush to it, reminding him of her shuddering climax last night.

The desire to make love to her still stinging his body, Ian made himself enter the room. It was her uncertain smile, however, that seared him. For a suspended moment, his heart beat oddly as their gazes touched.

Ian swore mentally. He wanted to feel detached from her; he didn't—not in the least. Particularly when he passed her chair and bent to kiss her cheek for the benefit of his servants.

"Good morning, my love," he said as he took his seat beside her.

Tess murmured "Good morning" in return, but Ian noted the color blooming in her checks.

While his footmen proceeded to pour coffee and fill his plate from the sideboard, he politely introduced a neutral topic of conversation.

"Would you care to take a tour of the estate this morning?"

"Thank you, I would," she replied just as politely. "And I hope to meet the household staff also."

Ian had little doubt Tess would fill the role of his duchess to perfection. She'd been reared to be mistress of a genteel household, and her dealings with her diverse charitable organizations had only increased her experience in managing large staffs.

Yet he had no desire to add to her obligations. To Ian's knowledge, Tess allowed little time for herself, devoting most of her waking hours to benefit others. And since his cousin's death, she'd rarely engaged in any idle, frivolous fun.

She might not welcome the suggestion, however, that she think of herself for a change instead of her numerous responsibilities. Thus, he waited until he'd dismissed the servants before saying casually, "There is no rush for you to take over the management of Bellacourt."

"I know, but I like to keep busy."

He could give her more pleasant occupations for her time besides work, Ian reflected, although he refrained from saying so. "We ought to remain at Bellacourt for a few more days, but I have business in London that needs tending. Would you care to accompany me there sometime this week?"

She met his gaze eagerly. "Yes, very much. I will feel at loose ends here with nothing to do."

"You are welcome to invite any or all of your friends to Bellacourt, of course. Their visits might make your exile in purgatory a bit less onerous."

At the reminder of her complaint, Tess blushed again, yet there was a hint of humor in her reply. "It might at that, your grace."

"Perhaps you should call me by my given name," Ian suggested. "You often use 'your grace' as an epithet. And when you address me as 'Rotham' in that certain tone of voice you reserve strictly for me, I always wonder if you are about to challenge me to a duel."

Amusement did curve Tess's mouth then. For a moment as she returned his gaze, her eyes held genuine warmth, not coolness and wariness as they usually did with him.

When she didn't immediately reply, Ian prodded her. "You can always reserve my title for whenever you are out of sorts with me—which is likely to be often—but perhaps we can call a temporary truce over breakfast."

She continued smiling at that and relaxed back in her chair, appearing to capitulate for the time being at least. "Very well . . . Ian. A temporary truce. Although I doubt it will last much past breakfast."

Ian relaxed as well, and for the next short while, their truce seemed to hold. By tacit agreement, they both made an effort to minimize the level of discord between them.

The moment of harmony ended abruptly and unexpectedly, however, before they were halfway through the meal.

A small boy, little more than a toddler, ran into the breakfast room, heading straight for Ian.

"My grace, my grace . . . Eee-ahn!" the tot chimed in a singsong voice. "You came back from Lon'on."

Seeing Tess start in surprise, Ian stifled an oath at the poor timing. He was fiercely glad to see the young boy, but he hadn't wanted for his new bride to be confronted with this fresh issue quite so soon.

The towheaded child raised his arms, however, asking to be held, so Ian pushed back his chair and scooped Jamie onto his lap.

Just then the boy's nurse hurried into the room after her charge and halted in consternation upon catching sight of Tess.

Looking harried and flustered, Mrs. Dixon curtsied and began apologizing profusely. "I beg your forgiveness, your grace. Jamie got away from me when my back was turned. We were eating breakfast in the kitchens, but he wanted so badly to see you. He could scarcely sleep last night, knowing you had arrived home."

"It is all right, Mrs. Dixon. I know what a handful this little scamp can be."

Grinning, Jamie threw his little arms around Ian's neck, hugging with all his might, while Ian watched Tess. The resemblance had clearly dawned on her, for a hint of shock flashed in her eyes, followed by an even more fleeting look of hurt.

Yet she quickly masked her reaction and kept her expression carefully neutral, merely raising an eyebrow in question, silently asking for an explanation.

Ian's attention was promptly claimed by the child, though.

"You bring me present, my grace?"

Jamie was incorrigible, outspoken, and supremely confident of his unshakable place in Ian's affections.

"Of course. Mrs. Dixon will deliver it to you shortly. But you will have to learn manners, my boy. You know it is bad of you to worry her."

Ian shifted his gaze to Tess. "This is my ward, James Mortimer, and his nurse, Mrs. Dixon."

Tess sent the woman a polite smile, but returned her focus to the boy. Jamie turned shy for a moment and hid his face in Ian's shoulder, then peered back at Tess.

"She won't bite you, scamp," Ian said, adding in an undervoice, "she reserves her bites for me."

Tess visibly swallowed her retort at his provocation and offered her hand. "How do you do, Master James? I am pleased to meet you."

The boy giggled and clasped her hand briefly, then buried his face against Ian's chest again.

"Say good morning to Miss Tess, Jamie. She is my new duchess. She will be living here at Bellacourt from now on."

He raised his head to gaze worshipfully up at Ian. "With *us*?"

"Yes, with us. It would be kind of you to welcome her."

James considered Tess seriously before pointing at her. "Pretty lady."

"Yes, she is," Ian agreed. "But a gentleman does not call attention to a lady's looks if he knows what is good for him." His tone turned more firm as he held the child's blue-eyed gaze. "Mrs. Dixon will bring you your present shortly. For now I must attend to some matters with Miss Tess. But I will visit the nursery later today."

"So we can feed the ducks? I want to feed the ducks, Eee-ahn."

Ian glanced out the window at the gray autumn day. "There are few ducks left this time of year, imp. But if it doesn't rain again, I will show you how to build a fort out of leaves. The gardeners have saved a large pile especially for you."

Jamie squealed and clapped his small hands. "You promise?"

"Yes. Have I ever broken my promises to you?"

"No." The toddler beamed, then abruptly changed the subject. "I have a new friend her name is Sheila and she has a lamb, his coat is so *soft* when you pet it, you should pet it Eee-ahn and you will see how soft."

"I want to hear all about your new friend and her lamb, Jamie, but for now you should go back to your breakfast."

"Yes, my grace!"

Ian relished the violent hug the child gave him. Then, still grinning, Jamie scrambled down and ran back to his nurse, who led him from the room after giving the duke another curtsy and a humble, apologetic look.

When they had gone, a profound silence reigned.

Tess stared down at her plate, avoiding Ian's gaze. It was several moments before she finally spoke. "Why did you not tell me about Jamie?"

Ian hesitated, knowing he had to choose his words with care. "I planned to eventually, but there has scarcely been time in the past two days."

She looked up, her dark eyes measuring him. "Is he your son?"

Ian parried her question as he picked up his coffee cup. "Why would you assume he is mine?"

"He looks very much like you."

Although he didn't reply directly to her observation, he responded with a significant part of the truth, not wanting to lie to her. "Jamie is not a by-blow, Tess. When his mother bore him, she was wed to one of my London footmen. Jamie was a mere baby when he lost her to the same influenza epidemic that took your mother. I legally made him my ward to give him a better life."

Tess's sympathy was immediate at the tale of a helpless baby growing up motherless, yet he could see the distress on her face. Any genteel young lady would be angry and hurt to think her husband had sired a child out of wedlock, which was clearly what she had assumed of him.

"I never heard any rumors that you had a ward, natural born or not," she murmured.

"My servants are protective of Jamie and shield him from the gossips as much as possible."

"How old is he?"

"Three, nearly four."

Ian saw her making the mental calculations . . . determining that Jamie had been born the year after her London Season and that he'd lost his mother in December of 1814, the same hard winter that Tess had lost her own mother.

"I don't know why I am surprised," she added quietly. "Richard always said you were a wicked rake."

It irked Ian that she would leap to conclude he was the one who had sinned. It irked him more that Tess had always relied on his cousin's account of events to make her judgments of him. But he clamped his lips shut. He didn't intend to offer her meaningless defenses, nor would he shatter her illusions. Prevarications would hurt her much less than the truth.

"Do you mean to acknowledge Jamie as your son?" Tess asked.

"No," Ian answered carefully. "He has a father, although one who doesn't want him."

"Who is Sheila, the owner of the pet lamb he mentioned?"

"The young daughter of one of my tenant farmers, I believe. I charged Mrs. Dixon with finding regular company for Jamie. It is lonely here at Bellacourt for a young boy, and I want him to have children his own age to play with."

"Is that why he breakfasted in the kitchens this morning?"

"Yes. He usually takes his meals there. The nursery is too secluded for a child. My cook and her staff dote on him, so he considers eating in the kitchens a special treat."

Biting her lower lip, Tess shook her head as if still trying to come to terms with Jamie's existence. "Your kindness toward him *does* surprise me, your grace," she remarked, pointedly returning to her irksomely formal form of address. "You are not generally known for your softheartedness."

It was not only softheartedness that had made Ian decide to take the boy in, although he couldn't tell her so.

Tess reclaimed her fork to resume eating her breakfast, but she only toyed with her food. Watching her, Ian felt a sharp ache twist in his chest. He didn't want to feel this fierce need to comfort her, yet he did.

He wasn't being exceptionally noble, though, in desiring to shield Tess and spare her pain as long as possible. She was the kind of woman that men instinctively respected and protected.

At the thought, Ian repressed a humorless smile. Tess had always aroused contradictory impulses inside him, with her paradoxical images of both strength and vulnerability.

She could take care of herself quite well, however. Jamie could not. Ian was determined to protect the young lad and provide a real home for him. He himself had never had love in his life, and he wouldn't let Jamie grow up the same bleak way he had.

"I suppose your vices simply caught up to you," Tess commented when he was silent.

"I never claimed to be a saint," he pointed out more curtly than he intended.

"I know. And what you do with your own life is your own affair. But it troubles me when innocents suffer for it."

"Jamie is hardly suffering, Tess."

"But he has no family who will even acknowledge him."

A muscle in Ian's jaw clenched. He well knew Tess's opinion of him. She thought him selfish and wicked, a dissipated nobleman who had wasted his entire life. It was not too far from the truth. He was known for his many deliberate youthful indiscretions. As a young man, he'd spent his days pursuing reckless adventures and his nights indulging in wild carousing. He deserved her condemnation in most instances.

Ian attempted to swallow his frustration, knowing his young ward was just one more strike against him in Tess's eyes. Whatever progress he'd made last night with his overtures toward her had been wiped away in a single moment.

Indeed, the air between them practically vibrated with suppressed tension as she studied him.

"What do you expect of me in regard to Jamie?" she asked. "Do you wish me to accept him as my own son?"

"No, I don't expect that of you," he answered honestly. "I would like him to continue living at

Bellacourt—although I would understand if you wish him to leave."

"I don't wish him to leave. This is his home. A child is innocent of his father's sins."

Ian felt a strong measure of relief. He should have known she wouldn't take her wounded pride and resentment out on a child. Tess was too tenderhearted and kind. She would never banish a young boy from the only home he remembered.

He had little doubt that Jamie would take to her quickly. Tess had always drawn people to her because of her warm nature. It was also an indication of the kind of mother she would be when she had children of her own—

Ian quelled the unwanted thought, but didn't try to conceal his sardonic humor. It was unlikely they would be having children any time in the near future, not when even the consummation of their nuptials was in doubt. Apparently their marriage bed would be as contentious as the rest of their relationship.

Yet he couldn't change the past now. His course had been set years ago when he'd assumed responsibility for Jamie. The ward of a duke would be far better treated than the unwanted castoff of a London footman. More importantly, the boy would have ample warmth and affection in his life.

He'd come to love Jamie as his own son, Ian reflected. He'd had to fight tooth and nail for his own father's love and attention—futilely, as it turned out—and he'd be damned before condemning Jamie to his same bitter fate.

For now, however, he would keep the details about

the child's birth to himself. There were some secrets that simply could not be shared.

And as he'd told little James, he honored his promises.

Tess managed to continue eating breakfast, but it required fierce determination on her part to maintain a semblance of composure with her thoughts in such turmoil.

She'd woken this morning feeling strangely optimistic. The taste of desire Rotham had given her last night had been sinfully hot, while the emotional aftershock of his lovemaking had left her with an even keener physical awareness of him. She would have difficulty, she knew, pretending that he hadn't made her yearn to share his bed for real.

His nearness at the breakfast table further addled her already muddled thoughts. And when Rotham had offered to tour his estate with her this morning, Tess had begun to hope they might eventually—someday in the distant future, at least—have a friendly marriage, if not a loving one.

She should have known better. Her optimism had been dashed the moment his young ward had scampered into the room.

It should not have bothered her, this living proof of Rotham's licentiousness. She'd always known the kind of man he was. Richard had claimed his cousin was the wickedest nobleman alive.

Rotham hadn't actually denied the child was his natural son out of wedlock, merely parsed his words to insist that Jamie was not a bastard in the legal sense. But if the boy was not his, why had he not just said so to keep her from thinking so poorly of him? And why would he make Jamie his ward if not to accept responsibility for his profligacy?

It wasn't that she cared about Rotham himself, Tess vowed to herself. It was just that she'd been taken off her guard seeing this side of him—a side that was both shocking and more endearing at the same time. There was clearly a deep affection between the ordinarily arrogant duke and the adorable, adoring child.

The silence in the breakfast room now was charged and heavy. Rotham's expression was unapologetic, his countenance implacable, almost as if he were angry at *her*. Which was as bewildering as it was vexing, Tess thought, annoyed all over again.

Perhaps she should not have ragged him about his hedonistic tendencies. In truth, it was admirable that he had taken in a motherless baby to raise as his ward. His generosity had nearly melted her heart, as had his obvious affection for Jamie—an instinctive, involuntary response that infuriated and dismayed her. She didn't want her heart softening toward Rotham. She found it difficult enough to resist her deplorable weakness for him as it was.

One thing was becoming clearer. She needed to escape this tightening coil, and soon. Spending the next fortnight or more here at Bellacourt with him would be disastrous to her willpower. Learning of Jamie's existence had only underscored the danger she was in. She had to get away from Rotham before she succumbed to his tempting offer to show her passion.

Her best course was to go to Cornwall at once, Tess decided. She could take Fanny with her, and Basil, too. Not only would her friends keep her company and take her mind off her irresistible husband, but Fanny and Basil would finally have the chance to be together and fall in love irrevocably.

Convincing Rotham to let her go, however, might prove difficult.

While swallowing the last of her coffee, Tess cast about for the best approach and decided simply to announce her intentions without giving him the chance to argue.

Setting her napkin on the table, she rose. "I believe I must decline your invitation to tour Bellacourt this morning, your grace. I must go upstairs and pack just now."

His head rose sharply as he surveyed her. "Pack? What do you mean?"

She gave a casual shrug. "I intend to set out for Cornwall this afternoon."

His lips pressed together. "You are upset at learning about Jamie."

"I am not upset in the least," Tess lied through her teeth. "I simply want to implement my plan to help my friend Fanny in her courtship with Basil Eddowes, and I realized there is no reason to wait. Pray, will you write me a letter of introduction to your servants at Falwell Castle so I will not descend upon them unexpectedly?"

Rotham frowned up at her, his gray eyes intense, penetrating. "I am afraid I cannot support your plan, sweeting. It is too dangerous a journey for you to make alone."

"I will not be alone. I will have Fanny with me." *Or hopefully I will once I write to her and beg her to accompany me.* "She knows quite well how to take care of herself. And my coachman and footmen will protect me from any danger. One of my footmen was once a pugilist and employed as a bruiser at a gaming club, did you know?"

"As it happens, I do know."

Before she could ask Rotham to explain his cryptic admission, he voiced another objection. "I also don't want you putting yourself in danger at Falwell. There could be trouble if there is any truth to the ghost sightings."

Tess nodded. "I truly hope there *are* ghosts. As I told you, a haunted castle will provide the perfect atmosphere and inspiration for Fanny to write her next Gothic novel."

"Even so, I don't want you journeying there until I can investigate the matter for myself."

His refusal struck her the wrong way. "You cannot prevent me from going, Rotham."

"Actually I can, love."

As their glances clashed, Tess bit back a hot retort. She would not permit him to turn her into a shrew. She was always agreeable and even-tempered; indeed, she never raised her voice to anyone but Rotham. Letting him provoke her was *not* the way to win this argument. No, she intended to remain on the offensive.

Taking a calming breath, she forced herself to say sweetly, "So you mean to act the tyrant and refuse me?"

Rotham hesitated before a faint scowl crossed his features. "I am not acting the tyrant."

"No? Then what do you call this high-handed, autocratic manner of yours? Do you honestly believe you can browbeat me into following your commands?"

Rotham opened his mouth to respond, then closed it again. Mutely, he leveled a look at her, his eyes containing a gleam of mockery, even exasperation.

Evidently he understood her strategy, since he took a different tack. "How will it look if you bolt from Bellacourt after only one day of marriage? Who will believe that we made a love match?"

Tess arched an eyebrow. "So that is what worries you. The ton will think you have driven me away and you will look the villain."

"Oh, yes, I live in fear of looking the villain," he said, very dryly. In a softer tone, he added, "I admit I would rather not have the entire world think I have sent my new bride fleeing from me, but my concern for your safety is the more pressing reason for my objection."

She smiled brittlely at him. "We have had this argument before, Rotham. Your concern is unwarranted."

"I disagree. I promised Richard I would look after you."

Her smile fading, Tess gave him a puzzled look. Then her gaze narrowed. "Is *that* what your recent interference in my affairs has been all about? Because you made Richard a promise to keep watch over me?"

Rotham's eyelids lowered to shade his striking eyes. "In part. I was the one who bought Richard his set of colors. I owed it to him to see that you remained unharmed."

"So you felt guilty for sending him off to war?"

Rotham didn't reply, but Tess knew she had struck a nerve in him—and herself as well.

She had never consciously acknowledged her feelings about the part the duke had played in his cousin's military service, but truthfully, she had always resented Rotham a little for purchasing Richard's commission, even though she knew such resentment was irrational. Yet how could she feel otherwise when her fate had been impacted so cruelly by the decision? Richard had planned to sell out his commission after they were wed, but then he'd been called back to war and had lost his life in battle.

With effort, Tess swallowed the sudden ache in her throat and managed to keep her voice light. "You never fail to astonish me, Rotham. To think that you actually have a heart."

Her taunt made him wince. But at least she achieved her initial goal. Rotham exhaled a heavy sigh of annoyance. "Very well, I won't object if you go to Cornwall."

Before she could celebrate, however, he added in a stern tone, "However, I intend to accompany you."

Tess shook her head. How was she to fight her attraction for him if he went with her? "That will never do," she said hurriedly.

"Why not?"

"For one thing, you promised Jamie you would teach him to build a fort of leaves today, remember? You cannot disappoint him now. And for another, there is Basil's pride. We discussed this last night, Rotham. For Basil to be able to wed Fanny, he must earn a significantly greater salary than he does now, but the offer of better employment must come from you so he will not think it charity on my part. Therefore, you need to remain here in order to hire Basil away from his current employer. You will, of course, send him to Cornwall as soon as the deal is struck—and you can even accompany him if you must—but I am traveling ahead with Fanny *immediately*. This afternoon, if I can arrange it."

He was not pleased about her scheme, clearly. Yet something in her tone must have warned him that after the emotional upheaval of being forced to wed him, and the shock of seeing his young ward, Tess had reached the end of her tether.

"As you wish," Rotham said finally. "I will write a letter of introduction to Falwell and have it sent by courier at once."

Tess eyed him warily, surprised that he had capitulated to her terms without further battle. But she wouldn't give Rotham time to change his mind.

"Thank you," she said swiftly, graciously, and sincerely. "Now if you will excuse me, I must send a message to Fanny and tell her of my plan."

She turned and escaped the breakfast room, feeling Rotham's gaze following her all the while. When she reached the corridor, Tess breathed a sigh of relief and vexation.

Relief because she would soon be on her way to Cornwall, far away from her dangerous new husband.

Vexation because of her contrary, tumultuous, maddening feelings toward him.

Sparring with Rotham always got her blood up, but now she had softer, more tender assaults on her heart to contend with—namely, his unexpected bond of affection with his young ward. She also had a dull ache in her chest induced by this fresh evidence of Rotham's wickedness.

Tess muttered a low oath. She had wanted to bring sparks and fire and feeling into her life, and she had undeniably done so with her unwanted marriage. The damnable truth was that for the first time in two years, she felt truly alive. She'd been living half a life, sacrificing joy and excitement for freedom from emotional pain. And after such a long numbness, she yearned to experience simple emotions other than sorrow again . . . to know joy, pleasure, excitement, passion. . . .

Without a doubt, last night's passion with Rotham had been exhilarating, thrilling, amazing—and he had given her only a fleeting taste of what she could expect if they became lovers.

But it infuriated her—galled her even—that of all men, it was the wicked Duke of Rotham who stirred her blood and made her vulnerable again to pain.

Chapter Seven

❧

I do not believe in ghosts, and yet Falwell Castle is plagued by eerie sounds that cannot be readily explained. Hopefully the mystery will provide a distraction for me should Rotham arrive, as he threatened to do.

—Diary Entry of Miss Tess Blanchard

The dull ache in Tess's heart only intensified two hours later. She was packing her trunks yet again, this time for a much longer journey, when she spied the Devil Duke and his young ward from her bedchamber window. The two were bundled up warmly against the chill, tramping across the immaculate west lawns toward a verge of mostly bare-limbed woodland.

A large pile of autumn leaves awaited them, along with a wheelbarrow full of objects that Tess couldn't quite make out from such a distance.

Halfway there, Rotham swung Jamie up on his shoulders and carried him the rest of the way, but upon reaching their destination, tossed him gently into the mound of dried leaves. Tess could almost hear the child's delighted shrieks of laughter as he struggled to extricate himself from the slippery pile. However, she could clearly see Jamie's happy grins as he ran around wildly, kicking up leaves with his small boots while his guardian inspected the contents of the wheelbarrow.

Eventually Rotham allowed himself to be pulled down into the pile by the joyful child, and they proceeded to roll and wrestle with abandon in the soft bed of leaves. For the life of her, Tess couldn't look away.

Her gaze remained riveted on the pair, even when they began the serious business of constructing their fort. Apparently a leaf fort entailed making a sort of low tent out of several blankets and wooden staffs, and then covering the tent with leaves and crawling inside, so that only their faces showed.

For one wistful moment as Tess observed their frolics, she had a poignant flash of a possible future with Rotham. She could envision him playing with their own children, lavishing the same heart-melting affection on them—

Crushing the notion, Tess forced herself to turn away. Making a family with Rotham would be impossible when they only had a forced marriage of convenience, and watching him with his young ward was too painful a reminder.

Determinedly, Tess returned to her packing with her maid. Fortunately, she had just heard back from Fanny, who claimed to be thrilled to accompany her to Cornwall, so in a very short while she would make her escape from Bellacourt.

Tess knew without a doubt she had made the right decision to leave this very afternoon. The sooner she put some distance between her and her damnedly endearing husband, the better.

The journey to Cornwall was uneventful, chiefly because it was made in easy stages over three days.

Tess's coachman and footmen took excellent care of her and her fellow passengers, Fanny and Alice. They changed teams at regular intervals and laid over each night at small but comfortable inns along the route.

Thankfully, Tess found her frayed nerves easing the farther they got from Richmond. It was impossible to quell her memories of Rotham and his unforgettable lovemaking, but at least she was not locked up at Bellacourt with him, having to face him over the breakfast table, or worse, sharing a nuptial bed with him.

It was easier also, Tess knew, to defer dealing with her unsettled emotions aroused by Rotham's adorable little ward, who might very well be his son. She needed time to come to terms with the situation—or at least enough time to discipline her outward demeanor. The last thing in the world she wanted was to make the darling child feel spurned, and Tess feared her distress might convey itself unwittingly to the young boy, no matter how earnestly she tried to conceal her reactions.

She hadn't had much difficulty persuading Fanny to accompany her to the wilds of Cornwall. The denizens of Falwell Castle had likely never heard of the notorious courtesan, so Fanny's worry about tarnishing the new Duchess of Rotham's reputation was not a significant risk. And Fanny relished the opportunity for Basil's courtship to blossom under more favorable conditions. Thus, she was both anxious and hopeful about Tess's matchmaking scheme.

Tess was mutually glad for her friend's support. She disliked taking Dorothy Croft away from her beloved painting. And if Rotham *did* join them at Falwell as he'd pledged, her sweet, gentle companion would offer her little protection from her irresistible husband. Fanny's extensive skills and knowledge of men, on the other hand, could be her best defense.

During the first evening of their journey, when she and Fanny dined alone in her hired parlor and Tess confessed what had happened on her wedding night, she received a thoughtful frown from her friend.

"It is unfortunate that you didn't complete the consummation," the ever-practical beauty responded. "Now you will continue to fret over what is still to come."

Yet Fanny heartily approved of Tess leaving Bellacourt and likened her battle with Rotham to military action: Retreating temporarily would provide her the chance to regroup and rearm herself before returning to fight another day.

The temperate weather also helped lift Tess's spirits. They left behind the cold, dreary dampness of Richmond and found more and more sunshine as they traveled south.

"The warmth is remarkable," Fanny commented on the second afternoon as she lowered the coach window a few inches to let in the fresh air. "I have never visited Cornwall before, have you?"

"No," Tess replied. "I have been to Bath and Brighton several times, but never Cornwall. I understand the climate in the lower reaches of Devon and most of Cornwall resembles the Mediterranean more than England. It is balmy enough even in winter that palm trees grow."

They rode through wooded river country, a lush patchwork of thick forests and verdant valleys. Reportedly, Rotham's castle was situated partway down

the eastern coast, near the small port of Fowey. By
noon of the third day, they could smell the salt-fresh
scents of the ocean and were occasionally afforded
glimpses of vast silvery-blue waters.

Because of the convergence of rivers and creeks,
Tess's coachman, Spruggs, took a circuitous route for
a time before making several turns to approach the
estate from the south. Then, halting the carriage a
few miles from their destination, he pointed out the
distant castle above them.

Situated on a low bluff stood an enormous edifice
of gray stone, complete with towers and crenellated
battlements, set off by a backdrop of dark woods. To
the southeast, Falwell boasted a breathtaking view of
the sea and overlooked a lovely cove and golden sand
beach below.

A bit further up the coast was a headland that
formed a small bay. From the coach window, Tess saw
a charming fishing village perched on the steep hillside
that was crowded with whitewashed, thatched-roofed
cottages.

They drove another ten minutes through a hilly
woodland park, then along a sweeping gravel drive,
before coming to a halt at the front entrance of the
castle. The main wing was recessed around a paved
courtyard, Tess saw, and flanked by two octagonal
towers. The lichen growing on the granite walls gave
the gray stone a slightly rose hue. Clearly older than
Bellacourt by a century or two, Falwell Castle was
not as splendid or impressive, but still striking.

Miles, one of her two strapping footmen, handed
the ladies down, while Fletcher—the former pugilist—
ran up to the ornate front door to seek admittance.

Both servants had shadowed Tess during the journey. And since Rotham knew her coachman and footmen by name, she suspected he'd charged them with closely protecting her. When asked directly, Spruggs had confirmed her suspicions, saying that the duke had ordered them to take special care of her and her friend, Miss Irwin. Once more, Tess didn't know whether to be piqued or touched by Rotham's continued interference on her behalf.

She and Fanny stood for a moment, drinking in the magnificent vista. The sparkling blue-gray expanse of ocean seemed to stretch to the ends of the earth. A soft breeze blew from the sea, amazingly warm for early November.

Tess reluctantly turned away when her attention was claimed by the castle's massive front door opening. Evidently Rotham's introductory letter had already arrived, for an elderly couple emerged, bowing and beaming.

They made themselves known as the Hiddlestons, steward and housekeeper for the castle. Both husband and wife were plump and ruddy-cheeked with a lively, informal air that was quite different from the dignified formality shown by the head retainers at Bellacourt.

Mrs. Hiddleston, apparently, was also far more outspoken. She seemed excited to have a new mistress and claimed to have been preparing for the new duchess's arrival since yesterday.

"Oh, your grace, do forgive us for not greeting you the very instant you arrived," the woman gushed. "We were polishing the silver to make ready for you. We had such short notice, you know, but we wish to make you welcome. We never expected his grace to wed, to be truthful—" After a warning glance from Hiddleston, his missus clapped a hand over her mouth. "Not that we mind his marrying, certainly, and not that it is our place to judge his affairs. . . . Listen to me running on so. You must be weary after your long journey and in need of rest and refreshment. If you will come this way, your grace. . . ."

Tess liked the Hiddlestons at once, she decided as she and Fanny followed them inside and handed over their bonnets and pelisses.

"I fear we have only a small staff serving here," the housekeeper chatted on. "The new duke never visits this big pile—well, almost never. . . . Oh, that was not a criticism, my lady, no indeed. I am sure the duke is exceedingly busy. I only meant there is little need for a multitude of servants with no lord or lady in residence. But yesterday I hired some girls and lads from the village to help out during your visit."

Over the course of the next two hours, Tess and Fanny were served a hearty tea and then given a lengthy tour of the castle. Falwell was originally built in the 1500s, they were told, but refurbished extensively in the middle of the last century by the current duke's great-grandfather, who added the battlements and the two flanking towers.

The castle supposedly had over twenty bedchambers, as well as a great hall and portrait gallery, with many of the main rooms decorated with tapestries and paintings and even armor and weapons. The towers had several small chambers each, and were four stories high.

"I understand you also have a large dungeon," Tess prodded for Fanny's sake when Mrs. Hiddleston ran out of praise for the living quarters. "We would like to inspect it, if you would be so kind."

The housekeeper first looked surprised, then made a face. "Well, to be truthful, it is more a monstrous wine cellar, my lady. But of course Hiddleston will gladly show it to you, although you may be offended by so much accumulated dirt. We do not go down there much, except on rare occasions. Are you *certain* you wish to see it?"

"Quite certain. Miss Irwin is a novelist," Tess explained, "and so has a particular interest in such things as dungeons. She also has an avid interest in ghosts. Is it true that Falwell is haunted? We would enjoy hearing anything you can tell us."

Both upper servants frowned, before the housekeeper smiled weakly. "Aye, we have a ghost that is said to be the duke who built the towers during the renovations. By all accounts, his grace came to an untimely end when he fell from the west tower, although some say he was *pushed*."

"So the Falwell ghost may be the spirit of the current duke's murdered ancestor?" Fanny interjected.

Mrs. Hiddleston looked to her husband, who had not been given much chance to get in a word edgewise, and then fell oddly silent.

"We have heard some disturbing noises," Hiddleston answered for her, "since the beginning of summer, but it is only now and then."

"What sort of noises?" Tess asked.

"Oh, a few bumps and bangs and whatnot— something like the rattle and clank of chains. But it is likely the wind. And in any event, the castle has been silent for the past fortnight at least."

His wife clearly looked uncomfortable, perhaps even afraid, but she held her tongue.

Deciding not to push, Tess said they would save a tour of the dungeon for the morrow. For now, she thought she should comply with Rotham's demand that she let him know they had arrived safely.

Thus, she penned a letter to his town house in London and had Hiddleston post her missive in the village of Fowey.

That evening, she and Fanny dined in a cozy parlor rather than the enormous dining room. And when they retired for bed, Tess chose a bedchamber just down the corridor from her friend, saying she wanted to be close to her guest as an excuse to avoid sleeping in the lord's chambers.

The first two nights, there was no sign or sound of any ghost. During the days Tess and Fanny settled in the library, which had an inspiring view of the sea cove below the castle. While Fanny wrote on her manuscript, Tess saw to her extensive correspondence; she had brought her large case of files pertaining to her charities. Although she had no official role in any of the organizations except that of chief advocate, she wouldn't shirk her responsibilities simply because she was two hundred miles away.

Nor would she abandon her work merely because she had married into the aristocracy. She'd seen too much poverty and hopelessness to turn a blind eye now. There were still countless families in need, many to the point of desperation. Women and children and elderly parents especially, who were barely surviving after their men were killed or maimed in nearly two decades of war.

Tess also made an effort to learn about her nearest neighbors, particularly those who would expect a formal call from the new duchess. There were several nobles in the district, plus a dozen families who could be considered gentry, but since she was of higher rank now, she would have to initiate any visits.

Her first meeting would be with the local vicar, Tess decided. And she would have Alice accompany her instead of Fanny. For years Tess had futilely battled society's strictures regarding ladylike conduct, but she had to agree with Fanny's assessment—that flaunting their friendship could be detrimental to the very causes she was urgently trying to promote. Her neighbors, including perhaps even a man of the church, would likely be appalled to know she was associating with a lightskirt, even a reformed one.

Tess hoped her friend's prospects for acceptance would improve shortly. If Fanny could marry Basil, she would automatically gain a measure of respectability. Marriage covered up a multitude of sins with the ton, and associating with the Duchess of Rotham would increase her gentility even more.

Beyond wanting to help Fanny, Tess welcomed the challenge of matchmaking for personal reasons. From long experience, she knew that keeping busy was the most effective way to avoid dwelling on her troubles. Unfortunately, her strategy of occupying every waking moment did not seem to work very well with the problem of her marriage. To Tess's frustration, shutting out her memories of Rotham proved impossible, particularly at night when she lay alone in her bed.

By day, however, her efforts at distraction were more successful. She took long walks with Fanny, strolling along the bluffs and breathing in the marvelous sea air or exploring the surrounding woods that were only now showing significant signs of autumn. They had yet to attempt the steep footpath that led down to the village, but on their other sojourns from the castle, Tess's footmen always accompanied them while keeping a respectful distance behind.

Tess was also glad to serve as literary advisor to her friend. She had read Fanny's first manuscript and offered her thoughts then, and was now reading completed pages of the current novel. Usually they spent the afternoons discussing plots and protagonists while taking tea.

The courtesan hoped to become as popular and prolific as Mrs. Ann Radcliffe, Frances Burney, or Regina Maria Roche, who were great favorites with patrons of booksellers and circulating libraries.

"I don't aspire to be a star in the literary firmament," Fanny contended, "but only to make a comfortable living."

Her publisher was the Minerva Press, a printing establishment that had successfully capitalized on the lucrative market for Gothic romances. "Horrid" novels, as they were frequently termed, often featured wicked villains and hapless young damsels chasing each other about gloomy mansions or drafty castles.

Fanny insisted on holding her characters to a certain standard, however. "It is all well and good to have lovelorn, romantic innocents for my heroines," she explained, "but I won't have them swooning at the slightest provocation. They must possess a modicum of wit—at least enough to be instrumental in their own salvation."

It was a common fallacy that romance novelists could scribble cheap Gothics in their spare time, but having watched Fanny's labors, Tess knew the process was much more difficult than she'd imagined. Besides, this was only Fanny's second attempt at fiction, so it was not unreasonable that the manuscript was progressing in fits and starts.

The principal reason, however, was that Fanny had her own distractions to deal with. On the second afternoon at Falwell Castle, she admitted that she had grown too nervous to write much or well. "I cannot stop thinking about what I shall do if Basil comes," Fanny confided.

"*When* Basil comes, you mean," Tess said in a bracing tone. "I have faith that Rotham will get his way and send Basil here to us."

"But what do I do once he is here? How should I behave? I don't want to be too forward with him for fear of reminding him of my wicked past."

Tess smiled teasingly in an effort to reassure her friend. "You conquered the entire London demimonde, Fanny. Surely you can charm one single, eager gentleman. I'll wager that by this time next week, you will have Basil eating out of your hand. You may very well even be betrothed by then—and you will be, if I have anything to say to the matter."

Fanny's expression turned hopeful. "Do you truly think so, Tess?"

"Yes, indeed. You may have more experience in

carnal matters than I do, but I know more about matrimony. I have had two proposals of marriage, remember?" Catching herself, Tess gave a soft laugh and wrinkled her nose. "Although the second offer was entirely unwanted . . . and I suppose I cannot call Rotham's arrogant declaration that I would have to wed him a true *proposal*. Nevertheless, you need to quit fretting, dearest Fanny. Your romance with Basil will work out, I am certain of it."

Fanny seemed grateful for the encouragement, but still she worried her lower lip. "I do not have your confidence, Tess. I am afraid even to kiss Basil, and I don't dare try to make love to him. What if he doesn't like it?"

Tess laughed outright at that absurdity. "There is absolutely no possibility of Basil not enjoying your lovemaking. Your problems with him are monetary, not amorous."

"I suppose so," the courtesan agreed. "But I mean to let him take the lead in our relationship so that I don't frighten him off. And my conduct must be believable. My acting like a virgin will make him feel more manly, no doubt, but my innocence has to seem real, don't you think?"

"I think you are worrying for no reason. Wait until Basil arrives and then see how things stand between you."

It was amazing to see Fanny so uncertain of herself. She had sold her sexual favors for outrageous sums and reigned over the demimonde for years. Then again, she had never before been vulnerable to love, as she was now with Basil, Tess conceded.

For Fanny's sake as well as her own, therefore, Tess

was almost glad to have her first experience with the castle ghost that very night. Waking suddenly in the dark, she recognized the eerie disturbance that had put the servants so on edge.

Her heart pounding, Tess quickly lit a candle. The clanking noises did indeed resemble rattling chains and sounded as if they were coming through the walls, or perhaps from the chimney. It was warm enough that she hadn't needed a fire, and the contrasting quiet of her bedchamber only seemed to amplify the metallic racket.

Summoning her courage, Tess climbed out of bed and checked every nook and cranny of her room but found nothing unusual to explain the cause. When the mysterious noises stopped abruptly, she threw on her dressing gown and hurried down the corridor to Fanny's room.

Fanny was sitting up in bed, apparently having been startled awake also.

The rattling did not resume, however. And after a time they discussed the phenomenon to help calm their shaken nerves.

"There must be a rational explanation," Tess ventured to say, to which Fanny agreed.

"Yes. Perhaps it was just the wind."

"Perhaps. There probably is no point in searching the castle tonight in the dark. We will have to wait until daylight to investigate."

Fanny nodded, but stopped Tess from leaving. "Will you stay with me here, Tess? I would rather not be alone until we know what we are dealing with."

Tess was of a similar mind, so rather than return to her room, she claimed the other side of Fanny's bed.

When no more commotion threatened their peace, they eventually managed to fall asleep and didn't wake again till dawn.

After breakfast the next morning, they searched the entire castle from top to bottom looking for clues, but could find no hint of what had caused the unsettling disturbance. Both of Tess's sturdy footmen accompanied them, particularly when they searched the "dungeon," but all they gained for their troubles were dirty gowns.

The housekeeper apologized profusely for the condition of the cellars, perhaps fearing for her job, but Tess reassured her.

"Please don't worry, Mrs. Hiddleston. As you said, no one uses the cellars anymore. As for exploring the depths of the castle, we think of it as research for Miss Irwin's novel. I doubt there are real ghostly spirits lurking down there or anywhere else."

In the light of day, Tess found it easier to dismiss the absurd possibility of Rotham's murdered ancestor haunting his palatial home. Yet to her consternation, an hour later she had a new concern to occupy her: A brief message came from Rotham, saying that he had succeeded in hiring Basil Eddowes and that they would arrive sometime the following afternoon. Thus, instead of worrying about confronting a ghost, Tess had to worry about facing her new husband.

She told herself that the restless flutter in her stomach had nothing whatsoever to do with eagerness or anticipation of seeing him again. Of course she was delighted for Fanny, but she'd hoped to avoid Rotham for a good while longer.

It was unfortunate, Tess thought wryly, that she

couldn't simply refuse him entry so she wouldn't have to deal with him. Yet she couldn't exactly kick him out of his own castle. And if she tried, she could only imagine the grief Rotham would give her.

Fanny was even more unnerved by the realization that her moment of truth was at hand. For the remainder of the day and all the next morning, the two of them tried with only mild success to calm each other's agitation.

Long before the expected hour, they gave up working in the library and settled in the drawing room to read. Despite their effort to appear composed, however, when the gentlemen finally did arrive around two o'clock, Fanny only had eyes for Basil, and Tess could not look away from Rotham.

It was deplorable how all her senses came alive the moment he strode into the room. His gaze was fixed on her in return, she saw. He was studying her closely, perhaps wondering what sort of reception she meant to give him . . . perhaps also remembering their one passionate night together, just as she was.

Tess felt the impact as Rotham's gray eyes raked slowly down her figure. She had deliberately chosen lighter colors and fabrics to wear for her visit to Cornwall, and he seemed to approve of her gown of blue sprigged muslin—not that she cared what he thought of her, Tess reminded herself.

Yet her body was instantly, profoundly aware when Rotham stepped closer. And when he took her hand to press a light kiss to her fingers, she shivered at even that slight touch.

With effort, Tess withdrew her hand from his grasp and shifted her attention from Rotham to her friends, who were staring at each other as if they had been parted for a decade rather than merely a few days.

Tall, lean, and lanky, Basil was blond, brown-eyed, and wore spectacles that gave him a scholarly appearance, which provided a striking contrast to Fanny's lush, raven-haired beauty. Tess knew theirs was a clear case of opposites attracting; Fanny, the gay, vivacious, pleasure-seeker, and Basil, the earnest, bookish law clerk. His studious air was fortunately relieved by his sharp dry wit, though. And reportedly he'd been fun-loving in his youth, acting as Lily Loring's childhood compatriot in her sporting endeavors and rebellious escapades.

Fanny and Basil had been childhood friends, too, but they'd been at loggerheads over her shocking decision to enter the flesh trade at sixteen. His disapproval, Tess suspected, in addition to his fierce anger, disappointment, and outright jealousy, stemmed from the probability that even back then, he was head over ears in love with Fanny.

Basil certainly seemed eager to see her again. Indeed, the desire and longing in his eyes was unmistakable.

When Fanny gazed at Basil in return, the tender look they shared only confirmed Tess's conviction that they both wanted a future together.

She had watched the change in Basil over the course of the past summer. He'd dressed in homely attire until Fanny's elderly courtesan friends had taken him in hand, intent on turning him into a fashionable gentleman. Under their direction, Basil had begun to look the part of a nobleman's secretary. Just now he wore a tailored brown frock coat and pantaloons and shiny Hessian boots, and he carried himself with manly confidence, as if he were worthy of a beautiful Cyprian like Fanny.

While they greeted each other, Tess drew Rotham aside and spoke in a low voice. "Thank you for bringing Basil here. I gather he is now in your employ?"

"Yes, as my newest secretary. Did you doubt my success?"

"Not in the least." She would never doubt Rotham's ability to gain anything he truly wanted. "What reason did you give for requiring him to accompany you to Cornwall?"

"Just that it was difficult for you to wed me so suddenly and that you wanted your friends around you."

That much was true, Tess thought wryly. "I presume Basil will have specific duties as your secretary?"

Rotham nodded. "To start with, he will take charge of my library at Bellacourt. I told him that the collection here at Falwell needs cataloging to determine if there are any rare editions I want to bring home with me."

"And does it need cataloging?"

"Not to my knowledge, but it won't hurt. However, the library here is not extensive, so it should take no more than a week for Eddowes to complete his work. After that I will run out of excuses. You should tell your friends to hurry and fall in love before my patience runs out."

Suspecting that Rotham was deliberately provoking her, Tess returned an unwitting smile. "I realize you have an aversion to lovers, but this is for a good cause."

"You say that about all your causes, sweeting."

"Yes, but this one is particularly important to me."

"Then by all means, I will endeavor to enforce your will. It would pain me greatly to disappoint you."

She refrained from retorting to his light mockery. Rotham was helping her with her friends' problems, even against his inclination, and she was very grateful.

Tess glanced over her shoulder at the lovers. Fanny looked like a blushing schoolgirl as she contemplated the object of her affection. It was amazing to see her so nervous and uncertain around any man.

"Fanny is anxious for Basil's visit to go well," she observed quietly to Rotham, "and so am I. You do know that you cannot monopolize all of his time? He must have the chance to conduct a courtship . . . and yet we shouldn't leave them alone together too often, either. I don't want the arrangements to seem too contrived."

Rotham's gray eyes showed a flash of amusement. "I imagine he already suspects a conspiracy."

Tess started to reply, but forgot what she meant to say as she got caught up in Rotham's eyes. Eventually she dragged her gaze away, but only to the rest of his face.

His hair still wanted cutting, she thought absently. She found herself longing to smooth an unruly lock back from his forehead.

Then her gaze dropped to his mouth. She remembered that sensual mouth making love to her body only a few nights ago. A vision filled her mind of his nakedness, of his smooth, hard muscles and sleek, warm skin—

Abruptly, Tess shook herself and forced herself to respond. "You didn't need to accompany Basil here, you know. You could have allowed him to come on his own."

"Perhaps, but hiring him served to explain our separation after your sudden departure from Bellacourt."

"What excuse did you give for my absence?"

"I claimed that we were taking a wedding journey to Falwell, but that I sent you on ahead while I completed some necessary business in London. I had no desire to give the impression that you had left me after one night of marriage."

"Of course not. We would not want your outsized male pride to suffer."

Rotham responded with a short laugh, but countered her. "I am more concerned about your reputation than my pride, darling. I don't want to give the gossips any more fodder to chew on."

Tess sighed audibly. "I suppose we still must keep up appearances, even if we would both prefer to remain apart."

To her surprise, Rotham hesitated. Tess had the oddest feeling that he meant to deny his desire to remain apart from her. But he changed the subject instead.

"Did you find the ghosts you were seeking?"

"In a manner of speaking."

She told him about the strange clanking sounds they'd heard recently and of their futile efforts to search the castle. "We found no leads, but I am determined to solve the mystery."

Rotham sent her a narrow look. "That is another

reason I came to Cornwall. I wanted to be here if you deliberately went seeking trouble."

Tess refused to be intimidated by him. "I told you, I do not require your protection."

"Nonetheless, I am better able to handle danger than you are."

She lifted her chin and stared back at him challengingly. "Is that so?"

"Certainly. I will take a turn in searching the castle tomorrow."

"Do you think you can do any better than Fanny and I did?"

"I'll warrant I can. I haven't visited Falwell much, so I don't know it well, but as you said, there must be a rational explanation."

Once more Tess failed to reply as she became conscious of a damning thought: She had greatly missed sparring with Rotham.

In truth, these past few days she had merely been passing time at the castle until he arrived. It was as if all her senses had been slumbering, waiting for the heady rush of awareness that made her feel so vividly alive.

And now that he was here, exhilaration was charging through her like an electrical current—just as if she had never learned of the painful likelihood that Rotham might have a son she had never known about.

Her silence went on for too long. Finally Tess cleared her throat. "We can discuss our differences later, your grace. For now I think we should join our guests."

She turned away toward her friends, seeking safety in numbers. But as she felt Rotham's presence behind her, Tess shivered once again, wondering how she would manage to endure the next week or more with her husband in residence. As enormous as Falwell Castle was, it still would not be large enough for the both of them.

Chapter Eight

*Am I foolish to be so dissatisfied with the barren state
of my marriage?*
— Diary Entry of Miss Tess Blanchard

Ian raised no objection to the living arrangements
when Tess insisted on sleeping in her own bedchamber rather than share the master's apartments with
him. So far from London, it hardly mattered if anyone knew their marriage was not a love match. Moreover, Ian wanted to avoid the maddening frustration
of having his alluring wife in his bed without being
able to touch her.

Thus, on his first night at the castle when he escorted Tess to her rooms, he merely bowed politely
and murmured a brief good night.

The obvious relief in her dark eyes irked him. He'd
thought Tess would change her mind about carnal relations once she understood the pleasure he could
give her, yet she clearly had no desire for a real marriage between them. He would not insist on a consummation, though.

Despite his pledge, Ian found it hard to leave Tess
there and make his way to his own suite in another
wing entirely. It was even harder to purge the memory

of her silken skin as he attempted to fall asleep alone in his bed.

He was not enamored of her other than natural male lust, Ian promised himself, but that alone was dangerous. Lust was a powerful force; it weakened a man's willpower and clouded the mind.

So did the contradictory feelings Tess aroused in him. He'd felt an unanticipated gladness upon seeing her again after only a few days of separation.

He could have remained in London, of course, but he'd thought it best to join her in Cornwall, rationalizing that with Eddowes and Fanny Irwin as houseguests, he should be able to control his craving for his beautiful new wife. He was too jaded and experienced to fall victim to his own desires.

But if so, then why was he having such a damnably hard time forgetting his marital troubles and falling asleep?

The next morning, Ian rose at daybreak and met his newest secretary to discuss strategy for undertaking the library inventory. They had just concluded their conversation and settled in the breakfast room when Tess made an unexpected appearance.

Eddowes stood with alacrity, while Ian politely followed suit. She offered her friend a cheerful greeting, and when they were all seated once more, she explained why she had joined them at this hour.

"I know you are an early riser, Rotham, but I didn't want you searching the castle without me."

Before Ian could object to her planned involvement, Tess turned back to Eddowes. "Fanny says she will be down shortly, even though she is accustomed to sleeping a good deal longer. Do you mean to begin work in the library this morning?"

"Yes, Miss Bl—I mean, your grace. The duke and I were just discussing the particulars of our plan."

"If it will not inconvenience you, Fanny can continue to write in the library so she will have company while I am away. I don't like to leave my houseguests to their own devices, you see, and I will be occupied most of today. After our search of the castle, I mean to pay some courtesy calls on my new neighbors."

Ian broke into their conversation. "It isn't necessary for you to search the castle again, love."

Tess offered him a beatific smile. "Perhaps not, but I can show you the ground we have already covered. Shall we discuss the matter after breakfast?" Without waiting for Ian's reply, she gave her full attention to his secretary. "Mr. Eddowes, pray tell me how Fanny's friends at the boardinghouse go on. Are Fleur and Chantel keeping out of trouble?"

Eddowes sent his new employer an apologetic glance and launched into a discussion about two women, which Ian eventually learned were elderly courtesans whose acquaintance Tess had made during the summer when she'd taught special classes on diction and manners at Fanny's London boardinghouse as a favor to Lily Loring.

When breakfast was over, the secretary asked to be excused to begin his cataloging and left Ian alone with Tess.

She evidently expected an argument, for her gaze narrowed as she took up the issue of searching the castle again.

"You cannot expect me to sit idly by, Rotham,

while you take over the investigation of those mysterious clanking sounds."

"Oh? Why not?"

"I might be of help, for one thing. As I said, I can show you exactly where we have already searched and save you from wasting time. The sooner we expose the 'ghost' the better. It is terrifying the servants, and me as well."

"I doubt you are terrified," Ian said in a languid drawl.

"Well, Fanny is. She was afraid to sleep alone the other night. And I won't put her through that fright again."

From the stubborn set of Tess's shoulders, Ian suspected that he was fighting a losing battle. He raised his gaze to the ceiling for a moment, before giving her an exasperated look.

"Why did I think for one moment that you would behave like any other female of my acquaintance?"

Perhaps she could tell he was relenting, for her mouth twitched with the effort to repress a smile. "I cannot imagine. But I doubt you object because you think ghost-hunting isn't a task for ladies. I think the trouble is that you are far too accustomed to having your own way. Your nose gets out of joint when anyone has an opinion contrary to yours."

"But you particularly delight in having opinions contrary to mine."

Her eyebrow lifted. "Is that not an outrageous case of the pot calling the kettle black? Besides, I need an excuse to leave Fanny and Basil alone together. If I am occupied with you all morning, then their courtship can proceed that much faster."

Ian shook his head in resignation. Tess was fiercely loyal to her friends and loved ones and wouldn't be deterred from her plan except by sheer force.

"Far be it from me to stand in the way of your matchmaking," he grumbled. "Very well, then. Where do you suggest we begin our search?"

"Where I first heard the ghostly sounds, naturally."

Ian exhaled an exaggerated sigh, but there was a smile on Tess's lips when she led the way from the breakfast room.

They searched the castle room by room, starting with her bedchamber where she had heard the clanking noises. The sounds, Tess said, had seemed to come from one side of the room, near the hearth, or possibly down the chimney.

However, they found nothing of interest in any of the castle's upper floors, or in the towers or cellars either. Their failure seemed to gratify Tess, judging by her good-natured gibe once she had dismissed all the servants who had aided in their exploration.

"I am glad you had no more luck than we had the first time, Rotham. I would not have liked to be upstaged."

The teasing note in her declaration captured Ian's attention more than her actual words, and when he hazarded a glance at Tess, he found himself transfixed. They had finished their search up on the battlements, where she had paused to drink in the view.

When she lifted her face to the morning sun, letting the glow caress her ivory skin, Ian's breath caught at the enchanting picture she made. She wore her hair down instead of piled atop her head as usual, and the dark richness reflected the sunlight, making him want to bury his hands in the silken mass.

Her quiet smile held that same joyful touch of warmth, like the first rays of a sunrise.

Ian felt a hard tug of sheer lust in his gut. With fierce effort, he clamped down on his primal urges. He refused to act the fool, lusting after Tess when the desire was so one-sided.

Fortunately, she seemed not to notice his momentary paralysis, for she changed the subject entirely. "Now, if you will be so kind, I would like for you to accompany me on my morning calls."

Ian winced at her suggestion. "You are asking a great deal of me, you realize?"

"Perhaps, but our absence from the castle will continue to allow Fanny and Basil to be alone together. And because of your exalted title, our neighbors are likely to receive me more cordially if you are with me. I confess I am eager to meet them, especially the vicar."

"That is because you know little about him," Ian replied sardonically. "I guarantee that spending even ten minutes with the good reverend will be torture."

Her eyes danced with restrained amusement. "You can suffer for one afternoon, I imagine," she replied sweetly, her smile full of magic and mischief. "It is time you owned up to your obligations, Rotham. You've led a life of dissipation for so long, you have no inkling how to aid your fellow human beings."

Ian refrained from arguing with Tess again about his dissipation. Thus it was that while Fanny wrote on her manuscript and Eddowes began cataloging the Falwell library, he found himself paying duty calls on his neighbors, beginning with the vicar for the parish, Gideon Potts.

Ian was far from happy, however. It was bad enough that he'd been embroiled in Tess's matchmaking against his will. Traveling over a large part of Cornwall with her was even worse, since it gave him far too much time alone with his entrancing new wife. And before Ian realized it, he was being drawn into Tess's newest cause.

At her first meeting with Vicar Potts, she explained her plan to organize a charitable fund for the poorest parishioners. During the next several days, they visited every single genteel family in a thirty-mile radius of Falwell, as near as the neighboring village of Fowey, and as far away as St. Austell to the south and Liskeard to the north.

Ian found it intriguing to watch their unsuspecting neighbors fall under Tess's spell. Whatever she did, she poured her heart and soul into, and this instance was no different. She charmed and wooed them all, as tenacious in her campaign as Boney had been in conquering much of Europe.

When he labeled her "Saint Tess," she took his ribbing with good grace.

"You may disparage me all you want, but I find it deeply satisfying to help people and make a difference in their lives. It wouldn't hurt for you to engage in a bit of philanthropy yourself. . . . Beyond the wedding gift you recently gave me, I mean. Just think of all the good you could do if you put your vast wealth and power to a useful purpose."

It was one of her greatest strengths, Ian knew; Tess inspired others to try their best to please her and live up to her lofty standards. He was undeniably affected himself. Yet he was also drawn in by her physical allure . . . the sensual pitch of her voice, the creamy glow of her skin, her easy laughter.

His attraction was becoming harder and harder to resist, Ian admitted. Especially since on every visit, they pretended to be a happily married couple—although each night he continued to escort Tess to her bedchamber, where he left her alone.

On the fourth night, however, she hesitated with her hand on the doorknob and turned to gaze up at him.

"I want to thank you for all your help these past few days, Rotham. I know you would much rather be occupied elsewhere. . . ."

When her voice trailed off, Ian realized he had involuntarily lifted his fingers to touch her cheek.

He felt a sudden tension shimmering between them, a certain sexual awareness in the air. From the look in Tess's dark eyes, he knew she was as acutely conscious of him as he was of her.

Ian dropped his hand as if scalded and stepped back. "You needn't worry that I will force my way into your chamber and ravish you," he said, resorting to a sardonic tone. "I told you there will be no consummation of our marriage vows. Not until you beg me."

Tess swallowed and then seemed to regain her composure. "We will both be gray from old age before *that* happens," she replied with a challenging smile before disappearing into her room and softly shutting the door in his face.

Ian stood there for a moment, undecided whether

to laugh or swear. He wasn't certain he could wait so long for conjugal relations with Tess. Not when he was becoming obsessed with the notion of bedding her. Every night she invaded his dreams, making him burn for her.

He blamed Tess for being so damned captivating and leaving him in a constant state of aching arousal. Relieving the physical pain with his own hand wasn't nearly as satisfying as assuaging his needs in her lovely body. If he wasn't wed to her, he could turn to another woman, but he intended to remain loyal to his marriage vows.

Therefore, Ian vowed, he would continue to deny himself the right to hold her and touch her, to arouse her to passion and to sleep with her wrapped in his arms.

The thought of bringing Tess to passion made his loins grow heavy and hard—which did have the effect of making Ian curse.

Sexual obsession made bloody fools of its victims, and he refused to become Tess's victim . . . although he had the sinking suspicion that it might already be too late.

If their relationship left Rotham moody and irritable, Tess felt a similar frustration. It was her own fault that she was trapped with her handsome husband in a carriage for the better part of each day as they traveled throughout the district soliciting funds for her latest charitable project. But Rotham pervaded her dreams by night and taunted her with remembered passion.

The pleasure she found in his company was another enormous point of vexation for Tess. She would rather quarrel with him than engage in mere polite conversation with anyone else. How contrary was that?

Even more contrary was the dissatisfaction she felt because Rotham was keeping his word and not pressing her to consummate their union. Absurdly, she resented that he was leaving her strictly alone. She was a married woman now, but still a virgin in essence. And she was just as lonely as before her marriage—perhaps more so, since most of her friends were far away and Fanny was currently preoccupied with Basil.

Tess had vowed to banish the emptiness from her life, but here at Falwell, the same hollow ache continued to plague her, while a new restless energy thrummed through her entire body.

Her weakness for Rotham was to blame for her sexual frustration, of course. Merely being near him aroused stirrings of physical need inside her . . . particularly since she knew that if she wanted to share his bed, she had only to ask. It was growing harder by the moment to anchor herself against temptation.

Even her carefully planned distractions were proving less effective than she'd hoped, although their search for the Falwell ghost took an interesting turn.

To Tess's surprise, Rotham hunted down the scholar who had supplied information on Cornish spirits to Patrick Hennessy when the actor had researched ghosts for his play.

"You spoke to Hennessy about the rumors of Falwell Castle being haunted?" she asked Rotham when he mentioned a change of plans for that afternoon.

"Yes, the day before I left London. I wanted to know how he had learned of it. Hennessy told me about his correspondence with a noted expert who lives in Polperro—a Mr. Norris. So I arranged an appointment with Norris today at two o'clock. We can consult him in between our other calls. I want to know what he can tell us about Falwell's ghost."

Mr. Norris was indeed an expert on local lore, they discovered when they sat down with him.

"Godolphin House near Falmouth is said to be haunted by the White Lady," the elderly gentleman told them. "The wife of the first earl died in child-birth, and she reportedly appears on the anniversary of her funeral."

When asked, however, Norris had little to add to what they'd already learned from the castle's house-keeper and steward about Falwell's phantom—that their ghost was supposedly a murdered ancestor of Rotham's.

"But we have our own legendary spirits right here in Polperro," Norris added. "Battling Billy was a smuggler who transported his contraband brandy in-land in a coffin. When he was shot and killed by a Revenue officer, the tale goes, Billy's dead body con-tinued to drive the hearse for some distance, all the way through the town and into the harbor."

Tess and Rotham left Norris's cottage more knowl-edgeable, but disappointed.

"You don't believe Falwell is haunted, do you?" Tess asked as he handed her into the carriage.

"No, not for one minute. It's more likely that some person or persons are slipping around the corridors undetected. This area of Cornwall is known for supporting and protecting smugglers, so residences along the coast—great houses in particular—often have secret passages and tunnels to provide hiding places to escape detection by the Revenue Service. I wouldn't be surprised if Falwell has its own share of hideaways. To that effect, I tasked Eddowes with keeping an eye out for architectural renderings of the castle when it was modernized a century ago."

Tess eyed Rotham with admiration. "That was clever of you. I would never have thought of examining how the castle was rebuilt."

"I do have my uses sometimes," he said dryly.

Tess conceded the point in silence. Strangely enough, she felt safer with Rotham there. She wanted his protection if there truly was an entity haunting the castle, either real or supernatural.

Unwilling to admit her concession, though, she changed the subject slightly. "I would say that your new secretary is proving useful already. I understand that he has unearthed several rare volumes to add to your library at Bellacourt."

When Rotham confirmed as much, Tess couldn't refrain from needling him. "So hiring Basil was worth all the trouble you went to?"

"I wouldn't go so far," he replied, albeit with a smile.

She knew Basil at least was grateful to be at Falwell. The next morning before she left to make her daily calls, he sought Tess out.

"I wish to thank you, your grace. I know you arranged this opportunity for me to woo Fanny."

Tess's smile was genuine. "I was glad to help. How is your courtship proceeding, if I may ask?"

"Well enough, I suppose. We are arguing far less now, and even when we sometimes squabble as we did in our youth, we make up our disagreements quickly." Basil hesitated, then ran a hand through his fair hair in frustration. "But I hardly know how to act with Fanny. Do you have any notion what she expects of me?"

"I suspect she is only waiting for you to take the first step," Tess confided.

"Do you really think so?"

"I do indeed. Fanny is trying very hard to change her ways for your sake."

He apparently took her advice to heart. When Tess returned to the castle that afternoon and went upstairs to dress for dinner, Fanny burst into her bedchamber, clearly in alt.

"Basil kissed me, Tess!" the courtesan exclaimed, beaming with excitement.

"Oh?" Tess murmured, hiding her delight. "And did he respond with revulsion as you feared he would?"

"No. He seemed to enjoy it immensely."

"And what about you? Was kissing Basil what you imagined?"

Fanny's blissful sigh was answer enough. "It was so much better," she said softly. "One of the sweetest kisses I have ever known. I never expected to feel that way, considering my past. But I realize now that my affection for Basil is what has changed between us. Love makes all the difference."

Fanny gave another dreamy-eyed smile before wandering off to her own rooms.

Tess was also smiling as she shut her bedchamber door. Even though her happiness for her friends was tempered by caution, it was a good sign that they enjoyed kissing each other. And she had to agree; love did indeed make an enormous difference to felicity.

Her smile faded as she thought about her own unsettled situation with her husband. Fortunately, there was little chance of her falling in love with Rotham. She would never allow herself to risk it, since giving her heart to so wicked a man would only open her up to pain—and she had experienced more than enough pain in her one and only romantic relationship.

Still, Tess reflected, it was best that she hold strictly to her plan to avoid Rotham's bed and avoid temptation altogether.

It was the following evening after dinner when her willpower was tested. She had just repaired to the drawing room with Rotham, Fanny, and Basil, when Hiddleston nervously informed them that a mysterious light had been spied in the castle's west tower, shining from one of the topmost windows overlooking the cove.

Rotham and Tess quickly led the way to the tower, accompanied by Hiddleston and Tess's two footmen, Miles and Fletcher. By the time they reached the upstairs chamber, it was dark and only a slight scent of burned candle wax remained.

Obviously no apparition had lit a candle, but an exhaustive examination of the entire tower and roof offered no clues as to the culprit.

Fanny, however, cleverly made use of the threat to advance her romance by exaggerating her fear of ghosts and pleading with Basil to share his room for the night.

The courtesan whispered her plans to Tess before they retired for the evening. "I don't want to be too forward with Basil, so I won't attempt to seduce him. I only want to make him feel manly by protecting me."

Tess approved, although she was not afraid to sleep alone. That is . . . until she became the ghost's target herself.

She fell asleep without much difficulty, but sometime in the middle of the night, she dreamed that Rotham was stroking her cheek. When a low whisper came to her, the discrepancy puzzled her. The rough voice sounded nothing like her seductive husband's.

Restlessly, Tess rolled onto her side and muttered a reply. Still in that twilight between waking and sleeping, she heard soft footsteps, then a moment later a low, scraping sound followed by a distinct "snick."

The final noise startled her fully awake.

"Who is there?" Tess demanded as she sat up in alarm.

An ominous silence greeted her. Her bedchamber was faintly illuminated by slivers of moonlight seeping from beneath the draperies, but she could see no one there. And yet . . .

Her heart racing, she raised her hand to her cheek. The touch on her face had felt very real, like fingers brushing her skin. Boney fingers. Not cold, but warm and human. Not ghostly, but not Rotham's, either.

As she lit her bedside lamp with shaking hands, Tess noticed an odor that didn't belong: the smell of an unwashed body. Even if Rotham had entered her room and left again, his clean masculine scent would not have disturbed her.

Someone or something had been in her room, she was certain of it—a realization that actually did frighten her for real.

Knowing she would get no sleep if she remained there, Tess climbed out of bed. Taking up her lamp, she hurried down the corridor to Rotham's wing of the castle, telling herself she would only take refuge there until morning.

Her soft rap on his door was initially met by silence, then by his sleep-roughened voice bidding entrance.

Hastily, Tess slipped inside his room. Closing the door to shut out the threat behind her, she exhaled an uneven breath at finding Rotham sitting up in bed. Just seeing him already made her feel safer. Even though he was bare-chested, the covers thankfully concealed his lower body. His gold-streaked brown hair was tousled from sleep, convincing her that he hadn't been the one to pay her an eerie late-night visit.

"What is it, Tess?" he demanded, his tone now alert, but strangely wary.

"I . . . I am sorry to disturb you," she stammered, "but I think there was an intruder in my room. Something touched my face when I was sleeping, and I don't believe I was merely dreaming."

There was a long pause while Rotham observed her standing there in her nightdress, barefooted, her hair spilling down around her shoulders.

"I am afraid to return, Rotham," Tess insisted when he was silent.

"I cannot imagine you being afraid of anything," was his noncommittal reply.

She swallowed. "It is one thing to disbelieve in ghosts. It is another to deny a real, physical manifestation. I am not returning to my room tonight. Fanny is in Basil's room, though, so I cannot stay with her. I will be more courageous in the morning, but until daylight, I want to stay here with you."

He looked at her for another long moment. "You are not using the ghost as an excuse to torment me?"

"What?" Her brow furrowed. No, she was not pretending to be frightened for her own purposes, as Fanny had done. "No, of course not. Why would you think that?"

"If you remain here, I cannot vouch for my control. I cannot spend another chaste night with you in my bed. I don't have the willpower."

It surprised Tess that he would admit to having any vulnerability to her, particularly that she could make him lose control.

She slowly crossed the room to his bedside. "I want to stay, Rotham," she repeated.

"Do you know what you are asking?"

Understanding his question, she hesitated. If she remained, the long-delayed consummation of their marriage would take place.

Was that what she wanted? Tess wondered, her gaze roaming over him. The lamp glow played over his bare torso, over sleek skin rippling with muscle.

Tess shivered, yet her reaction had nothing to do with fear and everything to do with her unwilling desire for Rotham. She craved his warmth, his sheltering arms. She wanted him to protect and hold her and keep her safe from harm.

But she also wanted so much more.

The dryness in her throat made her reply a rasp. "Yes . . . I know what I am asking."

His gray eyes sparked with unmistakable fire as he drew the covers down beside him, while his voice grew husky.

"Then stay."

Chapter Nine

※

Incredible is the only way to describe it.
—Diary Entry of Miss Tess Blanchard

Tess hesitated for another long heartbeat, yet she could not possibly have turned away. Rotham's powerful, hypnotic aura held her spellbound—that same captivating allure that had made her heart flip over when she'd first set eyes on him at nineteen.

His eyes just now were heavy-lidded and unexpectedly soft as he regarded her, waiting silently for her final decision. Yet she knew this moment was inevitable. They had danced around each other for days now, ever since their first, ill-advised, explosive embrace had resulted in forced matrimony. But it was time to end the battles between them . . . at least momentarily.

Releasing the breath she was holding, Tess carefully set her lamp down on the bedside table. When she started to extinguish the flame, however, Rotham stopped her with a gentle order.

"No, leave on the light."

Propping the pillows against the headboard behind him, he sat back and held out a beckoning hand to her. "Come here, love. Let me warm you."

Wordlessly, she obeyed. She had agreed to his terms, even though after tonight, not only would their marriage be irrevocable, her body would no longer be her own.

When she climbed onto the high bed to sit beside him, he slid an arm around her waist and drew her close. Accepting Rotham's embrace, Tess let her head rest on his shoulder.

For a while he merely held her, his heat seeping into her. She could feel her chilled body warming against the satin of his bare skin. His hand drifted soothingly over her hair, down over the long sleeve of her nightdress and back up again.

For a time she was content to remain in the hard masculine shelter of his arms. She felt cloaked in warmth and safety . . . yet undeniably aroused as well. Being with Rotham like this, sharing his bed, brought back potent memories of their wedding night. His slow caresses reminded her of how skillfully his hands and mouth could play over a woman's body . . . over *her* body.

Tess bit her lip, keenly aware of the contradiction. He was offering her comfort yet stirring chaotic feelings of longing and desire inside her. Feelings she would no longer—*could* no longer—resist.

After a moment, his lips pressed against her hair. "You should take off your nightdress," he murmured.

Without argument, Tess eased away from Rotham and rose up on her knees. Her palms damp with nerves, she unbuttoned the bodice of her cambric nightdress, then caught the hem and drew it over her head, letting the garment fall to the carpet beside the bed.

When, self-consciously, she made to cover her breasts with her hands, he shook his head. "Let me look at you."

It was arousing in itself, she realized, to have Rotham studying her nude body. She never would have believed a simple look could be so titillating. The expression in his eyes made her breathless.

He was a riveting figure himself, she thought, taking in his physical masculine beauty . . . his gold-brown hair, thick and wavy, glowing richly in the lamplight. The proud bones and angles of his aristocratic face. His firm, sensual mouth. His strong, vital body. His enchanting, mesmerizing eyes.

Her gaze was caught helplessly in his, even before he reached out and traced a fingertip over her cheekbone and along her jaw, then lower, down the column of her throat to one bare breast. Her nipple peaked instantly, making Tess gasp at the delicious sensation. And yet she felt shaky, trembling inside.

"Are you afraid of me?" he asked as if he could read her thoughts.

Not afraid of him, no. Rotham had been extremely considerate of her innocence that first time together, Tess reassured herself, so surely he would offer her the same consideration now. She feared herself, though. She was afraid of her relentless, deplorable need for him.

"I am a little nervous," Tess admitted honestly.

"Then you should take the lead."

Her brow furrowed. "What do you mean?"

"Why don't you learn my body? Your trepidation will decrease with familiarity."

His suggestion was unexpected, and she didn't immediately reply.

"You are completely in command, Tess," Rotham added, his voice low and casual.

She understood and appreciated his tactics. By allowing her to control the pace of her deflowering, she was likely to conquer her nerves more quickly.

"How do I begin?" she asked.

"Use your imagination. You are not a complete novice any longer."

No, she wasn't actually a novice. Fanny had helped her to prepare for her nuptial bed, including lessons in self-defense regarding how to arouse a man. And Rotham had shown her the incredible pleasure to be found in his arms. She could attempt to work the same seductive magic on him, Tess decided.

When she drew down the covers to expose his entire lower body, her heartbeat hammered in her throat. He was an overwhelming man, lithe and virile, but it was the foreign sight of his loins that drew her gaze. His long male member stood thick and darkly rigid, fascinating her with its sheer proportions.

"You may touch me, Tess," he urged. "I won't break."

She leaned closer, placing her palms against his bare chest, feeling the warm, strong resilience of his muscles as she trailed a tentative path lower to his hard, flat abdomen.

When she stopped short, Rotham took her hand and brought it to his loins. Her breath went shallow at the feel of that huge, swollen arousal.

Wrapping their joined fingers around his erection,

he moved her palm slowly along its length, stroking himself with her hand.

"Can you imagine having me inside you?" he asked. "Filling you with my flesh?"

Tess's lips parted at the enticing image he'd awakened in her mind.

"I would like very much to be inside you, Tess, giving you pleasure."

Yet *she* wanted to give *him* pleasure this time, Tess realized. The thought strangely excited her.

"You said I should lead," she reminded him, surprised by the husky intensity of her voice.

"As you wish. What do you propose doing?"

"I want to taste you."

His lips curved in a slow, sensual, heart-stopping smile. Something inside her stirred, responding as naturally, as inevitably, as breathing.

"Then taste me," he said.

He relaxed back against the pillows, giving the appearance of surrender. Yet evidently she affected Rotham, too. She could feel the fine tension in his body as she bent over him and pressed a kiss to the bare skin covering his heart.

And when she cupped the soft, velvety pouch of his loins, his body tensed visibly. Then her fingers curled around his hard shaft, and the thick length surged in her hand. Encouraged by his involuntary reaction, Tess couldn't help a gratified smile.

Still kneeling, she kissed her way further down Rotham's body, letting him feel the drag of her heavy sable hair over his stomach and groin. When she took him in her mouth, his rampant member jerked reflexively, and she felt another faint measure of triumph.

Control was somehow empowering, Tess realized, and liberating as well.

More eagerly, she slid her lips fully over the thick head of his shaft, swirling her tongue lightly over the taut, heated skin. His body clenched, and although his resulting groan was soft, she felt his hand twist in her hair.

After enduring several more moments of her seductive ministrations, though, he issued a ragged protest. "I knew it . . . you came here to torment me."

"Am I tormenting you?" she whispered.

"Yes . . . and I cannot take much more."

She relished the thought of making Rotham lose control. Yet apparently he wouldn't cede all the power to her.

Holding her upper arms, he eased his rigid length away from her caressing mouth. Then, pulling Tess up to him, he guided her knee over his thighs so that she sat straddling him, face-to-face.

At her look of surprise, his gray eyes smiled into hers. "This way we can both enjoy the pleasure," he said huskily.

Tess couldn't find her own voice, however. The searing heat of his arousal against her stomach had made her throat dry and deprived her of speech.

Reaching up, he took her breasts in his hands, lifting the swelling weight in his curving palms. Then leaning closer, he covered her mouth with his.

Just the taste of him sent her pulse leaping more erratically. He invaded her mouth with bold strokes of his tongue while his fingers plied her nipples with a gentle plucking motion. The eroticism of it stole her breath. His mouth, his tongue, his hands—all combined in a powerful assault on her senses.

Wanting grew inside her. Her heart pounded as he sent waves of heat to every part of her body.

Then Rotham unexpectedly drew back. His eyes had darkened, Tess saw before he glanced down at her breasts again.

His lids lowered, he deliberately bent his head and closed his mouth over one engorged peak. At the same time his hand dipped between her legs to find the creamy wetness there.

She gasped as his teasing fingers stroked her sex. The strong pull of his mouth on her nipple created a hot, echoing throb deep inside her very center . . . a throb that intensified when he paused to whisper huskily against her skin, "You're wet for me. Your body is eager for mine."

It was true. Her cleft was already slick and swollen and aching for him. And Rotham was clearly intent on making her longing even greater. Still caressing her, he left off suckling her breasts to watch her face. His smoky gaze held hers, never wavering as he explored her more thoroughly, his fingers probing between her feminine folds, the rough pad of his thumb gliding back and forth over the sensitive bud of her sex.

She nearly moaned at the sweet torment. "Rotham . . . you are making me so . . ."

"So what?"

"Hot. . . . Like I will burst into flames any moment."

"I want you to burst into flames, sweet Tess."

When he sheathed two fingers in her pulsing

warmth, a half gasp, half moan spilled from her lips as she shivered with wanton pleasure.

Oddly, her response only made him give up his delectable torture. But Tess realized why a moment later. Easing her thighs open wider, he closed his hands over her buttocks and pulled her hips even closer, so that her belly and feminine cleft cradled his heavy, swollen shaft. The pressure on the sensitive core of her sent a shock of fire rippling through Tess, making her clutch at his shoulders.

Unable to restrain her desire any longer, she rose up on her knees, intending to lower herself onto the velvet-smooth head of his manhood. When she felt his thick hardness begin to press inside her, though, Tess stiffened at the invasion, drawing a deep breath.

"Slowly," Rotham whispered, stopping her from going any further. "Let's take our time."

She paused, shutting her eyes, wondering if her body could accommodate his enormous size. For a dozen heartbeats, she felt the heat of his fingertips brush her face, her throat, her shoulders in soothing caresses. And after a time, her damp sheath seemed to open in readiness for him.

When she nodded, his hands moved to her thighs to guide her. She sank down another fraction, slowly enveloping him. The pain was not too great, more a burning sensation than real pain, and even that subsided in another few moments.

"Look at me, sweet angel."

She obeyed and found herself drowning in the shadowed glimmer of Rotham's eyes. How had she ever thought those gray depths cold and cynical? They smoldered hot and hungry now.

Tess felt an answering hunger burning inside her. Yearning for him to fill her more completely, she sank all the way down, so that he was seated fully inside her.

He held her there unmoving while he gently kissed her. His lips stroked over hers tenderly, as if she were rare and special and something to be savored.

His mouth was magical . . . and so was his touch. His kisses enchanted, and when she began to relax, he kissed her even more deeply, his tongue penetrating her mouth like his shaft was doing between her thighs.

An aching tightness coiled throughout her, spreading to her every nerve and sinew. Of its own accord, her inflamed body began to rock against his.

Rotham had given her the illusion of being in command, Tess realized, but she was not in charge at all; control was quickly slipping from her grasp. Her pulse turned wild as he began a slow, deliberate thrusting in turn. She moved her hips instinctively in a primitive, needful rhythm, trying to satisfy the hot, urgent longing clamoring inside her.

To her dismay, Rotham's beguiling lips left hers as he drew back again . . . yet it was only to watch her. There was a fierce tenderness in his eyes as he coaxed her with his hard body, heightening the erotic friction between them.

Her breath was coming in hoarse whimpers now. Her hands clenching spasmodically, Tess gripped his shoulders, clinging to him, seeking more of the fevered pleasure he was giving her. Her body felt deeply connected with his, so full that she was part of him. The feeling was intense, wonderful, and so was his dark, molten gaze. . . .

Suddenly, the pleasure was too keen, too fierce to be borne. Her heart pounding, Tess gasped at the bright flare of sensation that rocketed through her. She tried to press herself even deeper against Rotham—but then the shattering explosion came and swept away all her senses in a storm of fire.

His climax followed directly, as if he'd forced himself to wait for her. He groaned and shuddered and surged hard into her, catching her when she collapsed bonelessly onto his chest.

In the aftermath, his hand rose to cradle her throat, soothing her thundering pulsebeat, while his mouth feathered light, tender kisses over her face and hair.

His own breath was harsh and uneven, but after a long moment, Rotham lifted her and eased her down beside him. Letting his legs tangle with hers, he pulled the covers up over them both and drew Tess into his arms. He lay there, his body wrapped around hers, warming her, calming her, brushing her cheek with warm fingers.

"Are you all right?" he murmured after a time.

"Yes," Tess replied, savoring his hard strength. Her feelings for Rotham were still chaotic, creating turmoil in her heart and in her mind, yet her body had never felt so blissful. "Thank you for being so . . . considerate."

"Did you expect me to be otherwise?"

"I suppose not. But I did not think . . . this would happen tonight."

Ian himself had not expected to seal their marriage vows either. He hadn't meant to renege on his pledge to leave Tess strictly alone. Yet he could not possibly have resisted when she'd come to his rooms garbed only in a nightdress, looking anxious and alone.

He'd wanted to comfort her, yes, but he'd wanted more to claim her. The prospect had made him hard in an instant.

At that moment he was almost glad for the castle ghost, since it had driven Tess into his arms.

And then he had joined carnally with her. Her serene loveliness had taken his breath away . . . her exquisite body, her hair cascading down over her shoulders in heavy silken waves, her dark velvet eyes hot and pleading.

Her passionate response to his lovemaking had been everything he'd imagined and more, Ian admitted, remembering her sweet cries of pleasure. She was even more beautiful in her arousal than he'd anticipated, making all his past encounters with other lovers pale in comparison.

It was his own response that deeply concerned Ian. The pleasure he'd experienced with Tess had been shattering. Despite his extensive carnal experience, he'd felt the effects of their union as if it were his first.

And now he was lying here in the aftermath of passion, treasuring the quiet intimacy of holding her, relishing her scent on his skin.

Ian spread his fingers in the dark richness of her hair, luxuriating in the texture of it. Taking her innocence had left him hungry and aching for more of her.

Tess glanced up at him then. Her beautiful face was still flushed, her eyes hazy with sated passion, her thick sable hair a sultry tangle, her mouth swollen from his kisses.

Remembering the ripe softness of her lips, Ian felt a rush of desire that only made him want to be inside her again. He wouldn't use her body so harshly her first time, though. Yet he knew one night with Tess would never satisfy him. He wanted the rights of a lover, of a husband. He wanted to lose himself in the tempting fire of her—

"I will return to my own bedchamber in the morning, Rotham."

Her husky declaration coming so unexpectedly dashed cold water over his alluring fantasies.

Wondering if she was merely unnerved by the potent emotions sizzling between them, as he was, he kept his voice even when he replied. "You are welcome to sleep in my bed from now on."

"I see no need for us to share a bedchamber. You promised we could live separate lives, remember?"

Ian didn't dispute her, although familiar irritation clawed at him. It was bad enough that his own wife didn't want to share his bed. It stung more that Tess was pretending indifference after the remarkable passion they had just shared. How could she so blatantly ignore her obvious desire for him?

Then again, he would be wise to ignore his own fierce desire for *her*, Ian realized. Just now, self-preservation needed to be his chief concern. Particularly since after tonight, his feelings for Tess were even more raw and conflicted.

He was in perilous, uncharted waters; possessiveness had sunk its talons deep into him.

He meant to fight his vulnerability to her, though, Ian vowed. He'd seen her effect on other men, his own cousin most of all. He could well remember

Richard being reduced to a lovesick supplicant with Tess, behaving like an adoring puppy, hanging on her every word, her enchanting smile, her delightful laughter.

He had no intention of loving Tess, Ian promised himself. He wouldn't let himself be drawn into that desperate affliction as his cousin had been. Especially when she would never return any tender feelings of love for *him*.

Tess was still in love with his dead cousin, Ian reminded himself grimly. He couldn't compete with the beloved memory of a war hero.

At the reflection, he felt a muscle in his jaw harden. He didn't *want* to compete for Tess's affections.

But clearly he needed to make their battlefield more even. To ensure that his weakness for his lovely wife was not just one-sided.

There would likely never be love between them, but that didn't mean he wouldn't do everything in his power to make Tess want him just as fiercely as he wanted her.

Chapter Ten

Surely I can learn to control my desire for him.
—Diary Entry of Miss Tess Blanchard

Hoping to avoid the servants, Tess returned to her own room at daybreak, wearing Rotham's dressing gown. But as she reached her bedchamber door, she spied Fanny coming down the corridor from the opposite direction.

Her friend followed her inside, evidently eager to have a coze.

"I have been waiting for ages for you to return," Fanny said at once. "When you didn't answer my knock earlier, I presumed you were with the duke—and I see I was right." Her perceptive gaze took in Tess's nightclothes and passion-bruised mouth. "Well? Was the consummation what you expected?"

Color mounted her cheeks at the intimate question. *The consummation had been perfectly glorious,* was her silent response. To Tess's surprise, however, Rotham hadn't made love to her again after that first time. She'd spent the remainder of the night sleeping wrapped in his arms, and he had let her go this morning with nothing more than a casual, almost lazy kiss. Even so, she was acutely conscious of her lost virginity. She could feel the new sensitivity of her body . . . a tingling ache between her thighs, a swelling heaviness in her breasts.

"Yes, you were right about everything, Fanny," Tess admitted.

A rather smug smile touched the courtesan's mouth. "So, does this mean you will be moving into your husband's rooms?"

"No, it does not," she replied emphatically. "I only stayed with Rotham last night because I was frightened." Quickly Tess explained about being startled out of her dreams by eerie sensations and taking refuge in Rotham's rooms. "Our marriage is consummated now, but we have agreed to continue keeping separate apartments."

"A pity," Fanny responded. Yet she seemed to understand Tess's concern. "If you are careful, you can still enjoy passion without involving any tender emotions. There is no reason to deny yourself the pleasure of having Rotham as a lover."

Tess shook her head. "I don't want to risk it. What about you, Fanny?" she asked to change the subject. "Did you make any progress in your clandestine courtship of Basil?"

The courtesan's expression turned soft. "I believe so, Tess. I suspect he understood my ploy about fearing the ghost, yet he didn't object to my sharing his room. And it was the most amazing thing . . . all we did was converse before we fell asleep. I have never, ever done that before—shared a man's bed when nothing happened. It was . . . nice."

Tess's heart warmed at Fanny's confession, although it seemed droll that their situations were completely reversed. Fanny was discovering the pleasures of friendship and companionship while courting, and Tess was learning about carnal relations.

"I am even beginning to hope," Fanny added softly, "that Basil is coming around to the idea of marriage. But it is best to let him proceed at his own pace."

Tess agreed, and said so. "It is clear to me that Basil worships you and only needs a bit more encouragement. I predict it won't be long before your strategy bears fruit and you achieve your heart's desire."

She was not as confident that her own strategy in dealing with Rotham would work to her satisfaction. Particularly an hour later, when, after a long, hot bath, she joined him in the breakfast room along with Fanny and Basil.

Merely looking at Rotham aroused stirrings of unbridled lust inside Tess. When he scrutinized her with that penetrating gray gaze, as if remembering what lay beneath her gown, her breasts tightened with a delicious ache. And when he seated her at the table and made a point of brushing his fingers across her nape, the pulsing throb between her thighs instantly brought back memories of Rotham moving inside her and giving her the kind of stunning pleasure she had only imagined before.

All through breakfast, Tess was constantly aware of him and her own dilemma. She wanted Rotham, there was no doubt. In his arms she felt alive . . . gloriously, passionately alive. She cherished that feeling, yet she knew she was wise to keep their marriage strictly a legal union rather than viewing him as her lover.

Tess was therefore quite glad when Rotham said he

planned to spend the day searching for the castle's architectural renderings with Eddowes, and thus would not be making any calls with her that afternoon. The less time she spent with her handsome husband, the better—except that Tess couldn't help ribbing him about his motives.

"Are you certain you are not merely trying to avoid Vicar Potts? You know I mean to call on him today."

Rotham's response held wry amusement. "I admit, being spared the annoyance of listening to the loquacious clergyman prose on and on about his flock will be a relief. But in truth, my purpose is less selfish. Finding evidence of a hidden passage at Falwell will be our best chance at discovering how our 'ghost' is getting about the castle without detection. Invading your bedchamber was the last straw, and I mean to catch whoever it is."

Tess shivered in remembrance. She wanted to expose the ghost as much as he did, so she approved when Rotham retired to the library with his secretary and Fanny, whose manuscript draft was nearing completion.

Tess spent the morning in the drawing room attending to her neglected correspondence. It was perhaps two hours later when she was interrupted by Hiddleston, who said his grace wished to speak with her in the library.

Setting down her pen, Tess answered the summons and found the three of them—Rotham, Basil, and Fanny—poring over sketches of the castle's design.

"Eddowes unearthed the drawings we were looking for," Rotham informed her. "A remarkable feat, considering that they were buried behind some history tomes."

At his praise, Tess noted that Basil smiled modestly but looked pleased with himself. When they stepped aside to let her see the drawings, she realized she was looking at floor plans for each level of the castle and also for the towers that had been built in the previous century.

"Do the plans show any secret passageways?" she asked Rotham.

"No, but by measuring the inner and outer dimensions of various rooms and corridors, we may be able to determine discrepancies in the placement of the walls. You and I will begin by surveying your bedchamber."

"Just the two of us?"

"I think it best for Eddowes and Miss Irwin to continue their usual work here in the library. The 'ghost' could have some connection to the castle staff, and I don't want him to know we are trying to ascertain his method of access."

It was in that manner that they found the secret panel in Tess's room. By using a length of twine marked off in feet, Rotham proved that the inner dimensions of the chamber were not as wide as the drawings indicated they should be. And by examining the wainscoting closely, they discovered a movable panel near the hearth, with a catch that released upon applying pressure to a certain point.

The panel slid open with a soft scraping sound to reveal a narrow passage, and closed with a "snick" that Tess recognized from her dream.

She shuddered to realize that last night someone truly had entered her room by way of the panel and touched her face while she slept.

Rotham's expression turned grim as he evidently came to the same conclusion. "You are not sleeping here again until our damned ghost is caught," he said resolutely.

Tess gave him no argument. There was no way she would remain in this bedchamber tonight—although that didn't mean she would again take refuge in Rotham's room or bed. But she would deal with that problem later, Tess reflected as he lit a lamp. For now they had a hidden passage to explore.

It was an extremely tight fit for Rotham to squeeze into the dusty, airless space, and awkward for Tess, wearing skirts, to climb the rungs of a ladder that led to the floor above. And given the dirt that had collected over a century, her gown was filthy by the time they crawled into a cupboard in a linen pantry, where they narrowly missed startling a chambermaid at work.

When the maid left, they quietly retraced their path to Tess's bedchamber so they could study the architectural drawings and discuss their next steps without whispering.

They knew there could very well be other secret passages that provided access to various rooms of the castle—how many they weren't certain. But Rotham decided it was more important to discover how the intruder could enter the castle without being seen.

"There has to be a tunnel below the castle," he mused. "I want to search the cellars next, and then the towers."

* * *

Avoiding the castle servants while examining the cellars would be much harder, they concluded, as would justifying their presence without raising suspicions. Therefore, even though a duke and duchess needed no reason to explore their own residence, they gathered Fanny from the library to provide a logical excuse for scouring the castle depths, claiming they were plotting some new scenes for her novel.

Their search of the cellars came up frustratingly empty, however. It wasn't until they scrutinized the second of the two towers, on the lowest floor, that they finally found a panel in the wainscoting similar to the one in Tess's bedchamber that hid a secret passage. But while the concealed space off her room had been dusty and stifling, this narrow passage was cold and dank.

Taking two lanterns, they squeezed through the panel opening and proceeded single file, with Rotham leading. A steep flight of wooden steps led to an underground tunnel hewn out of earth and rock. The tunnel eventually spilled out into a dark, shallow cave, they discovered.

A sliver of daylight glinting before them pointed to the cave's entrance. Upon investigating, they found an opening in the rock that was shielded by a wall of lush vegetation and further hidden behind the tumbling cascade of a waterfall.

Beyond the waterfall, they could see the cove below Falwell Castle in the distance and hear the quiet rush of waves swelling against the sandy shore.

"This cave would be ideal for smugglers," Rotham said, voicing what they were all thinking.

Turning back to explore the interior, they found a stash of contraband at one side, behind a low wall of boulders—a dozen casks of brandy as well as three sizeable chests that were padlocked.

"This evidence suggests that our 'ghost' is real," he added with satisfaction, "and not the haunted spirit of my murdered ancestor. I'll wager that whoever left this bounty has been using the tunnels to gain access to the castle."

"Should we try to open the chests?" Tess asked.

"Not at present. We would have to break the locks, which could forewarn our culprits when they return to claim their goods."

Tess nodded in understanding, although disappointed that the contents of the chests would have to remain a mystery for now.

Fanny spoke up then. "So what do you propose, your grace?"

"I want to catch our intruders in the act of stealing into the castle. For now we'll use our own servants to set up a watch around the clock. We may have to trust the Hiddlestons, but I don't want to involve the other castle staff in case they're complicit."

Tess frowned slightly. "Do we have enough of our own servants to mount a full-time watch?"

"I expect so. We'll need at least two armed men per shift, but if Eddowes and I join our footmen and coachmen and grooms, that should be adequate to apprehend the smugglers if they reappear."

"I would like to help," Tess said earnestly.

"So would I," Fanny seconded.

"We'll see," Rotham said noncommittally. "For now, let's find the trail from the beach so we'll have an alternate route to and from the castle other than the tunnel. We don't know if the smugglers will be returning by sea or by land."

They soon found a path through the woods that climbed up the bluff to the castle. Rotham identified the best places to lie in wait for their quarry, and upon retracing their steps to the caves, decided to divide the watch into six-hour shifts, with a man inside the cave and another outside, judging that one could hold the smugglers at gunpoint to prevent them from escaping while the other summoned reinforcements from the castle.

He wanted Tess's two footmen to take the first watch, since Miles and Fletcher were trained in firearms and fisticuffs. Rotham was still hesitant to allow Tess to participate, however.

She was about to argue the point when she realized the time. "I have an appointment at the vicarage at two o'clock," she said, regretting having to leave.

"I'll accompany you," Rotham informed her, "since I want to speak to the good reverend. Potts may have useful information about the local smugglers, even though a man of the cloth isn't likely to be involved with the actual misdeeds."

After setting the two footmen to guard the cave, Tess and Rotham rode saddle horses to call on the vicar rather than take a carriage and require their servants to drive. When they arrived, the congenial, silver-haired Gideon Potts fawned over the duke and showered Tess with gratitude for her efforts to help the poorest of his congregation.

"It is just amazing, your grace," the vicar gushed to

her, "We have been getting contributions daily, and it is all your doing."

Rotham waited until Tess's business was concluded before inquiring about his main interest.

The long-winded vicar obliged with an extensive sermon on the subject.

"There are not as many Freetraders nowadays as in the past, you see. Smuggling has died down because customs duties were reduced significantly once the long wars with France ended—which made the trade far less profitable. But truly, smuggling has never been considered all that grave a crime in these parts, your graces. Most Cornishmen are sympathetic to the cause and often aid the Brethren in avoiding the excisemen."

He went on to explain that Freetraders were often seen as romantic adventurers performing a valued service.

"Outright thievery is another matter altogether, however." Potts's florid face grew solemn. "Sadly, we had a ring of thieves at work in the neighborhood over the past summer. Several of the great houses suffered break-ins, with valuable jewels and silver stolen. It is particularly worrisome, since innocents are being hurt. Only a week ago, two of Lord and Lady Shaw's servants were struck on the head and rendered unconscious. The thieves have yet to be caught."

Tess met Rotham's gaze just then. From the arrested look in his eyes, she knew they were entertaining the same suspicions—that perhaps Falwell's ghost might have some connection to the thieves.

When Rotham told the vicar about finding contraband in the caves below Falwell, Potts agreed it was possible that the miscreants were using the castle to hide their ill-gotten gains.

A short while later, Tess and Rotham politely took their leave. During the ride home, she asked him about proving that the thieves could be Falwell's ghost. "Perhaps we should break the padlocks after all, to see if the chests contain any of the stolen jewels."

"I intend to."

"If so," Tess mused aloud, "then it means we are dealing with an entire ring, and you will need more support to foil them. Surely now you will allow me to help watch the cave, and Fanny also."

Rotham shook his head. "You heard Potts. These thieves are known to be violent."

"All the more reason for us to be involved. We can provide strength in numbers."

"No, it's out of the question."

Tess felt herself stiffen at his commanding tone. "I warn you, Rotham. I won't just sit idly by while you confront an organized band of thieves."

"You will, love."

She regarded him in frustration. "You are acting the tyrant again."

"Oh, yes," he drawled in a voice heavy with satire. "It is tyrannical of me to want to protect you from danger."

Brown eyes clashed with gray—but then Tess bit her tongue. She would never persuade Rotham to agree to her participation by resuming their former hostilities.

Forcibly, she adopted a more reasonable tone. "You

seem to have no qualms about putting our servants at risk, or Basil Eddowes, either."

"They are men. They can shoot a pistol if necessary."

"Fanny and I both know how to shoot."

"I am *not* putting you in the middle of a gun battle."

"I am *not* suggesting any such thing," she replied sweetly. "We are perfectly capable of going to fetch reinforcements from the castle while you big, strong *men* hold the thieves at gunpoint."

When he only scowled, Tess continued. "I am not a fragile flower, Rotham."

"No, that you are not," he allowed grudgingly.

"You need us. Otherwise you will have to involve the castle servants, who may warn the thieves away."

Rotham sent Tess a quelling glance. "Your stubbornness is highly annoying."

"Well, you delight in purposely annoying me, your grace. Turnabout is only fair play."

He grimaced. "Your grace, this . . . Rotham, that. Your formality grows irksome." His tone held irritated masculine impatience. "Must I remind you again that you are my wife now? You may call me by my given name rather than my title, as I have mentioned before."

Tess pursed her lips thoughtfully. "I have thought of you as my nemesis for so long, it would seem strange to use anything other than your title."

"Ian is my name. I prefer you use it."

"And in return, Ian? Will you allow me to participate?"

A pained smile touched his lips. "I expect you will leave me no choice."

Tess's own smile was brighter. "No indeed, dear Ian."

Rotham eventually gave in, Tess decided, because he knew she was right. When they reached Falwell Castle, they left their horses on the bluff and made their way down the steep path through the woods to join Miles and Fletcher, who were lying in wait in hopes of catching the smugglers.

Inside the cave, they broke the padlocks on the chests and discovered an abundance of valuable jewelry, coins, and silver—mainly candelabra and dinnerware.

Fletcher gave a long, low whistle. "Cor, 'tis a fortune."

"Not the work of Freetraders," Rotham agreed grimly.

With that new intelligence, it was easier for Tess to gain his grudging approval in helping to guard the cave. After some further discussion, they formulated their plans. Rotham's footmen would assume the next shift, while he and Tess and another servant would take the third shift later that night, beginning at ten o'clock. Fanny and Basil would relieve them at four A.M., along with Tess's stalwart coachman, Spruggs.

Then they returned to the castle and informed the various parties about their duties. Basil was not keen on Fanny endangering herself, either, but although she was pleased by his protectiveness, Fanny used the same argument with him that Tess had used with Rotham—or Ian, as she had agreed to call him.

They dined together as usual that evening, and repaired to the drawing room afterward for cards and conversation. But when ten o'clock neared, instead of retiring for bed, Tess and Ian changed their formal attire for dark clothing—garments that were thick and heavy enough to protect against the nip in the autumn night air.

Slipping quietly through the dark castle then, they exited through a side door, where they met one of Rotham's grooms.

Rotham—Ian—had brought two loaded pistols and a lamp, although they couldn't use a light for fear of giving themselves away. The half moon was bright enough to illuminate the woods, however, as they negotiated the path down to the cove. And the soft rush of the waterfall was sufficient to cover the sound of their progress and even drown out the rhythmic swell of the surf surging against the shore.

Even so, when they encountered the first footman, they kept their voices low. Ian's groom took the footman's place, hiding behind a patch of shrubbery, and Ian and Tess moved on to relieve the second footman inside the cave.

The interior was nearly pitch-dark. Thus, Tess was glad Ian had paced off the dimensions earlier, since he was able to lead her to the rear of the cave. They settled behind the low wall of boulders, so that they could cover the cave entrance and the tunnel opening at the same time.

To avoid being heard over the babble of the waterfall, they spoke little as they waited for the thieves to show themselves. Tess rested her shoulder against Ian's strong arm, glad to feel his reassuring warmth.

She had dressed in a hooded cloak, woolen gown, and gloves, yet after an hour, the chill of the rock seemed to seep into her limbs.

Ian must have felt her shiver, because he murmured quietly, "Come here," as he drew her closer.

He repositioned her between his outstretched legs, with her back to his chest, his arms wrapped around her from behind. Gratefully, Tess leaned back against him and concentrated on staying awake in the darkness.

As the time slowly ticked by, she felt herself growing stiff as well as sleepy, but she was not about to complain since she had been the one to insist on accompanying him to the cave.

Perhaps another ten minutes passed before she shivered again. In response, Ian shifted his hold and drew down the hood of her cloak to expose her hair, which was still pinned in an elegant chignon from dinner. To her surprise, he lightly kissed her bare nape. Then he slipped one gloved hand between the folds of her cloak to cover her gown's bodice.

Tess drew a startled breath, and when he began caressing her breasts from behind, she asked in an incredulous whisper, "What are you *doing*?"

"I am merely trying to warm you."

The sound of his low voice scraped along her senses and flooded her with the warmth of memory, taking her back to the previous night spent in his bed. And when his hand slowly continued stroking her breasts, she knew he was purposely arousing her, despite his denial.

"You are trying to seduce me, aren't you?" she demanded hoarsely.

"That was not my original intention. If I wished to seduce you, I would do this. . . ."

Through her layers of clothing, his gloved fingers plucked at her nipple, sending a shock of sensation spearing through her.

"You cannot make love to me here, Rotham."

"My name is Ian," he reminded her, gently nipping her earlobe.

"You cannot make love here, Ian."

"Yes, I can," he answered, unperturbed. "Shall I show you?"

His free hand delved inside her cloak to stroke over her gown, sliding along the fabric covering her abdomen, then lower to cup her woman's mound between her thighs, pressing her skirts against the bare flesh of her sex.

Tess gasped at the pleasurable friction.

"Hush, darling. You don't want to give us away."

Yet it was difficult to hush. Even through her gown she could feel Ian pinching her nipples above while probing her feminine folds below. The combined effect of his dual assault sent a bolt of sheer sexual excitement through Tess.

As he pressed harder against her sensitive core, her own gloved fingers clutched on his hard thighs.

"You don't really want me to stop, angel, do you?" he observed in that provocative tone that never failed to rile her.

He was daring her to prove her dispassion, Tess realized; indeed, he was almost taunting her.

She should have been vexed, except that his caresses were driving any thought of anger from her mind. With her senses on fire, she couldn't seem to care that he was conducting his scandalous offensive in a dark cave, or that at any moment a band of smugglers could come storming in—although in that event they would likely have a warning.

She most certainly didn't want Ian to stop, however.

"I didn't think so," he murmured with amused satisfaction. When he urged her to spread her legs wider, she whimpered. "You have to be silent, Tess," he reminded her.

His wicked caresses were somehow even more erotic because she couldn't scream, and because his mouth joined in the seduction. His tongue swirled around the shell of her ear, then slipped inside, reminding her how he had thrust deep into her body just last night.

He continued stroking her through her gown, knowing just where to touch to increase her need. Soon her hips were rising and falling at the delicious friction he created, but Ian only increased the rhythm of his caresses.

Tess bit her lip hard, but when the fire mounted higher inside her, she couldn't stifle a sob of pleasure.

"Remember, you can't cry out when you come," he whispered huskily in her ear.

To make certain she obeyed, he grasped her chin and turned her face back to his. As her body shuddered and began to buck in his embrace, he captured her mouth with a deep, hot kiss to silence her scream of ecstasy.

When her climax finally was over, his magical hands remained where they were, lazily soothing her.

Panting and weak, Tess sprawled back against him. "You are a fiend," she muttered in a hoarse voice. "I cannot believe you did that."

"Did what?" he asked innocently. "As I said, I was only helping to warm you. Are you warm now, love?"

Yes, she was warm. She was feverishly hot.

Before she could answer, Ian echoed her thoughts. "I think you are hot for me." Catching her wrist, he guided her hand down to his loins so that Tess could feel the hard bulge beneath his breeches. "I know I am hot for you. I want to be inside you, sweet Tess."

Her thighs clenched at his suggestive tone, while her stomach contracted. "This is why they call you the Devil Duke, isn't it? Because you are utterly wicked."

"No doubt. But it is hardly wicked to pleasure my own wife."

"But I am not a real wife to you," Tess pointed out breathlessly.

"Even so, when our shift is over, you are sleeping in my bed for the rest of the night. We are legally wed. There is no reason we must endure this sexual frustration any longer."

Tess didn't reply at first, although her body was aching shamelessly for Ian. The damnable truth was, she wanted to spend the entire night with him, making passionate love to him, getting lost in his strength and his heat.

And what was so wrong with enjoying a sexual liaison with her own husband? She had yearned for passion to fill the emptiness inside her, Tess reminded herself.

Perhaps Fanny was right. She could have Ian as a lover without involving her heart. Indeed, for the past few years, she had shut out emotions in her life as self-protection. She could continue doing so if they slept together as lovers, surely.

She could remain cool to Ian, in complete control of her feelings.

"Very well," Tess agreed after a moment. "I will sleep in your bed tonight and ease your sexual frustration."

He laughed softly and pressed a kiss against her hair. "How kind of you, darling, to pretend you are granting me a favor. But you will enjoy sharing my bed as much as I do, I promise you."

Chapter Eleven

Connubial relations do not necessarily lead to more
intimate feelings, do they?
　　　　—Diary Entry of Miss Tess Blanchard

To her gratification, Ian made good on his promise that very night. With no sign of either smugglers or thieves, he turned duty for guarding the cave over to his secretary and servants and escorted Tess to his bedchamber. There, he spent the remaining hours till dawn showing her precisely what he'd meant when he pledged to see to her enjoyment, rousing her to depths of passion she never knew were even possible. They fell asleep entwined just as day was breaking.

It was nearing noon when Ian awakened Tess by pressing arousing kisses all over her body, culminating with a tender kiss on her lips as he slid into her. The beauty of it—the exquisite feel of his hardness molding to her softness—stole her breath.

At her husky gasp, Ian sank even deeper inside her, deliberately inflaming the shimmers of pleasure that were radiating from her in waves.

He moved in a rhythmic motion, with slow, hot strokes that she felt in her very core. Liquid wanting poured through her, her flesh absorbing the heat and strength of him, her tension mounting with his every sensual thrust.

In only moments, the quaking excitement in her body built to shattering proportions . . . until she shuddered and melted around him. As she shook and sobbed his name, Ian came also, emptying inside her in a powerful climax that left them both weak and gasping.

In the drowsy aftermath of their passion, he stroked the curve of her hot cheek with a soothing finger.

"I would say we are making progress," he murmured in husky satisfaction.

"What do you mean?" Tess asked hoarsely.

"You cried out my name rather than my title."

She sighed with grudging contentment. She couldn't regret surrendering to him. No doubt it had been inevitable after spending so much time alone together these past few days. The wonder was that she had managed to resist Ian's allure as long as she had.

But the almost smug note in his voice compelled her to reaffirm her position.

"I thought you claimed to be a man of your word," she breathed in an accusatory tone.

"I am."

"Then how do you explain going back on your pledge? You promised we would not consummate our marriage until I begged you, but I never begged."

When Ian lifted his head, she saw a lazy, heated smile glittering in the gray depths of his eyes. "Not yet, but you will. And I might point out that *you* are to blame for precipitating the consummation. You came to my room clad only in a provocative night-dress."

Although Tess couldn't deny his logic, she side-stepped the issue with a smile. "I will never beg you, Ian," she insisted.

His mouth lowered to hers with heart-stopping languor, then finally drew back. "I will refrain from mocking you when you renege on your vow, love. For now, however, I propose we ring for breakfast. All this passion has left me famished."

Tess was starving also, but she raised an eyebrow at his suggestion. "It would be more proper to dress and go down for breakfast."

"Propriety be damned. I mean to spend the remainder of the day here making love to you."

A fresh shiver of excitement ran through her. "Is that not rather decadent, as well as lazy and self-indulgent?"

"Perhaps, but newlyweds can be forgiven their inordinate carnal lust. And it is time you indulged your own needs for a change. You have acted the role of Saint Tess for so long, you have forgotten how to enjoy a leisure hour or two."

Acknowledging the truth of his charge, she gave Ian no further argument just then. They breakfasted in his room, wearing only robes, and while they were being served, he ordered a bath to be filled in the adjacent dressing room.

Tess waited until the footmen had left to do his bidding before lodging a protest. "You cannot mean for us to bathe together."

Ian sent her a taunting smile. "Are you afraid of a

simple bath, darling? Or merely afraid I will make you beg?"

"I am afraid of neither," Tess replied defiantly.

Ian was obviously taking her declaration as a challenge, and she thought it wiser to respond in kind. Keeping their marriage adversarial would go a long way toward maintaining her emotional distance from him, she rationalized.

For the remainder of breakfast, Tess tried to tamp down the anticipation and excitement welling inside her, yet she felt Ian stealing her breath every time their gazes collided.

His servants carried cans of hot water into the dressing room and eventually filled the copper bathtub. When the last one left, he shut his bedchamber door and locked it behind them, then turned to face Tess.

Awareness coursed through her with an intensity that made her burn. The air was crackling between them again, charged with a suppressed sexual chemistry . . . that blood-pounding, swept-away sensation that always made her feel so alive.

Then Ian shrugged out of his dressing gown, baring his nude body. Tess was unbelievably stirred by his striking beauty. He was strong and tall and handsome enough to take her breath away—but then, breathlessness was becoming a habit with her whenever she was near him. She wanted him with a greed that she had never experienced before.

He crossed the room to her, moving with a masculine grace that titillated the senses and only emphasized the leashed power in his long limbs.

"What are you waiting for, love?" he asked when Tess remained motionless.

"Nothing."

"Then take off your robe or I will do it for you."

The words were a gauntlet, a threat, and there was a distinct challenge in his gaze. But Tess mutely shed her robe and stood before him naked.

His expression turned frankly sensual as his gaze slowly swept downward, over every part of her. Raising his hands, he brushed his palms over her nipples, making all the nerves in her body shiver with delight. Then his fingers spread, fanning over her breasts.

His warm caresses sent a jolt of desire through Tess and set the inner passage between her thighs to aching. She wanted his magnificent length pressing deep inside her, filling her emptiness with heat.

A faint moan escaped her as he thumbed the taut peaks, but when she clutched at his shoulders to draw him closer, Ian stepped back.

"Not yet. The pleasure will be greater if we delay."

Hiding her disappointment, Tess accompanied him to the dressing room, where she pinned up her hair so as not to get it wet. Then Ian led her to the tub and supported her as she stepped into the water. When she sank down, he joined her.

To her surprise, however, Ian would not allow her to wash herself. "I intend to play lady's maid today," he informed her, taking the soap and cloth from her.

Then he proceeded to bathe her, making Tess understand why so many women longed to be his lover.

She had never seen this playful side of Ian, nor had she ever been the sole target of his wicked, seductive charm, even though undoubtedly he had used it to devastating effect on other members of her sex.

"You can be exceedingly charming when it suits you," she said tightly as he washed her aching breasts.

"Indeed."

The corners of his fascinating mouth turned up in a slow smile that was full of sin. Tess was nearly undone by that smile, but she forced herself to think of something other than his enchanting attentions.

"I suppose all your mistresses were exquisite beauties," she observed.

"Are you fishing for compliments, love?"

"Not at all."

"You compare favorably with any woman I have ever known. . . ."

As if to prove his point, he began commenting on each part of her body as he washed and rinsed her inch by inch, punctuating his observations frequently with his mouth as well as his hands. Her blood was pounding by the time he finished.

As his husky laughter caressed her nipple, Tess pulled back and commandeered the soap and cloth. She washed him in turn, pleased that Ian was obviously as aroused as she felt, judging from the size and hardness of his swollen male member.

When they emerged from the bathtub clean and dripping wet, he resumed control and used a towel to dry her off, paying particular attention to the sensitive folds between her legs. A shock of fierce pleasure shot through her nerve endings when he cupped her sex, then sank two fingers into her, his teasing slow and deliberate.

"Wicked man," she said in a strangled voice, closing her own fingers around his thick shaft.

"Wicked woman," he countered with a low, devilish laugh.

She held on for another moment, marveling at the hard length of him, before reaching for another towel to dry his skin.

When she was done, they left the damp towels behind and returned to his bedchamber, where they faced each other. Ian's gaze held hers, and Tess could only stare back, enthralled by the challenge in his eyes.

The battle lines were clearly drawn, but she intended to meet his challenge measure for measure. Ian was an expert at lovemaking; if she hoped to remain unscathed by their love games, let alone be victorious, she would have to become much better at arousing him.

Reaching up, Tess unpinned her hair and shook her head, sending the long tresses tumbling over her bare shoulders. His gray eyes darkened with a heated look that only fed the aching need inside her.

Taking a step toward him, she ordered him to lie down on the bed. After a moment's hesitation, Ian obeyed. Moving to the bedside, Tess stood staring down at his splendid nude form.

She had kissed his body briefly yesterday. Now she wanted to explore him at her leisure, to learn him with her hands, to taunt him until *he* lost control.

She wanted to make him feel the same wonder as she felt, the same melting need.

In short, she meant to make *him* beg for *her*.

*   *   *

Ian felt a sharp jolt of desire for Tess, but he clamped down on his own need for the time being. All his instincts warned him to allow her at least the illusion of control. He wanted Tess to know passion, to feel the savage pleasure he could give her, yet he could perhaps accomplish his aims best by allowing her to explore her wild side at her own pace.

Therefore, when she stood there looking enticing and oh so female, he kept his hands firmly at his sides.

She leaned closer, however, her full breasts dangling above him, pale and perfect, her dark hair swinging forward in a silky wave. He wanted to pull her down on top of him and kiss those lush breasts, to bury his face in that gleaming sable mass.

He reached for her then, yet her hands pressed down on his shoulders insistently. "No, I mean to do this."

He lay back, pretending quiescence.

Easing onto the bed, Tess knelt between his spread legs and bent over him. Ian nearly shuddered, feeling the silky strands of her hair against the skin of his chest. And then she pressed her lips against his bare shoulder.

She kissed his entire body slowly, deliberately sweeping her hair over him as she moved lower, letting her taut nipples graze him as well. He was already heavily aroused, his rigid cock rising toward his belly, but he hardened even further when she swirled her tongue over the sensitive area of his inner thighs. Then she moved back up his body, her lips trailing fire over his flesh.

When she bypassed his loins, he grasped her hand and guided it to his erection, wanting her to feel how ready and swollen he was for her. When Tess raised her head briefly, he could see by her pleased smile that she knew very well what her touch did to him.

Bending down once more, she attended to him again, her mouth sweet and hot and demanding as it covered his body, her tongue tentative at first, but then growing bolder. The pleasure that rippled through Ian in the wake of her taunting kisses was savage enough to make his heart pound.

It required almost Herculean effort for him to lie totally still while she attended him, licking, stroking, tantalizing. . . . She paused to flick his male nipples with her tongue before returning to his mouth, delivering a featherlight kiss that made his stomach clench in a mixture of tenderness and gut-wrenching desire.

The coiling tension tightened even further as Tess moved downward again, her tongue skimming along his throat, exploring his chest, dipping into his navel, gliding over his belly to his groin. When she finally touched his shaft with her lips, his breath caught in his lungs.

He sensed rather than saw Tess's smile of satisfaction. Her fingers cupped the heavy sac of his testicles, brushing the seam-like line underneath, then molded over his hardness. The thick length surged in her hand, sending a fierce, fiery ache shooting through him and making him reach for her.

"Be still," she commanded in a husky voice as she raised her head.

She held his gaze, looking directly into his eyes before she lowered her head once more. His heart slammed against his ribs as her warm, wet mouth closed around him fully, and he groaned with the sheer pleasure of it.

Tess suckled him, her grasp firm as she tasted his rigid flesh, her touch inflaming him with need. His fingers dug into the mattress as he fought for control. Every muscle he possessed was quivering, straining with hunger.

She went on arousing him, though, her hands a continuation of her mouth, stroking, squeezing, exciting, while her tongue stimulated him relentlessly. The lash of pleasure was almost cruel. His body shuddered under the exquisite impact of it.

Arching against the delicious torment she inflicted, Ian started to slide himself slowly between her lips, his hips rising reflexively off the bed.

"Tess." He grated her name between his teeth. "I want you . . . *now.*"

She only increased the searing rhythm of her mouth.

"Sweet God, Tess . . ." He said it like a caress, like a curse.

"Not yet," she paused to murmur, repeating his own words. "The pleasure will be greater if we delay."

His patience was limited, though, and so was his control. It almost hurt to breathe, he was holding himself so tightly in check.

Then Tess suckled him harder, and Ian lost even that tenuous thread of his willpower. His control breaking, he grasped her shoulders and drew her up to claim her mouth with an almost violent pressure. This kiss was not about power, though. It was all about hunger and need.

Tess was suddenly straining against him also, as if she'd die if she ceased touching him, ceased kissing him.

Reaching between her thighs, Ian stroked her sex, probing urgently. The cream of her arousal soaked his fingers in an instant. Tess whimpered, and when he delved even deeper, she gave a soft sob.

He rolled her over then and covered her body with his. He felt her sigh burst against his lips as he entered her in one long, slow thrust.

Ian sighed harshly himself as her lush folds enveloped him, creamy hot and wet. It was like plunging into molten honey, and it was his undoing.

His body bucked just as she went rigid and began to sob. Groaning, he preceded her shivering convulsions in a climax that was bright and brilliant and explosive, her sweet cries of pleasure mingling with his hoarse shout of release.

When their shudders at last subsided, Ian collapsed to one side of her shoulder, barely having the strength to spare Tess his weight. He could scarcely believe his lack of control. No other woman had ever affected him this strongly.

Yet he no longer marveled at his wild physical response to Tess. The powerful sexual drive churning in his blood was matched only by his possessiveness. Already he wanted her again—yet he had to remember her inexperience. He had to be gentle with Tess, at least until she could grow accustomed to the demands he made on her body.

Easing off her, he drew Tess's naked form against him, lying with her head on his shoulder.

The sigh she gave was sated and content, although her voice was hoarse and held a teasing note when she spoke. "Admit it, Ian, you came very close to begging me."

Indeed, he had. But he would not share that thought aloud. "I would say we came to a draw this time."

She glanced up at him, her mouth fighting a smile. "Very well, I will acknowledge a draw. But if I am to have a fair chance at winning, you must teach me more about passion."

"What more do you need to learn? Your knowledge seems more than adequate now."

"Not adequate enough. You have a vast advantage over me. If you show me the secrets of being an ideal lover, it will put us on more equal footing."

He pressed a light kiss on the crown of her head. "I will be happy to oblige, darling. I am surprised you know so little about lovemaking," he added absently.

Her eyebrow lifted. "Why would you be surprised? Setting aside the fact that ladies are supposed to remain chaste until after marriage, where would I have gained any experience?"

"From Richard. I would never have thought he would be slow in that arena."

Ian felt Tess stiffen at the mention of her betrothed.

"Richard was a gentleman," she replied in his defense. "He never attempted more than a kiss or two. And we never had much opportunity for anything else. He was away with his regiment for much of the time we were betrothed."

Ian's jaw hardened for a moment. He was infinitely glad his cousin hadn't had the chance to spoil Tess's innocence. But he should never have brought up the subject.

Seeking to distract her, Ian drew a finger over her swollen lips. "So you wish me to share my secrets, hmmm? Where would you like to begin?"

Tess allowed him to divert her attention, even though the reference to Richard had unsettled her. Eventually they fell asleep from sated exhaustion, but later when she woke from a doze, as she lay beside her sleeping husband, her thoughts returned to her late betrothed.

Her marriage was nothing like what she'd dreamed of when she accepted Richard's proposal. She had loved him a great deal, both as a friend and future husband, yet she honestly had never felt much *passion* for him. Certainly not the kind of fiery sparks she always felt for Ian.

Richard had been kind and gentle and sweet and compassionate. He frequently made her laugh, and even when she was vexed with him, he always managed to charm her out of her ill mood.

Ian, on the other hand, made her burn for him and yearn for something more exciting and fulfilling.

Still, despite the danger of being swept up in an ardor beyond her control, she could justify her decision to share his bed, Tess reflected defensively. Simply because Ian could arouse her body did *not* mean she would lose her heart to him.

Yes, he made her feel a fierce desire for him. It was also true that he fired her emotions by challenging her, that he forced her to *feel*.

But she relished that exhilarating sensation and

had no intention of giving it up. She would never return to that numb state she had existed in for the past two years, Tess vowed. She refused to let life pass her by, to grow old wondering what might have been.

Her hopes of having a loving marriage would likely elude her, but at least she could have passion.

Moreover, she was not as vulnerable now, Tess knew. It was quite possible that she'd fallen so earnestly in love with Richard because she had recently lost both her parents, but she was much stronger now, and fully on her guard.

Hearing Ian's quiet breathing, she opened her eyes and studied him as he slept. His striking features were softer in repose, but she would not make the mistake of thinking he had a heart.

After today's sensual battles, she felt much more optimistic that she could enjoy their nuptial bed, but keep their physical relations from leading to anything more intimate. Especially if Ian was willing to teach her how to be his ideal lover. She was a quick study, and she would use his expert skills to further arm herself against her handsome husband.

With that comforting thought, Tess once more closed her eyes and slept.

Chapter Twelve

Ian believes me to be softhearted and idealistic, but it is only right that we help those who most deserve our compassion.

—Diary Entry of Miss Tess Blanchard

Ian continued her lessons in passion that afternoon, although making allowances for the unaccustomed tenderness of Tess's body. Her overheated senses were still throbbing when she returned to her own bedchamber later to dress for dinner, and it required significant effort to focus on such mundane tasks as ringing for her maid and choosing what gown to wear.

Alice was arranging Tess's hair when Fanny knocked and wandered into the room. Giving a big yawn, Fanny said she had just risen from a nap after being up a good part of the night guarding the cave—which had all been for naught.

"It is disheartening that our efforts yielded no results," the courtesan complained. "We saw nothing of any smugglers last night, or anyone else for that matter."

Tess started to reply that it was too early to deem their plan to catch the smugglers a failure, but a sudden muffled cry interrupted her.

All three women started at the strange sound, although only Alice vocalized her fear.

"Was that the *ghost*?" the maid breathed in a hoarse whisper.

When the eerie cry came again from near the hearth—something between a groan and a tormented scream—the hair on the back of Tess's neck stood up.

Alice exclaimed, *"Heaven save us,"* while Tess rose from her dressing table and moved cautiously toward the hearth.

"Your grace . . . please, take care," Alice pleaded.

"I will," Tess murmured in return. "But I believe that was a human sound and not one made by a ghost."

She picked up a fire iron to use as a weapon and approached the secret panel they'd discovered the previous day. With a glance behind her, she saw that Fanny had also armed herself with a large china figurine.

Inhaling slowly to calm her pounding heartbeat, Tess pressed on the catch point and slid the panel aside. The passageway was fairly dark, but she could hear the rough rasp of labored breathing to her left.

Gripping the iron harder, Tess peered inside. To her astonishment she saw a form lying there, a man from the looks of it. Since he was shifting restlessly on his back, he clearly wasn't dead, but appeared to be asleep. Just then he cried out again, likely in the throes of a nightmare.

Repressing a wince, Tess called softly over her shoulder, "Alice, there is a man slumbering in the passageway. Go and fetch the duke—quickly. And send whatever footmen you can find. I think we have solved the mystery of our castle ghost."

After a moment's hesitation, Alice hurried to do her bidding. Tess sank down on her knees and inched a bit further inside the passage, although keeping the iron in front of her.

The sleeping man was dressed in a ragged coat and trousers and emitted the foul odor she recognized from her bad dream. She was debating whether to wake him when he abruptly opened his eyes and struggled to sit up. Upon seeing Tess, he shrank back in alarm.

The left sleeve of his coat was half empty, she noted. He was missing much of one arm, and his features were gaunt and grimy as well as being flushed with fever.

Tess's fear suddenly diminished a measure, to be replaced by a powerful rush of pity. She had seen too many such men over the past two years. Forlorn relics of humanity lying in hospital beds—if they were fortunate enough to even *have* beds. Former soldiers and seamen dressed in rags and missing limbs, their grimy, unwashed bodies mere skin and bones, their tormenting memories making them cry out in their sleep.

When her bedchamber door swung back with a bang to admit a footman, the one-armed man shrieked and cowered in fear. That, too, was indicative of soldiers who had seen the horrors of battle.

Tess quickly held up a hand behind her to stay the servant, and said in a low soothing voice to the frightened man, "It is all right, I won't let anyone hurt you."

He blinked in the dim light. "Sal, is that you?"

Tess hesitated, wondering if she should pretend to be someone else to ease his apprehension. "Won't you come out, please?" she coaxed instead. "You must be chilled sleeping in there on the hard floor."

"Eh?" He turned one side of his face toward her. "I canna hear too well in one ear."

Raising her voice, she repeated her request. When he nodded, Tess backed out but remained on her knees, trying to appear unthreatening.

The man eventually crawled out from the passageway, but stayed hunched down, like a wary animal, his eyes darting around the room until finally coming to rest on Tess. "You are not Sal."

"No, my name is Tess," she said gently.

"I thought ye were Sal . . . my daughter."

"What is your name, sir?"

"Ned . . . Ned Crutchley."

"Were you a soldier, Ned?"

"Aye, a gunner. Served with the Royal Artillery under General Lord Mulgrave."

Which doubtless explained his loss of hearing, Tess reflected. The continuous explosions from cannon bombardments had deafened many a gunner.

"You seem to be ill, Ned. Do you have a fever?"

"Aye, summat. Lost me arm at Wa'erloo. Never healed proper. Gives me a brain fever sometimes."

Tess felt her heart twist. From the terrible accounts she'd heard, the Battle of Waterloo, where Allied armies had finally defeated Napoleon Bonaparte once and for all, had been hell on earth. So much blood had been shed, so many lives lost, including her beloved Richard's. Even the men who had survived physically sometimes suffered from mental trauma.

She knew because she had spent countless hours sitting by the bedsides of wounded and dying war veterans, holding frail hands, sometimes reading aloud, sometimes singing, sometimes simply speaking in a low, soothing voice about nothing much at all.

Recognizing Ned's plight, Tess came to a decision. Her aim had to be to make him feel safe for now. They could sort out the issues of his ghostly behavior later.

Just then, however, she heard the sound of pounding footsteps. An instant later, Ian burst into the room, holding a pistol, his expression fierce.

When Ned jumped and tried to crawl back into the passage, Tess placed a gentle hand on his shoulder and said hastily, "It is all right, Ned. This is my husband, Ian. He will not hurt you either, I promise you."

Ned stilled at the soothing sound of her voice, but then he simply collapsed on the carpet. Curling into a fetal ball, he lay there cringing, his one hand covering an ear as he rocked back and forth, moaning.

Tess felt a sob well in her throat. It enraged her that this poor soul who had given so much in service to his country should be reduced to this quivering mass of fear.

Swallowing hard, she reached out to stroke Ned's good arm while she met her husband's eyes with grim determination.

"Ian," she said calmly, as if her heart wasn't breaking. "This is Mr. Ned Crutchley. He has a fever from his war wound, and I intend to care for him."

The fact that their "ghost" had turned out to be a wounded war veteran who suffered a touch of madness caught Ian somewhat by surprise, yet he was not at all surprised when Tess decided to champion the intruder. For her own safety, he wanted to forbid her, yet he couldn't help but respect her for her fearless compassion.

Despite his concern, therefore, Ian held his tongue and watched as she tried to soothe the trembling man.

When Ned's moaning eventually ceased so that he merely lay curled there on the floor, mute and shivering, Tess stood and fetched a quilt from her bed and covered his emaciated body.

By that time a small crowd had gathered out in the corridor. Catching sight of Mrs. Hiddleston, Tess quietly summoned the housekeeper into the room.

"Do you know this man, Mrs. Hiddleston?" she murmured.

"Yes, indeed, your grace. Crutchley came back from the wars a bit daft."

"Does he live near here?"

"In truth, I do not know where now. He once shared a cottage with his daughter in Fowey, but she died while he was away."

Fowey was the nearby fishing village, but it was still some distance from here. Tess's mouth tightened. "Then he will sleep here at Falwell tonight. Will you prepare a bedchamber for him, please?"

The housekeeper looked slightly aghast. "Your grace, are you certain?"

"Quite certain. He is ill and starving, and he needs warmth and sustenance and medical care."

Mrs. Hiddleston frowned, but pursed her lips in thought. "There is a small room off the kitchens that is always warm from the hearth fires. I could make up a bed for him there."

"That should do for now."

Still the woman hesitated, shooting a critical glance down at Crutchley before raising another objection. "No doubt he is crawling with vermin."

"We can burn bed linens later. When you have arranged a bed for him, I wish you to bring me some broth and a bit of bread and cheese to start with. And some cool water and cloths so I can try to bring down his fever."

Ian stepped in to give his own orders. "And have Hiddleston summon the nearest doctor at once."

Tess cast him a grateful look before returning to Crutchley and kneeling beside him once more. "Ned? Will you come with me, please?"

His bleary eyes opened. "Where?"

"To bed. You need to eat and rest."

He searched her face for a long moment. Then evidently trusting her, he nodded wordlessly.

When she made to help him rise, another footman, Fletcher, stepped forward to assist her. Wrapping the quilt around Ned's bony shoulders, Tess urged him toward the door, meeting Ian's gaze as she passed. She was clearly upset, yet there was no sign of distress or anger in her voice—indeed, nothing but gentle comfort—when she explained to Crutchley where they were taking him.

They led him downstairs to the kitchens where the Hiddlestons awaited. Directed to a small room nearby where a cot stood piled high with blankets, Tess had her patient tucked into bed in short order.

After dismissing the servants for privacy, she

perched on a stool beside Ned and applied a cool damp cloth to his fevered brow. Ian let her have her way, but ordered Fletcher to remain close by in the corridor. Ian himself stayed in the room to watch and guard her in the event the former soldier turned violent.

Ned's tremors eventually ceased, though, and Tess began asking easy questions as she spoon-fed him a bowl of warm chicken broth.

"Can you tell me where you live, Ned?"

"I 'ave no 'ome now."

Tess paused, obviously struggling to hide her dismay. "Then where do you sleep?"

He frowned as if trying to remember. "Sometimes a cave."

"The cave below Falwell Castle?"

"Nay . . . over to Fowey way."

She carried the spoon to his lips once more. "The village where you lived with your daughter? That is over two miles from here, is it not?"

"Aye, Mum."

"Then what brought you here to Falwell?"

When he shifted uneasily beneath the blankets, Tess gave him one of her gentlest smiles. "I will not be angry, Ned. I am merely curious to learn how you ended up in the secret passageway behind my bedchamber wall."

At his shamed silence, Tess prodded. "You entered my bedchamber the other night, did you not? You touched my face while I slept."

He lowered his gaze. "Aye, ye were so beautiful . . . I thought . . . you reminded me of Sal . . . me daughter. Sal is with the angels now." His expression turned contrite as he glanced up again. "I 'umbly beg yer pardon, Mum."

Her voice softened even further. "I forgive you, Ned. Indeed, I am flattered." Her questions ceased for a few minutes while she fed him. "There now, you have finished all the broth. Do you think you could eat a bit of bread and cheese?"

When his pained eyes sparked with eagerness, Tess set aside the empty bowl and broke up the food into small pieces on the plate. While Ned ate her offerings, she gradually coaxed him into explaining why he had pretended to be the castle ghost. Her patient warmth not only soothed him, he seemed to recognize her desire to help. Ian quelled his own impatience since her methods seemed to be bearing fruit.

"Were you the one to rattle the chains all those times, Ned?" Tess asked casually.

"Aye, I was . . . but I dint cause the voices."

"What voices?"

"The ones I 'eard. There are *real* ghosts in those towers, make no mistake."

Tess took her time replying, evidently not wanting to disillusion Ned, even though he'd very likely been hallucinating about corporeal spirits. "How did you manage to rattle the chains? That sounded very ghostly to me."

"Sometimes I climbed onto the roof and banged the chains ag'in the chimneys. And sometimes I 'id in the secret passages."

"But why?"

"To scare you away. Jolly dint want you snooping around. If you thought there was a ghost, you might leave."

"Who is Jolly?"

"Jolly Banks. 'E paid me a shilling to 'aunt the castle." Suddenly Ned clamped his lips shut, as if realizing he had betrayed a confidence. When Tess asked why Jolly would have wanted her to leave, Ned's grimy features turned shuttered. "I canna say more."

Ian spoke up then. "How did you gain entrance to the castle? By way of our cave and tunnel?"

Ned started, as if having forgotten there was anyone but Tess with him in the room. Surveying Ian warily, he nodded. "Aye. The tunnel leads to the tower, and from there ye can reach the roof."

Tess resumed leading the conversation in her gentle tone. "Who else knows about the cave entrance, Ned?"

"I dunno, Mum. Only Jolly's crew, I guess. His great-grandda' was head groundskeeper for the castle at one time."

"It worries me that any stranger could just break into our home, intent on doing us harm."

Ned's expression grew dismayed. "I would ne'er 'ave 'armed you, Mum, I swear. . . ."

Tess smiled. "I believe you, Ned. Truly. But that doesn't mean that Jolly feels the same way toward us. After all, he asked you to drive us away."

At her observation, Ned looked intensely remorseful and eventually allowed Tess to cajole more of the story from him—specifically that at the beginning of the summer, Jolly Banks had paid him to "haunt" the castle to scare the servants enough that they would keep away from the cave below the bluff, and then to double his efforts once the new duke and duchess arrived.

When Ian interrupted once more to ask if the three chests in the cave belonged to Banks, Ned's brow furrowed as he tried to recall. "Aye, Jolly told me to guard those chests well."

From Ned's wandering tale, they concluded that a ring of thieves led by Banks had used the old smugglers' hideout to store their stolen goods. Ned as much as confessed that he was connected to the thefts, although the exact role he had played was less clear.

He had finished the last crumbs of bread and cheese when he sank back wearily against the pillows. "I canna tell ye more, Mum, or Jolly will kill me."

Tess cast a worried glance at Ian but promptly ended the discussion. "Forgive me, Ned. I should not have pressed when you need to rest. You look exhausted."

"Thankee, Mum, for the food," Ned offered.

"You are quite welcome. Do you want more?"

"Could I p'raps 'ave some ale? I'm that parched, I am."

"Certainly you may have some ale. I should have thought of it."

Taking up the empty plate and bowl, she rose just as a tap sounded on the door.

An elderly man carrying a medical bag was admitted and bowed first to Ian, then to Tess. "Your graces, I came as soon as I could. How may I be of assistance?"

After assuring Ned that the doctor was only there to help, Tess followed Ian from the room so her patient could be examined. In the corridor, she handed over the empty dishes to Fletcher and asked that he fetch a pint of ale for Ned.

"It is beyond appalling," she muttered to Ian when they were alone, "that Ned should be homeless and dressed in rags. He was a soldier like Richard. We owe men like him more than we can ever repay. And to think those thieves may have drawn him into their crimes. . . . Do *you* believe Ned is a criminal?" she asked Ian worriedly.

"We don't have enough details yet," he replied. "We will have to question him further in the morning to find out more about Banks and his gang of thieves."

Tess nodded with reluctance. "I suppose so, but please remember, kindness will go much farther than threats."

His mouth curved wryly. "I wouldn't dare threaten him, love. Not with you standing guard over him like a mother tigress."

She gave him a faint smile, but then paced the corridor for some twenty minutes until the doctor emerged from the room to give his report.

"The stump of his arm is raw and inflamed, but not completely putrid. I washed and bandaged the wound and administered a sleeping draught. He should be out until morning at the very least."

It was only the doctor's assurance that convinced Tess to leave Ned to sleep. Ian swore the doctor to secrecy and made certain the door was locked with a footman standing guard outside.

Before escorting Tess to his study then, he asked both Hiddlestons to join them along with Basil Eddowes and Fanny Irwin.

They discussed the new revelations with the steward and housekeeper for a time. Hiddleston was familiar with Jolly Banks and identified him as a local smuggler from the nearby seaside village of Polperro. The steward was also unsurprised to learn that Banks might be the ringleader, since he had a vicious streak.

"Banks will not have much support in his new trade, however," Hiddleston ventured. "Not if he and his cohorts are hurting the common folk, stealing and wounding indiscriminately."

Ian eventually thanked both servants and dismissed them.

When they were gone, Tess broke the resulting silence first. "So how do we proceed? Banks is clearly dangerous. Someone needs to put an end to his thievery."

"I intend to," Ian replied.

"How? We haven't enough of our own footmen to go up against a large gang, do we?"

"We won't need to act alone. Hiddleston is likely right and we can trust that the servants here won't be in league with thieves. It's time to involve the local authorities, perhaps even the county militia. I'll send for Vicar Potts in the morning. I want his opinion on how best to proceed. But basically we need to catch Banks and his minions with their loot . . . or failing that, catch them in the commission of another theft."

"You mean, lure them out somehow?"

"Yes."

"What of Crutchley?" Eddowes asked. "If he participated in the thefts, then he is a common criminal and should be in prison."

At his logical question, Tess stiffened and turned an imploring gaze on Ian. "You have seen Ned. His mental facilities are clearly impaired. Even if he aided Banks, he should not be treated in the same manner as a vicious lawbreaker."

Watching Tess, Ian felt an odd twist of his heart. It was hard to remain cynical in the face of her genuine caring, which was why he'd decided to help her champion her wounded veteran.

"No, he should not," he agreed.

"And even if he is not innocent, we cannot just turn Ned out of the castle. You heard him—he said Banks might kill him for what he revealed to us."

"He can remain here at Falwell for a few more days while we work out a plan."

"Thank you," she said fervently.

His promise seemed to reassure Tess enough that she could eat dinner awhile later, although she mostly toyed with her food. During the remainder of the evening, Tess insisted on checking on Ned twice. Only when she found him slumbering peacefully the second time would she accompany Ian to his bedchamber.

Her thoughts were still with the veteran, however, as she readied for bed. "What will happen to Ned if he is guilty of those thefts?"

"He will be arrested and brought before the local justice of the peace. If arraigned, then he'll be bound over to the assize court for trial."

"There must be *something* we can do. Waiting for the assizes could take weeks, if not months, and he will be locked up for all that time. He is *ill*, Ian, and he needs proper medical care. I will not let him suffer that way—and I am *not* letting him go to prison where he could very well die."

There was a stubborn set to her mouth that Ian recognized. "You cannot save every poor soul who crosses your path, you realize."

"Perhaps not, but I can try. As can you."

She gazed up at him with a considering look. "I know you will do the just thing and help Ned. You are certainly clever enough to determine a way to save him."

Ian shook his head in unwilling amusement, realizing that Tess was once again using her persuasive arts on him. But he had no intention of arguing with her. "Why don't we learn the extent of his involvement before fretting overmuch about how to save him?"

"I cannot help it," she said with a sigh. "I am worried for him."

"I know, sweetheart. It is in your very blood to care."

He snuffed the lamps and joined her in bed. Expecting her to be too preoccupied for any sort of lovemaking, Ian drew Tess against him, intent on merely holding her. But she raised her face eagerly for his kiss.

The sweet passion she showed him during the following hour did not seem to be based on gratitude, either, but sincere desire.

They both managed to sleep afterward, but Tess rose well before daybreak, which meant Ian had to rise also.

Ned's fever was down and he looked much heartier than the previous evening. He ate a thin gruel with appetite and asked for more. Even so, his nerves were so raw that he started at any sudden movement or sound. And he was still exceedingly nervous about any mention of Jolly Banks.

Eventually, though, they drew out his confession, with Ned admitting that he'd acted as a lookout for Banks and his crew when they robbed more than a dozen houses over the past summer and autumn.

At least Ned claimed to know when Banks planned to return to the caves to retrieve the chests full of stolen loot—on Sunday night, three days hence, since Sundays were when the Revenuers were the least vigilant.

"Jolly would 'ave waited for another sennight, till the dark o' the moon, but 'e was worried about what the duke might do"—Ned cast a wary glance at Ian before continuing—"and so decided to move it forward."

When Tess and Ian left the room so that Ned could sleep, she gave vent to her anger. "It is so unfair," she exclaimed, her eyes dark with outrage. "They used him for their own foul ends, and now he could be imprisoned or even hanged."

"He will not go to prison," Ian promised.

"How can we prevent it? Ned could perhaps testify against Banks, but given his diminished mental capacity, his word alone may not be enough to make the charges hold. And Banks could even lay all the blame on Ned and leave him with no defense."

"If the information Ned provides helps us to apprehend the thieves, then the courts will show him leniency."

"But what if he cannot help us?"

"Stop fretting, Tess. A duke has extensive powers,

and I will put them to good use. I also have a fortune at my disposal. At minimum, I will persuade Banks's victims to leave Ned out of it. They are likely to be more forgiving if I can recover their stolen property and if I offer to reimburse them for any distress they suffered as a result of the burglaries."

Her anger arrested, she looked up at Ian hopefully. "You would do that for Ned?"

"No, I would do it for you."

Tess raised herself up on her tiptoes and kissed him warmly on the cheek. "I *knew* you were not as heartless as you always pretend."

With a semblance of her usual cheerful optimism, she turned and headed for the kitchens with the invalid's breakfast tray, leaving Ian with a dry smile hovering on his lips.

At least he seemed to have made progress convincing Tess he had a heart. More surprising still, he found himself *wanting* her to believe he had a heart, when for the past four years, he had been intent on proving just the opposite.

Chapter Thirteen

I confess, the strength of my desire has become a prime source of guilt for me, but perhaps my guilt is a good thing if it can help to protect my heart.
— Diary Entry of Miss Tess Blanchard

If Ned was right, they had only until Sunday night to prepare to capture Jolly Banks and his band of thieves, so there was little time to lose.

Ian, along with Tess, met first with Vicar Potts, then Sir Thomas Greely, the magistrate who meted out justice in that part of Cornwall. Upon deciding to call in the militia, Ian traveled to Falmouth—the closest large city and naval seaport—to make an official request of the Lord Lieutenant and was granted two dozen troops to aid in the effort.

In addition, he alerted the local Customs preventative officers to ward off any accidental interference. If Banks failed to appear Sunday night, they would have to devise another strategy, but for now they hoped to catch the thieves red-handed, in the act of retrieving the stolen property or breaking into the Duke of Rotham's castle.

They also attempted to discover Banks's current location in order to keep an eye on him, but he hadn't been seen in his home town of Polperro for several days. It was possible that he was scouting out another great house to rob. Since wealthy estates were widely scattered over the district, he would have to range farther than when operating in shires closer to London.

In the meantime, they continued to guard the cave below the castle and swore the Falwell servants to secrecy.

As for Ned, his health improved significantly with proper care, and with his fever gone, he was more lucid, almost in his right mind, in fact. But they refrained from mentioning their scheme to trap his cohorts in crime. It was doubtful Ned could keep any confidences secret from the castle staff, and they didn't want Banks to be warned off, or Ned to make himself a target for revenge.

Tess had appointed herself the veteran's guardian angel and was more optimistic that he could avoid incarceration of any kind. Moreover, she'd learned that the most recent victims, Lord and Lady Shaw, had offered a reward for the return of their jewels, and she was determined that the funds would go to Ned in reparation for helping expose the thieves.

Ian did not argue with her. In past years, he'd reluctantly been drawn into supporting Tess's causes, but this was one battle he would fight for her willingly—in no small part because her good opinion had become annoyingly important to him.

He was, however, somewhat surprised that she trusted him to deal with the complex arrangements involving government forces and wasn't afraid to tell him so.

"Truthfully," Tess confessed when he returned from Falmouth, "I am glad you are in charge, since I wouldn't know where to begin. I have every faith you will foil Banks and his men."

They generally agreed on the major points of the plan. The biggest bone of contention was the extent of Tess's participation on Sunday night. She wanted to take part in the thieves' capture, but although Ian was impressed by her tenacity and courage, he was not about to expose her to danger.

When she complained that he was being dictatorial and overly protective again, he remained adamant. "Your safety is my one condition, darling. You will remain behind in the castle. If you won't agree, then I will end this entire enterprise at once."

Tess sent him a look of frustration. "Why is it that women are never allowed to be of any use? It is hardly fair that *you* get to have all the excitement while I must be coddled and protected."

"You can watch the cove from the castle battlements."

"It will likely be dark, and I won't be able to see a thing." When that argument failed to sway him, she added crossly, "So what am I to do while you are off playing the hero, your grace?"

"You can keep Ned out of trouble. If something were to happen to you, who would take care of him?"

That argument at least gave Tess pause. "You have a point. Very well, I will agree to stay behind."

Ian eyed her suspiciously, wondering if she was being truthful with him. Still, from her sparkling eyes, he could tell she was relishing the challenge of bringing a gang of thieves to justice, and he enjoyed seeing her enthusiasm.

Their relationship seemed to be improving daily. They were no longer at daggers drawn, as they'd been for the past four years, yet there was still a measure of spirited opposition between them. And in the bedchamber, their heated physical relationship had become something of a sexual rivalry. It was a game they played, to bring each other to gasping pleasure. Ian was a master at it, but Tess held her own in the battle to see who could arouse the other best. Neither wanted to admit defeat.

By late Saturday afternoon, as they rode home from yet another conference with Sir Thomas Greely and Lord Shaw, Tess's spirits seemed quite high. When they reached the bluffs above the Fowey harbor, she drew her mount to a halt and waited for Ian to help her down, then stood beside him drinking in the splendid ocean view.

The recent rains had ceased, and a glorious sunset tinged the sky with rosy light. Seeing the glow bathe her lovely profile, Ian felt another fierce stab of desire for Tess. Watching her was a pure pleasure, yet seeing her delight was an even greater pleasure.

"Such power and grace," she murmured with reverence. "The sea is so beautiful, especially at this time of day."

"Not as beautiful as you are," he said without thinking.

Turning to eye him, she arched an eyebrow. "You said as much this morning when you seduced me, but I take such comments with a grain of salt."

Thankfully, she saw his compliment as mere flirtation, a weapon he used in their battle for supremacy.

"I'll remind you," Ian returned in that same bantering tone, "that this morning, I was not so much seducer as seducee."

A catch of laughter escaped her, and Tess leaned into him, more to tease him, he suspected, than because she needed support.

"I realize I have not properly thanked you for trying to spare Ned," she said huskily.

"You are free to do so now," he invited, smiling down at her.

She smiled back, and Ian felt a strange lifting beneath his heart. Her smile was a lethal weapon, he thought not for the first time.

When she tilted her head back, inviting him to kiss her, he responded by sinking his tongue into the welcoming richness of her mouth. Like many of their recent encounters, the kiss began as a taunt, but quickly turned tender.

It was that tenderness more than anything that unsettled Ian. He was beginning to lose his self-control, he realized, no matter how determinedly he fought against Tess's enchanting allure.

Heeding his warning instincts, he ended the kiss more abruptly than he'd intended and stepped back from her. And for the remainder of their ride home, he stayed on his guard. Yet his thoughts were churning at the alarms going off in his head.

His most powerful instinct was to protect Tess, to keep her safe from harm, but how could he protect himself from *her*?

* * *

Unexpectedly, he faced that question again upon arriving home. Tess went directly to the kitchens to check on Ned, while Ian retreated to his study to finalize some details of his plan.

He was writing at his desk when Fanny Irwin knocked on his study door a few minutes later.

"Forgive me, your grace," Fanny murmured. "I hoped I might have a private word with you."

Setting down his quill pen, Ian invited her to take a chair in front of his desk, which she did.

"I wished to thank you, your grace. I am more grateful than I can say for your kind hospitality."

"Think nothing of it, Miss Irwin. You are a friend of Tess's, and as such, you are a welcome guest in our home."

When Fanny remained silent, Ian raised an eyebrow in query. "Is there something else you wished to say to me?" he prodded.

She looked oddly on edge. "Well, yes. The thing is . . . I saw you with Tess from my bedchamber window this afternoon. And well . . . Do you love Tess, your grace?"

His stomach muscles tightened; it was a question Ian didn't want to ask himself. His first instinct was to deliver a sardonic retort, but he settled for drawling mildly, "That is hardly your concern, is it?"

The courtesan hesitated, then offered a conciliatory smile. "I know I am vastly overstepping my bounds with my presumption," she admitted, resorting to her famed charm. "But as you said, I am Tess's friend, and I care for her a great deal. I only want her happiness."

"As do I, Miss Irwin."

"Is that so?" she asked softly, searching his face. Whatever Fanny saw in his expression must have satisfied her, for she nodded. "I thought you might. I cannot help but notice how you look at Tess sometimes . . . as if you harbor some deeper feelings for her. If that is true, then I may be able to help you."

Curiosity warred with irritation inside Ian. "Help me how?"

"To break down her defenses and overcome her resistance to loving you. It will not be easy, given the pain and loss she endured her first time around. But Tess needs love in her life, your grace. Even her dearest friends are not enough to fill the hole in her heart left by her betrothed's untimely passing."

Fanny's expression turned solemn. "I do not think I would be betraying Tess's trust if I were to aid you, since I believe her future happiness depends very much on you. So if I might be permitted to offer some advice, your grace. . . ." She paused again, giving him time to reject her counsel.

"I am listening," Ian said curtly.

Finally she launched into the main purpose of her visit. "You may not have considered the question of love before, since your marriage was so sudden, but for a woman like Tess, the issue can be fundamental. A woman needs to feel wanted, but even more crucially, she needs to feel *loved*."

"So you wish me to admit to loving her?"

The courtesan lifted her shoulders in a graceful

shrug. "Not to me, no. But I think you must at least admit your feelings to yourself."

"Love is not an easy matter to comprehend, Miss Irwin."

At his evasion, Fanny's lips curved in a wistful smile. "On the contrary, your grace. As I have just recently come to realize, love is fairly simple, and you need only ask yourself some elementary questions. Does Tess make your life worth living? Would you feel desolate without her? And the opposite side of the coin . . . could she feel the same about you? I repeat, Tess needs to feel loved, not only desired, and if you truly love her, then you would do well to show her."

Ian leaned back in his chair, unprepared to make such an admission just yet, to Fanny or to himself. "I appreciate your good wishes for Tess, Miss Irwin, but I will deal with my wife in my own way."

"As you wish, your grace. But if you decide otherwise . . . I wanted you to know I will do everything in my power to help you."

"I will keep your offer in mind."

After Fanny was gone, Ian sat unmoving for a long moment, contemplating the courtesan's bold, blunt query. Did he love Tess?

Would he even recognize the sentiment if he felt it?

He had never had much love in his life, Ian reflected. His mother had died giving him birth, and by the time he outgrew his childhood, he'd felt neither respect nor love for his libertine father.

He felt a measure of affection for Lady Wingate and a particular few of his other relations, and a much stronger love for his young ward, Jamie. But he had never been *in love,* nor had he ever wanted to experience the affliction. The prospect of giving up control over his own will to someone else was even more intimidating than marriage, Ian believed.

Before wedding Tess, he'd enjoyed his solitary existence. He could do as he pleased, live as he chose. Now he had to take his wife's feelings and interests into consideration, even before his own.

Yet strangely enough, he found himself *wanting* to place Tess's interests before his own. He couldn't deny, either, that he was exhibiting some of the symptoms attributed to love; not least were the riotous emotions she stirred in him. Protectiveness, possessiveness, jealousy . . .

Was that love? Admittedly, his feelings for Tess hadn't been rational since he saw her kissing Hennessy behind the stage curtains at her godmother's house party. And without question, she made his blood surge and his heart beat faster. Yet he knew his attraction was driven by far more than lust. He felt happier in her presence. He missed her when she was away. He found himself craving just to be near her, whether they were sparring or conversing about serious matters or making love.

So yes, Ian acknowledged regrettably, he might just be past the point of no return.

And if he was willing to admit that Tess had invaded what passed for his heart? What the devil would he do about it?

Was he a fool to wonder if he could rouse similar feelings in her? Given his sinful past, he was as far from her ideal mate as possible. He didn't believe he could ever live up to her image of a proper husband, not with her memories of her saintly Richard to provide constant competition for her affections.

Still, there was no longer any question that he wanted to prove himself worthy of Tess. And no question that he wanted to make her forget her late betrothed. Unless he could manage that, he never stood a chance of winning Tess's love.

A muscle in Ian's jaw worked. Was her love what he wanted? Without question, he could make Tess desire him, but as Fanny Irwin had pointed out, desire was not the same thing as love.

Ian ran a hand roughly through his hair as he struggled to define his feelings for his beautiful wife. He wanted to make Tess smile, of course. He wanted her happiness more than his own. He wanted her to need him, not just for her causes, not just in his bed, but in her life.

And if that was not love, then what was it?

Fanny was positively glowing, Tess thought when they met in the drawing room before dinner. They were the only ones present as yet, and Fanny didn't hesitate to share her joy.

"Tess, I am so happy, I am beside myself. Basil proposed to me while you were away this afternoon!"

"I am elated for you," Tess said, embracing her friend warmly. She started to ask for details, but Fanny obliged before she could say another word.

"Basil says he love me . . . that he has always loved me and he doesn't want to live without me."

"Of course he feels that way. He has worn his heart on his sleeve for months now. I could see it, even if you could not."

"Yes, but my wicked past . . . I didn't dare let myself believe that Basil could overlook everything I have done. But he says he loves me, and since I love him, the rest doesn't matter."

Fanny paused to beam another ecstatic smile. "You were right, Tess. Basil was willing to forgive me because he loves me. And I was right about the other. This afternoon we made love for the first time, and it was different from any coupling I have ever experienced . . . much, *much* more wonderful. I know it was because of the love between us." The courtesan squeezed Tess's hands. "Love makes all the difference, Tess. I do so wish *you* could find love again."

Tess's smile faded as she tried to think of how to respond.

"I would say," Fanny added in a leading tone, "that the prospects for you finding love in your marriage are improving rapidly."

Fortunately Basil entered the drawing room just then and claimed Fanny's attention.

Glad for the diversion, Tess immediately congratulated him on their engagement. But while the two unlikely lovers were sharing a private moment whispering sweet nothings to each other, her thoughts returned to her conflicted feelings for her husband.

There was little question that her marriage was improving, Tess acknowledged, but that in itself was a problem. Her desire for Ian was growing daily. He could arouse her with just a glance. A mere touch made her blood heat, thick and rich. She had never had to fight such powerful, overwhelming lust before.

The fact that she wanted him so much roused an unsettling guilt inside Tess. She had never desired Richard that fiercely. She had loved her betrothed, however, and felt as if she ought to remain true to him in her heart, even though he was long gone.

Other comparisons between the two men continued to haunt her also. Richard had been wonderful and charming, but a bit young and immature, almost more boy than man. In contrast, Ian was all man, much more masculine and mature. As her lover, the physical pleasure Ian gave her was incredible.

Yet something was missing. The truth was, they were caught up in a game of passion and power, with little real emotion between. Their lovemaking, while explosive, was not as emotionally satisfying as it could have been. Nothing like the fulfillment that Fanny claimed to have found with Basil—

Tess abruptly quelled that subversive thought. She was quite happy—vastly relieved, in fact—that their marriage was founded on a strictly carnal basis. She was coming to believe that Ian was not as wicked as she'd always thought. The more she came to know him, the more good she saw in him. But loving him was out of the question. She would be mad to let herself succumb to his seductive arts.

When Ian appeared in the doorway a moment later, his intent gaze met hers across the room. Sensing danger, Tess glanced away quickly.

She would hold to her current strategy, she resolved firmly. She would do her utmost to hide her weakness for Ian and maintain their adversarial relationship.

She would continue to keep her memories of Richard in the forefront of her mind and heart and purposely stoke her feelings of guilt.

Really, she had no choice. For her own self-protection, she had to use every weapon at her disposal to prevent her desire for Ian from growing strong enough to captivate her heart.

Chapter Fourteen

Why has the threat of danger to Ian left me so shaken?
—Diary Entry of Miss Tess Blanchard

Tess shivered as midnight neared. For over three hours she'd waited on the battlements with Fanny and Basil and Ned Crutchley, hidden behind the crenellations. A chill wind cut through her cloak, while the cold from the stone seeped into her bones.

Ned was close beside her, watching the cove through another arrow port, and Fanny and Basil were a short distance away. In the dim moonlight, Tess could make out the beach below the castle, although visibility was further reduced by a thick cloud cover that portended rain. Occasionally, she could even see the dark shadows of militia troops.

Ian had stationed the government soldiers around the castle, disguised as groundskeepers and various other servants. Half a dozen men were inside the cave, secreted in the tunnel. Several more troops were concealed at the base of the bluffs, out of sight of the cave entrance. There was also an armed Revenue cutter standing offshore to cut off escape by sea. If the thieves managed to elude the ambush, the cutter would be alerted by lantern signal.

Tess shifted restlessly, trying to ease the ache in her limbs from remaining motionless for so long. Her nerves felt acutely on edge, for although they had planned as well as humanly possible, she had difficulty believing that nothing would go wrong.

Beside her, Ned seemed surprisingly calm. He'd been included in the proceedings, since he could identify Jolly Banks and his men and determine if any were missing, and he had sworn to help.

"Ye need a spot of patience, yer grace," Ned whispered now at her movement. "In the Army, we had to wait days, even weeks, for a battle to begin."

Feeling humbled at the reminder of all Ned had endured, Tess steeled herself for another long interval of inactivity.

It was perhaps twenty minutes later when he pointed down at the water. Tess recognized the dark shape of a fishing smack sailing silently into the cove.

"'Tis Jolly's boat, I'll wager," Ned said.

A short while later, the smack dropped anchor. Squinting, Tess could make out the outline of a rowboat gliding toward shore and counted a half dozen men inside, more shadows than forms. When the prow touched land, the rowers climbed out and dragged the rowboat higher onto the beach so that the waves couldn't wash the vessel back into the water.

Then four shadows headed directly for the bluff, leaving two behind.

Tess couldn't tell if they spoke to each other. The low sound of the surf, along with the more delicate rush of the waterfall below, drowned out any voices from that far away—and she knew, in turn, that the castle inhabitants couldn't be heard from this high up on the battlements.

But Ned kept his voice to a whisper all the same. "'Ere we go."

Tess held her breath as the main group of shadows disappeared beneath the castle walls, out of her line of sight. The plan was to wait for the thieves to claim their stolen bounty before swarming them all at once.

"See the two left on shore?" Ned said quietly. "That short fellow by the boat is Jolly. Ye can tell by 'is 'at."

Tess did see. The others wore knit stocking caps, but Jolly wore a tricorn. She also noted his stance—legs spread, one arm raised as if aiming a weapon.

"Is that a pistol he's holding?" she asked, suddenly alarmed.

"Aye, Mum, Jolly always goes armed."

Tess felt her heart jolt. Ian had warned her of the danger, but she hadn't quite realized that apprehending Banks's band of thieves could possibly be *lethal*.

She started counting seconds then, trying to gauge how much time would be needed for the main group of thieves to enter the cave and claim the chests. When she reached one hundred and twelve, the silence of the night was abruptly ended by muffled shouts that carried even to her post on the battlements.

For an instant, the two figures on shore remained frozen. Then the thief with Jolly scurried to drag the rowboat into the water.

More shouts reached Tess as some of the government troops outside the cave spilled onto the beach, heading toward the rowboat to prevent the thieves' escape. When Banks realized he couldn't make it to the boat in time, he turned and sprinted in the opposite direction, parallel to the shore.

A lone figure broke away from the militia and raced after him. Seeing he was being pursued, Banks cut left, making for the bluffs. No doubt he hoped to climb his way to freedom and disappear into the thick woods.

Tess recognized the distinctive height and lithe, muscular form of the man in hot pursuit. *Ian,* she thought with renewed alarm.

Ian changed course when Banks did, and then he, too, disappeared from view, below the battlements.

Tess's breath faltered, then failed altogether when a small explosion shattered the night—the crack of a pistol shot, she realized.

When another gunshot rang out seconds later, Tess felt her heart go cold.

Dear God, Ian.

A small cry escaped her before she could stifle it, while Ned swore "Gor" under his breath. She'd felt a grave disquiet all evening long, but she had never imagined Ian might actually risk a shooting match with the leader of a gang of thieves.

She clutched hard at Ned's remaining bony hand, watching as militia troops surged in Ian's wake.

It seemed an eternity before anyone emerged from the shelter of the bluff. The soldiers were half carrying, half dragging a man between them, she saw.

"Lookee, Mum . . . that's Jolly."

The wounded man must be Banks, since she recognized Ian's long, powerful stride in another shadow. He seemed unharmed, Tess thought, her relief so profound that her knees almost buckled.

Basil exhaled audibly, while Fanny said, "Thank God."

Eventually the thieves were successfully rounded up and herded toward the path that led up to the castle, while more soldiers rowed out to the fishing smack, no doubt to commandeer the vessel and arrest any remaining culprits.

When the beach was once again deserted, Basil spoke up. "They will be brought up to the castle courtyard, your grace. Perhaps we should go and meet them."

Tess swallowed the tight knot in her throat. She had not expected the threat to Ian to affect her so strongly. The danger was over now, but he could have been killed.

It was a terrifying thought.

Tess shuddered. She could have lost Ian just as she had lost Richard.

"Are you all right?" Fanny asked at her elbow.

"I am fine, just a little cold," Tess lied.

As if sensing her lingering horror, Fanny tried to reassure her. "I had faith that Rotham would prevail. He is accounted a crack shot."

The courtesan's confidence soothed Tess marginally, but she wanted to see Ian for herself, to touch him, to convince herself that he was unharmed.

They made their way down through the castle to the courtyard, which by now was lit by lanterns, but they remained with Ned in the shadows, not wanting to expose him to his former colleagues' wrath.

They had to wait for another long interval before the armed militia appeared with their prisoners. Banks was groaning in pain and unable to support his own weight, Tess saw. Evidently he had been shot in the upper leg, for his thigh had been bandaged.

She watched as the thieves were loaded into a wagon that had been brought around from the stable-yard to transport them to Fowey. Then their arms and legs were bound to prevent their escape.

Yet she only felt able to breathe once Ian joined her a few minutes later, even though his focus was on Ned rather than her.

Ned had supplied the names of all the thieves already, but Ian asked him to confirm the culprits. "Do those men account for all of Banks's gang, Mr. Crutchley?"

Ned scanned the prisoners. "Aye, yer grace, that's the lot."

In response, Ian gestured at the militia lieutenant, who gave the command to proceed.

As the wagon rattled away, guarded by a dozen mounted troops, Ian's gaze at last turned to Tess. "I trust now you understand why I didn't want you involved tonight?"

"Yes," she conceded, drinking him in. "For several moments there, I feared you had been shot."

A humorless smile curled his mouth. "Banks fired and missed—but in actuality, I am glad he attempted to shoot me, since assault on a peer will only cement the other charges against him." Ian gestured after the departing wagon. "I mean to accompany the prisoners to Fowey, to see they are properly secured for the night. It will likely be an hour or two before I return.

Why don't you retire? There is no need for you to wait up for me."

"Very well," Tess agreed, managing to keep her voice even.

Ian gave her an intent glance, as if trying to divine what she was thinking, before turning away and mounting his own horse.

Repressing the urge to follow him with her gaze, Tess went inside the castle. The entire household was awake, waiting anxiously to hear the results of the operation. Upon learning of the successful conclusion, Mrs. Hiddleston clapped her hand over her heart. "Thank heavens for the duke, capturing those criminals. We can all sleep safe in our beds now."

The housekeeper was particularly solicitous of Ned, and when he had been put snugly to bed, she turned her motherly concern on Tess.

"Would you care for a glass of warm milk, your grace, to take the chill off your bones?"

Tess declined, however, deciding that something stronger was warranted. After all the turmoil, she felt too restless to retire, so when castle staff began to settle down for the night, she accompanied Fanny and Basil to the drawing room, where they poured glasses of wine and discussed the case against Jolly Banks and his cohorts. Since Basil had been a law clerk for several years, he ventured a prediction.

On the morrow, the thieves would be arraigned by the Justice of the Peace and conveyed to Falmouth, where they would be jailed until the next assizes were convened. If indicted by a grand jury, they would go to trial immediately. Since the lieutenant of the militia had made the official arrests, the Crown would prosecute the crimes, but the victims of the thefts could bring charges as well. And a conviction for assault against the Duke of Rotham would bring the most serious punishment of all.

"At the very least, Banks will be imprisoned for a very long time," Basil assured Tess. "He may even be transported or hanged. And Crutchley's testimony will not be needed, since the thieves incriminated themselves. His cohorts will likely never know that he turned on them."

Tess felt a surge of relief, knowing that Ned would be safe. His future was still uncertain, but she hoped to persuade him to accompany her when she left Cornwall for home. Thanks in large part to her cousin Damon, Viscount Wrexham, there now was a hospital in London where Ned could get much better medical care than here, not only for his physical wounds but for his mental ones as well.

A few moments later, Fanny changed the subject to her own future. "Would you mind very much if I returned to London soon, Tess? I am nearly finished with my novel, and I need to tie up any number of business matters." Fanny shared a loving look with Basil before adding, "We want to be married as soon as possible. We have already waited far too long for our chance at wedded bliss."

Of course they were eager to begin their married life together, Tess thought to herself.

"Certainly, I don't mind," she assured her friend. "In truth, it is time I considered returning home myself. There are countless details that impact my or-

ganizations which have been left unattended because
I am not there to deal with them myself."

As for her own future, she didn't like to remember
that her marriage to Ian was still so unsettled.

A short while later, Tess said good night to her
friends and made her way to her husband's bedchamber. A welcome fire burned in the grate, and after
changing into her nightclothes, she went to the hearth
and held out her hands, drawing on the warmth from
the flames.

She knew Ian was right; there was no reason for
her to wait up for him. She ought to go to bed, yet she
couldn't possibly sleep just now. Her thoughts were
still much too restless, her stomach churning with a
vague feeling of dread.

She hated that gnawing dread, Tess thought as she
stared into the fire. Hated the uncertainty, the endless
waiting, never knowing if the future would hold
tragedy or hope.

That unspoken fear was what the wives and families of soldiers endured every moment that their loved
ones were away at war.

What she had endured while Richard was away.

What she had felt for Ian during several endless
moments tonight.

No doubt she was more sensitive now precisely because she had lost her betrothed, Tess knew. Logically, she had no reason to worry about Ian. He was
perfectly safe now. And yet . . .

Tonight she had faced a disturbing revelation, she
acknowledged unwillingly: The emotions she felt for
Ian were far stronger than she had let herself admit.

Wincing, Tess turned away, although she still

couldn't make herself go to bed. She tried to read, but wound up pacing the room, pausing now and then to stare out the window at the dark night.

It was some half hour later when she spied several horsemen riding toward the castle. Ian had returned home, Tess realized, yet she still didn't know how she would deal with him.

She settled in a chair to read, determined to pretend indifference. But when eventually she heard his quiet footsteps in the corridor, she abandoned her book.

As the door swung open, Tess rose to her feet. Then Ian met her gaze and the air was suddenly charged with suppressed emotion.

She didn't mean to react so foolishly, honestly she didn't. She meant to remain calm and totally in control of herself.

Yet when Ian stepped into the room and shut the door behind him, Tess lunged forward and ran straight into his arms.

She had surprised him, Tess realized, burying her face in his broad chest—and worried him as well. Ian's voice was rough and low in her ear as he demanded, "What is wrong, sweetheart?"

Her muffled reply was shaky. "Nothing is wrong. I am just glad that no harm came to you."

He held her for a moment longer before putting a finger under her chin to make her lift her head.

When their gazes locked again, the air crackled as if an electrical pulse arced between them. Ian's face was enigmatic, impassive, but his muscled body was tense and rigid, his eyes silver-hot.

His blood was up, as was hers.

Tess's heart began to pound as she read the purpose in his eyes: He wanted her and he meant to have her.

Yet she wanted him just as much.

She didn't protest when Ian turned with her and backed her against the wall. And when he brought his mouth down on hers, she responded by raising her hands to clutch at his hair and draw him even closer.

His kiss was hard and urgent. Tess whimpered gratefully, her lips burning, aching, needing to be soothed. At the needy sound, he increased the pressure, roughly cupping her face, holding her still so that he could have his fill of her.

His kiss, as fierce as fire, smoldered with pent-up emotions that stopped her breath.

She was trembling when suddenly Ian broke off and lifted his head, his eyes burning with intensity. The gray depths had darkened into something both primitive and powerful, and Tess could sense the coiled need in him, feel the passion throbbing between them, hear the clash of their excited breaths in the quiet hush of the room.

When Ian's hard body pressed hers more forcefully against the wall, Tess realized that he meant to take her then and there. A thrill coursed through her that made her stomach clench. She already felt swollen and ready for him to claim her and wished he would hurry.

"Please, Ian . . ." she whispered.

Obligingly, his mouth fell on hers again, hungry and hot. Not content with merely kissing, however, Ian lowered his hands from her face to mold her breasts through her nightdress, kneading, arousing.

The shape of his wicked hands branded her and made her gasp. Then abruptly his fingers curved over the neckline of her gown and ripped the buttons away, rending the fragile fabric to bare her breasts.

His wildness found an answering chord in Tess. She moaned when he bent his head and circled a nipple with his rasping tongue. And when he sucked the pebbled peak into his mouth, she arched into his hands, straining for his touch.

Her senses were knife sharp and almost as painful; the need to be joined with him was unrelenting. Unconsciously, her hips began to move, grinding against the bulge at his groin, her body urging him to fill her.

Thankfully, Ian responded to her need. Her naked breast still in his mouth, he rucked up the skirt of her nightdress and cupped the heat between her thighs. She felt her own slickness as his fingers rimmed her cleft, seeking and finding the throbbing bud of her desire and making her moan again.

She was shaking now, Tess realized. Feeling frenzied, she fumbled at the front flap of his breeches, but Ian pushed her hands away impatiently and swiftly unbuttoned his breeches himself, releasing his manhood. The swollen arousal surged into her hand, thick and hard and pulsing.

Tess sighed with relief and anticipation.

Abandoning her breasts then, Ian slid his hands under her buttocks and lifted her. His breath thickened as he spread her thighs wider with his own and bent his legs so that he could part her moist flesh with his shaft.

When he thrust inside her in one, long, sleek motion, Tess gasped, overwhelmed by each thick inch stretching her, filling her until the pressure was beyond exquisite.

Her longing was raw-edged, nearly out of control.

When she tilted her hips, drawing him deeper, Ian penetrated her even more fully and took possession of the rhythm, stroking inside her again and again, igniting sparks of pure passion.

She shuddered with ecstasy and knew it spurred him on.

"Tess . . ." His thick voice was hoarse with desire, a plea and demand both.

In answer, she wrapped her arms tightly about his neck and her legs around his hips as she struggled to drag air into her lungs. Her body welcomed him with frenzied need, savoring the power of him as he withdrew only to impale her again.

Their lovemaking was almost frantic. His fingers clenching on her bare buttocks, he stared into her eyes and drove harder, faster, the corded fabric of his breeches chafing her inner thighs with a friction that only heightened the ruthless sensations tearing through her. Ian's eyes burned bright, hunger sharpening his features as he pounded into her. He wasn't gentle, yet Tess craved his violent intensity, for she felt it herself.

This wasn't a fight, wasn't a battle. This was confirmation of life. This was gratitude and relief and reassurance. This was passion at its most elemental . . . a passion that threatened to burst inside her at any moment.

Caught in the tempest of desire, Tess blindly found

his mouth. Ian answered rapaciously, kissing her with fierce need, as if he couldn't get enough of her, meeting urgency with hunger, heat with fire. His tongue plunged into her mouth like the driving rhythm of his flesh sheathed deep in the burning-hot core of her body.

Their hips thrust together wildly until abruptly the heat exploded in an incendiary rush of flame.

Her cry was nearly a scream, his groan a shout as he poured his seed into her.

The searing wave finally crested, then slowly, slowly calmed. Eventually, Ian sagged against her and gathered her close. Tess heard the air rasping in his throat, but it was a long while before he stirred enough to lift one hand to her cheek.

The sweep of his finger was a whisper as he gave a hoarse, tender laugh. "I confess I never expected such a welcome reception."

Tess felt another kind of heat flood her body, this one of scalding embarrassment. Chagrined to have flung herself at Ian in that desperate way, she tried to make light of her hunger.

"You should not read too much into my response, your grace. I was merely celebrating now that the danger is over. A release of tension, nothing more."

"Is that all?" he murmured skeptically, his lips nuzzling her ear.

"Of course. I was concerned that you might have been shot."

He hesitated a moment. "Should I be flattered, love?" he drawled. "I never thought you would care enough to worry about my fate."

Chapter Fifteen

I was mistaken to think I could escape with my heart unscathed.

— Diary Entry of Miss Tess Blanchard

Ian must have sensed her dismay, for he lifted his head to examine her face intently. When her silence dragged on, his expression clouded.

Belatedly, Tess attempted to conceal her feelings. "It was only natural for me to worry about your fate this evening," she claimed, averting her gaze as she shaded the truth. "I was accustomed to fretting about Richard constantly. I spent two years wondering if he would come home from the war in one piece. No doubt I reacted tonight out of simple habit."

It was the wrong thing to say, judging from the way Ian's body stiffened.

"How charming," he observed in a mocking tone, "to know that you are dwelling on your late betrothed while your husband is still inside you."

Tess bit her lip, realizing that she had angered him.

Yet Ian gave her no chance to express regret for her callous choice of words. His face was irritated and frowning when he added cuttingly, "You can always close your eyes and pretend that I am Richard making love to you."

She couldn't pretend any such thing, Tess thought, feeling a fresh wave of despair. She'd never been intimate with Richard, but if she had, her body would certainly have known the difference between the two men. Ian fulfilled her needs as a woman. He gave her the wild passion she had always dreamed of, completing her in a way, she now realized, Richard never could have done.

This time, however, her silence had an even stronger effect on Ian. His gaze turned hard and cold.

Wordlessly, he pulled out of her body and eased Tess to her feet, then abruptly turned away.

Feeling the aching emptiness of his withdrawal, she wanted to reach out to him and pull him back into her arms. Instead, she leaned weakly against the wall behind her for support.

It shook her to realize the distressing truth: She wouldn't want Richard in her bed even if she could have had him. She only wanted Ian.

Tess shut her eyes, feeling a terrible guilt even while acknowledging the danger she was in. Her desire for Ian frightened her. If she was this feverish for him, he would burn her to cinders. He was a man who had never been in love, who had never *wanted* to love anyone, particularly not a woman he had long disdained and had been forced to wed.

She heard him mutter a low oath as he began to undress. Tossing his coat on a chair, Ian shot her a dark glance. "I realize you've enshrined your saintly Richard in your memories, but someday you will have to accept that he is gone and move beyond him."

Tess swallowed, knowing she had to apologize for giving him the wrong impression earlier. "I am sorry, Ian. I did not mean to imply that I was only thinking of Richard. Of course I care what happens to you—"

He waved a hand to cut her off. "It hardly matters. Do you mean to remain up all night?" he demanded, his tone impatient and commanding. "If not, you should go to bed. I would like to sleep for a few hours. I have to travel to Falmouth early tomorrow morning to lay charges against Banks and his fellow thieves."

Tess felt her own body stiffen, but she raised her chin, refusing to be cowed by Ian's anger. Perhaps his harsh reaction was for the best, for she could use the acrimony simmering between them in order to protect herself.

Pushing away from the wall, she went to the washbasin to clean herself of his seed wetting her inner thighs. Then Tess crossed to the bed and climbed in. Pulling the covers up to her chin, she managed to keep her tone surprisingly even when she spoke.

"Since you will be away tomorrow, could we discuss our immediate future? For several reasons, I would prefer to return to London as soon as possible. Ned needs better care, for one thing, and I know of a brilliant physician in London who understands the special needs of veterans. And Fanny is eager to return, since she must sever her relations with her past life before she can wed Basil. Moreover, I should begin planning my next charity event soon. It will be another musical evening, and there are a thousand details to see to if it is to be successful."

"Very well," Ian said tersely as he shed the last of his clothing.

"What does that mean?" Tess asked.

"I agree, you should return to London. In fact, you should go tomorrow—and take Eddowes with you. My library has been fully cataloged, so we no longer need to maintain the pretense of him being needed here. You don't require me to accompany you, I presume? I have served my purpose, playing matchmaker for your friends."

At Ian's icy proclamation, Tess made no reply, telling herself she was grateful that he wouldn't protest her abrupt departure. In all likelihood, she had imagined the hint of bitterness in his voice when he'd pointed out that his usefulness was at an end.

Moments later, he extinguished the lamps and joined her in bed. Yet he didn't draw her into his arms, as was his recent habit. Instead, he gave her his back.

Tess also rolled onto her side, away from him, glad for the space that separated them. The darkness that fell over the bedchamber was relieved only by the faint glow of the hearth fire. Rather than close her eyes, however, she watched the flickering shadows made by the flames.

She still felt greatly shaken to realize she couldn't control her desire for Ian. She'd wanted to believe the hunger that had befallen her was merely a weakness of the body, an obsession of the mind. But she had been deceiving herself.

What she was feeling was a frailty of the heart.

Fanny was wrong for thinking that passion wouldn't lead to more tender emotions, Tess now knew. She couldn't simply cut off her feelings for Ian. It was too late to hope she could remain unscathed.

He was a demanding, alluring, dangerous lover who made her feel things for him that she'd never felt for Richard . . . which only increased her burden of guilt.

As she lay there staring at the wall, Tess flinched to realize another bitter truth.

They might have vanquished the castle ghost, but Richard's ghost still haunted them.

Much to her relief, Ian was gone before Tess woke the next morning. After breakfasting, she had Alice pack her bags while she wrote farewell messages to Vicar Potts and her other Falwell neighbors. Then Tess thanked the Hiddlestons and the castle staff, promising to visit Cornwall again in the near future.

A chill rain was falling by the time her carriage departed for London. Ned had resisted riding inside like gentry, claiming it was more proper for him to share the driver's seat with her coachman, Spruggs, and more comfortable besides, insisting that "a spot of rain will not fash me." Therefore, there were only four passengers inside the traveling chaise. Alice sat beside Tess, with Basil and Fanny in the opposite seat.

Tess tried to keep up a pretense of cheerful spirits rather than staring out the window and dwelling on her morose thoughts. Yet she couldn't help noting that the sea resembled a dull sheet of rumpled metal . . . gray and cold like her heart.

She was profoundly glad for the chance to be apart from Ian, however temporarily. By the time he followed her to London, perhaps she would have devised a better plan to save herself the pain and heartache she knew was coming.

At least her friends' prospect for happiness had improved greatly. Very shortly Fanny would leave the glamorous, desperate world of the demirep behind her forever. Once the marriage took place, Tess intended to use her new social connections as Rotham's duchess to help the courtesan become more respectable. With such a high rank, she should have considerable influence over Fanny's acceptance by society, especially when combined with the power and influence of their other close friends—namely the Loring sisters—who had recently married into the peerage.

Meanwhile, Fanny meant to persevere in her return to propriety. She had recently sold her large London house, which had been her place of business, so she would live and write at her much smaller private home in St. John's Wood, north of Hyde Park. Until the wedding, Basil would maintain his lodgings at Fanny's boardinghouse and travel daily wherever he was needed by his new employer—either Rotham's London mansion in Cavendish Square or Bellacourt in Richmond.

Fanny also planned to make renewed overtures to her remaining family members in Hampshire. Her mother in particular had barely spoken to her since she'd launched her wicked career as a Cyprian all those years ago.

As for Tess, with her marriage on such shaky ground, she was unsure where she should live, at least until she decided how to proceed with Ian.

No doubt it would be unwise for her to reside at Bellacourt just now, particularly without Ian present. His young ward, Jamie, could easily be confused by her uncertain role in his life. A motherless child seeking love could become too attached to her, and Tess knew she could become much too fond of the darling toddler in return. It would be painful for them both if they formed a bond that then had to be broken because she and Ian lived apart.

Her larger fear was the pain Ian could cause her. Sharing his bed, his breakfast table, his everyday life, was perilous enough. But if she risked creating a family with Ian, she would be that much more vulnerable to hurt, Tess reminded herself. She longed for children of her own—and even now she could be with child, given the passionate frequency of their lovemaking. But if not, then she desperately needed to keep as much physical and emotional distance from her husband as possible.

Moreover, her business affairs required that she remain in London for a few days at least. She had dozens of calls to make on the chief benefactors to her charities, to shore up their support after her abrupt marriage.

Even more immediately, Tess wanted to remain close to Ned so he wouldn't feel abandoned among strangers when she delivered him to Marlebone Hospital. Most likely her best choice of residence just now would be Ian's home in Cavendish Square, although she wasn't particularly eager to face another strange staff of servants in her new role as the Duchess of Rotham.

At the thought, Tess winced inwardly and forced herself to rejoin the discussion regarding the ending of Fanny's novel. Helping plot a fitting comeuppance for the villain was a welcome distraction for her, particularly when she feared her own story would end badly.

They reached London two long days later. Tess's carriage dropped Basil at the boardinghouse, then took Fanny home to St. John's Wood before proceeding to Marlebone Hospital with Ned.

Tess's connections to preeminent physician Mr. Otto Geary garnered the veteran an immediate examination and admittance as a patient. Yet the alarm in Ned's eyes was unmistakable.

"You have nothing to fear, Ned," Tess promised, adopting her most soothing tone. "My cousin Damon chiefly built this hospital, and I have raised funds to establish a wing for veterans, so Mr. Geary is happy to help our special friends. And you are certainly my special friend, Ned. Mr. Geary will take excellent care of you, is that not so, sir?"

The portly, ruddy-cheeked gentleman responded by smiling fondly. "Indeed it is, your grace. If not for you and Lord Wrexham, I would still be a poor country hack and this hospital would not even exist."

"You see, Ned?" Tess said, patting his hand. "You

will be an honored guest here—and not only because you are my friend. You are a valiant soldier and a recent hero besides. I mean to tell my many acquaintances how helpful you were in foiling a vicious gang of thieves at our home in Cornwall. And if you have need of me for any reason whatsoever, you have only to ask Mr. Geary to send a message and I will come immediately."

At her reassurances, Ned seemed finally to relax and even managed a wan smile. "Thankee, Mum. You're as kind as me daughter, Sal, that you are."

Tess squeezed his bony hand. "That is a high compliment indeed."

Before leaving Ned a quarter hour later, she pledged to call at the hospital the following afternoon as soon as she returned from Chiswick.

Although weary of travel after the hard journey from Cornwall, Tess decided it best to return to her own home first. She not only needed to collect her companion, Dorothy Croft, to lend her countenance when she called to reassure her benefactors, but she also wanted to fetch what she knew would be a mountain of correspondence that had gathered dust in her absence.

Spruggs drove her carriage the remaining hour through a pouring rain, and Tess was grateful to arrive home to a heartwarming reunion with Dorothy. The absentminded elderly lady claimed to have missed her dearly and ordered a hot supper prepared at once, treating Tess like a beloved prodigal daughter.

After a long coze with Dorothy, Tess retired to her rooms for the night. She should have been pleased to sleep alone in her own bed, but despite her fatigue, her dreams were fitful, and much to her dismay, she found herself yearning for the nearness of Ian's hard, warm, sheltering body.

Seeking a distraction the next morning, she tackled her correspondence with ruthless determination. But Tess's mouth twisted with self-deprecating irony. Throwing herself into her work was her normal mode of dealing with her darkest emotions, and her emotions just now were every bit as conflicted as her initial distress at being forced to wed her longtime nemesis, Ian Sutherland, the Duke of Rotham.

It was nearly noon when Tess came across a bank draft that oddly reminded her of her marriage. The large charitable donation was from one of her most generous benefactors and was dated the day of her amateur theatrical at her godmother's estate in Richmond, the same day she had kissed Patrick Hennessy and set in motion the events that had disastrously changed her future.

When Tess examined the accompanying letter more closely, the signature at the end made her frown. She had seen that same hurried scrawl very recently: Mr. Daniel Grimshaw, Esquire—the same solicitor who had signed the documents detailing her marriage settlement.

When Ian had given her the sheaf of legal papers his first night at Falwell Castle, she'd been too preoccupied at the time to notice the particular details.

"What a strange coincidence," Tess murmured. Mr. Grimshaw regularly contributed to the Families of Fallen Soldiers as well as an orphanage she championed, but she hadn't realized his firm represented her husband's legal interests.

Tess set aside the bank draft, even though she couldn't quell the niggling feeling that there was something she had missed. When she returned to London later that afternoon, she decided, she would pen a note to Patrick Hennessy and arrange an appointment. She needed to confer with him about her next charitable event—a concert to be held at Drury Lane Theatre in early December—and she would use the opportunity to ask him what he knew about Mr. Grimshaw's contributions.

Thankfully, Ned didn't appear any worse for wear when Tess visited him at Marlebone Hospital that afternoon. His physician was not yet ready to offer a prognosis, but Ned seemed almost at home among his fellow veterans, playing cards one-handed while swapping tall tales about his exploits during his army days.

When he caught sight of her, Ned jumped up from the table and hurried over to greet her. A new light shone in his eyes that filled her heart with gladness, as did his report on his previous night's slumber.

"I was dead to the world, yer grace. Slept better than I can remember in o'r two years. Dint hear the voices once. No bad dreams, not a single one."

Tess was still smiling by the time her visit ended. According to Mr. Geary, the ghosts in Ned's head might never go away, but with proper care, the debilitating effects of his trauma should lessen over time.

Upon leaving the hospital, she decided to call on Patrick Hennessy at once rather than wait for a formal appointment, and so directed her coachman to Covent Garden, where the actor had converted a small warehouse into a theater for his troupe's rehearsals and productions.

When she was shown into his office, Hennessy appeared glad to see her, yet his restrained greeting was significantly more cautious than in the past. Clearly her marriage had impacted their relationship, Tess concluded—perhaps because he was now wary of rousing the Duke of Rotham's ire.

Hennessy relaxed somewhat when she began the conversation with a topic near and dear to his heart: His investigations into the spirit world.

"I regret that the rumors of Falwell Castle being haunted by ghosts were slightly exaggerated," Tess said lightly, before recounting her adventures over the past fortnight—how Ned Crutchley had posed as the ghost of Rotham's murdered ancestor to scare away the castle servants so that a local band of thieves could store their booty beneath the dungeons undetected.

Hennessy chuckled at the conclusion of her narrative. "I cannot say I am not disappointed," the actor commented. "But this one incident still does not disprove the existence of spirits."

Tess then asked him how the planning for the Drury Lane concert was proceeding.

"The program is coming together well, your grace. Indeed, your new title has unexpectedly opened doors, garnering renowned performers and patrons alike. I did not think it shameless, however, to use every advantage we have."

Tess smiled faintly. She was not above using her new, albeit unwanted title, either.

Finally, when they had finished discussing which acts to hire and which to cross off the prospective program list, Tess opened her reticule. After showing him the bank draft signed by Daniel Grimshaw, she asked if Hennessy knew why the solicitor had always been so generous.

"I beg your pardon, your grace? I do not understand the question."

Tess watched Hennessy thoughtfully as she explained. "Until now, I never wondered why Mr. Grimshaw was so eager to part with his fortune. Do you perhaps know what motivates him?"

The actor looked strangely uncomfortable. "I wouldn't venture to guess, your grace."

"It seems curious," she mused aloud, "that his firm handles Rotham's legal and financial affairs. Are there other connections that you are aware of?"

When he remained silent, Tess added casually, "Tell me, has Rotham ever contributed to any of our theatrical endeavors without my knowledge?"

Hennessy's face became shuttered. "Well . . . he has not contributed any funds directly that I know of."

"What about indirectly?"

After a marked hesitation, he grimaced. "Perhaps you should discuss the matter with the duke, your grace."

Tess's gaze turned penetrating. "I prefer to discuss it with you now, Mr. Hennessy. I should like an honest answer, please."

"It is not my place to say anything."

"Why not?"

"The duke bade me keep my mouth shut."

Tess would not relent, however. "What were you not supposed to reveal to me, Mr. Hennessy?"

"Honestly . . . I don't know for a *fact* what the truth is."

"But you have your suspicions, do you not?"

He sighed heavily, as if acknowledging that she wouldn't give up her questioning until she got the answers she sought. "Very well, your grace, if you insist. I *suspect* that Grimshaw's involvement in your charities was a pretense . . . a charade to hide your true patron's identity. It was never admitted in so many words, but I fancy Grimshaw has been acting for the Duke of Rotham all along."

Tess's mouth opened in startled disbelief. "You mean, Grimshaw made all those donations at *Rotham's* behest?"

"I suspect so. But from the very first, Rotham made clear to me that he didn't want you knowing about any role he played as your benefactor."

She stared at Hennessy in bewilderment. Had Ian truly supported her philanthropic endeavors anonymously all this time, contributing large sums to her charities from his own vast fortune?

"Perhaps you are mistaken," she protested in an unsteady voice. "Grimshaw could be acting entirely on his own. What makes you think he is not?"

Hennessy hesitated. Evidently, however, he realized the futility of silence, for he heaved another sigh. "Chiefly because Grimshaw always seemed to know exactly when we needed large sums for our productions. I believe the timing was not mere coincidence, since I regularly kept Rotham informed of our needs. And I know for certain the duke aided us in the past, in ways other than financial. I had only to mention to him that we required a thing and he saw that it was done. Do you recall when the Prince Regent attended the benefit at the Theatre Royal in September? That was the duke's doing."

Tess sat there in mute astonishment. Prinny's attendance that evening had assured the event's success, but she'd never known Ian had interceded on her behalf.

"How long has this been going on?" she finally asked.

When her tone remained calm instead of irate, Hennessy's expression went from anxious to sheepish. "Since you first hired me two years ago. Rotham appeared the very next day and made his wishes known. I was to apply to him if we ran into difficulties on any front."

Tess raised a hand to her temple. "How would he even know that I had hired you?"

"I gather that some of your servants may report to him about your affairs. Your footman, the former pugilist, for one. I believe that big strapping fellow was in the duke's service before he came into your employ."

Fletcher had been in Ian's service? Was *still* in Ian's service, doing his bidding? He had commissioned her servants to *spy* on her?

Tess didn't know whether to be outraged or grateful. Ian had always claimed that it was his duty to protect her because he considered her family. Perhaps controlling her servants was his chosen way of imposing his will on her and ensuring her safety at the same time.

But his furtiveness made little sense to her. Why would he keep his good deeds a secret? Because he didn't wish her to know he had a soft heart?

This was not the first time, either, that she had wondered if Ian was hiding his inner goodness, Tess recalled. Without question, he'd kept secrets from her before this. He had never told her about his young ward, for one thing.

But in that instance, he most likely hadn't wanted her knowing that he had a son from an adulterous affair with a married woman. . . .

Tess shook herself and returned her gaze to Patrick Hennessy. "Why would Rotham contribute to my charities, but let his solicitor receive all the credit?"

"I couldn't begin to guess, your grace."

Neither could she, Tess realized, feeling swamped again by conflicting emotions.

She was still stewing over the baffling question when she concluded her meeting with Hennessy and returned to her carriage. Fletcher was there to hand her inside, but although she gave him a piercing look, Tess refrained from interrogating him just yet, not wanting to accuse her servants of betraying her without proof.

She would have confronted Ian directly on the matter, but she had no notion when he planned to return from Cornwall. Furthermore, she hoped to find some sort of evidence of her suspicions so that he could not simply deny his involvement.

Perhaps Basil could assist in her search for the truth, Tess reflected. As the duke's newest secretary, Basil could likely help her learn more about Ian's past business dealings. And as a former law clerk, he might even know Daniel Grimshaw.

If so, then she could possibly confirm what she was beginning to believe: That for some inexplicable reason of his own, Ian had spent years aiding her causes through his lawyers.

She directed Spruggs to take her to Fanny's nearby boardinghouse at once. While waiting for Basil to return home, she visited with Fleur and Chantel, the two aging courtesans who had mentored a young Fanny at the beginning of her career and who now supervised her lodgers.

When Basil arrived shortly before supper time, Tess explained her suspicions about the duke's solicitor. And since he was a quick study, he instantly understood her desire to know if her husband was the enormously generous benefactor who had anonymously supported her charities for years.

"What do you wish me to do, your grace?" Basil asked simply.

"Can you tell me where Rotham's account books are kept?" she replied. "I maintain a record of the major contributions my charities have received over the years. If I could check his accounts and compare entries to see if the same sums were paid to his solicitor around various dates, then it would confirm my theory."

Frowning, Basil shifted uneasily in his seat. "I only hold a junior position in the duke's household, so I don't yet know where his staff keeps his account books. I could inquire, certainly, but I dislike betraying the duke's trust. And then there is—"

Even before Basil stopped abruptly, Tess could see his obvious reluctance. "There is what, Mr. Eddowes?" she prodded.

"You do realize I could be dismissed for prying into the duke's financial affairs?"

It was Tess's turn to frown. She was not asking him to pry, only to help *her* to pry. But perhaps there was little difference.

Then Basil hastened to add, "But of course I will do anything you ask. Indeed, I would not even have the post of his secretary if not for you."

"No, I have changed my mind." She didn't want to cause trouble for Basil, especially not when he was just beginning his new life with Fanny. "Never mind. It isn't important."

"I can see it is exceedingly important to you, your grace."

It was desperately important to her, but rather than say so, Tess fell silent. Basil knew her marriage to Ian was not a love match, but that didn't mean she felt comfortable discussing her marital problems with anyone but her closest friends.

"Is there no other way to gain the evidence you seek?" Basil asked, still intent on helping her.

"Perhaps." She could question Mr. Grimshaw, but his loyalties doubtless lay with his employer, and he would probably not be forthcoming. Worse, he might report her peculiar interest to Ian before she had a chance to question him.

She wanted the element of surprise when she confronted her husband. Ian might try to fob off her queries, and she urgently needed to see his expression and judge his reaction for herself.

"With all due respect," Basil added with obvious concern, "could you not simply ask the duke directly when he returns to London?"

"I intend to," Tess said, pressing her lips together with resolve.

One way or another she meant to get to the bottom of Ian's secrecy and discover if and why he had been deceiving her all these many years.

Chapter Sixteen

It is shocking to learn why Ian hid the truth from me all this time.

—Diary Entry of Miss Tess Blanchard

From the moment she began suspecting Ian's subterfuge, Tess felt fretful and on edge. Doubtless she was a fool to long for his return, but she was anxious to understand his motives if he had deceived her. *Not,* Tess firmly told herself, because she keenly missed him.

Perhaps her unease was due in part to the fact that she had to settle into Ian's magnificent ducal mansion in Cavendish Square. She claimed her own suite of rooms, but without his presence, she found it awkward to establish herself with the large staff, who were much more formal than the friendly servants in his remote castle in Cornwall.

At least she had Dorothy for companionship. When Ian finally did arrive home Friday afternoon, Tess was out making calls with the elder lady. Upon being informed that the duke was in his study, Tess excused herself to Dorothy, then handed over her outer garments to the lofty butler and went in search of her husband.

The study door was closed, but when she rapped

lightly, she was bid entrance at once. She found Ian seated behind his desk. His expression remained shuttered as he greeted her, although he politely set down his quill pen and stood.

Not wanting to seem too eager to welcome him home, Tess kept her tone dispassionate when she said, "I trust your business in Falmouth went as planned?"

"Yes. Banks and his confederates are in jail awaiting a hearing."

"Good," she responded.

"How is Crutchley?" Ian asked in a detached tone of his own.

"His mental state seems to have improved a bit, I think. He no longer quakes at his own shadow. And now that he has proper care, I hope he can heal enough to find productive employment someday. Earning his own keep may help Ned recover his dignity and give him a reason for living."

When Ian gave an impersonal nod, Tess hesitated. The stiff formality of their exchange felt supremely uncomfortable, although she should have been glad for the cold barrier between them. It was precisely what she had wished for, wasn't it?

"Did you desire something particular of me?" Ian prodded.

"Well . . ." Hearing the tentative quaver in her voice, Tess chastised herself. She had no reason to feel ill at ease. She had a legitimate right to question Ian about his possible involvement in her affairs.

She just wasn't certain she wanted to know the answer. Not if it meant that he had been her anonymous benefactor all this time. She didn't like to think

she owed him such a great debt, or that she had mis-
judged him so profoundly. But Tess took a deep
breath and began calmly.

"I recently realized that Mr. Daniel Grimshaw is
your personal solicitor," she commented.

"So?"

"So, for the past several years he has been a major
contributor to my two most important charities."

At first, Ian gave her no response at all. When eventually he raised an eyebrow, as if waiting for her to
proceed, she blurted out her suspicion. "I believe you
have been making those contributions all along, and
that Grimshaw was merely acting at your direction."

Ian's silence spoke volumes, but Tess wanted to be
certain. "Do you deny it?"

"No."

Her brow furrowed. "Why would you let Grimshaw take all the credit for your philanthropy?"

Ian delayed his reply, obviously reluctant to explain
his involvement. "It seemed wise at the time. Had I
used an alias, you would have been overly curious
about an anonymous donor. Thus, I had Grimshaw
make the donations so you could put a face to a
name."

"That explains *how* you hid your altruism, but not
why."

When Tess's gaze remained steadfast, Ian finally offered a justification. "You are so conscientious, you
might have felt obliged to refuse my donations if you
knew their source."

Her eyebrows rose in disbelief. "You thought I was
so closed-minded and priggish, I would turn down

funds to feed and clothe destitute women and children because I *objected to your wicked reputation*?"

Ian remained silent.

"I think you had another reason," Tess said slowly. "You didn't want me to know you had a heart."

"There is that," he agreed with an ironic, humorless smile.

"And it was not only monetary support you provided either," she added. "You have intervened in other ways, haven't you?"

"Why would you think so?"

"I spoke to Patrick Hennessy yesterday."

Ian's jaw hardened. "Hennessy should learn to honor his word."

"He did. He refused to tell me anything of worth. I had to prod him relentlessly before he would even acknowledge the possibility that you were behind your solicitor's generosity."

Ian's mouth twisted cynically at her resolve. "I am not surprised you deduced my role, Tess. You always were too clever and inquisitive for your own good."

"In this instance, I was not clever at all," she retorted. "You deceived me for years. I should like to know why."

"I told you why."

"No, you did *not*. Not really." She took a step closer to him, her hands reaching out in an unconsciously imploring gesture. "Why have you always been so protective of me, Ian? Since the moment we met, we were always more enemies than friends, and you made clear your disdain for me and my hopeless idealism."

"You were betrothed to my cousin."

It was still an inadequate explanation, and Tess's mouth tightened with frustration. "But I was never a member of your family."

Ian's eyes grew more hooded. "As I told you, Richard asked me to look after you in the event something happened to him."

Tess hesitated, knowing he had a point. "Even so, that doesn't explain the enormous sums you provided. A hundred pounds would have sufficed. You gave thousands to my organizations."

Ian sighed faintly and looked away, as if wanting to avoid her penetrating gaze. "We have discussed this before, Tess. I was the one who sent Richard off to war, so it shouldn't surprise you that I wanted to make amends. In some way, my contributions were in reparation for you losing your betrothed."

"You purchased Richard's colors, Ian, but it was not your fault that he died."

"No, I didn't directly cause his death," he agreed solemnly.

"Then there was no need for you to feel guilty. Richard was eager to serve in some dashing regiment. You did not force him to go."

Reluctantly, Ian turned his attention back to her. "Actually, I did force him."

Tess frowned in puzzlement. "Why?"

The gravity she saw in his eyes was somehow unsettling. "At that point in Richard's life, I thought he needed to grow up and learn to take responsibility for his actions."

"What actions?"

Ian's expression remained guarded, enigmatic, as he shrugged. "It isn't important now."

"It is to me," Tess pressed.

Several moments passed before he finally answered. "Richard made a serious mistake a few years ago."

"What mistake? When was this?"

"During the spring of your comeout season."

Tess thought back, remembering. Spring of 1813 was when Richard had first begun courting her, and when she had first met Ian. She moved closer so that she stood directly in front of his desk. "So what was Richard's big mistake?"

Ian's eyes were shadowed. "He didn't wish you to know about it. He wanted to try and make up for his transgression before you learned of it, and I agreed then not to share his secret."

Tess's hands clenched at his cryptic reply. "I am so weary of everyone always wrapping me in cotton wool," she exclaimed in frustration. "Why all this secrecy? What is it that Richard didn't wish me to know?"

Ian grimaced, then sighed softly again. "I think you should sit down, Tess."

"Thank you, I will stand."

To her surprise, he moved from behind the desk and crossed the study to the window. His back to her, he stood looking out at the square of elegant Mayfair residences. His voice was low when he spoke. "Jamie is not actually my son but Richard's. He never acknowledged the boy because he didn't want to disappoint you."

Tess felt herself gasp. *Richard's* son? Richard had a *son* he had never told her about?

Her incredulous silence filled the room, but not because she thought Ian was making up the tale. She remained speechless while trying to absorb the shocking impact of his revelation.

That explained why Jamie's features looked so familiar to her, she realized. Because the toddler was the spitting image of Richard as a boy. But why had he purposely kept the truth from her? And why had Ian abetted him?

Her hand stole to her heart where a sudden sharp pain had lodged.

"He should have told me," Tess murmured hoarsely. "I cannot believe he would have kept such a significant secret from me."

"He wanted to spare you pain," Ian explained. "And he feared if you knew the truth, you would terminate his courtship when it was just beginning."

"Richard thought I would have repudiated him if I learned about his licentious behavior? Because he had fathered a child out of wedlock?"

"It was not only the child," Ian said quietly.

"What more could there be?"

He glanced over his shoulder at her. "It was also how the child was conceived."

"I don't understand."

"That spring . . . Richard seduced one of his young maidservants. A young female dependent in his own household."

Tess stared. "Surely you are mistaken." Yet in her heart she knew he would never make such a charge if it wasn't true.

"It is no mistake," Ian responded. "Her name was Nancy and she was only fifteen at the time."

Reaching out, Tess held on to the desk for support.

How could the gentle, laughing, charming friend she had known for much of her life have committed such a disreputable act? No honorable man would behave so deplorably. . . .

When she remained mute, her gaze imploring him for a denial, Ian continued. "In his defense, Richard claimed that he was foxed when he succumbed to temptation, and that the girl was eager to share his bed. Despite her age, Nancy was a coquette and was trying to attract the notice of a handsome, charming gentleman like Richard. She admitted as much when I questioned her later."

"But how could he possibly excuse taking advantage of a girl that young? A defenseless dependent who deserved his protection?"

"He could not—and he eventually accepted the blame. Richard had continued the liaison even after he began courting you, but several months later, when Nancy discovered she was with child, he ended the affair and came to me for help."

Her mind in chaos, Tess could barely focus on what Ian had said. "Why would he come to *you*?" she asked after a moment.

"Because I was the head of his family. He was third in line to be my heir, and he could have been duke one day. I gave Nancy a position at one of my smaller estates, since obviously she couldn't remain in Richard's employ any longer."

"Obviously," Tess echoed with bitter sarcasm.

Ian held her gaze intently. "Richard swore that he regretted his actions and begged me to keep the ugly truth from you. He feared how you would respond to his sins, given your idealism."

He was right on that score, she thought numbly. She would have ended their courtship at once.

"So you agreed to keep his secret," she said in an accusing tone to Ian.

"Yes. Richard didn't want to lose you, but he also didn't want his child to grow up a bastard and wished to do right by the girl. So I arranged for Nancy to marry one of my footmen. I insisted Richard enter the army, though. He joined his regiment by summer's end, shortly after the wedding took place."

With her heart thundering in her ears, Tess scarcely heard that last revelation. She felt light-headed and queasy in her stomach.

She must have swayed, for suddenly Ian was beside her, his hands on her shoulders, steadying her.

"I told you to sit down," he said gruffly, although his gray eyes were dark with concern.

"For once I regret not obeying you," she whispered, her throat dry enough that the words came out a mere croak. When Ian guided her toward a chair, she went weakly.

"How did you end up with Jamie?" she asked after a long, brittle silence.

"Nancy died a year or so later . . . the same winter that you lost your mother, in the same epidemic. So I took Jamie in as my ward. He was a blood relation, after all—he shares the Sutherland lineage. And he was innocent of his father's sins. Moveover, he was unwanted by his stepfather, and I judged he would fare better as the ward of a wealthy duke than the castoff stepchild of a servant. Lady Wingate was able to find a reputable nurse for Jamie, which was fortunate since I knew nothing about caring for a baby."

Her godmother knew about Jamie? Tess wondered. She raised her stricken gaze to Ian. "Does Lady Wingate realize that Jamie is Richard's son and not yours?"

"Yes."

"She never said a word to me."

"Richard pleaded with her not to. And she agreed it was best for Jamie's sake to conceal his parentage. Very few people know the truth, and I intend to keep it that way."

She searched his gray eyes, which were dark and solemn. "Did you ever intend to tell *me*?" Tess asked in a faint voice.

"I don't know," Ian replied somberly, his gaze honest. "I might have someday. I wasn't certain how you would react. Some ladies would punish a child for the ignoble circumstances of his birth. I have come to love Jamie like my own, and I want to keep him at Bellacourt if I can. I don't want him growing up like I did, brought up by servants and shipped off to boarding school at the tender age of five," Ian said with conviction.

Still stunned by the blow she'd been dealt, Tess rubbed her throbbing temple. At least she understood now why Ian hadn't defended himself three weeks ago when she'd first learned about the boy.

He was watching her with caring and concern now, as if regretting the pain he had caused her. But *she* had insisted on knowing the sordid truth.

She could still scarcely credit it, though. She felt a cold, numbing shock along with a deep, aching distress to learn that her beloved Richard was not the honorable man she'd always believed him to be.

Tess clutched a hand over her heart, finding it difficult to breathe. The man she'd thought was so loving and honest and trustworthy had used his charm to debauch and impregnate a young maidservant.

And all that time Richard had deceived her, Tess reflected. He'd pretended to esteem and cherish her while carrying on an illicit liaison behind her back. He'd fathered a child with another woman while professing his love and devotion to her. And he'd purposely lied to her and covered up his betrayal.

Ian had deceived her also, but at least his deception had been for unselfish reasons: He'd been trying to protect her from hurt, and he'd wanted to protect a young child as well.

How should she react to the revelations about the boy's parentage? Jamie was part of Richard, and she had loved Richard. Yet her love had been built on a deception. Now she didn't know what she felt for him.

And what about his hypocrisy? How many times had he railed against his elder cousin, deploring Ian's wickedness? Richard had been every bit as wicked as the Devil Duke, perhaps more so. Ian was known for his scandalous gaming and carousing in addition to his ruthless business dealings, but even at his worst, she felt sure he would have drawn the line at seducing young girls under his protection.

"Are you all right?" Ian asked urgently when she remained silent.

Tess shook her head mutely. She couldn't speak. She was too shaken, too devastated. She wanted to seek solace against Ian's broad chest, but she couldn't seem to move.

After a few more moments, however, she roused herself enough to speak. "I think you should have told me before this."

"I didn't want to shatter your illusions," Ian replied in a low voice. "Richard was a saint in your eyes, and I felt obligated to preserve his memory. Moreover, he seemed truly repentant. He recognized his mistake and spent the two years before his death trying to redeem himself—to make himself worthy of your love. The army was the making of him."

Perhaps so, Tess thought, remembering General Lord Wellington's letter commending Richard for heroism under arms. Reportedly, he'd been a brave, gallant soldier, recognized for his valiant and honorable deeds. Was his heroism a direct result of his dishonorable past?

She was still debating the question when Ian returned to his desk and retrieved a folded parchment from a drawer. Crossing to Tess, he held it out to her.

"Richard wrote you a letter in the event he didn't make it home and you learned the truth about Jamie."

"A letter?"

"Yes."

The seal was still intact, Tess noted as she accepted Ian's offering. Seeing her name there in Richard's familiar handwriting, she closed her eyes, trying to keep the worst pain at bay. She had been raw with grief at her betrothed's death, and now, seeing his letter brought all the old pain rushing back.

Her eyes blurred with tears, she broke the seal and opened the letter.

My lovely, loving Tess,

If you are reading this, then you know about Jamie and his mother—the girl I wronged, just as I wronged you. Please know that I have striven to become a better man every day since. I knew I was not worthy of you, that I needed to earn your love and respect.

I hope you can find it in your heart to forgive me. And if not, then I pray I haven't destroyed the affection you once bore me.

I have one last favor to beg of you. Will you look after Jamie for me? Rotham has agreed to raise him, but a child needs a mother, and I know you will be wondrous in that regard.

Always your loving Richard

Feeling the tears slip down her face, Tess bowed her head.

Watching her, Ian balled his hands into fists. He wanted to hit something, preferably his damned dead cousin. He wanted Richard alive again so he could strangle the bloody bastard for putting Tess through this renewed pain.

He knew approximately what was in the letter: Richard was begging her for forgiveness. A forgiveness he didn't deserve.

Seeing Tess like this, weeping silently, made Ian hurt deep down in his chest.

This was exactly why he'd kept the truth from her all these years. He hadn't wanted to be the one to hurt her—and shattering Richard's halo only added to the loss she'd already suffered. From her stricken expression he could tell he had devastated her once again, just as he'd done two years ago when he'd broken the news of her beloved betrothed's death.

Ian breathed forcibly, battling a surge of emotion at his own impotence. He ached with the urge to comfort Tess, his heart wrenching at the crushing vulnerability he'd seen shimmering in her eyes. He wanted to hold her until that terrible look went away.

"Tess," he entreated, taking a step toward her. "Please, love, don't cry. . . ."

At the sound of his voice, she stiffened and dashed a hand over her wet cheeks. She wouldn't accept his comfort, Ian knew.

The next moment she proved him right. Tess rose abruptly to her feet, clutching her hands together to steady their shaking.

"I cannot . . . forgive me, but I cannot stay here just now. I need to be alone."

"Very well, I will leave you," Ian offered.

He started to turn away, but Tess stopped him. "No. This is your house, Ian. I want to go home. To Chiswick."

Ian went still. Of course she considered Chiswick her home, and not this London mansion where she was residing only to fulfill expectations of his duchess.

He searched Tess's face, wishing in vain that he could wipe that lost, grief-stricken look from her eyes.

Then stepping back, he let her go, even though it was one of the hardest things he had ever done.

Tess hurried from the room, and when Ian heard voices a moment later, he knew she was summoning her carriage. When eventually he heard the sound of horses' hooves outside on the street, he moved back to the window and watched Tess run down the front steps to the waiting vehicle.

A feeling of emptiness, of dread, washed over Ian. Her despair had only confirmed his fears: She was still too much in love with his cousin's memory to ever love *him*.

He'd wanted, hoped, to make her forget her former ardent feelings, but her heart still belonged to Richard.

No doubt she would forgive Richard in time, Ian surmised. Tess was too kindhearted not to. But more crucially, she would forgive his sins because she had loved him.

Ian's jaw clenched. *His* own wicked past was another matter entirely. He doubted Tess could overlook his own sins as readily. Especially not now when her trust had been violated so painfully.

And therein lay the rub.

He'd known from the moment he laid eyes on Tess four years ago that he wanted her, but now he truly wanted her for his wife, his life's mate. What was more, he desperately wanted her love. He wanted her to look at him with respect and affection and trust. He wanted to arouse the kind of deep, passionate emotion in her that she aroused in him.

The same heart-deep love she had felt for his cousin.

Yes, Ian was finally willing to acknowledge, he loved her passionately. In truth, Tess had invaded his barren heart long ago.

He'd always thought it would be difficult to open

himself to love, but he'd had no choice in loving Tess. She had obliterated his legendary dispassion from the very first.

Fear of losing her made him ache. . . . Except that he couldn't lose what he had never had, Ian reminded himself savagely.

Tess didn't love him and likely never would. Their marriage was a sham. No doubt she wanted more than separate bedchambers; she wanted them to live separate lives, as he'd originally promised they would.

And he would let her do so if that would make her happy.

When had her happiness become so vital to his own? Ian wondered. Perhaps it had always been so.

He swore a vicious oath—a curse rife with anger, frustration, and despair of his own. Once again he had lost out to his saintly cousin. His saintly *dead* cousin.

Ian gave a harsh, bitter laugh as he watched Tess's carriage disappear. After two years of watching her pine for her lost love, he should have learned by now that it was futile to fight a damned ghost.

Chapter Seventeen

Why am I not surprised to learn the truth about Ian's character? He is not nearly as wicked as I have always believed, or as he himself led me to believe.
                    —Diary Entry of Miss Tess Blanchard

Tess's tears continued to spill silently down her face as her carriage left London and wended through the countryside toward Chiswick. She felt betrayed, sick at heart upon learning the shameful truth about her late betrothed's failings.

Perhaps she should not have left Ian so abruptly, but pain had rushed up to swamp her. She'd needed to get away, to be alone while she reassessed her beloved memories of Richard.

When Spruggs eventually drew up before her house, Tess sat there unseeing, feeling the bleak weight of sadness. Moments later, her footman opened the carriage door and let down the step.

Suddenly realizing she would find no solace inside her empty house, however, Tess no longer wanted to be alone. "I have changed my mind, Fletcher. Please have Spruggs drive me to Wingate Manor."

The footman looked concerned, but tugged on his forelock. "As you wish, your grace."

Fletcher shut the door quickly and soon her carriage was moving again.

Retrieving a cambric handkerchief from her reticule, Tess attempted to dry her eyes and cheeks and strove to calm her distraught emotions. She was acting on impulse, but she wanted her godmother's counsel and the comfort of a dear, familiar face. Even more, she wanted an explanation for Lady Wingate's decision to shield her from the truth.

When they reached her ladyship's estate in Richmond, Tess was admitted and shown into the elegant rose parlor, where Lady Wingate was finishing her tea.

"Ah, you deign to visit me at last," her ladyship said with more than her usual acerbic bite. "I heard you had returned from Cornwall, Tess, but I expected you to call on me before this—"

She stopped abruptly, evidently deducing from Tess's red eyes that there was something gravely wrong.

"Cheevers, please bring more tea for the duchess," the baroness commanded her butler. To Tess, she said more gently as she patted the brocade sofa cushion beside her, "Sit down, my dear."

When the servant had gone, Lady Wingate said simply, "So you know about Richard."

Tess nodded, feeling her eyes well up again. "I wish I had known four years ago," she declared in a hoarse voice.

"He did not want to risk losing you."

"So Rotham claimed. But I don't understand why *you* kept the truth from me, my lady. It is not like you to coddle me."

The baroness held her gaze steadily. "Like Rotham,

I did not want you to be hurt, which would have been the case had you learned that Richard had feet of clay."

That much was true, Tess reflected. Her initial disbelief had quickly turned to repugnance and dismay. Now she mostly felt a deep, aching sadness.

"At the time," Lady Wingate continued, "it seemed best to let sleeping dogs lie, so to speak. I did not know about the affair until months afterward, when the girl realized she was with child and Rotham sought my advice about caring for her and her expected infant. By then you were already in love with Richard, and he swore by everything holy that he rued his sins. Then he entered the army and the duke was able to marry the girl off. I decided that no good purpose would be served by exposing Richard's despicable behavior to the world. We had the family reputation to consider, you know."

Tess shook her head dully. "I feel like such an ignorant fool. You knew all along, but never said a word in warning."

Lady Wingate's mouth pursed in a remorseful grimace. "At my age, I know a good deal about a lot of things, Tess—but I also know it is sometimes better to hold my tongue. Still, I am sorry to have distressed you so. Perhaps I was wrong." The baroness sighed. "None of this would ever have happened if you had just chosen Rotham in the first place."

"I beg your pardon?" she asked absently.

Just then, Cheevers returned with a second tray, and the ladies had to pause while he arranged the tea table. When they were alone again, Tess spoke.

"What did you mean about my choosing Rotham in the first place?"

The baroness busied herself pouring a cup of tea for her guest, but she clearly grasped that Tess wouldn't give up, for she sighed again in resignation. "I would have much preferred that you wed Rotham four years ago." She gave a humorless smile of remembrance. "If you must know, I invited the duke to your debut ball and insisted he dance with you in hopes that you would take a liking to each other. By that time, Rotham had turned his life around enough that I considered him suitable material for marriage."

Taken aback, Tess eyed her with bewilderment. "So you were attempting to play matchmaker? You wished me to marry *Rotham,* of all people?"

"You needn't look so shocked. You are my goddaughter. It is my duty to look after you and to act in your best interests. But to my regret, Richard engaged your affections first. And when Rotham saw your decided preference, he withdrew from the lists for your hand without even putting the question to a test. I suppose it was the honorable thing to do, but it was excessively disappointing to me. Richard was a charming boy, but Rotham was a *man.* Unlike my dearly departed husband," the baroness added tartly. "Wingate was such a weakling, I could run circles around him."

Her ladyship shrugged then, as if dismissing her unpleasant memories of her late spouse. "I thought you needed much more of a challenge in your marriage, Tess. And I confess, I have always had a soft spot for rakes. I hoped you could be Rotham's salvation—or at least aid his reformation process. And that is just what happened, even though it took a good while longer than I expected."

Tess stared at her in puzzlement. "What in heaven's name are you talking about, my lady? What reformation?"

The elder lady's expression turned softer. "How much do you know about Rotham's boyhood, Tess?"

"As much as most, I imagine. His mother died in childbed, and he did not get along well with his father."

"That is a *vast* understatement," Lady Wingate declared curtly. "Did you know that Rotham faced financial ruin when he inherited the title?"

Tess continued to stare. "No, I did not."

"Well, it is true, I assure you. His father had depleted the entire family fortune on lavish extravagances and then compounded the crisis by losing outrageous sums at a notorious gaming hell."

"Like father, like son," Tess murmured.

Lady Wingate's chin rose sharply in disagreement. "Indeed, there was an immense difference. The younger Rotham gambled to stave off destitution. When his father died, Ian was saddled with crippling debts of honor, and he had to fight tooth and nail just to save Bellacourt. Since the main property was entailed, it could not be used to raise capital. His only other choice was to sell all the surrounding lands and furnishings, leaving his ancestral home no more than a shell. An ignominious fate he refused to allow."

Tess remained mute, trying to absorb her godmother's vigorous defense of Ian.

"I am not saying he did not deserve his wicked reputation," Lady Wingate temporized. "Yes, he led a life of dissipation and excess in his youth. But I believe much of his rebellion stemmed from his animosity toward his father. Once Rotham inherited the title, all that changed. It was only to repair the dukedom's dire fiscal situation that he turned to gaming. And thankfully, he had the Devil's own luck at the card tables. Then he built an empire with his winnings, employing a remarkable business savvy that clearly was not inherited on his father's side. His detractors say he was ruthless in his ventures, but I expect that was merely sour grapes and envy."

Pausing for breath, the baroness sniffed with a measure of her usual hauteur. "I confess, I did not approve of Rotham's methods. It is ungentlemanly to engage in commerce. But he never cared much about society's good opinion. It is his biggest failing, if you ask me."

Tess's thoughts were still on Ian's past struggles, however, rather than his rebel tendencies. "I never realized," she said quietly. Ian had kept even more secrets from her than Richard had.

At Tess's response, Lady Wingate came down from her high horse and softened her expression. "Rotham is not one to air his dirty linen in public, so you could not be expected to know. But I sincerely believe he has changed his sinful ways. To my knowledge, he has given up gaming, at least. And to the extent that he has become concerned about his reputation, I credit you, Tess."

"Me?"

"Yes. I have little doubt that Rotham wished to earn your respect, much as Richard did."

Tess shook her head in disbelief. "You cannot be right, my lady."

"Why can I not? Rotham has looked after you all this time."

"Because I was betrothed to his cousin. He felt it was his duty."

"It was not his duty to support your charities. I kept him informed about your various endeavors, true, but when he learned about the causes you were championing, he bolstered your efforts with absolutely no prodding from me."

"That is rather puzzling," Tess conceded.

"Rotham is a much better man than most people realize," the baroness said firmly. "Consider his young ward, for instance. I helped a small measure by finding the child a nurse, but it was the duke who insisted on providing the boy a home, even against my advice and protestations. Rotham certainly did not have to take responsibility for raising his cousin's by-blow. Furthermore, he allowed everyone to think *he* was the child's father. He took all the blame solely for your sake, Tess, to keep you from learning of Richard's transgression."

"He admitted as much this afternoon," Tess commented.

Her godmother went on as if she hadn't spoken. "When you wed him, I wanted to tell you about young Jamie then, because I didn't want you to think Rotham a complete rake, but he refused because he did not want you to be hurt."

"I know," she admitted.

"I was never happy with how you were led to view Rotham. In my opinion, Richard was jealous of his cousin and feared you would favor a duke over him. He wanted to court you himself without any competition, so he painted Rotham much blacker than he was in order to turn you away from him."

Tess frowned. Much of her unfavorable opinion of Ian had been spurred by Richard. And since his own cousin had deemed the duke wicked, she had readily believed it. Yet she'd been greatly mistaken.

"Perhaps," Lady Wingate added, "I should not have been so insistent that you marry Rotham, Tess, but honestly, I don't believe my adamancy was the deciding factor. He could have refused to offer for you, and I could not have forced him if he truly objected. Rotham saw the virtue in saving your reputation, unquestionably, but I think his reasons were much more complicated than that."

"What do you mean?"

"I think he cares for you, Tess. The moment you enter a room, his countenance changes. It is a subtle difference, but he becomes more alert, on edge. His eyes follow you—although as soon as you look his way, he averts his gaze. That is certainly not a sign of indifference."

Tess suspected her skepticism showed in her expression. "I never thought him indifferent to me, but we have always been adversaries, if not enemies."

"I know you are constantly at loggerheads, but that does not mean he wishes to continue as such. He attended my recent house party because it was your birthday. I am positive he would never have come otherwise."

When Tess remained silent, Lady Wingate searched her face. "Is it not possible that given time, your feelings for him might soften just a little?"

"Yes, it is possible," Tess answered faintly, knowing the baroness had already gotten her wish. "But our marriage is only a legal contract."

"I know it began that way, but will you at least *consider* accepting Rotham as your husband in truth? For my sake, if not for your own?"

Tess returned a wan smile. Lady Wingate was playing her trump card, knowing her loyal goddaughter would always strive to please her whenever possible.

Surprisingly then, the noblewoman leaned closer and kissed Tess's cheek in an uncustomary outward display of affection. "I will leave you now to finish your tea alone, my dear. I expect you have a good deal to think about."

Rising from the sofa, the baroness exited the parlor as promised. Tess could not find it in her heart to object, for she did indeed have much to ponder.

A kind of bemused numbness settled over her as she considered what she had just learned about Ian. How could appearances be so deceiving? She had been wrong about him all along. He wasn't nearly as wicked as she and the world believed.

It seemed a bitter irony, though, that the wicked duke she had wed to avert scandal was truly a good man, whereas her late betrothed wasn't nearly as good as she'd always thought him.

Granted, she had always been too idealistic, but now she was forced to see Richard in shades of gray.

Tess gazed off in the distance as memories of their youth and courtship flashed through her mind. Falling in love with Richard had been so easy. They'd been friends since childhood, and their mutual affection had only deepened with maturity. Despite having to face disillusionment now, she knew he was not a bad man. He'd made a detestable error and tried to atone for it, even giving his life for his country. That had to count for something.

A renewed wave of sadness and remembered grief swept over Tess, yet it was tempered by her newfound knowledge of Richard. Still, he had asked for her forgiveness . . . although the pain was too fresh for her to grant it just yet.

And then there was Ian. Apparently she hadn't known him at all, Tess acknowledged. Had he actually considered competing for her hand at one time? Or was it merely wishful thinking on her godmother's part?

Tess thought back, trying to recall those months directly after her debut ball. Admittedly, she'd felt the increased discord between the cousins during the summer before Richard went into the army. It made better sense now that she understood the cause of their friction.

And it was certainly possible that Richard had exaggerated his complaints against the Devil Duke for his own personal reasons.

She was partly at fault, however. She'd been deliberately blind to Ian's true nature all this time. She had *wanted* to see him as a wicked rake for her own self-protection. To paint him black, just as Richard had done.

She'd been determined not to fall in love with so heartless a man, to open herself up to pain again. But now that she knew the truth, how could she justify not loving Ian?

The fact was, she couldn't, Tess conceded, her head suddenly reeling in a fresh daze. Her feelings for him had been rapidly evolving since their first shocking kiss, when they were discovered by Lady Wingate and forced by propriety to wed. But now Tess no longer had any doubt in her mind—or more crucially, in her heart.

She loved Ian. Deeply, irrevocably. The kind of breathless, aching love she had always dreamed of feeling for her husband. In contrast, her girlhood love for Richard had been sweet and innocent, not the passionate love she felt for Ian.

But it was not just his incredible passion that had won her. She loved him for all the reasons Lady Wingate had just enumerated:

Because Ian would act to protect a child who was not even his. Because he possessed the kind of honor that was quietly selfless. Because he had protected *her* in innumerable ways all these many years, with no thought of himself. Because he had brought her back to life after an eternity of numbness.

A helpless smile touched Tess's lips. That was likely the foremost reason she loved Ian.

Because he fired her emotions by challenging her. Because he forced her to *feel*. Because he had banished the emptiness inside her once and for all.

She'd resisted loving him with all her might, but her resistance now seemed foolish. She'd really had no choice in the matter once she had become his wife and been obliged to spend intimate time in his company.

But the question was, what did Ian feel for her?

Suddenly beset by gnawing dread, Tess clenched her hands together. The possibility that her love might never be returned frightened her.

Although Lady Wingate maintained that Ian's feelings went beyond mere duty, Tess had grave doubts. He wasn't the sort of man to fall in love. His past experiences had been very different from her own, starting with his childhood. He had never known a mother's love, or a father's. Indeed, had he ever known any kind of love at all?

If not, then how could he feel love for *her?* Tess wondered. The kind of deep, abiding love that warmed the very soul. The kind that lasted forever. The kind of love she felt for him.

She had given Ian no reason to believe she'd had a profound change of heart, Tess bleakly reminded herself. She had pushed him away from the very first, demanding a marriage in name only. Even when their physical attraction had kindled to white-hot desire, she'd insisted that any carnal relations serve only to mitigate their mutual sexual frustration—and Ian had readily agreed.

What was worse, he thought she still loved another man. Only hours ago she had fled his presence while weeping over Richard . . . mere moments after Ian had finally admitted the secrets he'd held close for years.

Tess's stomach tightened as panic curled inside her. Was she too late to convince him of her changed feelings? To ask him to give her a second chance?

She wanted his love, more desperately than she had ever wanted anything in her life. She wanted a real marriage with Ian. But now any overtures she made might be futile.

Chapter Eighteen

Do I dare believe Ian when he says he loves me?
        —Diary Entry of Miss Tess Blanchard

Ian's strongest inclination was to follow Tess to Chiswick immediately, but he forcibly controlled the urge. Compelling her to share his company just now would only compound her distress. He would be making an even greater mistake, Ian knew, by revealing his fierce jealousy of his dead cousin and demanding that Tess choose between them.

His impotence was galling, however. When his butler appeared at the study door to ask if he wished to be served tea at his desk, Ian nearly took the servant's head off with his growled refusal.

For a moment, Phyfe's usual impassive countenance slipped enough to show astonishment. Ordinarily the Duke of Rotham never took his ill moods out on his underlings.

But at least the interruption snapped him out of his own despondency. When Phyfe murmured a meek "As you wish, your grace," and turned away, Ian called after the butler.

"One moment, Phyfe. Do you know Eddowes's present whereabouts? Is he at Bellacourt?"

The butler shook his head. "No, your grace. Mr. Eddowes is here at Cavendish Square, in the library. He has been working there for the past hour or more, sir."

"Has he? I did not hear him arrive."

"He used the servants' entrance, your grace, as he regularly does. Shall I summon him for you?"

"No, I shall seek him out myself. That will be all, Phyfe."

Ian paused only to clear his desk of his most sensitive business documents before rising and heading for the library. His frustration had reached the boiling point. Sitting on his hands would get him absolutely nowhere, so he had to act.

But the question was *how*?

He couldn't let Tess leave him. He wouldn't. He intended to fight for her. Four years ago, his cousin had had prior claim to Tess, but he'd deferred long enough. Too long, Ian thought, gritting his teeth. He'd kept his promise to Richard even after death, but now it was time to move on. To convince Tess to let go of the past.

He knew there was only one way for her to get over Richard, though. He had to make Tess love *him*. It was the only reason she would be willing to stay with him as his wife. The only chance for them to have a future together.

Fortunately, he was wise enough to know that he needed counsel—and he knew just the person to ask. Fanny Irwin had attempted to advise him once before, but he had brushed off her good intentions. Now, however, Ian planned to take the courtesan up on her offer, which meant asking where she might be found of her betrothed, who just happened to be his newest secretary.

As expected, Basil Eddowes was in the library, poring over the catalog of volumes he'd made of the collection at Falwell Castle. He jumped to his feet when Ian suddenly appeared, looking strangely solemn. Then, when Ian eyed the open ledger on the table, the secretary started to explain about having begun work on the library at Cavendish Square.

"I am not here about the cataloging," Ian interrupted. "Just now I wish to know where I can find Miss Irwin. I need to speak with her on a matter of importance."

Eddowes stared, then nodded. "Certainly, your grace. She has a private residence in St. John's Wood . . . Number Eleven Crawford Place."

Thanking him brusquely, Ian turned to leave, but Eddowes called after him. "Your grace, if I might have a word with you?"

Ian paused to glance back. "Yes, what is it?"

"I am very grateful that you engaged me for such a distinguished position, but perhaps I should not continue in your employ any longer."

Ian frowned. "Whyever not?"

"Well, you see . . . I never realized I could be facing a case of divided loyalties. I am loyal to Miss Bl— I mean, the duchess."

"I should hope so," Ian replied. "I have no plans to dismiss you, though, unless you give me good reason. Have you done anything to deserve dismissal, Mr. Eddowes?"

"Er . . . not yet, your grace. But I know you hired me only at the duchess's behest, so if you should—"

Ian raised a hand, not having the patience to deal with his secretary's odd themes. "I prefer to continue this conversation at another time, if we may, Eddowes."

"Of course, your grace. As you wish."

Ian resumed making his exit, but threw a comment over his shoulder at the last moment. "Oh, and Eddowes? From now on you are to use the front door. You are not a regular household servant, to be relegated to the tradesmen's entrance."

The secretary called after him once more. "Thank you, your grace. I will—"

But Ian was already striding purposefully from the library.

His coachman found Fanny's home with little difficulty. The young maid who answered the front door looked intimidated when Ian said, "The Duke of Rotham to see Miss Irwin."

The girl bobbed a timid curtsy, however, and showed him into a small but elegant parlor. To his surprise, the courtesan already had company—three ladies whom he recognized as the Loring sisters.

Having walked involuntarily into a den of genteel females, Ian considered withdrawing, but quickly changed his mind. He needed allies in his effort to win Tess, and her friends could probably help him if they could be persuaded to join his cause.

Fanny looked just as taken aback by the duke's sudden appearance. She rose swiftly from the sofa, her countenance a mix of puzzlement and alarm. "Your grace, is something amiss with Tess?"

"No, nothing is amiss," Ian hastened to reassure her.

Composing her features, Fanny offered him a doubtful smile. "You honor me by visiting. I believe you have met my guests, the Duchess of Arden and the Ladies Danvers and Claybourne?"

Ian sketched a polite bow to the three beauties. The eldest two Loring sisters—Arabella, Countess Danvers and Roslyn, the Duchess of Arden—were tall, slender, and fair, while Lily, the Marchioness of Claybourne, had dark-chestnut hair and a more compact, although still lithe and feminine, figure.

"My friends are here to help plan my wedding, your grace," Fanny added in explanation. "But if you are looking for Tess, she is not here."

Before he could respond, Lady Claybourne spoke up in a tone that was decidedly unfriendly. "*Are* you searching for your wife, Rotham? I would not be surprised if she has fled you. Indeed, I suspected it was only a matter of time before you drove her away."

Ian shifted his gaze to the youngest Loring sister and found her fixing him with an accusing stare. "I assure you, I did not drive my wife away," he began bitingly before conceding he had done precisely that.

"But you have made Tess unhappy," Lady Claybourne pressed. "Can you deny it? What else would send her rushing back to London without you when you are supposed to be enjoying a wedding journey?"

Ian sent her a sharp glance, while Fanny—who was looking uncomfortable at the unexpected altercation—stepped toward him. "No doubt you wish us to speak in private, your grace. I have a smaller parlor upstairs, if you will follow me. . . ."

However, their departure was forestalled by Lady Danvers entering the conversation. "As it happens, we were just discussing you, Rotham." Her tone sounded authoritative, possibly because as the eldest sister, she was accustomed to taking charge.

"Yes," Lady Claybourne interjected again, "we were debating whether to call upon you. I wanted to give you a piece of my mind, but Roslyn dissuaded me."

Ian halted. "Oh? Why would I deserve a piece of your mind?"

"I thought you needed to be reminded of the consequences of mistreating Tess. You will answer to us—and her cousin, Viscount Wrexham, as well. Perhaps threats of retaliation made by mere women will not move you, but Damon is another matter. He will protect Tess to the death, I promise you."

Ian eyed Lady Claybourne piercingly. "All I have ever wanted was to protect Tess."

Her delicate chin jutted out with a stubbornness that reminded him of Tess at her most determined. "I beg to differ, your grace. You compromised her so that she was forced to wed you—"

"Pray calm down, Lily," the Duchess of Arden interrupted in her serene way. "You go too far." Roslyn then offered Ian a smile and an apology. "Forgive my younger sister, your grace. Lily has yet to learn that not all noblemen are foes. She only just recently wed, and Claybourne has not yet totally convinced her. Please, will you be seated?"

Ian hesitated, then settled in the only vacant chair left, while Fanny resumed her place on the sofa.

Yet Lily would not give up, it seemed. "Just what are your intentions toward Tess, your grace?"

His mouth twisted with a mix of exasperation and ire. "What is this, an inquisition, my lady?"

"Perhaps it should be. Are you afraid to explain to the friends who love Tess dearly just why we should not come to her rescue?"

"I am here, aren't I? In point of fact, I came to seek Miss Irwin's advice on how to win Tess."

His declaration took the wind right out of the marchioness's sails. When she stared, slightly slack-mouthed, her middle sister Roslyn smiled again and said sweetly, "I commend you for braving the four of us together, your grace. We can be like mother lionesses when it comes to our close friends."

Ian nodded in appreciation, while Arabella asked curiously, "What do you mean about seeking advice on how to win Tess?"

"I love her and want her for my wife," Ian admitted with far more ease than he'd expected.

A look of glee claimed Fanny's features, and she clapped her hands together. "This is beyond famous! I knew it! I have a good instinct for these things. Have you told her of your love yet, your grace? That is the first step, you know."

Ian met her gaze evenly. "I don't believe it is so simple."

"I think it is. Tess fears you will only cause her more pain, so she needs to know how you feel before she will risk returning your love."

"Yes," Lily agreed. "She believes you will break her heart, and she has already had it shattered once."

Ian grimaced. "That is a large part of the trouble. Tess is still in love with my late cousin. Richard was a saint in her eyes."

"Whereas you are a devil," Arabella commented in an audible undervoice.

"Just so," Ian said dryly. "But it is beyond time for her to move on with her life."

"Tess was prepared to move on with the right man," Lily pointed out, obviously still skeptical. "Perhaps you are not the right man for her."

Ian turned a blazing glance on her, but said nothing.

When he remained silent, Lily searched his face intently. "You are positively certain you love her? You have no doubts?"

"No doubts whatsoever," he said emphatically.

Her expression softened a tiny measure. "You will have to prove that you will be a good husband to her."

"I realize that. But my bigger dilemma is to make Tess love me as much as she loved my cousin."

"So how can we help you accomplish your aim, your grace?" Arabella asked genially.

His attention shifted to the eldest sister. "I am willing to entertain any suggestions you might have."

"I should hope so," Lily muttered. "We know Tess better than anyone. You would be wise to take our advice."

Ian couldn't help but be amused by her reluctant about-face. "I agree, Lady Claybourne. I am accustomed to putting experts in charge of my business enterprises, and you are certainly more expert than I when it comes to Tess."

The four women glanced at one another, before Roslyn answered for them all. "Fanny is right, your grace. First and foremost, you must tell Tess that you love her. She is too wary to give her heart when her love is not returned. If you like, we can speak to her and ascertain her feelings, to see what you are up against."

Ian nodded, relieved by her offer.

By the time he left Crawford Place, the sisters as well as Fanny had all pledged to do everything in their power to aid him, including pleading his case for him with Tess if necessary. Most surprisingly, he had managed to convince even the dubious Lily that he was serious about winning Tess's love.

Ian still felt anxious and apprehensive about his prospects for success, but their counsel had given him reason to hope. Moreover, he'd faced and conquered enormous challenges before, although none where the stakes were so high.

Therefore, he directed his coachman back to Cavendish Square rather than go after Tess just then. He would give her the night to come to terms with her new knowledge of Richard's shortcomings. But first thing in the morning, he intended to head for Chiswick.

His restlessness didn't abate, however. Before his marriage, Ian might have dined at his club or invited friends or colleagues to his home for dinner. Having no desire for the company of mere acquaintances, though, he ate alone at his empty dining table.

He missed Tess badly. Missed her warmth and her verbal jousts. Missed her sweet smiles and even sweeter touch. Realizing how swiftly he'd shed his bachelor ways, Ian laughed softly at himself.

Most assuredly he was in love. Why else would he be craving his wife's presence the way a parched man craved water?

After finishing dinner, Ian drank his port in front of his drawing room fire. It was perhaps ten minutes later when Phyfe informed him that the duchess had returned home.

Ian's heart started thudding erratically, but before he could do more than set down his glass and stand up, Tess appeared in the doorway.

Phyfe bowed himself from the drawing room and shut the door for privacy, but Ian scarcely noticed.

His heart felt lodged in his throat as he drank in the sight of her. She was no longer weeping at least, although she looked pale and her expression was gravely serious.

Ian started to speak, but Tess interrupted him by holding up a hand. "Please, let me say something first, Ian."

She bit her lower lip, then hesitated. Her dark eyes looked huge in her face.

He forced himself to wait, hardly daring to breathe for fear of what she might be planning to tell him.

Finally, she murmured in a low voice, "I did not mean to give you the impression that I am still pining after Richard. I am not."

"You aren't?" he managed to ask, his throat tight.

"No, not at all." Tess twisted her hands together, as if gathering her courage. She looked nervous, anxious, fearful even. At last she broke the silence again. "I love you, Ian, and I want you for my husband."

Joy slowly burgeoned inside Ian, although he wondered if he could trust the feeling. "You love me?" he repeated rather densely.

"Yes. And I want a true marriage with you."

The fearful ache inside him eased for good. "I suppose that is just as well, Tess, since I have loved you for years, even if I never acknowledged it to myself until very recently."

She stared, searching his face with a fierce intensity. After another long moment, hope lit her dark eyes. Then the same joy Ian was feeling swept over her beautiful features and with a glad little cry, Tess launched herself into his arms.

Chapter Nineteen

I never believed I would know such joy.
            —Diary Entry of Miss Tess Blanchard

The taste of Ian's mouth was pure heaven, but it was his admission of love that made Tess delirious with happiness. Clinging to him with all her might, she kissed him ardently, showing him without words what she felt inside: Relief, elation, wonder, joy, love. . . .

Eventually, however, Ian pulled away, leaving her lips bereft. A fresh tinge of apprehension surged through Tess until he took her face in his hands.

"Say it again," he demanded, his voice husky and urgent.

She stared up into his heated gray eyes. "You mean, say that I love you? I do love you, Ian, so very much—" Tess declared, only to be interrupted by another fierce kiss.

Her breath fled as he lifted her off her feet and took her mouth rapaciously. She welcomed his ferocity, though, returning his ardor measure for measure.

It was a very, very long while before Ian allowed her any respite by setting her down and ending their embrace. Dazed as she was, Tess made no protest when he guided her backward and settled upon the sofa with her.

Drawing her into his lap, Ian cradled her against his chest and simply held her, his forehead pressed against hers while their racing pulses slowly began to calm.

Tess was the first to speak. "You truly love me?" she asked, seeking reassurance just as he had done.

He drew back to meet her gaze. "Truly. I love you dearly, my sweet Tess. More than I can say."

She shook her head in wonderment. "I never expected to hear those words from you, not in a thousand years." She reached up to touch his beloved face. "Lady Wingate thought you might be harboring some unacknowledged affection for me, but I wouldn't believe her."

Ian's smile was slow and tender. "She was right, love, although I did my utmost to pretend otherwise."

"It seems you have been concealing other secrets as well," Tess pointed out, feeling a trifle more confident now. "When I spoke to her this afternoon, she revealed any manner of interesting details I never knew about you."

His eyebrow lifted. "Details such as . . . ?"

"Such as the state of your finances when you inherited the title from your father. I never realized you were facing ruin, Ian, or that your gaming was born out of necessity."

Ian's expression sobered. "It's true. I was drowning

in debt from my father's reckless extravagances and calamitous misfortunes at the gaming tables. But I happen to have an uncanny skill at cards, and gambling was the only way I could survive financial disaster and save Bellacourt, as well as all the other money-gorging properties that accompanied the dukedom, including Falwell Castle."

Very glad he'd been able to save his ancestral home and the smaller castle in Cornwall, Tess remembered what else her godmother had told her. "Lady Wingate suggested you are not only skilled at cards, but that you have a Midas touch when it comes to business."

"That may be a slight exaggeration," Ian replied, his mouth curving. "But I invested my winnings wisely and eventually managed to restore the family fortune to its former glory."

Tess slid her arms around his neck again. "And here all this time I thought you were a wicked libertine, following in your father's footsteps."

Despite the teasing note in her voice, Ian returned a somber answer. "I well deserved my wicked reputation, Tess. I squandered my youth in rebellious escapades and shirked my responsibilities out of spite. I could have easily ended up like my father. But I have changed my wicked ways. I no longer need to gamble, and I certainly no longer indulge in amorous affairs. I haven't for quite some time."

"No?" she asked somewhat dubiously. "Why not?"

"Because I want no other woman but you, my lovely Tess."

She felt a warm glow welling inside her. "I can scarcely believe you love me, Ian. I was convinced you lacked all heart."

"I do have a heart. It's just that you twisted it and tied it into knots."

Tess smiled to think she had such power over him, but then her amusement faded and turned to sadness. "I doubt your notoriety was solely of your own making. I suspect Richard helped by embellishing your sins at every opportunity."

"I am certain of it." Ian's mouth tightened a moment. "I'm clearly no saint, Tess, but it always frustrated the bloody hell out of me that you believed Richard to be one."

Hearing the grating note in his voice, Tess searched his face. "I know differently now, Ian."

His eyes held sympathy. "Still, I regret you ever had to find out about his foibles."

"No, I needed to know. I *wanted* to know." Tess frowned. "I now understand why my godmother seemed unhappy when I became betrothed to Richard. Yet she told me today that even before then, she favored you, in spite of your rakish ways, or perhaps because of them."

"Did she?"

"Yes. She confessed that she wanted us to marry four years ago and that she tried to play matchmaker at my comeout ball."

"I know," Ian replied, not trying to conceal his amused irony. "I had every intention of evading her efforts, but then I saw you for the first time. You were laughing with Richard, and the sight cut right through me. But when you fell in love with my cousin, you became off-limits. It was damned hard for me to be near you, Tess, always wanting what I couldn't have."

"Lady Wingate thought you might be jealous of Richard."

"I was, savagely so. But like Richard, I wanted to be a better man because of you. To win your admiration and respect. I wanted to see that same look in your eyes that you always had for him."

"You *are* a good man, Ian. You have proven it in countless ways."

"Have I?"

"Indeed. It was remarkably admirable for you to take Jamie in as your ward."

Ian shrugged. "My reputation was already tarnished. What was one more blot on the whole?" His features lightened. "And then I came to love the little fellow." Ian's gaze held Tess's. "I will send him away from Bellacourt if you wish it, but—"

"Good heavens, no. I don't want him sent away. As you said, he is an innocent child. And he needs a mother as well as a father."

"Lady Wingate thinks I coddle Jamie too much, but I want him to grow up knowing he is loved."

"He will be. By us both."

Ian briefly kissed her temple, then drew back. "You are amazing, did you know?"

His eyes were so vivid with warmth, it made her own eyes smart. "*I* am amazed you think so. I thought you despised me for being a starry-eyed idealist."

"Never. I love your passion, Tess. Your fierce devotion to your causes is part of who you are." His mouth curved. "The truth is, I had recently resolved to try my hand at courting you, since according to your godmother, you were finally coming out of mourning for Richard. And then I walked in on you kissing Hennessy. Speaking of savage jealousy . . . he was fortunate I didn't pummel him to a pulp."

"He only kissed me on impulse, Ian. And I only responded because I wanted to know what it felt like to be kissed by a man other than Richard. If it will make you feel any better, I did not enjoy kissing Hennessy one whit. I was impatient for him to be done with it."

Ian planted his own tender kiss on her lips. "At least your wanton experiment spurred me to act. I couldn't let you get away twice. I was actually glad when Lady Wingate insisted we had to marry."

"I never knew," Tess said softly.

"I didn't want you to know. For my own self-protection, I needed to keep up the barriers between us. I cultivated your animosity on purpose for years."

"Is that why you didn't want me to know about your generosity?"

"Yes. Because you would have looked at me more kindly. I wanted you to think me your adversary so I could better resist you."

Tess couldn't help but laugh. "You succeeded admirably, Ian. It always infuriated me, how you always got under my skin so easily."

"You got under my skin as well. You were in my head, my loins, my heart. . . ." Ian chuckled softly at himself. "I didn't want to love you, but my plan failed miserably. The more I fought you, the more I wanted you."

"It was the same with me," Tess acknowledged.

He exhaled in relief. "I wish I'd had an inkling of your feelings before this. You could have saved me a good deal of agony this afternoon. I was desperate enough to visit your friends, to seek their advice on how to win you."

"Which friends?"

"Fanny Irwin and the Loring sisters."

"Seriously? You asked their advice? What did they say?"

"That I should confess my love to you, first and foremost."

"They were right, you know," Tess agreed sweetly. "I suppose I can contrive to forgive you for keeping the truth from me, Ian. But please, no more secrets between us?"

"That goes for you as well, love."

Tess arched an eyebrow. "What secrets did I keep from you?"

"You concealed the fact that you loved me. That is an outrageous omission."

"I was not even aware myself, so how could I tell you?"

He pressed another tender kiss on her lips. "You have no more excuses. From now on, I want to hear regularly how much you love me."

"That will be no hardship, my love."

He started to kiss her again, but stopped. "Oh, and another thing. No more 'your graces' when you address me. It perturbs me to no end."

"Why do you think I do it?"

Ian kissed the teasing smile off her lips and made her sigh in surrender.

When he allowed Tess to breathe again, however, she fixed her gaze on him. "I meant what I said, Ian. I want a true marriage with you, despite how disastrously we began. I don't want a bloodless union where the only intimacy is based on physical passion."

"Nor do I."

Determined to drive her point home, she curled her fingers around the lapels of his jacket. "I want to be your wife in every way possible. I want a mate, Ian, not just a lover. I want a husband and friend and confidant."

"I think I can safely promise you that."

His perceptive gray gaze cut straight to her heart, his expression so brutally honest, she couldn't mistake his feelings of love for her.

Yet she needed to make him understand her own feelings, Tess realized. "You said I should move on with my life, Ian, and I am ready to do so, totally and completely. I don't want to waste any more time. If I have learned anything these past two years, it is that happiness and love are too precious to let slip away."

She paused. "And I don't want Richard to come between us ever again," Tess added in a softer tone, remembering their last night at Falwell. When she'd brought up Richard's name while making love to Ian, he'd responded angrily, almost bitterly.

She tightened her hold on his neck, wanting to offer reassurance. "I swear to you, Ian, there is no reason whatsoever for you to be jealous now."

He nodded solemnly. "I intend to hold you to that promise. I don't want Richard in our marriage bed."

"I should hope not," Tess said lightly, believing they could now lay their ghosts to rest.

In response, Ian brushed the crown of her head lightly with his cheek, then pulled her to his chest and held her, his strength palpable, surrounding her, protecting her.

She remained there for a score of heartbeats, with her head resting on his shoulder, savoring the tender moment. Soon, however, she could feel heat rising between them.

"Ian?" Tess murmured against the side of his neck.

"Yes, love?"

"At Falwell, we agreed to share a bed merely to reduce our sexual frustrations, but I want to sleep with you every night from now on."

"You read my mind, Tess."

"Do you think we could begin right away?"

"I expect so. I seem to recall never giving you a proper wedding night. I promise to make up for my lapse tonight."

"Must we wait until tonight?"

Raising his head, Ian gave her a wicked, heart-stopping smile, then stood with Tess in his arms. "I thought you would never ask."

He carried her upstairs to his bedchamber and stoked the hearth fire to ward off the chill of the November evening. Then they undressed each other in between tender kisses and languorous caresses and soft laughter.

Their marriage was no longer a battle, no longer a rivalry, Ian reflected gladly. Instead, for the first time, they would be sealing their union as true husband and wife, showing their love for each other. The prospect filled him with heat and pleasure.

He held Tess's gaze, savoring the perfect beauty of her smile, the giving warmth. Her generosity of spirit was what had drawn him to her from the first, but she awed him in so many ways.

He would never get enough of her, Ian knew. Yet physical desire was only part of his attraction. There was something deeply satisfying about just sharing her company. Even simple things somehow seemed new again to him. Every moment with Tess was like discovering something he'd never known was missing.

When he had bared her lovely body, he kissed her nape as he let down her hair, luxuriating in the sable tresses that fell in lustrous waves down her back. Then he attended to the delectable skin of her shoulder, which naturally led his lips down her arm to the ripe swell of her breast.

As he laved the budded nipple with his tongue, Tess sighed and wound her fingers in his hair.

"I always thought you the most vexing man alive," she admitted in a breathless murmur, "but now I am inclined to think you the most wonderful man alive."

"I am not quite the arrogant devil I once was," Ian agreed, lifting his head. "In fact, I've been humbled by love."

"*You*, humbled? I'll never believe it."

Her smile tantalized him as always, but the loving

laughter in her eyes was new. He relished that look, relished the hint of challenge in her tone. He suspected she would have continued provoking him, but he kissed her again, seducing her mouth into silence with his ardor.

Tess reciprocated, her lips melding with his, her hands touching him in a way that made him breathless with need.

When the heat grew nearly unbearable, Ian led her to the bed and drew her down. For a time they held each other . . . embracing, kissing, caressing, cherishing, leaving arousal everywhere they touched.

He ached to be inside her and yet he wanted to go slowly, to make this moment last. They fondled and stroked until they were both flushed and aroused to the point of trembling.

Only then did Ian shift to cover Tess's lithe, lush body. Easing between her thighs, he braced his weight on his forearms so that he could gaze down at her, wanting to watch her eyes as she went wild beneath him.

She was already awash with wanton desire, he could tell from her quivering response. And she was incredibly hot and wet for him, Ian discovered as he tenderly thrust inside her.

Yet it was the way Tess watched him that took his breath away. Golden firelight bathed her face and turned her dark eyes brilliant, the expression on her face one of joy.

The sight made his chest hurt with love.

"I've waited forever to love you like this," he said reverently.

Her features etched with passion, Tess clasped her legs around him and arched her back, drawing him in further.

"So have I," she admitted, her fever-bright eyes shining into his.

Caught in the magic of her dark gaze, he began to move, feeling Tess surround him, feeling Tess love him. Stark hunger and tenderness poured from him as they rocked together in ancient rhythms, intensifying the fire between them, the raw wanting.

When Tess softly moaned his name, Ian sank even deeper, claiming her as his own, filling her until she was gasping, until she was pleading, until they were both shaking with desire.

"My wife, my love . . ."

"My husband . . ."

Tess gave herself to him, body and heart and soul. Her moans turned to sobs that were echoed by his deep, guttural groans. Their bodies twisted feverishly together, writhing, clenching, until at last the powerful explosions left them gasping and replete.

As the pulsing ecstasy receded, Ian slowly withdrew and turned onto his back, pulling Tess with him, holding her possessively. It still stunned him, how powerfully she affected him. No woman had ever shattered his sense of reality the way Tess did. She consumed him, enchanted him.

Too sated to move, he lay with her, their limbs tangled together, their heartbeats slowing. After a while, Ian brushed his lips against her temple and peered down at her. The fire glowed, gilding her lovely face. Her eyes were closed now, but the blissful contentment on her beautiful features spoke volumes.

Ian felt the same contentment, along with a fierce, primal satisfaction, knowing that Tess's passion was something he alone could summon.

When he traced his fingertips along the rise of her cheek, she stirred enough to open her eyes.

"Fanny was right," she said dreamily. "Lovemaking is even more wonderful when you are in love."

Ian smiled. "I couldn't agree more . . . although it still startles me to hear you spout romantic wisdom from a notorious Cyprian."

Tilting her head back to see him better, Tess smiled up at him. "I'll wager Fanny will become much less notorious in the near future. She has abandoned her wicked ways in order to settle down in staid matrimony, just as you have."

Ian's humor deepened. "I fervently hope there will be nothing staid about our marriage, Tess."

"You have a point," she conceded. She paused. "I don't believe I thanked you yet, Ian. I am so grateful that you made it possible for Fanny to marry for love."

"I confess my motives were completely selfish. I only wanted to make you happy."

Reaching up, she twined her arms around his neck. "You *have* made me happy, darling. Deliriously so. You filled the emptiness in my heart."

Her simple declaration humbled him.

"I could say the same about you, my lovely Tess. I never realized how empty my life was until I met you."

She smiled radiantly, the same precious smile that had captured him the first time they'd met—only this time her joy was solely for him.

In response, Ian pressed a reverent kiss on her mouth. His heart was full of emotion for her: lust and love, caring, protectiveness. His fierce desire for her was only eclipsed by his even greater desire to protect and cherish her.

Suspecting that Tess still needed proof of his love, however, Ian wrapped his arms around her and deepened their kiss, determined to show his adoration with deeds and not mere words.

He succeeded admirably, if her blissful cries a short while later were any indication.

Epilogue

My friends have all been remarkably lucky in love, but I am the most fortunate of all, having my not-so-wicked duke for my husband.

—Diary Entry of Tess Sutherland,
Duchess of Rotham

Richmond, England: December 1817

Pride and delight surged through Tess as she watched Fanny and Basil being united in holy matrimony. The bride looked amazingly beautiful, her long-sleeved gown of forest green lustring boasting a high-necked bodice embroidered with gold threads. The groom, though almost handsome in a long, lanky sort of way, seemed a trifle awestruck at his good fortune. Yet the love in his eyes was unmistakable, as was Fanny's love for him.

The couple's friends had gathered in Bellacourt's small, elegant chapel behind the manor for a private ceremony, since society was not yet ready to publicly embrace the nuptials of a former lady of pleasure.

This was the last in a rash of unexpected weddings from among Tess's close circle. Indeed, Fanny's unlikely romance was the culmination of a remarkable year of love matches, which had begun in May when Marcus, Baron Pierce, inherited the Danvers earldom along with his unwilling guardianship of the Loring sisters. Now Marcus and Arabella were expecting the birth of their first child in the spring.

The thought warmed Tess's heart. So did the nearness of her own handsome husband sitting in the pew beside her.

She had actually seen little of Ian since breakfast, having spent the morning at Danvers Hall helping the bride dress and primp with the rest of Fanny's dearest female friends. Tess had then accompanied the ladies to Bellacourt, where, following the quiet chapel service, she and Ian planned to host a large wedding breakfast and ball to celebrate their own recent marriage.

The guests present in the chapel were an interesting mix of commoners and gentility, Tess noted. Several of Basil's bachelor friends from his law clerk days had come to support him. And not surprisingly, Fanny's beloved Cyprian friends, Fleur Delee and Chantel Amour, had been invited and appeared to be thoroughly enjoying themselves.

It was highly unusual, however, to see so many high-ranking members of the ton at a courtesan's wedding. In addition to Arabella, Roslyn, Lily, and their three noble husbands, Tess's cousin Damon, Viscount Wrexham, was there with his vivacious wife Eleanor, who happened to be Marcus's younger sister. Also in attendance were Arabella's nearest neighbor, Rayne Kenyon, the Earl of Haviland and his charming new wife, Madeline, whom the sisters had taken under their wing this past autumn.

Yet it was only fitting, Tess reflected, for them to honor Fanny this way, since she had aided them all in their courtship wars at one point or another.

Winifred, Lady Freemantle, was in attendance also, seated at Tess's other side. The plump, plain, middle-aged widow had been born into the lower classes, but her industrialist father's fortune had purchased her marriage to a baronet. Winifred was the original patron of the Freemantle Academy for Young Ladies, funding the school entirely before Marcus bought it outright for Arabella as his wedding gift to her this past summer.

Tess's godmother was not at the chapel, although she meant to attend the festivities afterward, once the notorious lightskirt and her groom had left the premises and set out on their wedding journey to Hampshire. Lady Wingate had her reputation to uphold, after all.

Lady Freemantle was not so fastidious. After warning that she always cried at weddings, Winifred sat sniffing happily throughout the ceremony. When the vows had finally all been spoken, she heaved a dreamy sigh while clutching her hand to her generous bosom. "That was simply beautiful. Weddings are such a joyous occasion, especially this one."

Tess nodded in agreement, wiping away her own tears of happiness with the handkerchief Ian had loaned her. She couldn't help comparing Fanny's wedding to her own hasty, forced marriage, however.

Ian must have been having similar thoughts, for he bent to murmur in her ear. "Do you regret not having a church wedding?"

Tess smiled up at him. "Not at all. How our vows came about hardly matters as long as I have you for my husband."

It was clearly the answer he hoped for, judging from the tender sheen in his gray eyes—a tenderness that warmed her from the inside out. By the time the wedding guests spilled out of the chapel into the chill gray day, the first snowflakes of the season had begun falling, yet Tess felt as if she was coming out of a dark winter.

She was filled with gratitude that she had found Ian. Knowing full well that happiness could be snatched away in the blink of an eye, she intended to make the most of the present moment and their time on earth together.

Life was all about being alive, and with Ian, she was constantly, gloriously alive. He had taught her to feel joy again, single-handedly banishing the hollow, empty feeling inside her. Even before their union, their battles had given her a focus other than grief. And the continued sparks between them only added spice to their spirited marriage. Yet their disputes never held anger; there was too much love.

Gazing up at Ian as they waited for the bridal couple to appear after signing their marriage documents, Tess felt cherished and protected and desired. What more could a woman ask for?

She had no chance for private conversation with him, however, since she was soon occupied with saying fond farewells to the newlyweds. For their wedding journey, Basil was taking Fanny home to Hampshire to visit his family and, hopefully, to reunite with hers.

After much embracing and laughter and sharing of good wishes, Fanny turned back to Tess.

"I cannot thank you enough, dearest Tess," Fanny

said, her gratitude positively heartfelt. "And you, your grace."

"I believe the appreciation is mutual," Ian assured her.

Basil added his earnest thanks and then bundled his radiant bride into the waiting traveling chaise, where he plied her with lap robes and hot bricks at her feet to keep her warm during their journey. As the carriage drove away, the wedding crowd broke into small groups in order to walk the short distance along Bellacourt's elegant graveled paths to the main manor, with Dorothy Croft and Lady Freemantle accompanying Tess and Ian.

Never one for silence, Winifred took the opportunity to thank the duke for his generosity. "We are all grateful to you for promoting Fanny's interests, your grace. She has been so instrumental in helping so many of our friends find true love that she deserves the same chance at happiness."

"I cannot take credit for her happiness, Lady Freemantle," Ian demurred politely.

"But you hired Mr. Eddowes, which improved his financial prospects considerably. One must be practical when it comes to marriage, you know. Lovers cannot live on romance alone. And Fanny's second novel will soon be published, which should nicely supplement their income. Of course, her work cannot compare to such literary geniuses as Lord Byron and Sir Walter Scott, but I vow her stories are nearly as exciting. And you aided in her research, your grace. Fancy you having the ghost of your murdered ancestor haunting your castle."

Walking beside Winifred, Dorothy Croft gave a delicate shudder. "I am quite glad you did not ask me to accompany you to Cornwall, Tess," Dorothy said with conviction. "I would have fainted dead away at the first hint of a ghost. In truth, I doubt I will ever be able to visit there for fear of encountering Rotham's murdered ancestor."

Kindly, Tess concealed her amusement at her faint-hearted companion. "I think you needn't worry, Dorothy. Falwell's ghost proved to be very much alive and human. The housekeeper, Mrs. Hiddleston, wrote this past week to say there have been no more ghost sightings, or smugglers, either."

"I should hope not," Dorothy replied fervently.

Winifred was not of the same mind. "Well, *I* should like to visit Falwell someday, Tess. I think a good night's haunting would be delightful. I often wonder if Freemantle Park is plagued by spirits—each time I hear rattles down the corridor, in fact. But no doubt it is just the drafty chimneys. What of the soldier who was pretending to be the duke's ghost?"

"Ned Crutchley is doing rather well," Tess answered. "The reward he received for helping recover the stolen jewels should provide for his care for a long time to come. And Mr. Geary may employ him at the hospital, aiding other veterans to deal with their traumas."

Dorothy chimed in again. "I am not surprised that the chain-rattling ghost was all a hoax. Honestly, I do not even believe in ghosts," she declared, blithely contradicting her assertion of only moments ago.

Tess had not changed her own beliefs about spirit hauntings, but like Winifred, Patrick Hennessy was

disappointed that the Falwell ghost had been exposed
as a real human entity. The actor would not admit
defeat, however, and his investigations had since expanded to Derbyshire in search of proof that other-
worldly shades were real.

"So all's well that ends well," Winifred concluded
happily, having a soft spot in her heart for downtrod-
den souls such as Ned Crutchley. "And the future is
bright for all my dearest friends . . . although it is a
terrible shame that Richard perished at such a young
age. Thankfully, you are blissfully wed to the duke
now, Tess."

"Yes," Tess said softly, feeling a familiar sadness
and regret at the mention of her late betrothed. Yet
she purposely caught Ian's eye to convey her silent reassurance.

She still mourned Richard and always would. Despite his failings, he'd been her friend and first love
and would always be a part of her.

But her feelings for Ian were different. She wanted
him with a woman's desire, not a young girl's romantic idealism. Her love for Ian was richer and deeper,
more abiding.

He seemed to read her unspoken message, for his
expression remained relatively tranquil, yet she made
a promise to herself to remind him of her devotion as
soon as they were alone together.

That moment was a long time in coming. When
they reached the manor, Tess was not surprised to
find that a throng of guests had already begun arriving, even though it was barely noon. An invitation to
Bellacourt was highly sought-after, in no small part
because of the Devil Duke's sudden marriage. In this

case, he and his new duchess were celebrating their good fortune and showing the Beau Monde that they were very much in love.

Tess's second aim for the festivities was to thank her charities' many contributors. She also wanted to laud the eminent physician, Mr. Geary, and to introduce her patrons to Lady Claybourne. With her husband Heath's assistance, Lily was following in Tess's philanthropic footsteps, having recently opened a home for destitute, abused, and fallen women—helping young girls escape the cruel life of a street-walker and unwed mothers provide a decent future for their children.

Tess had composed the primary guest list, but Roslyn had used her extraordinary social talents to help organize the wedding breakfast and ball. Thus, it promised to be a splendid affair. In the dining rooms, a veritable feast had been laid out on buffet tables for the guests, while musicians were tuning their instruments in the ballroom to offer dancing, and card tables had been set up in the drawing room for the whist enthusiasts.

A crowd had already gathered in the ballroom, Tess saw. She and Ian moved around the enormous room, welcoming their guests to their home. She soon found herself separated from Ian, however. Thus he was out of earshot when Damon and Eleanor approached her to discuss the happy state of her marriage.

"It is fortunate that you and Rotham settled your differences so delightfully, Tess," Eleanor said with a laughing look up at her husband. "Now Damon won't have to call him out."

"Yes," he agreed, amused. "I was not looking forward to shedding his blood or mine."

Exceedingly glad herself, Tess sought Ian's gaze through the sea of guests and shared another intimate smile with him.

A short while later, the new Lady Haviland broke away from her own beloved husband's side to take Tess's hands. "I am delighted your marriage turned out so wonderfully," Madeline said warmly. "You deserve happiness, Tess, more than anyone I know. When I heard that you had to wed Rotham, I feared it would not end well."

"So did I," Tess replied in heartfelt agreement.

It was perhaps two hours later when Ian found her again. "Are you ready, my love?"

"Yes," she answered, before excusing herself to her guests. She and Ian had promised to bring Jamie a treat before his afternoon nap.

They stopped by the buffet tables to collect a plate of meringues baked in the shape of swans, then made their way upstairs to a much quieter wing of the house where the nursery was located.

"I am not sorry to escape the intense scrutiny," Ian admitted. "Your friends have kept a close eye on me all afternoon, were you aware? No doubt they want to verify that I am adoring you properly."

"I know," Tess said with a smug smile. "They are highly protective of me. But they are coming to trust that you love me. And they are also grateful to you for helping Fanny by hiring Basil."

"He is turning out to be a fairly admirable secretary," Ian said before fixing her with a curious look. "I never did discover what came over him the afternoon I returned from Cornwall. Eddowes offered to resign his post while proclaiming his steadfast loyalty to you."

Remembering, Tess gave Ian a somewhat guilty glance. "I asked him where I could find your account books. I hoped to learn if you had made all those generous contributions while giving the credit to your solicitor. But Basil would not betray your trust and suggested that I confront you directly."

Ian pursed his mouth in solemn thought. "Perhaps he is worth keeping on after all."

Tess eyed him with concern. "You would not dismiss Basil now, would you?" When she recognized the glimmer of amusement in Ian's eyes, understanding dawned. He was baiting her again—and enjoying it thoroughly. "You are trying to provoke me, aren't you, your grace?"

"Of course. What did you expect?"

When an endearingly arrogant smile spread across his lips, Tess had to smile in return. "I would not have it any other way."

They found Jamie in his bedchamber, in the company of his nurse, Mrs. Dixon. The toddler was eagerly awaiting their arrival, for he began jumping up and down as soon as they entered. "My grace, Miss Tess! You 'membered!"

"Of course we remembered you, scamp," Ian said, ruffling the boy's blond curls.

Jamie's eyes grew huge when Tess offered him a swan. At first he didn't want to eat the confection and destroy the delicate design, and at the same time, he exhibited his generous nature by making certain Mrs. Dixon got her own swan, too. Then, assured that he could save one simply for viewing, he hungrily bit into the sweet.

When Mrs. Dixon worried aloud that he would spoil his appetite so that he wouldn't eat his supper, Tess intervened.

"I believe we can make an exception just this once."

When he had devoured two of the treats, Tess washed his sticky face. Then together, she and Ian put Jamie to bed.

Before snuggling under the covers, the child gave first Ian, then Tess an ardent hug—a loving gesture that brought a mist to her eyes.

Over Jamie's head, Tess shared a poignant glance with Ian as happiness ran through her. They were a family now, and someday they would be tucking their own children in to sleep.

When Jamie obediently closed his eyes and Mrs. Dixon settled down to watch over him, they left the room quietly. Out in the corridor, Ian paused to claim a lingering kiss from Tess.

"It has been much too long since I last kissed you," he complained before leading her back to their myriad guests.

Agreeing wholeheartedly, Tess refrained from mentioning that Ian had kissed her passionately just this morning before she left to join Fanny's bridesmaids. Nor did Tess remind him of the hours of searing tenderness they'd spent in their marriage bed the previous night.

Upon returning to the ballroom, they spent the next several hours fulfilling their duties as host and hostess, including opening the dancing with a minuet.

Finally, with a glance at the glittering crowd, Ian suddenly took Tess's hand and whisked her from the ballroom.

"Where are you taking me?" she asked.

"Someplace where we may be private. I am famished for a taste of you."

Anticipation and eagerness rippled through Tess. She was more than happy to slip away from the crowd to share an embrace with her stunningly sensual husband.

Finding a spot to be alone, however, proved difficult. In every corridor, they passed small knots of chattering guests and busy footmen carrying trays to and from the buffet tables.

After trying several rooms, which were also occupied, they discovered the library deserted. When they slipped inside, Ian shut the door firmly behind them. Instantly the gay sounds of the gathering became muted.

"Alone at last," Ian said, taking Tess in his arms.

"Just what are your intentions, wicked sir?" she asked, laughing up into his eyes.

"I have yet to decide. How wicked would you like me to be, my love?"

"A little ravishment might be gratifying."

"I might comply if you beg prettily enough."

Tess flashed him an arch smile. "You are still laboring under a severe misapprehension, your grace. I would be delighted to have you ravish me, but I will not beg you, prettily or otherwise."

His half-lidded gaze was amused. "I seem to recall you reneging on that vow on several occasions . . .

although I admit, you have had me pleading for mercy once or twice."

Her eyebrow lifted. "Only once or twice?"

"Well, perhaps somewhat more frequently than that."

"Yes, *much* more frequently. Your memory is sadly lacking, I fear."

"Then by all means, we must remedy my deficiency."

Thankfully, Ian bent to kiss her, his mouth hot and tasting of passion. That exquisitely hard, hungry mouth could drive her wild and fill her with pleasure, Tess thought as his tongue tangled and dueled with hers. So could his hands. When those marvelous hands rose to caress her breasts through her gown, she moaned at the delicious sensations streaking through her.

She was only vaguely aware of the library door opening moments later.

"There you are," a haughty female voice suddenly interrupted. "I should have known I would find you trysting."

They broke apart and turned to face Tess's disapproving godmother.

"Honestly, Rotham," Lady Wingate complained. "Can you never manage to quell your sinful urges in public?"

Unperturbed, Ian slid an arm around Tess's waist. "I have every right to tryst with my wife in my own home, Lady Wingate," he said mildly. "We have been wed for more than six weeks now, in large part thanks to you."

"Perhaps so, but it is deplorable, the way you disregard propriety when there are so many witnesses present. And you, my dear," she said, fixing her gaze on Tess. "Have I taught you nothing about proper behavior in all these years?"

Despite her godmother's avowed dismay, Tess suspected that Lady Wingate's expression of shocked rectitude was largely feigned.

Her own tone turned wry when she replied. "I think you protest a bit too much, my lady. You were quite glad to catch us in an illicit embrace at your house party, since you could demand that Rotham marry me. It all worked out exactly as you hoped. Come now, admit it."

The hint of a pleased smile on Lady Wingate's lips confirmed that she was only pretending to be scandalized now. "I admit that I was clever enough to take advantage of the opportunity you presented."

Ian answered for Tess. "You were indeed clever, my lady. And you are also astute enough to know when you are unwanted . . . as you are presently."

Lady Wingate pursed her mouth for a moment but gave in with good grace. "Very well, I will leave you to your shameless dalliances. I want a god-grandchild to keep young Jamie company. But I trust you will not make a habit of exposing Tess to scandal every time you venture out in public together, Rotham."

"Not every time," Ian pledged. "Only now and then."

Tess stifled a laugh as the baroness shook her head in exasperation.

When the noblewoman had left the library and shut the door firmly behind her, Ian turned to Tess.

"Now where were we?" he asked, drawing her against him again.

"I believe you were kissing me witless."

Tess thought he would resume his delightful attentions, but he hesitated. "She does have a point," he observed. "Jamie needs a playmate or two to keep him company."

Tess completely agreed. She was coming to love Ian's young ward and knew he would make a wonderful older brother to their own children someday . . . hopefully someday soon.

"What are you suggesting, dear husband?" she asked innocently.

"That I endeavor harder to sire an heir—merely to please your godmother, of course."

Tess laughed softly, feeling a sunburst of joy inside her. "Of course. But I would like nothing better than to bear your children, my beloved Ian."

Catching his hands with her own, she held them to her breast, where her heart thrummed with love for him.

Naturally, her gesture earned Tess another heated kiss that sent shuddering thrills through her pleasure-flushed veins and made her hurt with longing.

"You were right," she panted when he finally raised his head. "We do owe Lady Wingate our thanks for bringing us together."

"I am not so certain," Ian responded, short of breath himself. "She gave us a decided push weeks ago, but in the end, I would have eventually married you."

"Would you now?" Tess asked, delighted by the thought.

"Yes. My heart was captured long ago by a beautiful romantic who fascinates me, arouses me, inspires me. . . ."

Ian claimed her mouth in another cherishing kiss, letting her feel the fierce burn of his love.

Tess melted into his embrace. *Her* heart had been captured by a vexingly arrogant duke who fired her emotions and challenged her to reach for depths of passion she had never known were possible.

After a lengthy interval, Tess drew back far enough to murmur against his lips. "Love me forever, Ian."

"I will, I swear it," he promised—and then proceeded to show her precisely how he intended to keep his vow.

Dear Readers,

I've had a marvelous time embroiling the Loring sisters and their friends in their spirited Courtship Wars and helping them find their perfect mates. Thank you for joining me in their romantic adventures.

Next up is a brand new Regency series entitled Legendary Lovers, where the passionate, pleasure-loving Wilde cousins vie to follow in the footsteps of the world's greatest lovers.

Best wishes and happy reading!

Nicole Jordan

Read on for a look at book one in Nicole Jordan's
exciting new Legendary Lovers series

Chapter One

London, May 1816

The flash of amber silk intrigued him, although not as much as the lovely woman wearing it.

Lounging negligently against a column in his crowded ballroom, Ashton Wilde, eighth Marquis of Beaufort, narrowed his gaze as the blond beauty disappeared through the French doors and onto the terrace beyond.

Maura Collyer, his younger sister's bosom friend. What the devil was she up to?

Curiosity warred with odd disappointment as Ash speculated on her intent. It appeared as if Miss Collyer was trysting with one of his noble guests, Viscount Deering.

For all her beauty, he would never have taken Maura for the scarlet woman sort. As far as he knew, she didn't even *like* most men, and at four-and-twenty she was long on the shelf. And yet she had pursued Lord Deering onto a moonlit terrace in the middle of a grand ball for what looked like an assignation.

His boredom suddenly evaporating, Ash pushed away from the column and forged a path through the glittering, bejewelled sea of company. He had expected better of Miss Collyer.

Wry amusement twisted his mouth at the quaint thought. How the leading member of the scandalous Wildes could condemn a lady for flouting propriety with a lovers' tryst was the height of irony. The Wildes were legendary for their passionate exploits, their surname synonymous with a blatant disregard for the rules governing the Beau Monde, and Ash himself was currently his family's greatest offender.

Still, he couldn't entirely banish his contrary stab of displeasure at the notion of his sister's closest friend taking the likes of Deering as a lover.

The terrace doors had been flung open to alleviate the heat from the chandeliers and the crush of perfumed bodies. Upon reaching the threshold, Ash paused to let his eyes adjust to the dimmer light on the terrace and focus on the couple near the stone balustrade.

Although not embracing, they were standing close together—or rather the lady was standing before the gentleman. Her position offered Ash a view of her profile, so he could see that her delicate jaw was set while her hands were tightly clenched.

It did not appear to be a romantic tryst but a confrontation, he decided. He could overhear her low, impassioned voice imploring the viscount, although the noise from the chattering, dancing throng behind him drowned out most of her words.

Ash moved a step closer just as a momentary lull in the music brought Miss Collyer's urgent declaration to him.

"Emperor did not belong to her, I tell you! She had no right to sell him to you."

"I have a legal deed of sale that says otherwise,"

Deering responded in an arrogant drawl that evidently grated on her nerves.

The beauty inhaled a deep breath as if she were trying to maintain control of her emotions. "Then allow me to buy him back. . . . *Please*."

"You cannot afford my price, Miss Collyer."

"I can raise the funds somehow. I will sell the entire stables if I must."

When Deering laughed in that supercilious way of his, Ash felt the same grating irritation.

He knew Rupert Firth, Viscount Deering fairly well. Of similar ages, they had attended Cambridge at the same time. And like Ash, Deering had dark curling hair, a noble title, and a significant fortune. But there the similarities ended. Most notably, the viscount was a head shorter, with a body that was turning to flab from an overindulgence of fine port wine.

Ash had never liked Deering, mainly because of his attitude of snide superiority. That dislike only increased as the discussion continued.

"I might be persuaded . . . for a price," Deering said with a smirk that made Ash itch to intervene.

"What price?" Miss Collyer asked warily.

In answer, the nobleman reached out and trailed a languid finger along her bare throat to the low neckline of her gown.

When she visibly gritted her teeth, Ash felt some satisfaction that she wasn't soliciting the viscount's advances, far from it. Yet he was surprised by his own violent reaction: The urge to wrap his hands around Deering's throat speared through him.

Then Deering gave a low, seductive laugh that raised his ire even further.

"I see you take my meaning, Miss Collyer. If you are truly interested in regaining your property, you will accommodate my wishes. You are quite lovely. I find I want you almost as much as I wanted your magnificent stallion."

Flinching, she took a step backward, out of reach, distaste written in every line of her face. "I regret I must decline your proposition, my lord."

"You should realize that beggars cannot be choosers."

"I am not a beggar quite yet, Lord Deering."

The viscount moved closer, but she stood her ground. When his fingers covered her breast and squeezed, Ash took a reflexive step toward them.

But Maura Collyer evidently did not need defending, for she brought her heel down hard on the viscount's instep. Even with her soft evening slippers, the impact must have hurt.

It did, if the viscount's pained growl was any indication.

"Your stubbornness reminds me of your damned father!" he ground out through his teeth. "I could not persuade him to sell, but I found a way to win in the end. Your stepmother was far more accommodating."

For a moment Miss Collyer froze, her expression one of devastation. Only then did Ash recall the bad blood between her family and the viscount. Deering had accused her father of cheating at cards two years ago, but Noah Collyer had died before the matter could be resolved.

When Deering reached for her breast again, she broke out of her paralysis with ferocity. Uttering an audible curse, she brought her knee up to contact the viscount's satin breeches at an especially vulnerable point.

Deering gave a harsh groan and doubled over, clutching his ballocks. Then Maura stamped down on his other instep for good measure.

Ash didn't know which of his emotions was strongest just then—amusement, admiration, or anger.

Amusement because he'd wanted to do the same thing to Deering for years.

Admiration because very few females outside those in his own family had the spirit or courage to engage in a physical brawl with a significantly larger man.

And anger because a genteel young lady had been accosted in his own home. Specifically this young lady, who was Katharine's friend and therefore deserved his protection.

Deering was clearly angry also; in fact, he was in a fury. "You . . . will regret this . . . you damned witch!" he panted, still bent over.

"The only thing I regret is thinking you were honorable enough to let me plead my case! I was fully prepared to purchase my horse back, not sell myself to you!"

She was panting as much as her suffering adversary, but her breathlessness stemmed from outrage instead of pain. Ash could practically see sparks flashing from her eyes. When she balled her fists as if she might strike a blow at the viscount's sneering face, Ash decided it was time to intervene.

"It is time you took your leave, Deering," he declared, striding across the terrace toward them.

At his sudden appearance, Miss Collyer gave a start, while the nobleman straightened painfully.

"This is none of your affair, Beaufort," Deering snapped.

"It is very much my affair. You assaulted one of my guests."

"I assaulted her?" he sputtered. "That she-devil was the one who assaulted me!"

Ash bit back a smile. "I would not advertise that fact if I were you, Rupert. You will only invite scorn and make yourself a target for the cartoonists. Do you need assistance calling for your carriage?"

"Bloody hell . . . no, I can summon my own damned carriage."

"Then pray do so. You are no longer welcome here."

The viscount shot Ash a look of extreme dislike. "This is no way to treat a man of my rank, Beaufort, ordering me to leave while taking that witch's side."

"Spare me your protests. You got exactly what you deserved. I would have hurt you myself if she had not."

Deering's expression only darkened. After another fierce glare at Miss Collyer, though, he limped off in the direction of the ballroom.

Alone on the terrace with her, Ash turned and found his gaze arrested by the enchanting picture she made. Maura stood with her fists still clenched, her cheeks flushed with anger, her bosom heaving softly. In the candle glow spilling from the ballroom windows, she looked fiery and beautiful, her honey-colored hair only a few shades lighter than the gold-embroidered amber silk gracing her tall, lithe figure.

He was not accustomed to seeing Miss Collyer so stylishly garbed. Her ball gown was an elegant confection, with short puffed sleeves and a low décolletage that offered meager coverage for the ripe swells of her breasts. Usually she wore plain muslin or kerseymere or—since her father's unexpected death from heart failure two years ago—black bombazine.

Her long, white kid gloves shielded her arms from the cool night air, but she was still shaking, no doubt in the aftermath of rage rather than from the chill.

Seeing all that trembling intensity, Ash could imagine her in his bed, shuddering in the throes of passion.

Aware of the primal surge of lust streaking through him, he tamped down on his inappropriate urges at the same time he noticed that one sleeve of her gown had been pulled down to bare her pale white shoulder.

Stepping close to Maura, he straightened her sleeve, trying to make his helpful gesture appear casual and brotherly.

Her flush deepened, as if she suddenly recognized that he'd witnessed the entire event, including the viscount's ignoble sexual advances.

When Ash finished repositioning her sleeve, she turned quickly toward the French doors. But he stayed her with a light touch on her gloved arm. "You should remain here for a moment. You cannot return to the ballroom looking so disheveled and distraught."

"I am not distraught, I am furious."

"Don't quibble. It amounts to the same thing. You are breathing fire. You will frighten all my guests."

She grimaced in frustration but apparently agreed with him, for after a short hesitation, she went to stand at the balustrade, her gloved fingers clutching at the gray stone. "Why are you even out here, Lord Beaufort? You are supposed to be hosting your sister's ball."

Joining her at the railing, Ash answered honestly. "You roused my curiosity when you followed Deering here. I thought you might be having a liaison with your lover."

"With *Lord Deering*?" She sounded appalled, disgusted. "I would sooner take a snake as a lover— Not that I would ever take a lover of any kind," she hastened to add. "Or that it would be your concern if I did."

Ash let her intriguing denial go unremarked. "I realized your dislike of him when I overheard your conversation."

"Did no one ever teach you that it is impolite to eavesdrop?" she muttered.

He smiled at her question. "Any number of people have tried to teach me polite manners, but I fear little of their instruction took hold. In your case, however, it was not rudeness that led me to eavesdrop."

"No?"

"No. I relish a mystery, and I was suffering a near fatal case of ennui. When I saw you disappear, I was delighted that finally something interesting was happening this evening. And then I remained here on the terrace because I thought you might need my protection."

She shot him an irritated glance. "I did not need your protection. I can defend myself."

"Obviously," Ash said with dry amusement. Her hazel eyes were still shooting daggers. "If looks could kill, Deering would be six feet underground by now. As it was, you temporarily unmanned him."

"I wish it could have been permanent," Maura said through gritted teeth.

Her agitation was still visible, and she seemed intent on shredding her kid gloves against the rough stone.

Just then, voices from the ballroom grew louder, wafting through the open doors behind them. Not wanting an audience, Ash reached out on impulse and peeled Miss Collyer's fingers away from the balustrade.

"Come with me," he ordered, catching her hand in his. Turning toward the terrace steps, he tugged her behind him.

"Where are you taking me?" she demanded, trying to pull back.

"Only down to the garden so you can cool off. You need time to recover your composure."

She accompanied him then, although rather unwillingly.

As he led her down the wide marble steps, Ash tried to analyze why he felt so protective of her, and more inexplicably, why he felt this unexpected poss-essiveness toward her.

Her statement moments ago about not wanting a lover of any kind gave him a strange satisfaction. He'd never heard of Maura Collyer engaging in any romantic affairs, yet that didn't mean she hadn't indulged discreetly.

He supposed his protectiveness was a result of her close connection to his sister Katharine and his cousin Skye. The three girls had become fast friends years ago at an elite boarding academy.

Like Katharine, Maura was unique in that she enjoyed more masculine pursuits than was typical of their peers. Breeding race horses was most definitely not a ladylike profession, either. After losing her father so unexpectedly, Maura had retired to the country and thrown herself into improving the breeding stables she'd inherited so that she could support herself.

Ash had always been impressed by her fire and spirit. Yet he'd kept his hands off her because he considered her off-limits.

Unquestionably he had noticed her, though. From the time she had turned sixteen, in fact. What red-blooded male wouldn't? He'd have to be dead not to feel the rush of attraction for a beauty like Maura. But a gentleman did not go around seducing innocent schoolgirls, particularly a classmate of his sister's.

Maura was clearly no longer a girl. Ash was intently aware of her lithe, ripe body as they reached the garden below the terrace. She was also out of mourning for her father now, which made her fair game if he chose to pursue her.

The notion intrigued him, yet he set it aside for the time being as he guided Maura along a path illuminated by the occasional lantern.

"Perhaps you should sit down," he advised, leading her to a stone bench shadowed by a lilac tree.

She took no notice of his suggestion but pulled her hand from his and began to pace back and forth along the flagstone path.

Amusement tugged at Ash's mouth as he settled on the bench in her place. Prepared to indulge her, he stretched his long legs out before him and crossed his ankles. Despite his pleasure in watching her, though, he knew it would be more gallant if he attempted to distract her from her agitation.

Accordingly, he broke the silence after a moment. "Allow me to offer you my apologies, Miss Collyer."

"For what?" she asked absently.

"I regret that you had to suffer Deering's lechery."

"You are not to blame for his disgusting behavior."

"No, but this is my home, and I am responsible for the actions of my guests."

"Perhaps, but Deering is as far from a gentleman as it is possible to be. The gall of him," she muttered under her breath, "thinking I would have any interest in selling myself to him."

"You handled him well. I am all admiration. Where did you learn that trick of incapacitating a man?"

"From my steward, Gandy. There are some unsavory characters in the racing world, and Gandy wanted me to be prepared should I encounter any."

"I thought Katharine and Skye were the only gently bred females who were skilled in self-defense. I taught Kate that move myself."

When that brought no response, Ash continued casually. "I should thank you. Your altercation spiced up my evening and saved me from excruciating boredom."

His admission seemed to gain her attention for a moment, or at least she paused to glance at him. "Why did you even hold a ball if you are so jaded by them?"

"You know why. Because Katharine asked it of me."

"And you can never refuse her?"

"Oh, I regularly refuse her, but in this instance, I was

doing my duty as her elder brother. She claimed she was finally ready to look for a husband, much to my surprise."

"It surprised me also," Maura allowed, resuming her pacing.

Frankly, it had startled Ash two weeks ago when Katharine suddenly announced her desire to find a husband and requested a ball to aid her search for eligible candidates.

But he was not interested in his sister's matrimonial prospects just now. Instead, he wanted to know what had led to her closest friend's confrontation with one of his noble guests. Most particularly, why Deering would assume that Maura Collyer's charms were for sale. . . .